Jaguar

Painter Place Saga 3

Pamela Poole
Inspiring Southern Ambiance

Published by Southern Sky Publishing

Southern Sky Publishing
southernskypublishing.com

This book is a work of fiction. While references may be made
to actual places, events, historical people and their influences, and music,
the names, characters, incidents, and locations within this story
are from the author's imagination and are not a
resemblance to actual living or dead persons, businesses,
or events. Any similarity is coincidental.
Scripture references are from the Holman Christian Standard Bible unless
otherwise noted.

eBook ISBN 978-1-956089-05-9
Print ISBN 978-1-956089-06-6
Print ISBN 978-1-956089-12-7

Dedication

This novel is dedicated to my little sister Donna,
whose Barbie doll was often kidnapped during many hours we spent
pretending.
May God's light pierce the darkness wherever you encounter it.

To readers

May you shine the light of Christ in the darkest of places.

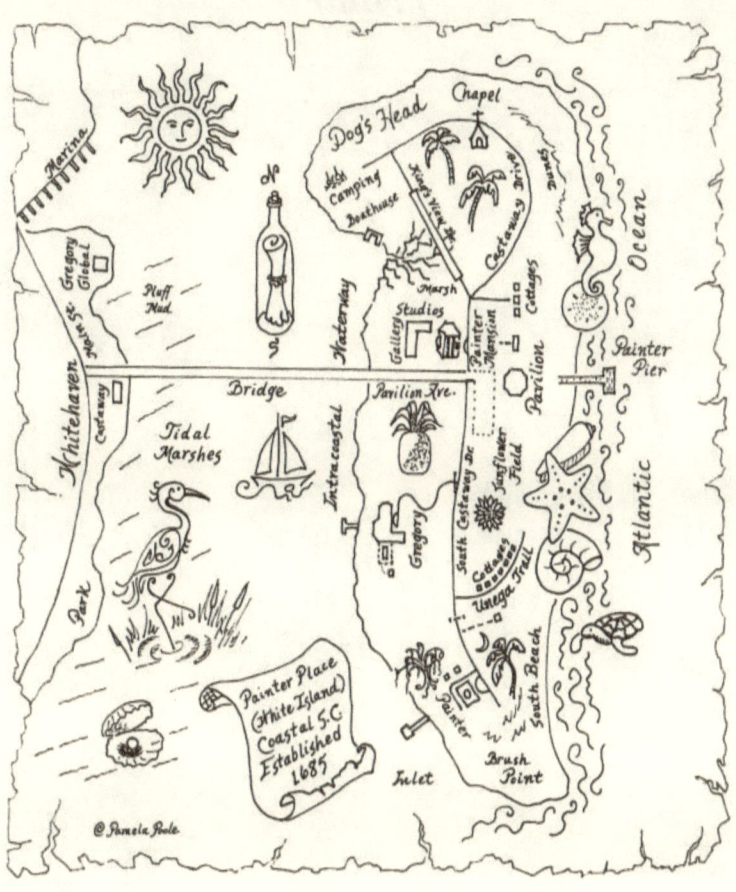

Map of Painter Place before Hurricane Hugo in 1989

Jaguar

Part One

Game On

Chapter One

Wilfred Rothschild's wrists burned, chafed in his struggle against their bindings. His meaty shoulders and back ached under a soiled white dress shirt that rubbed the metal slats of a cold, rusty chair. He pulled his knees together in another futile effort to ease the discomfort of the straps around his ankles, quaking from the damp chill and lack of a strong drink. A rumble in his stomach reminded him he'd been here for several hours, waiting for his captors to set him free from this filthy warehouse as they promised.

He had thrashed through his thoughts of the bad business deals that led to his current humiliating situation. The trouble boiled down to one person—Phillip Chadwick Gregory, Jr., head of the distinguished Gregory Global Corporation.

Wilfred had begun his own career with high expectations back in 1960, but Phillip Gregory took advantage of some complaints about his perceived drinking problem. To launch his own place in his dad's company, Phillip steered investors for a huge project over to Gregory Global. The blow to Wilfred's ego at the hands of that insufferably arrogant American was bad enough, but it was only the beginning. The hit to his reputation led to the necessity of taking seedy clients, and he was even more apt to drown his smoldering resentment in a glass.

That cocky Southern yokel drove him to drink. No one should have everything! Phillip Gregory was worth more than almost anyone in the world. At fifty-seven years old, the guy was still handsome and fit like some Greek demi-god. Everything he touched either made money or turned out right, and he had no vices to gossip about. It wasn't natural.

In fact, the only thing Gregory didn't have was a sparkling personality. But no one ever seemed to care about his lack of charm.

Wilfred ground his teeth, seeing those arresting blue eyes in his mind. He despised the pity they always held for him. But once, they were wild with a flash of fury, right here in England, on a yacht docked on the Thames.

Hatred ripped a hot streak through Wilfred. The owner of the new super yacht named it *Dominator*, and the elegant reception was the same day Phillip had wrested the King's Road project from him. The Gregory family attended as guests, and others on board celebrated Phillip's victory by nicknaming him the *Dominator*.

With a snarl, Wilfred's memories transported him back all those years. True, Phillip merely endured the nickname and considered it vulgar to celebrate a victory over a competitor in public. Wilfred was not so soused to remember the guy could never be shaken over business matters. His weakness was a woman, and Wilfred contrived to dance with her.

He grinned, recalling how he had touched her dishonorably and then insinuated to the guests that she was fair game as Phillip's leftovers. If the elder Gregory had not held his son in check, Wilfred and Phillip would have settled the matter in a fistfight in front of all the high society attendees and Global's clientele.

Later, Wilfred raged to hear that Phillip Gregory was blissfully married to the woman he set so much by. Then he had an heir. He smirked now at the dank, windowless wall of his temporary prison. Who names their son the family name for the third generation? Only someone with an ego the size of the American continent, in Wilfred's estimation. Phillip Chadwick Gregory III—it was ridiculously long and snooty. And then calling him 'Chad'? Not many people could pull that off. Sounded like a pretty boy, some boyfriend for a girl's fashion doll.

But the magazines were still eating it up, like Phillip's son was some pop idol, begging for interviews with him. He looked uncannily like that movie star in that sexy crime drama, the one in Miami where the vice cop drove a Ferrari and had a pet alligator. No doubt some Wall Street goons were naming their own sons after the guy.

What better way to get revenge on Phillip Gregory than to endanger his heir? Wilfred's shady connections knew how. The threatening notes delivered to Phillip were untraceable, and if the men directly involved in the hands-on part of the plan were caught trying to nab the baby boy, they did not know who hired them. They were never supposed to get away with it, only to create the illusion that they tried.

No matter that they were confused over which blonde baby was the right one and snatched both the Painter and Gregory boys just in case. Phillip would live his life knowing that his son, and therefore the future of the company, was in perpetual danger. It was what he would think of when he said his pious prayers every night.

And then ten years ago, there was that incident in Mevagissey. The newspapers here in London helped Phillip and that dashing son with the numbers after his name ruin Wilfred further, ending the decent level of success he spent years fighting for. He went to great lengths to pay a kid to get information from Gregory's careless younger son so he could hack into their accounts and set off an alarm that would land them in court, maybe even with a conviction for Cole. He thought every passing day with Global's security in question meant permanent damage to their reputation. Who could have foreseen that the captivating Pollyanna from Painter Place would show up over here in England, stumble into a media hotbed over that rock star, steal the media's imagination, and gush to the world about the integrity of generations of the Gregory family?

His scowl crumpled the deeply etched lines between his brows and the downturn at the corners of his mouth. Granted, Phillip Gregory could have made Wilfred's drunken misstep at British artist Dante Kent's yacht reception much worse. In his arrogance, he acted like he would get dirty by twisting the knife. No matter, because Wilfred gained another weapon. The same fury in Chad's eyes was in his father's eyes years before, over the same thing—a woman. His weakness.

And like de-ja-vu, just as Phillip's dad had checked him to stop a brawl with Wilfred, Phillip coolly did the same with his son Chad. The whelp would not charge ahead once his dad gripped his arm. The young man was like an obedient dog on Phillip's leash, but Wilfred saw what he needed to know. Chad had his father's bent toward a temper flare that could ruin him, like uncorking a bottle of fine champagne.

Wilfred licked his cracked lips at the thought of his favorite champagne before tracking back to his memory of revenge. The new associates he hired five years ago were pros and promised him a healthy cut from a ransom for Chad's sons, the prized twin grandsons that Phillip must look to as another generation to carry on with Gregory Global.

But that plan in France failed, and he sweated being connected to it. He never expected one associate to attempt killing Chad, the same baby boy he nabbed years earlier. Wilfred squirmed again and grimaced at the ache in his back, muttering to a mildewed wall, "I'm not a murderer." His obsession with Phillip was strictly about making him live in torment about the future and to be the Gregory under whom Global finally failed.

Despite his torturous misery in the metal chair, Wilfred allowed himself a malicious grin. After that threat by Chad's assailant that he would be back, Global was covering the cost of that over-the-top bodyguard. Wilfred's dreams and schemes ultimately damaged the company he hated, diverting resources for intense security and private planes, because Phillip wanted no one in the public endangered in a kidnapping attempt. Wilfred vowed that while he had a breath left in his body, the Gregory family would never know a day's true peace, and a financial faucet would gush out of Global for security. He was so clever that they had no suspect!

He gloated. The latest opportunity to set more trouble into motion had just fallen into his lap, like a gift from a god of revenge. His long-time enemy would soon be investigated, maybe even arrested. Wilfred rolled his bloodshot eyes and smiled. Phillip was predictably noble and would insist on taking full responsibility, getting his younger brother Justin out of the line of fire here in London. All the negative press would slap him and Global down, and that Golden Boy son of his would have the struggle of his life to overcome the setback.

A convulsive shiver reminded him of the unexpected cost of the dirty blow he was dealing. Last week, he found a new investor for an illegal venture, a badly needed injection of capital. His spying connections reported that the guy had dealings with Global under a different identity. He couldn't get the other name, but if the guy was laundering ill-gotten gain, he was good business for Wilfred. The plan was to get his money from the deal with the Columbian cartel *Temoso*, plant some evidence on the investor, and then anonymously tip off the authorities. They would untangle the link to Global.

Only, the deal with *Temoso* went sour when *Puña*, a rival cartel, intercepted the shipment, throwing lighter fluid on the raging fire between them. *Temoso* blamed Wilfred for setting them up or leaking information, though they had no proof, and they still wanted their payment. He had no product to collect the funds with and no idea how *Puña* got wind of the shipment for their raid. So, he had to adjust his plan, giving *Temoso* the information on the other investor, promising that the guy would cover the amount owed.

Now Wilfred was here, temporarily detained by what must be the roughest members of the *Temoso* cartel while they went to collect their money from the investor. The guy would fork it all over rather than risk having his family killed, Wilfred was sure of that. When the cartel got their money, it was still a successful venture, and they'd set him free. They might even want his business again.

He jumped as the bolt lock on the outside of the door behind his chair slid open and the rusty hinges screeched. He heard a rapid-fire interaction in Spanish among his returning captors. "Did you get your payment? Can I leave now?" rasped Wilfred hopefully, turning his head stiffly to his shoulder to address them.

"I promised you could leave, didn't I?" asked a man with heavily accented English. He only needed one shot at this range. As Wilfred slumped forward, the man snapped orders to his companions. "He's ready to leave now. Get 'im wrapped for delivery."

Flames waved their arms in a merry dance of light, warming a spacious family room that was fulfilling its purpose. Books, puzzles, and games were shoved helter-skelter under a low sofa table on which forgotten bits of apple wedges, kiwi slices, dried dates, cheese cubes, and cracker crumbs remained scattered on a ceramic platter.

Phillip Gregory lounged in sky-blue fleece sweats that had seen too many workouts. His running shoes were piled with the others next to the over-sized ottoman where he propped his athletic-socked feet. His twin grandsons flanked him in his favorite spot on the deep-cushioned leather sectional sofa. Although only five years old, they could read many of the simple words in the new book from their Christmas treasure trove. But it was the bright pictures of machines and how they worked that spoke to them. Their grandfather knew how to explain the pulleys and gears, so the twins listened and rested their blonde heads against the worn cotton of his sweatshirt.

Granddaughters Savanna Caroline and Brooke surrounded Camellia Gregory, who made suggestions in her melodic Charleston drawl about how to change their dolls into pretty polka-dot pajamas and brush their teeth and hair. Donning the imitated air of a parent, the toddlers put the dolls through the motions of their own nightly routines and assured them that bedtime was an unavoidable fact of life. If the dolls did all this without complaining, they'd have a story and some songs when they were tucked in. The girls had many of the same dolls and toys in different colors and were almost as inseparable as the twins. When their cousin Summer Painter was with them, it was a tight threesome.

Cole Gregory's son, Sean, giggled as his father and uncle Chad were wearing him down with a romp on the generous rug. Soft dark curls clung to his forehead, sweaty from staking an early mark on the rowdy reputation of a two-year old. Chad's wife Caroline and Cole's wife Shannon sat cross-legged in sweaters and jeans before the hearth, open notebooks spread on their laps and pens in hand. With cheeks blushing prettily from the warm fire and cuffs pushed up their forearms, they scheduled the week ahead. The children on the island were all homeschooling their early years, with the parents and grandparents pitching in. They spilled over into the small coastal town of Whitehaven to coordinate gathering with the Grayson and Wallace families, and others in the local churches.

"Natalie and I have it covered," Shannon assured Caroline decisively over the rich-toned chimes from an antique grandfather clock. She tilted her head in the direction of an open closet door, where shelves were laden like a teacher's cabinet and baskets were stenciled with the Gregory children's names. "Just leave the twins' workbooks and projects in their baskets. You'll only be gone two days."

"Time for dreams! How about snakes, and snails, and puppy-dog tails?" Chad exclaimed, pushing his nephew Sean up into the air over his chest like a barbell. The toddler had finally conked out on top of him, panting for breath after all the roughhousing.

When Sean protested, his uncle tickled him, so he peeled away toward his dad with his giggle-box-turned over. Cole rose to his feet and tucked his son under his arm like a sack of flour.

"Time for a good night kiss," Camellia told her granddaughters as they put the finishing touches on their dolls' bedtime fashion ensembles.

"Love you, Mimi Melia!" the girls sang out sweetly in chorus. They reached around her neck to kiss her as Cole hauled Sean in for a giggling sideways hit-and-run kiss.

The twins reluctantly, but good-naturedly resigned themselves to their fate as Phillip closed their book and gathered their hugs and kisses. They waited quietly for the girls to move so they could bestow the same on their Mimi Melia, then turned to follow Chad through the door to their family's wing of the estate. Caroline rounded up her daughter, who was having her doll kiss everyone all around.

Phillip and Camellia sighed contentedly and looked at one another. The heart of their home was now so quiet that the tick tock of the grandfather clock and the snapping flames in the hearth were the only sounds. The books and games had been tidied away and Shannon had taken the cups and empty platter to the kitchen.

Phillip's expression became a beckoning gaze across the table. With a slow spreading half smile, he patted the leather sofa cushion beside him. Camellia raised a delicately arched eyebrow. When she didn't come to his side, he pursed his lips and let his blue-eyed gaze grow more intense. Apparently, all the games hadn't been stashed away in the closet after all. "I've never known you to waste a romantic fire," he ventured.

"I noticed that romantic fire you're stoking, but you've forgotten how to convince me it's a worthwhile way to spend the evening."

A grin sprang to life on his face, making him look ten years younger. "Just checkin' to see if I had ya trained after all these years."

She assumed an airy attitude and gracefully crossed her arms, her cool green eyes soft as they reflected the elusive flicker in the fireplace. "A well-bred Southern lady doesn't chase a man. He proves he's worth the time and attention he's askin' for."

Phillip sighed, admiring his wife's profile. "That's the same attitude you had the night we met at the Battery, where you sparkled with as much class as the diamonds you were wearin'. You're still the impossible-to-get girl I fell in love with the moment I saw you. But you chose me, with a look I'll never get over, remember? And I didn't let you down."

Her lips curved slightly into a smile, and she gave him a sidelong glance before turning again to the fire. "Then don't start now."

He groaned and raked his graying dark hair back with both hands before he took two long-legged strides to land comfortably beside her. He pulled her back into his chest. "I'll always chase you. And about that romantic fire..."

Chad let the door to the master suite latch softly, smiling and sighing contentedly before settling back against the varnished wood. He turned the lock behind him with an audible click. Caroline was brushing her long blonde hair and looking at a nearly full moon through one of the glass French doors. A sheer peacock blue robe made her hair seem luminous. It was a gift he asked her to open recently on Christmas Eve, after the kids were asleep and they had placed packages under the tree. It became a night he liked to remember.

Now, he stood admiring her silhouette, his imagination stoking heat into the memory of the fluid drape and cool feel of the satin that night. The bedroom was filled with romantic music and lyrics that slid like liquid silk from the stereo. "Always and forever, each moment with you is just like a dream to me that somehow came true."

She held her brush down by her side and turned to speak over her shoulder. "Come and see! It's a beautiful night. The moon's sparkling all over the water."

The lead singer cooed through unseen speakers, singing, "We've got a life of love that won't ever change."

Chad sauntered slowly over with a short laugh, savoring the sight of her and catching all her signals with practiced ease. The music was fueling a mood that thrilled him.

"You think too much like an artist, Darlin'. Get inside my head and see what I see. I won't notice that view when I have this one."

She let him gently take the brush from her hand before he tossed it onto a nearby chaise, then his arms encased her possessively. He slid one hand over the drape of fabric he imagined at the door. "That same moon brings out my inner wolf," he murmured against her neck. "Save my place for a few minutes while I change?"

"Oh, I don't know," she tried to sound uncertain. "I only put this on because it's a national holiday. You know, like savin' the Lamborghini for Sundays and special occasions. And of course, I feel guilty that I have to leave you alone for a couple of days this week."

Chad made a low growling sound deep in his throat before sweeping her confidently into a slow dance, their steps falling within the moonlight that stretched over the hardwood floor. He skillfully made it to the lamp and clicked it off without missing a step, murmuring against her hair. "It's too late for excuses."

The lyrics were perfect. He learned long ago to pay attention to them, because Caroline did. Music put her in a romantic mood, and he liked to tease that song and dance were the keys to romance. He sang softly near her ear, "We'll share tomorrow together, I'll always love you, forever."

Chapter Two

You know you're in love when you can't fall asleep
because reality is finally better than your dreams.
– Dr. Seuss

As Chad gathered with his family on Tuesday morning for the usual boisterous breakfast in the main kitchen, his grin announced his mood like a billboard. But he couldn't help it, and wondered if he looked goofy, because his dad tried to duck away with an amused expression after their eyes met over a plate of steak strips, scrambled eggs, a blueberry muffin, and fresh pineapple juice.

Life was great. No, it was fantastic! He felt on top of the world, unstoppable. Today, he felt like the Golden Boy he was accused of being. He was ecstatically married to the woman he had always wanted, and she still adored him. She gave him kids who were finally past two and not yet teens; he lived on the island where generations of his family had settled, and business was good.

The irrepressible grin was still on his face while he drove his dark blue convertible Porsche 944 over the waterway bridge into Whitehaven. It faded when one of his lifelong best friends, Joey Grayson, announced over the radio in a news break that an earthquake had damaged a city in Japan.

Wincing, Chad said a quick prayer for those affected by the devastation, especially for his business acquaintances there. He would call to check on them when he arrived at the office.

The newsflash wrapped up and a love song perked Chad up again. "You make me happy baby, so I can say, Sha la la la la la la, I love you."

He pulled up to the traffic light at Main Street and belted out the contagious lyrics, though he'd face torture before he'd ever sing this around the guys. "It's something that just gets down in your bones, Baby, and once I see you, I can't leave your love alone, yeah, hah, baby, aw, make me happy, baby."

To his left, he eyed the Castaway, beaming at his brother-in-law Patrick's dream. He enjoyed driving by it every time he came off the island into Whitehaven and looked forward to lunch there today. The restaurant and the local radio station were the most satisfying investments his group of personal friends had made so far.

Still singing, he turned the steering wheel to the right, heading down Main. The streamlined windows of the sleek new Painter Gallery reflected blue sky overhead and his car cruising by in front. Caroline would not be there today. After getting the kids settled with her sister Marina for their homeschooling schedule, she would work on a new collection of paintings at the island studio she shared with her Uncle Wyeth.

Joey Grayson's southern accent filled Chad's Porsche again. "We just got a special request from Cole Gregory for his big brother. He won't say what the occasion is, so we'll just wish them a great day at Global."

"Eye of the Tiger" pounded the speakers, prompting Chad to laugh out loud as he checked his rear-view mirror to see where his brother's car was. He hit the button to open the sunroof, then waved his forefinger as a sign for the number one. Behind him, Cole tapped his horn and pulled closer.

The owner of Antiques on Main placed a sale plaque with wood-burned letters on hooks near the red front door. At the sound of Cole's horn, he twisted around to see the Gregory brothers drive by. Cole's hand was out of his sunroof so his big brother could see Spock's Vulcan sign for "Live Long and Prosper." The store owner chuckled and waved, shaking his head as Chad's

GLOBALX3 and Cole's ITSLEGAL license plates disappeared down the road.

Chad grinned as he sang and drummed the steering wheel. Gregory Global's security guard let him pass into the parking garage under the tallest building in Whitehaven. He shifted the car into park in his marked space beside his dad's still-warm Mercedes, and Cole slid his Porsche in beside his brother's. They headed to the elevator together, carrying themselves with the same confident, athletic stride as their father. Except for Chad's blonde looks from his mom, the Gregory brothers and their dad were enough alike that they were often called three peas in a pod.

Cole handled a nervous client on his mobile phone with characteristic wit and disarming charm, discussing the adverse effect the earthquake would have on Japanese stock and why God hadn't thought to put Cole in charge of natural disasters. When the elevator door slid open quietly on the seventh floor, Cole was taking another call from a client about Japanese stock and Chad was wearing a relaxed smile.

Inside his office, Chad hung his tailored sport coat and glanced at the expanse of his spotless desk, where the phone and answering machine were blinking like it was still Christmas. He went straight past to the sky view in his wall of sparkling windows, stretching out the muscles of his long arms before tucking clasped hands behind his head. He surveyed the shimmering horizon of the Atlantic Ocean. The calls about the Japanese stock market could wait another minute. He gazed watchfully at Painter Place. His home.

Caroline would be at her studio now, creating a body of work to celebrate their tenth wedding anniversary this September. She planned to paint their special places from memory and photos, though it meant experiencing a pendulum of contrasts between exhilarating and painful emotions. He expected her to be a little moody until these paintings were completed.

The island was still in recovery from the hurricane that destroyed it over five years ago, a different landscape than the one they grew up with. But they started over with the new generation in mind. There were more children on the island than at any point in its three-hundred-year-old history, and his own three were the first of the Gregory line to inherit portions of the Painter's part. His grandfather had prayed for that all his life, because it meant the resources of both families were officially blended. Now it was unlikely that the island would ever be lost.

Chad closed his eyes and drew a deep breath, as if inhaling the peacefulness that filled his soul. *Thank you, Lord, for these years of calm after the storm. I know life will always have mountains and valleys, and that we're enjoying the refreshing air on a high mountain right now. Help me remember this through the next shadowy valley.*

Phillip Gregory's office door was always open when his secretary was there. He heard his sons exit the elevator and head to their offices while he was being briefed about the schedule for the day and getting messages. When she went down the hall to give Chad his messages, Phillip leaned forward to flip his daily planner.

The Bible passage printed across the top for today was so familiar he merely noted it, murmuring it out loud from memory as he picked up his favorite fountain pen and prepared to move along. But he did a double take when he saw another verse referenced under it. Pausing with his fountain pen poised, he re-read Ephesians 6:11-12, NIV. "Put on the full armor of God, so that you can take your stand against the devil's schemes. For our struggle is not against flesh and blood, but against the rulers, against the authorities, against the powers of this dark world and against the spiritual forces of evil in the heavenly realms."

Now he looked under it again to see how 1 Chronicles 5:20 fit into the context. "They were helped in fighting them, and God delivered the Hagrites and all their allies into their hands, because they cried out to him during the battle. He answered their prayers, because they trusted in him."

He paused and knit his dark brows, arrested by the message. But his brother Justin's phone line from London lit up, so he slowly reached for the receiver, his eyes still on 1 Chronicles 5:20.

A stab of dread ripped through Chad's stomach when he saw his dad's face. Phillip herded Cole into the office and briskly closed the door. Chad stood abruptly, sending his chair rolling on its castors. At a gesture from their father, he and Cole sat down on twin blue leather sofas in the airy, spotless room.

Phillip paced for a few moments, absently touching his lips to the Gregory family crest on his platinum signet ring. When he stopped, he crossed his arms over his chest and stood resolutely, feet spread. Beside Chad, Cole squirmed on the sofa.

"A young client set up an account with Global just before your Granddad retired," began Phillip. "It was a sensitive account in which the client has alias identities in their line of work. The account's been growin' for years, but today, the man's attorney went into the London office on his behalf with a notarized letter and closed it. The client was not in the country to handle the transaction himself. Justin asked if he could reach the client by phone, and the attorney said the client was unavailable."

Phillip paused, turning to the window view of the serene azure sky juxtaposed against the restless white caps of the sea. Crinkled lines at the side of his blue eyes deepened into a scowl as he continued.

"Justin handled the protocol by law, but it nagged at him. After the attorney left, he followed up by phone with the client's family. They said the client was traveling with work and would be in touch when he could, but they had no idea where he is. Justin called the attorney's office on the pretense of following up to see if he needed anything further from Global, and a secretary said he'd left London for an impromptu vacation. That's when Justin and I got Dad and the authorities on a conference call."

Cole watched his father closely, then cleared his throat. "This is one of those accounts you hide from us."

"Right. You two will never be linked to the account, but Global will be quietly investigated to make it official that we have no part in money-laundering for drug-lord crossfire in South America. Chad, step up to the helm for me. Keep up an appearance of business as usual, and just tell the truth: that I'm in some unexpected meetings."

He turned to his younger son. "Cole, run the London office while Justin cooperates with authorities. Your cousin will help you get re-oriented. Take your family, since I don't know how long you must be there. Shannon's parents will be glad to see her and the kids, but you must stay at Justin's for security reasons. Go on home to pack for an immediate private flight. There'll be special security at the airport when you land, but in the meantime, Azariah will escort you."

Chad and Cole gaped at one another, eyes popping, and Cole blurted, "Dad, you're scarin' me! Could you or Uncle Justin be arrested? Is my family a target for drug cartels?"

"Just focus on your role with Global London." Phillip's deep voice resonated with his usual air of authority. "Justin and I will handle this. As an extra precaution, guards are on their way to Granddad's house in Charleston, so Caroline should be safe there tomorrow."

Chad shot to his feet, hands outstretched as he interjected, "But I planned for her to take Azariah! What about the reception at Grandpa Montgomery's?"

Now his father's composure cracked, which sent another stab of fear into Chad's pounding heart. He watched Phillip put his fingertips to his temples, draw a deep breath, and close his eyes a few moments. He dropped his hands to his sides with a thump and met Chad's eyes. "Frankly, son, you're the one in dire need of Azariah right now."

A chill ran down Chad's spine and he wet his lips, staring. The speaker on his desk spurted out the secretary's pleasant voice, asking Chad if his father was in his office. Phillip turned to answer her. "Yes, I'm here."

"Sir, you have an emergency call from your brother Justin in London."

"I'll take it in Chad's office." Phillip leaned to extend a long arm clad in a crisp, tailored shirt sleeve, pushing a button for Justin's line and then another for the intercom so his sons could hear. "Justin, I'm with the boys to explain our next steps. Any updates?"

"Hope you didn't think this day couldn't get any worse," came Justin's smooth drawl. Phillip groaned and wiped his hand over his forehead, bracing himself.

"A while ago, masked men with Spanish accents drove an unmarked white van up to Global London's front door, where they dumped a body bag. People on the sidewalk screamed, and the bobbies rushed over as the van sped away. There was a message pinned to the bag, and I've been questioned about both the message and the identity of the body. Expect an official call soon from Scotland Yard."

Chad and his brother gasped, watching their father's face as it paled. He straightened his sea-green tie and walked around the desk to plop down into Chad's chair.

Through the intercom, Justin asked, "Phillip, are you ready for this? You'd better sit down."

"I just did. Please, tell me this has all been a sick joke. I want to rewind my life back to breakfast this morning and hit the reset button."

A long sigh issued from the speaker. "You didn't rewind far enough, big brother. It would've still been too late for poor Wilfred. He was shot in the head last night, execution style, and delivered to Global's doorstep as a callin' card to prove how serious his murderers are. They're demandin' a scandalous amount of money from the account of the client we lost this mornin', so they don't know he's withdrawn it. We're ordered to gather the cash per their terms, and they'll contact us with more instructions."

Phillip was already on his feet, shouting in astonishment. "Wilfred? Not Wilfred Rothschild!" He pinched the fine lines across his forehead with one hand. "What's his connection to our client?"

"Precisely what I asked, to no avail. Tryin' to get anything out of British authorities is like questionin' a lamp post."

There was a brisk knock on the door, and Phillip nodded that Chad could answer it. Two men in dark suits stood politely in the hallway, introducing themselves impassively as they flipped open badges.

Phillip instantly transformed back into the cool, unflappable leader of Gregory Global. He set his shoulders and said, "Justin, the authorities are here now. I'll call you later."

Caroline abandoned her studio to rush home after a frantic call from her sister-in-law, Shannon, who picked up their children from Marina's home. She quickly packed for Sean and Brooke while Shannon filled suitcases for herself and Cole. Camellia gathered the children with a storybook and kept Sean engaged with a stuffed animal as one character.

Cole soon arrived home, shaken and brusque with only the barest details to his wife and Caroline about why they had to leave so urgently. Sean heard his dad's voice and ran to find him, submitting to being swept up into a desperate hug. His giggles ceased when he saw the expression in his dad's eyes, and Caroline's heart ached to watch her brother-in-law squeeze them shut against the stinging tears. The toddler gently touched his tousled dark curls to his dad's face, then patted a little palm on Cole's cheek. He mimicked a soothing tone learned from him. "It's okey-dokey Daddy, I'm right here."

Azariah was all business as he came to grasp the suitcase handles. Cole sniffed and told Sean it was time to kiss Mimi Melia goodbye so they could go fly up in the sky in an airplane. He hugged Caroline and herded his family out the door in an emotional whirlwind.

Like her mother-in-law, Caroline masked how upset she was at this abrupt, mysterious upending in their lives. Something was utterly, dreadfully wrong. Camellia's trembling lips betrayed her as she said brave goodbyes and waved until her youngest son and his family were out of sight. Then she grasped Caroline's hand and covered her mouth to hold back a sob.

Caroline glanced at the twins, whose ever-observant blue eyes were uneasy. Their Mimi was frightened, their mother upset, their uncle and aunt left with their cousins, and their homeschool routine was in chaos. The housekeeper ushered the twins and their little sister inside for juice and a snack.

Camellia whispered, "If the cartel goes after Cole's family, this could be the last time I see them alive! Phillip would only do this in a terrible emergency."

She stopped, rubbing the tension in her neck. "He needs me with him, but I can't show up at the office with all the authorities there, as if he's a child."

Grasping her daughter-in-law's hand again, her Charleston accent squeaked when she blurted, "He'll protect Justin with his last breath, Caroline! He won't allow his brother to take any blame. What if he faces criminal charges, or goes to prison?"

Caroline choked back her own rising fear and caressed the older woman's hand soothingly. "There now, I'm the one around here with the vivid imagination! I don't know what's happening, but I do know we have a God bigger than our troubles."

"Of course," Camellia whispered. "I'm sorry, I'm just so rattled." Sniffing, she smoothed her hair and composed her face. "God will hear a lot from us for a few days."

When Chad arrived home, Camellia watched the children so he could talk to Caroline. They went into the living room in their wing of the house, but he added little to the sketchy details Cole and Phillip had already given. A man she shuddered to remember was murdered and his killers were demanding money from Gregory Global after dumping his body at their door. There was a nefarious connection between Wilfred and a client who mysteriously closed his secretive long-standing account that morning. Chad was in danger because a drug cartel behind Wilfred's execution would think he was an easier way into the account than his resolute father, so he'd have to stick close to their bodyguard Azariah for a few days. While they waited, Phillip, and Global were under investigation for possible ties to money-laundering for a notorious drug lord.

All the public knew this early into the affair was that a man with shady financial dealings and a hatred for Phillip Gregory was murdered and dumped outside Global London's office, and a notorious drug cartel was claiming responsibility. While Phillip and his brother Justin were cooperating with authorities, Chad and Cole were leading the company as if everything was normal.

Chad tried to convince his wife to take their trained German shepherd with her to Charleston, but she firmly refused. "You know I'm not goin' to leave with Lancelot, even if I'd ever dream of puttin' a dog in my Ferrari! Your mom and the kids need him watching outside. I'll only be in the car for a little over an hour until I get to your grandparents' house."

She pulled back from Chad's arms to look up at him. His brow furrowed over a look in his eyes that she couldn't remember seeing since the night they faced Hurricane Hugo.

It was fear.

This was her rock, the guy who was always ready with assurances, on top of every situation, fixing things for everyone around him when trouble came up. If he feared something, then the monster really existed, and it crouched nearby, waiting to spring.

Realizing she read his feelings, he pulled her back into his chest, as if shielding her. His distracted urgency left her alarmed and a little breathless, so she clung tighter.

"I don't have to be at the reception," she said, her voice muffled against his shirt. "Did you explain to the officers it's just a fancy tea, with an art show to benefit a good cause? Guests would attend without me. At least let me drive back tomorrow night after dinner."

"No. We're ordered to act as if nothing has happened," Chad reminded her, absently running his hand through her hair. "It'll be dark by five-thirty this time of year, and I don't want you on the road alone at night. Our moms can't go with you now because we need them to look after the kids. Besides, my grandparents did a lot of work to host this tea."

He clutched her shoulders and said huskily, "Believe me, I want to lock you up here, but I have to do as I'm told right now. Guilty or not, no one will ever forget if Global is tagged to somethin' shady."

Caroline sighed as the room grew darker, remembering their plans for the evening. A relaxing date night would have been the right time to mention something she'd been meaning to tell him. Now it would have to wait.

"Your dad will need to discuss all this with your mom when he gets home, so our date tonight is off," she murmured into his collar. "My mom's babysitting for Natalie and Patrick, and Gran Vanna has dinner guests at the Big House."

Chad's hands slid down her arms. "This will disrupt our lives for a while. You and the kids shouldn't have to live like this. It's ludicrous, all this drama, security, bodyguards, dead bodies on the doorstep! Bein' married to me—"

"Is what I always wanted." Caroline reached up to push his blonde hair back from his face, then lightly caressed the clenched jawline. He relaxed slightly. Now that she'd accepted that they were in deep trouble, his distress stirred a protective feeling inside her. "Whatever's happening, Chad, God entrusted it to us. He will see it through, no matter how inept we are, because it's not really about us after all."

"If somethin' happens to me, Care, it's okay to move on with someone else, preferably someone insanely boring and to whom nothin' remotely interesting ever happens. Then maybe you and the kids will be safe."

Caroline's eyes narrowed at his words and the thick tone of voice. He was parroting something he knew he should say and adding something clever to disguise that he didn't mean it.

Wilfred's murder had shaken him. He saw his vulnerability to the unthinkable.

"You've forgotten how hard it is for anyone to fit into a life here at Painter Place. No, Chad. Without you, I'd be like my Gran Vanna. She could've remarried and left, but she carries on Poppy Noble's legacy here, helping Uncle Wyeth and Chrissy. As the next heir, I can't leave. The mansion will be mine. But you're not bound to the Big House anymore if I'm gone. You can leave the island to start a new life with someone else after the kids are older."

"No!" Chad shook his head vehemently and set his hands on her shoulders. "You're forgettin' the promise I made to you on the night of the Island Summer Dance. I said I'd always look after your home and gave you my signet ring to seal the deal. While I'm alive, no one else can do that like I can, and I'll never walk away from that promise. It's my home, too, and our children's home. We finally mixed the Painter and Gregory bloodlines—we're the answer to both our grandfathers' lifelong prayers. We aren't like other people, Caroline. We have a different way of life, and it controls our future, even down to who we can love."

They were only silhouettes in the gloom as she wrapped her arms around him. She murmured into his chest, "Then we'd better be pray like crazy that the Lord lets us grow old together."

Chad pulled her closer. His voice choked when he replied, "I've done that every day since my parents taught me how to pray."

Caroline knew all too well that sensation of a tightening knot in her middle, her pulse rate spiking up, and a slight breathlessness. It was her intuition. Yesterday's drama at Gregory Global was only the beginning.

Not for the first time in her life, she almost wished not to have this family trait. Amazingly, all the Painter family artists so far had passed it along from generation to generation, like part of the package that came with the island. Her grandmother and her mom said the reason she was even more sensitive to it than her Uncle Wyeth and Poppy Noble was because most females have an intuitive side anyway.

She stopped short of wishing away the gift because she knew it was part of how Christ used her in the world, for His purposes. Her blessings came with a higher risk than most people, and the new trouble at Global proved it.

But as an irrepressible optimist, she looked at the advantages of being married to Chad Gregory. He was driven to excellence, and his role as a husband was no exception. Once, he overheard her say the fire and flash in an emerald cut diamond was what she wanted in her marriage, so he gave her one as an engagement ring, then made her dream of fire and flash among his missions in life. He was possessive and attentive when they were seen in public, intentional about the impression he was a one-woman man who would see to it she was a one-man woman.

She had more than she dreamed of in a husband and more to lose than she could endure, if the worst happened. Only the resolve to be strong for their children would ever get her through it.

Caroline reluctantly left her home and family on this Wednesday morning in mid-January to drive her Ferrari toward Charleston, South Carolina. Just when her hands became white-knuckled in tension on the steering wheel, she passed a large homemade sign near the side of the road. It was like an old friend waiting patiently for her to drive by again, faded, chipped, and re-painted faithfully over the years by an unknown landowner.

"Jesus Saves," the words proclaimed. "John 3:16."

For God so loved the world...

Caroline's spirit soared to agree. *Yes, He saves us. And if He loves us that much, nothing about our lives escapes Him.* Her family's situation mattered to the Lord, and He would use it in ways she had no ability to fathom. Few things in her life were certain, but that much, she was sure of.

God had once comforted her with a thought, and it popped into her mind again now. *Nothing is wasted.* The profoundness of those words always hit her afresh. Sometimes, the thought was accompanied by a dusty shelved memory.

Like now. Her mind flashed with Chris Shepherd's face, his generous smile, and a special look that filled his eyes when he turned them to hers. It was as if a box lid resting askew in a far corner of her heart was pushed aside. Glowing memories were packed away there, along with a faint ache for something indescribable because it was never meant to be.

She caught a faint smile on her lips as she checked the traffic in her rear-view mirror. Once, she wondered if the preppy, uncomplicated, heart-of-gold guy who courted her might replace Chad, who seemed to have left her and Painter Place behind. But Chris abruptly broke off their brief courtship to go to the mission field, and it had gotten him killed.

A shake of her head cleared the sudden vivid memory of the look in his warm green eyes as he told her he couldn't take her with him where he was going, and she couldn't wait for him to return. That was truer than either of them had fathomed, for he was in heaven.

Maybe she never said a final goodbye in her heart because she was so overwhelmed with losing most of Painter Place in Hurricane Hugo. But even as this rehearsed excuse came to mind, she dismissed it. It had been almost five years, and today was as good as any to just face it: without a body, she had no closure. Her heart would not believe he was truly gone.

She checked her mirrors again, something her bodyguard Azariah had trained her to do constantly for situational awareness.

The road was relatively quiet and the pickup truck behind her allowed another car to pass and settle between them.

Shifting in her driver's seat, she pursed her lips at another familiar old feeling. Resentment. It was inappropriate for her to have direct contact with Chris after he left for the mission field and Chad returned, intent on marrying her. She had missed Chris and his easy, no-strings friendship. But there was wisdom in the wall erected between them. Chad was jealous of Chris, and anyway, how would she feel if Chad had an old girlfriend that checked in to say hello and occupied his thoughts now and again?

She impatiently brushed her hand across her fringy blond bangs. This was a fruitless pursuit, and irrelevant now. There was no gain in dwelling on things in the past.

Jesus Saves. The rustic homemade sign sprang once more into her mind. Did Wilfred Rothschild have time to come to terms with this truth before his life ended so violently? There were no more chances for him now. What a tragic ending, to be murdered and thrown on the doorstep of his despised enemy.

Her heart gave it a label. "Poetic justice," she whispered.

If he was lost forever, Jesus, I'm so sorry about Your heartache. I can't imagine Your pain when we turn our backs on You, and scripture says most of us choose the broad path to destruction. It also says You aren't willing for anyone to perish, loving us all, born and unborn, for all generations, so much that You sent Jesus to die in our place. Your heart's broken when we don't return Your love, yet You give us the freedom to walk away. That choice gives love value. It's the only way love can matter.

Caroline sniffed and blinked back unexpected tears for Wilfred before noticing that outside her car, the former lair of the Swamp Fox swept by. Francis Marion National Forest meant that Charleston was not much farther. She needed to be cheerful for Chad's grandparents.

Music would do it. She pushed in a cassette of one of her favorite Christian rock bands on the stereo. But the words to "Light A Candle" brought Chris Shepherd to her mind again. This song was how he both lived and lost his life. He gave up a career after college to be a light in dark places.

East Bay Street was always busy, even on weekdays in January. Caroline smiled politely at tourists when she was trapped at traffic lights, where they stopped on uneven cobbled walkways to admire her yellow Ferrari Testarossa. A group of men whistled and hit their hearts with their hand, and she quickly passed through the intersection before she could hear what they shouted.

She turned to the right onto Broad to get to Church Street. The Ferrari slid along the narrow way as she navigated between cars parked along the road, and she enjoyed the quaint views. Black gates in fanciful designs lured her with curling iron fingers to peek through into manicured gardens to see playful fountains. Historic homes in pastel colors with storm shutters, graceful piazzas to catch summer breezes, and window boxes that spilled color in a temperate winter made Caroline appreciate why Church Street was called the most romantic one in America.

At the drive of the Gregory's residence, she remembered Azariah's warning to be alert, to stay off the 'X'. That was also the first O in the OODA loop—*Observe*.

Tourists with cameras were enjoying their vacations and a mature couple read the historic marker plaque on the street side of the Gregory's home. No one seemed to loiter or watch the house.

Caroline shifted the Ferrari into park, ready to get out and open the gate, but a stocky security guard appeared and did it for her. She waved thanks to him and slid the purring sports car inside the property.

Stepping out onto the driveway pavers, Caroline extended a warm Southern greeting to the capable-looking guard. He wore an unassuming dark suit and an immaculate white shirt, sported a military buzz cut, and the set of his mouth told her it rarely curved upwards into a smile.

But this was Charleston, she mused, so he would learn to be lavished with kindness. "Hi, I'm Caroline," she said cheerfully, sharing a smile and her extended hand.

His darting brown eyes memorized her face while he nodded politely. "It's good to meet you, Mrs. Gregory. Just call me Jack. I've been briefed on your visit and I'm stationed here at the house. A local off-duty officer will watch things at the Heyward's home this afternoon for the tea. He's a friend of your grandparents."

Caroline kept her warm smile during his stiff greeting while she sized him up. All business, like her bodyguard Azariah used to be. She pinned him as ex-military, special forces, and his real name was not Jack. His accent was upper Midwest. Those alert eyes had the haunted look of seeing places and things that would give her nightmares.

She realized she studied him too long when he blushed and looked away. "Thank you, Jack," she said brightly. "Is there a Jill in your life?"

Disarmed, the guard jerked his head back around. An overpowering twitch pulled one side of his lips before he quipped, "Jill was tired of going up the hill all alone so often for a pail of water. When we tumbled down, she dusted herself off and walked away. I had to get over that fall by myself, while she ended up with 'Jack be Nimble, Jack be Quick.'"

Caroline tried to bite her smile in a straight line. "Ouch. She added insult to injury when you broke your crown. Women aren't all like that, you know. But much of the nonsense of real life can be learned in nursery rhymes, right?"

"You said it! Next time, I'd rather be a war-scarred knight who rescues a damsel in distress and gets rewarded by living happily ever after."

Caroline instantly beamed and wrapped the muscular bulk of him an irrepressible hug. "I'll pray that happens for you, Jack!"

Stiffly, the guard tried to be receptive without putting his arms around her or his hands on her. He managed a rusty smile when she pulled back from him to walk to the piazza. As she reached for the door handle of the restored historic home, she asked, "Where's Granddad? I don't see his car."

"The last guard on duty went with him on an errand up the street to First Baptist, overlapping our shifts. Mrs. Gregory is inside, though."

"Okay. I'll only be here for lunch, then I go to the Heyward's house."

"Yes, ma'am," answered Jack with a polite nod, all business once again. But he couldn't resist watching this charming young woman as the door opened. Instantly, she was wrapped in Lucinda Gregory's arms.

He wished she would chat with him longer. The sunshine seemed to leave with her, and the piazza felt vast and empty.

The ladies' exuberant greetings floated through the still-open door, joined by the pretty housekeeper he met earlier. She squealed in delight at Caroline's arrival like girlfriends at a sleepover, then promised something special for lunch with chocolate for dessert. He wanted to get to know that housekeeper better before this assignment was over.

A tight smile was playing tug-of-war with his mouth since meeting Caroline Painter Gregory. It felt good to use those muscles again, and with some practice, he might pull off something that could be considered friendly. When was the last time anyone had hugged him? He couldn't recall. He felt lighter, as if a weight he carried for too long was carried off in the warm breeze.

Jack had forgotten how different the people were in the South. Caroline was a modern Southern belle, and her accent dripped with sweet friendliness like the Spanish moss on the oaks out back. There was no question she was genuinely interested in what mattered to him.

Admit it, he told himself. *It's more than that. You don't talk about what happened, and she had no reason to pay any attention to you. Then she walks up like fresh air and sunshine through a window she nonchalantly opened in your soul, using a nursery rhyme to give you enough distance to express yourself. She got you to understand your own hopes and say it out loud. Voicing something is the first step to making it happen. Heaven help the guy who loves Caroline.*

His smile vanished. The guy who loves her was heir to Gregory Global, and he needed heaven's help all right—from a drug cartel named *Temoso*, the Spanish word for "fearless."

Jack tensed when a black sedan slowly pulled up on the Water Street side of the intersection in the Bend. He checked his weapon and stepped down to peer through the slats in the Gregory's gate. The sedan backed up to park in a short driveway, positioned for a quick chase. His earpiece came to life with confirmation that this was the street backup he was watching for.

Satisfied, he paced the perimeter of the property. No one was getting past him if they were coming for Caroline.

Chapter Three

Life is a spell so exquisite
that everything conspires to break it.
-Emily Dickinson

Phil Gregory, Sr. stood beside his black Mercedes with the front passenger door open, putting Caroline's overnight bag in the front floorboard. On the driver's side, she hooked a silky jade green dress on a hanger behind the front seat.

"You're sure you're okay with me drivin' your car?" Caroline asked as she walked back around to say goodbye and trade keys.

He laughed outright and put his keys in her hand firmly. "I've wanted to drive your Ferrari for five years! And to think, all it took was to block you into my driveway."

"Just take it easy on Jack's nerves when you race it over to the reception later," she said in mock sternness, handing over her key. She glanced at Lucinda while she walked back around to the driver's side of the Mercedes. "See you after Sandy gets here?"

"Absolutely!" answered Chad's grandmother, stretching out the length of the word. "It's a shame your mom and Camellia couldn't come, but never you mind, we'll take a lot of pictures."

Caroline waved goodbye, then got in and settled her purse. She adjusted the driver's seat while they went inside, beckoning Jack to step in with them for a quick bite of lunch before Mrs. Gregory cleared things away.

Caroline smiled to imagine the gruff bodyguard being pulled by the arm upstairs, where lunch waited, arranged on beautiful willow china and set on a wicker table with a view of the historic streets. She fiddled with the radio to change out the old Fifties station, then twisted to look behind, slowly backing out of the driveway into Church Street to navigate to Rutledge and Murray. The tinted windows in the Mercedes gave her an anonymity she didn't enjoy when driving the head-turning Ferrari.

Across the street from the Phil Gregory home, a man hiding in in Stoll's Alley pulled on a black ski mask and blurted into a radio. "The old man's leaving. Showtime!" He ducked behind an ancient rusty gutter downspout instinctively as the Mercedes crept back into the narrow street. He heard the tires shifting against the pavement as the luxury car began driving forward. His adrenaline surged, and he prepared to spring into action at the expected squeal of brakes and metal crunching metal.

"Go, go, go!" came the order over his radio, but he was already sprinting toward the intersection of Church and Water Street in the Bend. A black SUV rolled back from bashing the front quarter panel on the driver's side of the Mercedes and slamming it sideways into the traffic sign.

The crash of a fragile china plate coincided with the impact of the vehicles in the Bend as Jack flew from the upstairs veranda back in toward the staircase. Even from inside the house, he heard the van that screeched to a halt and knew it would block in the black sedan in the driveway on Water Street. He roared in dismay that his back-up would be distracted and neutralized.

Precious seconds ticked past as the officer in the blocked sedan dropped the cold fast-food burger he had in his hands to reach for his weapon. The van's driver left it running and fled through the passenger door, leaving the impression that there might be an explosive ready to detonate. The officer opened his door and quickly rolled out onto the ground for cover, as far as he could get from the vehicles. When the expected explosion didn't happen immediately, he squatted and scanned the scene before cautiously going from cover to cover toward activity at a black SUV.

From the second-story porch looking street-side, Lucinda and Phil Gregory watched in horror as a man wearing a ski mask roughly pulled Caroline from their wrecked Mercedes. He put an end to her elbow jabs when he covered her nose and mouth with a cloth. She went limp, even as Phil shouted angrily for them to let her go.

"This isn't the old man!" cried one of the armed men in ski masks to another. He grabbed Caroline's purse and overnight bag from the front seat.

"It's the right car! She's one of them. It's too late to change the plan!" shouted the first man, with no break in stride. "Leave her wedding rings."

Lucinda Gregory screamed Caroline's name while an abductor slid the rings from her left hand and placed them prominently on the front seat. Two men on the street in fatigues came onto the scene but stopped and raised their hands when the kidnappers leveled AK47s at them. Tourists shrieked and sought cover.

Three men ducked into the SUV with their helpless captive and tires squealed as they sped down Water Street toward Meeting. The well-orchestrated kidnapping was over before Jack could get through the gate. He ran to the open door of the driverless Mercedes as the flustered agent rushed from across the Bend. Jack swiftly gathered Caroline's rings and turned off the engine.

"I got the plates and radioed to get a tail. I couldn't see to shoot!" the man panted, fuming at being outsmarted. "They blocked me in and set up in front of a home. There were tourists and residents walking their dogs on the street. These guys knew

I couldn't shoot at someone's front door or into a crowd!" He slapped the smashed metal of the Mercedes.

A scream came from the second-story porch of the Gregory's home, and Jack looked up to see the pretty housekeeper covering her mouth in shock. Mrs. Gregory came to the railing. "Jack, please help!" she shouted. "My husband has collapsed!"

Jack ran back to the Gregory's house, barking orders to the other agent. "Get a bomb squad to handle that van and keep tourists away! Call local police while we have witnesses to interview and see if those soldiers will help with crowd control so I can get an ambulance in here. I'll call the Weaver."

With a tip of a hand through a lowered tinted window, a black SUV with a broken headlight and dented bumper passed through the entrance of the Port of Charleston. A few minutes later, a rig pulling a shipping container exited. The rig waited while flashing lights and sirens raced past on Concord, then slowly made its way toward the interstate. Downtown Charleston was exploding with raging sirens, and the rig was among the last vehicles allowed to go past onto I-26 before a police barricade was set up for traffic out of the city.

Phil Gregory Sr. was alive but unresponsive in the emergency room. Jack stayed close by, waiting for Mrs. Gregory to arrive with their in-laws, Montgomery and Charlyn Heyward, in whose home Caroline Gregory should be right now. She should have that beautiful jade dress on, sipping fancy tea and talking about her paintings to the guests.

A male voice amid the white screens commanded nurses to call a surgeon on duty and get Gregory prepped before they lost him. Jack gulped helplessly, watching the commotion as Mrs. Gregory rushed in and a nurse told her that her husband would need surgery. Lucinda pulled out a card from her purse and told the nurse to tell the physician on staff to call for Dr. Tony Rush.

"Dr. Rush? He used to be the best, but he's retired now."

Mrs. Gregory's hands flew to her mouth at seeing her husband lying so pale and unaware of her presence, but she recovered to answer with a steady voice. "Yes, I know, but Dr. Rush is family, and he's in town this week, to attend a reception with us tonight. His granddaughter was just kidnapped from my husband's car, and I assure you, he wants to know about this! My husband would choose him."

The nurse's eyes widened, and she promised to call as she chased the team with Phil Gregory down a hallway. When the doors shut, Jack stood awkwardly by Mrs. Gregory's side. She turned to him. "Are you a Christian, Jack?"

Her accent reminded him of stories of long summer days spent with a fishing rod under the sprawling embrace of ancient oaks. "Well," he finally replied, "I grew up going to a little church, but I left all that behind when I went into the military. It's hard enough to survive there without revealing your weakness."

Lucinda's delicate brows shot up in genuine surprise. "A weakness, Jack? Why, Christ is the only source of our strength. All else will fail us. When you've lived as long as I have, you'll look back and see the proof of that."

Jack was uncertain how to answer. "Mrs. Gregory let's go back to the waiting room."

Montgomery and Charlyn Heyward waited for her, distraught over Caroline's kidnapping and Phil Gregory's collapse. Charlyn hugged Lucinda as Jack's radio crackled again with updates on the futile search for the black SUV. Jack moved out of their earshot to listen, feeling desperate now and loosening his collar in an agitation.

The window of time to catch the abductors was lost. But he refused to accept the odds he knew were against Caroline Painter Gregory ever coming back.

Phillip Gregory couldn't keep up with the men that filled his and Chad's offices now, speaking in low, curt tones and coded communication into radios. His head hurt, his heart ached, and his eyes stung from crying like a baby. His dad had just suffered a serious heart attack, maybe a stroke, and he might not make it. Global was in emergency lockdown for security, so he could not leave to be at his mom's side at MUSC.

Worst of all, his daughter-in-law was kidnapped in a case of mistaken identity. Little wonder his dad collapsed. He would refuse to go on living if something happened to Caroline in his stead, knowing Chad and Painter Place would never be the same.

Azariah was ordered to drive Chad home, followed by a security team who would station themselves at the bridge and around the Gregory estate. True to his nature, Chad struggled, demanding to stay for information, but he was hoarse from crying and sounded more pitiful than powerful. A medic gave Azariah a small prescription bottle that rattled with several capsules. He murmured that it would "help Mr. Gregory sleep tonight." The bodyguard slipped it into his pocket, then he and Phillip led Chad out the door to the elevator.

Enduring his son's devastated expression as the door slid closed between them was one of the most heartrending experiences Phillip could remember, perhaps eclipsed only by the attempted kidnapping of Chad as a baby, or the night Hurricane Hugo might have killed him, or the night an intruder shot at him in France while attempting to steal the twins.

Standing in the hallway now, Phillip fought for composure, trying to shake the memory of Chad's eyes begging him to make everything right again.

Lights indicated the elevator had reached the parking deck. His son would be escorted to his car, as a passenger this time. Drawing a shaky breath, Phillip rubbed his hands over his face.

This might be the historic end of Gregory Global. And right now, he didn't care. "Nothing is worth this," he whispered fiercely.

As he returned to his office, the same medic handed him bottled water. "Sir, we'd like you to stay through the night, in case there's a ransom demand for your daughter-in-law or more instructions from the cartel who murdered Rothschild. We're bringing in dinner, but after that, you'll be more comfortable in your son's office while we set up a nerve center in yours. If you can't relax, I'll give you something. You're no help to your family if you don't rest."

Phillip nodded numbly and walked to the wall of windows with a view of Painter Place, which had effectively been turned upside down by Gregory Global. How this would affect relationships between the Painter and Gregory families remained to be seen.

Near a manhunt and roadblocks in the peninsula city of Charleston, South Carolina, a twenty-passenger Gulfstream prepared to take off. Abductors propped Caroline back in a seat cushioned with extra pillows and belted her in, with a slim pillow cradling her neck and head to hold it upright. A young woman with up-swept black hair sat beside her and grasped her wrist, taking her pulse. Her olive skin contrasted with the peach undertone of the hand in hers.

"*Halcones* say old Gregory had a heart attack," announced a man nearby. "Guess the boss was right that we needed your medical expertise in the get-away, Jadyn. At least we don't have a stiff to unload somewhere or a murder charge on our heads. Keep the *gringa* sedated, just like we planned for the old man. She can never tell what she does not know."

"She'll suffer motion and altitude sickness as she's waking up." The young woman's dark eyes were gentle on their prisoner, missing nothing. This *gringa* was taller than many males in South America, and they would scorn her slender, athletic figure. Men liked rounded softness, even plumpness. She glanced down at her own curves and breathed a sigh of satisfaction.

Looking back up to her patient, she couldn't resist brushing her hand on the woman's shoulder to push back a shimmering cascade of long blonde hair. It was straight and silky, not coarse like her own, and smelled like a summer breeze off the sea. It moved like a whisper. But the *gringa's* hair and clear, glowing skin could be her downfall before this was over. She would be a rare prize where she was being taken.

The man across from Jadyn watched her admire the prisoner, then he snorted. "You are too soft! Wear your mask as she rouses and be careful what you say. Make her eat and drink a little, then take her to the bathroom before you drug her again. I'll cuff her if we need to. She's supposed to be delivered undamaged, but she's a fighter. I cannot take her to your father beaten and marked up, no matter how much pleasure it would give me."

The nurse watched him smirk as his eyes ran over their prisoner. Hiding her revulsion, she set her patient's limp wrist on the armrest and adjusted a belt around it.

She looked out the window and let her mind drift like the clouds. This crime was exactly why she had to find a way out of the life she was raised into. It was not her expertise as a nurse that made her father include her on this assignment. When the fact that she took part in kidnapping this hapless young lady was strategically leaked to the rival cartel *Temoso*, Dominic might doubt her.

In the cockpit, the pilot listened to the co-pilot's communication with their *Puño* cartel dispatcher about what came next. As a security measure, even the pilots had no way of knowing how far they would carry Caroline Painter Gregory. She may be transferred to another mode of transportation in a crisscross path designed to scatter anyone trailing them. This could take as little as a few hours, but he had enough breadcrumbs if it took several days.

On Thursday morning, Chad staggered into the master bathroom where Caroline's fresh towel hung neatly beside his. Would she ever return to use it? Where was she? Was anyone hurting her?

Tears stung his eyes, though he couldn't fathom why there was any water left in his body for more. Bracing both hands on the marble vanity, he gasped for air to breathe. He must stay in control today, or Azariah would insist he swallow another one of those capsules that knocked him out last night.

Chad washed his face and reached for a towel, rubbing it over day-old stubble. Then he stared at his reflection, startled that he had aged overnight. The water wasn't washing away the tension on his face or the red from his swollen eyes, and he didn't want his children to see him like this. But their raised voices out in the living room meant he'd have to handle trouble.

Walking in, he saw little Savanna sweep her doll across a castle the twins were building with a million Legos, screaming that she wanted to play, too. Rhett grabbed the doll from her, shouting that she didn't understand what they were doing, and Mama said to be careful not to let her put the Legos in her mouth.

In despair, he surveyed the wreckage of the castle. With an infuriated cry, he tossed her doll over to a chair, shouting that Legos were not baby toys and she better stay out of their way. Rayce shot her a withering look, groaning in dismay and frustration, salvaging the strewn chaos that their castle had been reduced to.

Savanna cried out that her brothers were mean. She ran to her doll, climbing into the chair as she sobbed pitifully, calling for her mama over and over.

All three children stopped at once when they noticed their dad. Savanna quieted with a hiccup when she saw his face. He didn't trust himself to discipline them in the mood he was in, so he simply walked over to the sofa and sat down, his elbows resting on his knees and his hands covering his face.

His daughter climbed up beside him with her abused doll, wiping her damp cheeks with the back of her hand and patting his shoulder. Rayce sat down on the opposite side, putting his arm around his dad's back. Rhett knelt in front of him, timidly resting his hands on his dad's knees.

Chad sniffed and blinked back tears, then put his hands on Rhett's. His oldest twin son studied him and climbed into his lap, trying to stretch his arms around his dad's broad shoulders.

After planting a kiss on Rhett's blonde head, Chad rasped, "Rhett, I already feel like someone smashed my heart, the way Savanna smashed your Legos. If you all keep actin' like this, I'll have to spank you, and it will feel like someone's still poundin' my smashed-up heart."

"Your heart's smashed because the bad men took Mama. I don't like it when she's gone. You can get her back. You're in charge, Daddy."

In resignation, Chad shook his head. "Not this time, Rhett. I'm not in charge of this. God is."

"But God doesn't talk much." Rhett jerked around to spot his two-way radios, scrambling down to gather them. Savanna scampered into his space in Chad's lap, but after giving her an annoyed look, Rhett handed a radio to his dad. "I need you to be in charge, Daddy. Tell me where Mama is. And if God says somethin' you tell me that, too. Okay?"

Accepting a kiss on the scruff of his cheek from Savanna's doll, Chad studied Rhett's hopeful face. "Do I have a good battery in this?"

Sliding from the sofa cushion, Rayce exclaimed that he knew where the batteries were hidden from Savanna. She began her move from Chad's lap to go follow him, but her dad held her in place and shook his head. She started to pout, then thought better of it and kissed him instead.

Rhett climbed into the space Rayce left vacant. He reached up to take his Dad's haggard face in his hands, rubbing curiously at the stubble. Blue eyes just like Caroline's reached into Chad's soul, and like hers, his son's eyes were full of confidence in him. "Daddy, you're in charge. Go back. You send me words."

Chad blinked back more maddening, stinging tears, and Rayce came in with fresh batteries for the two-way radios. The twins changed out the batteries with a sense of purpose and hopefulness that he had no heart to discourage.

From behind them at the open double doors to the main part of the Gregory's estate, Camellia spoke, and he wondered how long his mom had been standing there watching. Her voice soothed him, even though it was hoarse, as if she had a sore throat or had been crying. "Breakfast is ready. I'll watch them, Chad. Valerie, Natalie, and Marina will help me. No one can leave the island right now anyway, and we want to do this for Caroline."

Her voice broke off, but she recovered to say, "Tony Rush called to say Granddad is stable. You go to the office. Put on that attitude of yours and insist that you're staying. It'll help you and the boys."

Chad looked at his son. "Okay, Rhett, I'll try to do what you want, if I can trust you to behave like a gentleman with your baby sister. She doesn't have Brooke here to play with. I need to focus on this problem, and it might take a while. This will mix our schedules up for a while. Can I count on you to be your best if I leave you and Rayce in charge here with Mimi Melia?"

"I promise," Rhett said solemnly, reaching for his dad's hand. "Shake on it. I love you, Daddy, and I'm sorry your heart is so smashed up."

Rayce characteristically echoed his brother and put out his hand to shake, too. Savanna wanted her turn to shake as if she understood and was in on the deal.

"No more smashin," she announced with finality.

Chapter Four

Great ambition is the passion of a great character.
Those endowed with it
may perform very good or very bad acts.
All depends on the principles which direct them.
-Napoleon Bonaparte

Showered, shaved, and dressed for business like any other day at work, Chad drove his Porsche past reporters kept at bay by security and barriers around Gregory Global. Cameras snapped glimpses of him through the car windows in his dark Ray-Bans. His mysterious bodyguard filled the passenger seat, his watchful eyes also obscured behind sunglasses. He wore the stony expression they expected.

Reporters clamored for camera time about the vehicle, speculating that Chad's license tag, GLOBALX3, might mean that he's the third Phillip Chadwick Gregory in direct lineage, though it was a family name in other generations. But they noted that others thought it was a statement that Phillip Gregory Jr. and both his sons ran the family business from this main headquarters in Whitehaven, South Carolina, so the 3 was about them all. Then they launched into speculating if Chad would get rid of that plate after this, since his company was the reason someone kidnapped his beloved wife.

Finding his office vacant, Chad went to his desk and picked up the sleek frame showing off his family. The photo oozed the wholesomeness he and Caroline aimed for, and he felt his heart gush with pain, love, and pride. He, Caroline, and the three kids were on a beach dune with sea oats and shells, the blue Atlantic creating a calm horizon. All blondes, all relaxed smiles and giggles, in white shirts, blue jeans, and bare feet.

Advertisers pursued him for portraits promoting their wares or services, hoping to make everyone wish that something magical would rub off the product to make their own families like his. His life had been nearly perfect life until yesterday, when it crashed into a shattered mess that could never be put right again, as if nothing happened. Even if Caroline was delivered safe and sound to him right this minute, nothing would ever be the same again.

He stared down at his planner, noting that someone had flipped it over to today, Thursday, January 19, 1995. The Bible verse for the day was Psalm 40:17. "I am afflicted and needy; the Lord thinks of me. You are my helper and my deliverer; my God, do not delay."

He read the verse again, then braced himself before pushing the button on the answering machine. His sister Sandy's voice was so much like his mother's, and it hit a soft place that was all hers in his heart. Tears stood in his eyes.

"Chad, nobody gets too tough for his big sister, you understand me? This is rippin' you apart and you need to call before you lose it and do somethin' you'll regret. I mean it, don't make me come up there!"

She broke off with a sob before launching into the rest of her message. "I just left Granddad's room. He's not out of the woods yet 'cause he's lost the will to live. He'll never get over this, Chad, never. I'm worried about Daddy, too. He blames himself. Anyway, my friends at church are organized a continuous prayer chain for us, and I have faith that God will use this bad event for some great good. Call me, I mean it! I love you, little brother."

The machine beeped and Cole took his turn at bat. "Chad, Mom tells me you aren't ready to talk yet, but I'm your brother. We do this together. Caroline—"

He lost his voice, cleared his throat, and rasped, "She was my sister before you made it legal, ya know? Shannon's so torn up, she's upsettin' the kids. I had to call her parents to come help. Uncle Justin's got to rest, or he'll be in the same place Grandad is. Our family can't handle more tragedy right now. I called Baker, Joey, and Derrick. I need to hear your voice, man. Call me!"

Chad grimaced, listening as his brother-in-law Patrick's voice poured out of the phone speaker next. "Chad don't blame yourself. Care talked to me about this one time, and she made me promise to keep the Painters from lettin' it come between our families. She claims this could only happen if God allowed it, which takes it out of Global's realm, and that she'd be in His hands. She loves you, man, she always has, and told me that's what makes the risk worth takin'. She wouldn't trade a minute of her life with you for safety. Call me or I'll set up a stake-out on the sofa at your house."

Chad's hands were over his face as he tried to keep control. He couldn't return any calls, not here. He sniffed and directed his mind to plan what to do next. Noticing the silent television screen, he checked his Rolex and dared to turn on the news.

The screen sprang to life with excited reporters and the first photos he'd seen of the abduction scene at the Bend, where his granddad's wrecked Mercedes was shoved against a street sign. He felt queasy. The open door, empty front seat, and the outline of Caroline's dress on a hanger hook in the back window stabbed his heart.

Unsteady now, he reached out to grip the top of his desk. Azariah scowled and moved closer to him, watchful, but Chad muttered that he was okay.

On the television, a woman walking down Church Street during the incident recalled what she saw, saying it was almost over before anyone understood what was happening. The interviewer asked if she heard a scream for help, and Chad clenched his jaw.

The witness answered, "No, but when a man pulled her from the car, she made a warrior cry with a sharp jab of her elbow—like somebody throwin' a punch in the movies. That girl has had some trainin' 'cause I wondered if this was real or if I was watchin' a show. But then a guy put somethin' over her face, and she just, ya know, collapsed against him and he put her in a black vehicle like a SUV."

A familiar publicity photo of a younger, vulnerable-looking Caroline filled the screen and Chad had to sit down. That sparkle was in her blue eyes and she wore that signature smile he never got enough of, the one that promised she was about to make something fun or interesting happen.

But what happened yesterday was not her doing, and while it was certainly interesting, he was sure she wasn't having any fun. He breathed another prayer begging God not to let anyone hurt her.

A reporter told citizens to be on the lookout to help find her. Authorities in Charleston would not comment on an ongoing investigation, except to say Mr. Phil Gregory of Charleston, the current patriarch of Gregory Global, was the intended target of the kidnappers. The crime was linked to the murder of Mr. Wilfred Rothschild, who was executed and delivered to the door of Global London. The reporter stressed that Caroline's captors were heavily armed and dangerous, and everyone in Charleston was praying her fate wouldn't be the same as Rothschild's.

A man with white hair strode into Chad's office and snatched up the remote control on the desk, clicking the screen off. He announced, "Mr. Gregory, if you want some real news, follow me." Then he turned on his heel and walked out.

Chad and his bodyguard exchanged looks under raised brows for a frozen moment, then Chad grabbed his briefcase with Rhett's two-way radio inside. They hurried after the man into Phillip

Gregory's office, which had been transformed into a headquarters of some sort. His dad looked up from papers he held and gestured for Chad to come over. Caroline's father, Andy Painter, sat on his other side, wearing the strain of a sleepless night. His Nike-clad foot shook nervously, crossed over the leg of his jeans.

Something was familiar about the frost-haired man with the commanding presence, and Chad tried to remember how he knew this wiry older gentleman with quick reflexes and alert eyes. Something about him said he'd been everywhere and belonged nowhere. His eyes were loaded with stories he could never tell, and Chad felt awed by what that must mean.

The man held out his hand. "I'm called the Weaver. I weave the traps that catch criminals."

There was still iron in the older man's handshake. "Just call me Chad. When Dad is beside me and someone uses 'Mr. Gregory,' I never know which of us they're talkin' to."

The Weaver nodded once with a blink. "Chad, I don't mean to be callous, but you'll hamper the process to rescue your wife if you're emotional. What happens here stays here. Family questions must be filtered to the barest details, like, yes, she's safe but we can't reach her yet. I know one of your best friends is Joey Grayson, but as an on-air radio personality, he gets no information but my press releases. Your friends Derrick Wallace and Baker Holmes will have the press after them for insider information. I know they're all upset, but we're playing by my rules. Understood?"

"I'm used to keepin' sensitive information, Mr. Weaver. Give me somethin' to do that will get my wife home."

Phillip broke in. "First, he needs to know about Global's true role in this."

The Weaver nodded, then explained that his team would direct a rescue from Gregory Global while coordinating with Scotland Yard, Interpol, DEA, and other groups involved. The supposed investigation of Global's involvement in money laundering was only a cover until his team could arrive. No such investigation existed, and it would never be on record or hinted at in public.

Justin Gregory's experience handling the mysterious client in London set off a signal that the officer was finally inside cover as an alias, and that a long-standing investigation of Wilfred Rothschild was substantiated. Global was a key player because it was Rothschild's second greatest weakness, after a bottle.

The Weaver's team was careful to arrange the sting operation so the agent would be the focus of interest for a ransom or other payoff against a threatened kidnapping, but there was always a risk that it could endanger a Gregory family member. They expected to deflect this threat by setting up an immediate ransom payoff. What they didn't expect was that a rival cartel would make that kidnapping move, with no known motive, unless they were trying to make it look like *Temoso* committed the crime.

"*Temoso* is delaying their demands out of confusion about your wife's kidnapping. They don't have her and the man whose account they expected to extort money from has disappeared. Our officer is under deep cover with their rival cartel, *Puña*, using these to alert us to his location."

Weaver held out his hand to Chad, who gingerly took an object in his palm. "It looks like a breath mint."

"Exactly. But when he breaks the coating with his teeth, he activates a technology that we can read. He spits it out and we follow his trail. He left one near Charleston, where he piloted an old Gulf Stream carrying your wife. That's overkill for an escape, but a twenty-passenger plane is ingenious for deflecting suspicion. It was his signal that gave us an area to search for a getaway vehicle. Strands of her hair are in it, but no blood. She didn't struggle."

Andy Painter winced and shifted his position on the sofa. Weaver glanced at him and paused, letting the information sink in before continuing. "We traced the rig back to the port, where we found the black SUV that hit your grandfather's car and fled with her."

He held up one of the breath mints, as if honoring it. "This is how we know exactly where the plane landed in Columbia. It's unlike *Puña* to take a straight path there instead of dodging around, so we're guessing they've planned a quick strike. Based on our ground game, we know who has your wife and where she's been taken. We're deploying a rescue team while there's a minimal guard around her. It will be nearly impossible to get her out once she's delivered to the *capo*, the head of the cartel."

"Can the pilot rescue her?"

Weaver pursed his lips, standing with his arms crossed in his dark tailored suit and watching the spark of hope in Chad's eyes. His expression softened at the desperate look of the handsome young man waiting at his mercy.

"He's not mine to command, Chad, and he's a valuable asset on the inside. His code name is The Fly, and he'll pretend to be a victim of my rescue effort. Frankly, he's in there for more than Rothschild's investigation and may never make it out. His job is to rescue a young couple who made a secret deal with two agencies to deliver them out of Columbia. They are the son and daughter of the rival *capos,* a real-life Romeo and Juliet."

Phillip ran his hands over his face and groaned. "What a mess. The couple's rescue puts Caroline in more danger."

"From our point of view. But your daughter-in-law is in grave danger no matter what we do, Mr. Gregory. The *Puña* cartel takes great care to be untraceable, and if my team finds her, the cartel knows there's been an information breach. From the other agency's view, Caroline's kidnapping is a monkey wrench putting their mission, and The Fly's life, at risk. Their asset gained the cartel's trust by setting up *Temoso* and Wilfred Rothschild. Rothschild's plans failed, but this was the tip of the iceberg on what he's been up to in his hatred of you, Mr. Gregory. You can read the report for yourself there on the table, in that stack of forms. Don't miss the compromising photo of your youngest son, Cole."

Weaver's gestured to the papers on the sofa table before them. His nod was grim at Chad's gaping expression when he heard his brother's name. "The photo was taken in 1985 in London at a party, when your brother passed out and his teammate got that note out of his pocket for Wilfred. Maybe you'll recall attending a hearing about Global's security measures. It was ten years ago, but Rothschild saved it to harm Global any day."

A round-faced man who had the flustered look of someone in a rush brought in a rolling cart laden with coffee cups and paper bags emitting enticing smells of biscuits, bacon, and eggs. He brought a few to the low sofa table to let Chad, Phillip, and Andy help themselves. Chad accepted the paper wrapped sandwich his dad commanded him to eat, but he put it down on the table. He opened the notch on his cup to let steam escape, then wrinkled his nose at a sip of the bitter liquid through it. He rarely drank coffee, but the caffeine could be handy today.

Weaver took a cup from the tray while everyone in the room settled to have their first chance at breakfast after a long night. He gave brief answers to requests from team members to evaluate data, then headed back over to the sofa.

"I will shoot straight with you, Chad. It looks like it will only be a matter of minutes now before you may regret coming in today. I'm expecting an update on a mission to extract your wife. It will be raw data off the field, not tidied up to make it easier to hear."

He took something out of his pocket and shrugged off his suit jacket, which he dangled on a finger to an assistant he'd been whispering with when Chad first came into the office. The aide took the jacket without a word, handing the man a large photo as if he read his mind about what came next. It was obvious the two had worked together for years.

Weaver held out his palm, in which Caroline's engagement diamond and wedding ring winked. "These were left by the kidnappers on the front seat of your grandfather's car. Consider them a calling card to announce she's no longer under your protection. She had quite an impact on the bodyguard on duty for your grandfather. He sent these rings overnight, asking to be re-assigned to a rescue team to go get her."

Chad drew a quick breath and stared at the rings, absorbing the reality that Caroline wasn't wearing them. The diamond was her dream engagement ring, a smaller version of the one Prince Rainier presented to Princess Grace Kelly. He heard her low, soft voice in his mind. *An emerald-cut diamond like a canvas to paint a lifetime together on, full of fire and flash...*

He clamped his lips into a line and reached out for this link to his wife, jamming the rings into his pocket. His expression said he'd deal with his feelings in private.

Weaver watched his reaction, then he thrust the photo in front of him. "Do you know this man?"

Chad's eyes popped, the rings forgotten, and his dad and Andy Painter gasped. A young man about his age looked back at him. If it weren't for the long hair, build, and expression...

"It can't be the guy that came to my mind," Chad muttered weakly. He reached for that cup of bitter coffee and took a long gulp.

Weaver seemed to expect Chad's reaction. "His family knows he's alive and serving others. He remembers nothing about his previous life and chose to leave it that way. He has a new identity and a whole new set of skills, the best operative I have in South America for rescuing your wife. But we have an obvious problem."

Chad couldn't take his eyes off the man in the photo, barely able to whisper the words, "He might remember her."

Weaver nodded and held out the photo. Chad hesitated before accepting it, then stared at a rugged, strong, and fearless face. The young man's expression was impatient and bored, as if he was on his way to somewhere else and had better things to do than stop for a photo. His long, light brown hair had blonde sun streaks scattered through it. He was beefcake compared to the sorrowful young man Chad saw break up with Caroline a decade ago. Shrugging off the impression of Tarzan, he felt a pang of jealousy that Chris Shepherd was not only alive, he was rescuing Caroline.

"Forget who you once knew," Weaver continued. "He was adopted by a man who's the head of the team I lead in Columbia. The man's biological son died in a cartel in a kidnapping rescue attempt similar to this one, and he looks like the twin of the guy in the photo you're holding. Chris Shepherd was rescued soon afterwards and only his team and agency know he's not the real son. They're a superstitious lot down there, afraid of him, thinking he's the blood son and can't be killed."

Weaver glanced over at Phillip and Andy, then back to watch Chad as he studied the photo. "His new name is Christian Chavarria. Chavarria means 'new house,' a fitting acknowledgment of his change in identity. But on a mission, he's known as 'The Jaguar,' after his predecessors, and the mere mention of his name intimidates people like the ones we're dealing with. He's highly trained, dangerous, and routinely rescues kidnapped government officials, wealthy civilians, and missionaries. He's under contract for five more years with us, if he lives that long. At that point, he can contract from year to year, as his age might put him at a disadvantage for injuries and he'll function in a more supervisory way."

Weaver took another sip of coffee and cleared his throat. "While Christian Chavarria instinctively uses talent, skills, and education he's always had, he doesn't recall learning them. He remembers little about his identity from before we rescued him. He had a head wound that would be mortal if we hadn't rushed him to get the latest and best in medical technology to keep him alive. When he has a memory, it strikes him with an immobilizing, blinding flash of pain that doctors don't yet know how to cure. It is mercifully quick, and he carries medication, but his family doesn't want to provoke that kind of pain by trying to make him remember them or hinder his mission. They say if it's God's will, they will be reunited eventually."

Andy Painter spoke up in a tremulous voice. "When the previous Jaguar was killed, was the victim rescued?"

"No, Mr. Painter. That mission to rescue a politician failed. And sometimes, the victim is tortured or murdered before we get in. My men are the cream of the crop, but sometimes they get killed getting back out, with no prize to show for their sacrifice."

Andy Painter's blue eyes were fearful, and his voice was rough with emotion. "Are you warnin' us that Chris—uhhh, the Jaguar—could die tryin' to get Caroline outta there?"

"Yes. Along with his team of very good men."

Chad read the look passing between them, and beside him, his dad rubbed his temples. They knew Chris as their former pastor's son. Another person they cared about was now ensnared in a deadly trail leading away from Gregory Global.

Weaver eyed his impressive watch. "I retired from a similar line of work and started this private organization to cooperate with governments and other operatives. We aren't military and we have our own radio code markers for the Jaguar's missions, just in case other organizations get entangled in our transmissions and need to sort them out. Your wife will be referred to as the Princess, for reasons of my own. If one of these rare debilitating incidents with the Jaguar's memory happens on a mission, we report that the Jaguar is 'mewing.' So far, it has never been a problem. If you overhear that he's mewing when he sees her for the first time, remember that we're prepared for that. Don't interfere. I'm his handler stateside, and I'll have you removed from this room. Do we understand one another?"

He locked eyes with Chad, who swallowed under scrutiny and slowly nodded. The Weaver gave a quick tilt of his head in Azariah's direction. "Show the photo to your bodyguard."

Chad glanced at Azariah, who was soaking in every detail of the briefing as he polished off a bacon and egg biscuit. He tossed the paper wrapper into the trash can from several yards away and stretched out a long arm for the photo.

In his first weeks on assignment with Caroline in France five years ago, Azariah was with her the moment she got the news that Chris Shepherd was presumed dead. He was among those who tried to comfort her that sleepless evening. Now, he memorized the picture and handed it back to the Weaver as a radio on Phillip's desk sputtered to life.

The Weaver spun around to go settle into Phillip's dark leather chair, removing impressive cufflinks and rolling back his sleeves.

Chapter Five

Being deeply loved by someone gives you strength,
while loving someone deeply gives you courage."
– Lao Tzu

"Weaver, this is the Panther. Acknowledge," a deep voice queried from a speaker into Phillip Gregory's office.

"Come in, Panther, you're loud and clear. Over."

There was a lag time before the radio came to life again. "Roger that. Six *Puña* guards down and the Fly and Juliet enjoyed a soft landing. The Princess is on the premises. I repeat—we found our Princess. But the Jaguar is mewing, Weaver, way off his game. The mission is compromised. Standing by for your signal to take charge. Over."

The Weaver's grimace made Chad's gut clench. He squeezed the edge of the sofa cushion in his fist. *The Jaguar is mewing* reverberated through his mind. *The Princess is on the premises... the mission is compromised...*

"Roger that," Weaver responded curtly. "Update status of the Princess. Over."

They waited for a full minute.

"Roger. Upper management and Juliet handled the Princess with minimal damage that we can observe. She's unconscious. We know she's been sick at some point because the clothing she was wearing at the time of her abduction is soiled and wadded up in the trash. She's been bathed and Juliet was dressing her in things from her overnight bag when the Jaguar had to put Juliet down. He managed to get the prize ready and has other evidence to send back, including a vial and syringe. Juliet assured him that any heirs would be safe with the formula."

The Weaver looked up sharply at Chad, his eyes questioning. Startled, Chad blinked before shaking his head to indicate his wife was not pregnant.

"Roger that," the Weaver responded into the radio. "No known medical risks. Get the package in the next drop. Is the Jaguar still mewing? Over."

"That's a colossal affirmative. I need new orders if you want this Princess. Over."

Weaver drew in a deep breath and his tone was decisive. "Roger. Panther, there's a new code in this mission. Tell the Jaguar I said that only the Plumber can save the Princess from Bowser. Ask if it's time for Luigi. Over."

He settled back into his chair. His aide scowled and moved closer. "Sir..." he trailed off softly.

Weaver slightly raised his hand to stop him, never taking his eyes from the radio. "I know you consider this to be useless information, but it's a secret weapon worth the gamble to get him into action again. He has a huge stake in this mission and deserves a chance."

The aide bit his lip and adjusted his tie. The radio crackled. "Say again. Over."

The Weaver repeated his order. Chad glanced at Azariah and saw the same question in his eyes. Had this old man played Mario video games? Why was he certain the terminology would awaken something in the Jaguar that would save Caroline?

The deep voice on the other end of the radio came back. "Copy that, Weaver. I've got an affirmative from the big cat on that new code, and a negative on Luigi. The Jaguar has landed on all fours. The Puma is covering him. Stand by."

Chad kept looking at his Rolex and clasping his fingers into one another with his hands together, absently rubbing over his wedding band and signet ring. He clenched his jaw at visions of Caroline lying somewhere drugged and throwing up. Then images popped in his mind of her lying helpless and unconscious in only her underwear while the Jaguar handled her. He honestly didn't know which vision bothered him most.

The radio sparked to life. "Weaver, the Princess is in the carriage and she won't wake up for a while. The Jaguar's wild. He says you deliberately held back vital information. He demands a mate, or you can come get her out of here yourself. Over."

Now Chad felt his jaw muscles clenching at his idea of the Tarzan in that photo in a rage. The guy had authority and Chad was unsure who was calling the shots.

"Affirmative, Panther," the Weaver agreed. "Tell the Jaguar he is cleared for a mate and a den. I repeat, the Jaguar has a mate. Over."

Chad shot to his feet with a gasp. The Weaver held up a warning hand and the speaker crackled on. "Copy that. Mission accepted under the big cat's terms. Next update at the checkpoint. Out."

"What does that mean?" Chad blurted.

The Weaver stood up with a sober expression. "The Jaguar has to assume a disguise now, so he lost his power of reputation to intimidate enemies. He's right, I withheld vital information, more than he knows yet. A blonde *gringa* in the jungle is a prize, something you can't comprehend here in Whitehaven, so you must trust me. Men along the way, maybe even scouting groups of opposing guerilla factions, will fight him for her. He can't protect your wife unless she's understood to be his woman, his possession, and then he'll be challenged to prove he can keep her. He must convince Caroline to play her part flawlessly under attack, because if she survives, she may never want her husband's touch again."

Chad felt like the wind was knocked out of him. He rubbed his hands briskly over his face and dragged them through his blonde hair before looking back into the Weaver's eyes. "What does she have to do?"

"That's the Jaguar's call. I cleared him for total control. There are no repercussions."

Chad squeezed his eyes tightly against the photo image burned into his mind. Chris Shepherd was dead, transformed into a living weapon called the Jaguar. He was nothing like the guy who left Whitehaven for the mission field. Whatever kind of man he'd become, he was in charge now, and he controlled Caroline.

If she survives, she may never want her husband's touch again. Chad envisioned a gang of ruthless men overcoming the Jaguar's team and molesting Caroline in succession. The Weaver's words were on a replay button. *Men along the way will fight him for her... guerillas...*

Chad's stomach lurched and he broke out in a cold sweat. His dad grasped his arm and pulled him quickly to his feet. "Let's take a break," he commanded.

As soon as he got out the door, Chad broke free and rushed to the nearby men's room, where he gave up the coffee he'd just sipped. His stomach continued to heave with nothing to offer up for relief. Tears poured off his face down into the toilet.

Phillip paced in front of the men's room door, clenching a fist, biting a knuckle between his teeth and listening to his son's misery. Beside him, Andy Painter covered his face against his own sobs. Azariah came out the door and braced his forearm against the wall before pressing his brow into it. He clenched his other fist by his side. Phillip stared at the bodyguard's distress, for it was the first time he'd ever observed a break in that cool demeanor. But in less than a minute, Azariah squared his shoulders and went back inside the office.

The next radio update for the mission was expected in the late afternoon. A fresh skeleton crew manned the equipment in the nerve center while the first team slept in cots set up like a camp in one of Global's conference rooms. Weaver napped in Chad's office.

Chad felt well enough to have brief phone conversations with his grandfather and sister. His dad hovered close, insisting that he eat the breakfast sandwich left untouched on the table, drinking water this time. He knew his dad was deeply upset by the radio transmission and Weaver's blunt description of what Caroline's situation was. Not only was her life and Chad's future at stake, but so was everything it had taken the Gregorys generations to build, and every relationship they had with the Painters.

Guessing the burden his dad was carrying and why it was comforting for him to have his son at his side, Chad settled back on the sofa. At his elbow, his dad handed him the shocking report on Wilfred Rothschild, and he looked it over until his eyelids drooped. Leaning back into the comfortable cushions in the quiet room, he fell asleep with a page about the episode in France resting in his lap.

His head came up with a bewildered start when the radio blurted into life. "Weaver, this is the Panther. Acknowledge."

Chad blinked several times, grasping for reality. A man jumped up from his seat at a computer screen and raced from the room. He brought in the Weaver, who found Phillip's chair and responded, "Roger, Panther. You're loud and clear. Over.

"Roger. Cancel that checkpoint route. Birds of prey circling overhead. The Princess is a diamond—the *capo* himself flew in to get her! Reporting from under the canopy in the closest den. The cat's still wild and the Princess is still unresponsive. Over."

The Weaver looked out into the sky over the Atlantic from Phillip's wall of windows. "Roger that. Identify the cat's problem. Over."

The Panther snorted into the radio, enunciating certain words for effect. "The Jaguar's problem is the Princess, and now he can't unload her at the bus station. He's stuck with her. Over."

The Weaver smirked and closed his eyes. After a few moments, he asked, "Is the cat approachable? Over."

"That's a colossal negative, Weaver. The cat mews intermittently, and he's sharpening his claws while he keeps a watch outside. The Puma and I didn't know he had this churlish dark side. We can't medicate him under fire. What are the orders? Over."

"Roger that. Pack for the trail and plan to sustain the Princess. Check off the den's supply list for females and add extra medical supplies. The Jaguar is cleared to re-route to the escape hatch, and I'll order the back-up team to meet you there. I repeat, follow the big cat if he can command, and take charge as per protocol if he's mewing. When the Princess awakens, she won't feel well and may panic. Explain that she's been rescued, and it's imperative that she stays calm and does what she's told without engaging the Jaguar. Assure her that her husband understands her status and everyone at home is safe. Convey to the Jaguar my full confidence in his new role as the Plumber. Over."

"Copy that, Weaver. Next report when we reach range. Will the two-way monitor be up? Over."

"Negative. The screen is delayed. That team member is wrapping up a mission to get here. Out."

Weaver looked across the office at the father and son duo, then at Andy Painter. "The cartel was closer than we hoped," he explained. "We're outnumbered. This means my three-man team can't deliver Mrs. Gregory to the American post to fly her home without being attacked. They must trek the jungle a day or so before we hear from them again, but I'll be right here, monitoring other efforts I'm firing up that will distract anyone from hunting down my team. You three should go home for now. Get some rest."

Chad's heart fell. He rose reluctantly, then picked up his briefcase and took out Rhett's two-way radio. "My sons asked me to radio them from here about the search for their mother. What can I tell them?"

Weaver held out his hand. "May I?"

Walking to his dad's desk, Chad put the radio in the Weaver's hands. The older gentleman looked it over to figure out how it worked, then pushed the transmission button. "Rhett and Rayce Gregory, this is the Weaver, with your dad at his office. Acknowledge."

Chad noted that he'd never told Weaver what his sons' names were. Was there anything about his life that this guy didn't know?

"This is Rhett, and Rayce is here, too. We're twins, always together. Do you work for my dad, Mr. Weaver?"

After a slight hesitation, Rayce's voice blurted from the speaker. "Over!"

Weaver pressed his lips together, then wet them as he answered. "Roger that, Rhett and Rayce. Your dad's letting me direct a rescue mission for your mama because it's a tricky business dealing with bad guys. My good guys found her and they're escaping now. This is top secret, so you can't tell anyone but your family. I'd like you to stay on your island for now. Your mama is in an enormous jungle, bigger than you can imagine, with lots of places to hide, but few places to reach me on the radio. Over."

Rayce radioed, "Roger! Are there wild animals there? Over."

Weaver grinned, an impish reflex that transformed his face into a grandfatherly expression. "Roger that. Look in your encyclopedias to find out about jungle animals in South America. Be sure to look for big cats called pumas or cougars, panthers, and jaguars. The next time we talk, I will ask if you know what kind of cat a panther really is. Over."

Rhett's voice answered, "Roger, Mr. Weaver. We will. Are you prayin' for my mama? We need her to come home. Over."

Andy Painter's hand went to his mouth, and he squeezed his eyes shut. The white-haired man's eyes softened when he looked at him. "Roger that, young man. I'm praying for her to come home soon, and for my rescue team to be safe while they help her. Will you pray for me, too, so God will give me wisdom to direct them? I always ask Him to help me know what to do next. Over."

They heard a deep sigh, then Rhett said solemnly, "We will. When you prayed, did God say anything back? Over."

Now it was Weaver who inhaled deeply. He leaned forward on one elbow and rubbed the wrinkles on his forehead. "Not in a sound like a voice on our radios, Rhett," he began slowly. "But I was just in your dad's office for a nap and read a Bible verse on his desk. It was like God spoke it into my heart. That's mostly how He talks, you know. So, I think God said something back. Sometimes, His answers to my prayers aren't words, just a sudden confidence that I know what to do, or a thought occurs to me. Other times, a preacher or someone will say something that is just what I needed to hear that day, or a song comes on the radio or into my head, and it helps answer my prayers. Do you know how to write something down if I tell you about a Bible verse? You and Rayce go find it after we're done. Over."

"Roger. O' course we can write! Just tell me the letters. Rayce is ready. Over."

Weaver spelled out P-S-A-L-M 40:17 over the radio. "It says God thinks of us when we need Him, and He helps us. Over."

"Okay. I mean, roger." Rhett sounded deflated. "Over."

"You already knew that, didn't you, Rhett?" asked Weaver. "But the things we learn every day in the Bible are the things we have to remember when we're scared. They're words for all time, not new words. Psalm 119:105 says God's word is a lamp to light our path. The time we need light is when things are dark. We don't need new words from God to tell us what will happen when we're scared. We're supposed to remember what He already told us and trust Him. Over."

There was a silence for a few moments, then Rhett answered politely. "Roger that. Thank you, Mr. Weaver. It's just that He said those things to other people first. I heard Pastor Payne say Jesus is the Shepherd and His sheep hear His voice. A voice is a sound. I wish sheep today could hear the sound, too."

Weaver looked up to meet Phillip Gregory's blue eyes before responding to the little boy. "Many Christians wish the same thing, Rhett. But until the day we get to heaven and understand all this, we should trust that the words are for us, too. Do you believe God is someone you can trust that much? Over."

"O' course. I mean, roger that. Can you work without my dad so he can come home? We're kinda scared. Lancelot's here on the porch, but he can't talk. My dad, he's big and strong, and he can read to us 'bout the animals. He's great at drawing them, too."

"Over!" blurted Rayce into the radio.

Weaver smiled. "Yes, your dad is big and strong. He's coming home now, and I'll keep working here to help your mama. Over."

Rhett's voice sounded relieved, but formal. "Roger. It was nice to meet you, Mr. Weaver."

Rayce blurted, "Nice to meet you, Mr. Weaver. I'm glad you're a good guy. Over!"

Weaver closed his eyes and smiled. "You're both welcome. Let's talk again soon. Out." He laid the radio down on Phillip's desk and sat back in his chair.

Solemnly, Chad said, "Thank you. I'll leave the radio here. Use it whenever you want to."

Chad's three children climbed all over him as they piled together on a rug in the family room with books about animals that inhabit the Amazon. They seemed to find security in clinging to him, though he felt inadequate to bring them any realistic measure of comfort.

The twins were fascinated to learn that jaguars mark their territory on trees by rubbing scent glands on the side of their faces into the rough bark. They pretended to be jaguars, acting this habit out with their cheeks on Chad's arms.

They were all unnerved by the hideous photos of black caiman. Savanna whimpered, burying her face in Chad's shirt. He stroked her hair, wondering if she'd have nightmares. The boys recovered from their revulsion and studied the animal.

Rhett pointed at the captions. "Daddy, what's it sayin' 'bout that alligator?"

Chad read silently. He'd need to translate to terms a five-year-old could comprehend. "Well..." he drawled, "it's like an alligator and a crocodile, but it's bigger. It's called a black caiman."

Rhett knit his brow in concern. "How big? Like this rug?"

"About sixteen to twenty feet, Rhett. It weighs almost a thousand pounds."

"How many feet are you, Daddy?" asked Savanna with a muffled voice, refusing to look at the book.

"I'm a little over six feet, baby."

Rayce scooted down to analyze the length of his dad's body on the rug. His eyes popped when he looked at his brother, who dropped his jaw. He looked back at his dad. "How many of you is that?"

"Three, all laid end to end."

Rayce gasped. "Would it eat people, Daddy?"

Chad sighed, knowing where Rayce was going with that information. "Yes, Rayce, it could. It's a predator that ambushes food, but it also likes fish like piranha so that's a good thing. I imagine it only eats animals, but not jaguars. Jaguars are their only enemy, besides the other caiman."

"They eat each other?" Rayce squeaked.

Rhett turned the page back to study the photos of jaguars, musing, "I like jaguars. They're my favorite. Other animals don't mess with them."

"Daddy, Mama won't be around caiman, will she?" asked Rayce, his little face scowling in concern.

A familiar stab of fear sank into Chad's heart, but he reached out to tousle his son's hair. "I don't know if she's near the rivers, Rayce. But I know God is with her, and she's very quick and smart."

"And God gave her a jaguar, and a panther jaguar, and a puma cougar," Rhett added confidently, still pouring over the photos in the book.

Caroline's brother Patrick and his wife Natalie brought their three children and some dinner to the Gregory family. After dessert, Patrick told Chad to grab a sweatshirt, then steered him out onto the deck for a private conversation.

Both pulled their sweatshirts on in the brisk winter darkness, walking to the edge of the deck to lean on the railing with a view of the glittering waterway. Patrick shook out his blonde hair as he said, "Dad told me about the Jaguar." He crossed his arms over his chest. "We need to jog tomorrow and blow off this tension. How about if you use one of Maggie Jane's sleep remedies tonight, go into the office early and see what the updates are, then call me with a time to meet back here? We'll take Lancelot out. He needs a good run."

"You should've seen his photo," Chad blurted with a dark scowl, settling into the same crossed-arm stance as his best friend. "He's nothing like the guy I saw break up with her. This guy—he's done things, seen things—hard-to-get-over things, like Ben and Azariah have done. Things very few people want to know about. Caroline was serious enough about their relationship to be distracted over her role here at Painter Place, and that was before he looked like the model in a Bowflex gym commercial."

"See! This is what I mean. Your imagination's runnin' wild. He was only a stand-in for you, just like Derrick was."

Chad's hair blew to one side in the breeze as he shook his head impatiently. He swatted it back in the general direction it came from. "I don't know, man. Remember, I saw them together when he told her he was leavin' for the mission field. She was gracious, but she was shell-shocked and hurt. Later, I knew she'd go out by the water, and I parked and watched her cry her heart out over him when she thought all of you were asleep. It ripped me apart."

Worked up now, he narrowed his eyes before turning to look out to the lights of Whitehaven businesses across the waterway. Patrick leaned toward him. "Your placeholder left, like you did! Neither of you were the type who just walks away. She didn't trust her own judgement anymore and wondered why God seemed to let her chase the wind."

Chad swallowed. Patrick sighed and ran his hand through his hair as if to straighten the jumble of words in his mind.

"Natalie helped me understand this back then. I'd been gone too long and didn't know my sister well anymore. Natalie watched her in Mevagissey when my parents asked Wyeth to take her to film the art video as a distraction from the breakup. Dad thought they'd put her out of your reach so she could clear her head and get used to you being back to stay. Caroline wasn't just grieving the loss of a close friendship with Chris. She was being forced back into enduring the emptiness you left. You caught her off guard the very next mornin' when she saw you for the first time in almost four years. Her heart was on her face and we both knew her reaction for what it was."

He pointed his finger at his friend. "Remember that moment every time you're tempted to doubt. With Chris, she looked for a way to move forward without you, with no idea you couldn't come home to her." He made a sweeping motion with his arm over the deck railing. "All this was put to rest before today, Chad. What is it that rubs you raw about him? Just spit it out."

Chad shifted his weight, brooding. "What if that hunky stunt guy Natalie used to date showed up to rescue her?"

Patrick slapped his forehead and groaned. "You had to go there! Misery loves company. Now I get to think about it for days."

"Okay, you're right, about everything. We'll jog tomorrow. I can't explain why that photo pushes my buttons, Patrick. His memories of her are affecting his ability to get her out. What if he falls for her all over again? During this mission, he can manipulate her to do somethin' that proves she's his 'mate,' and that better not mean to him what it means to me."

"No matter who the Jaguar is, Caroline hasn't changed," Patrick said with exaggerated patience. "Her heart and every inch of her is yours and always has been. I don't know how head or brain injuries change personalities, but Chris was once a deeply authentic Christian guy. He was a natural at sharin' his faith with other people. Surely that kind of conviction doesn't just fly out the window. He left her for the mission field, and he's still in it, just not the way he expected. As Caroline likes to say, nothin' is wasted. Maybe their previous relationship laid the groundwork for this event, when God knew her life would depend on him. But even if he falls for her all over again, it'll be more incentive to keep her safe. That's a win for you!"

Chad balled his fists. "It's a cruel irony that she's in danger because of me, and he's the one who gets to save her! Now he'll always be a hero in her life, maybe even some kind of fantasy."

Phillip opened the French door, then noticed Chad's fists. Chad relaxed his hands when his eyes met his dad's.

"Chad, sorry to interrupt, but Cole insists he won't hang up until you talk to him. Joey called again, too, and Derrick and Baker. Your mom told them you can't give them any information, but if you're up to it, maybe you can give them a chance to tell you they care."

"Okay. Thanks, I'll be right in."

Phillip closed the door and Chad looked back at Patrick. "Thanks. You always have my back."

Chapter Six

I cannot fix on the hour, or the spot,
or the look or the words,
which laid the foundation.
It is too long ago.
I was in the middle before I knew that I had begun.
–Jane Austen, Pride and Prejudice

Caroline was distantly aware of movement and unusual sounds, but these things quickly faded into the darkness she slipped back into. A familiar voice made her feel safe, so she relaxed until the musky scent of sweaty men and the fishy odor of a boat or dock aroused her curiosity. She stirred in a fight for a glimpse of reality. But the currents of a peaceful, timeless netherworld beckoned, enfolding her back into their depths.

A gentle rocking sensation lulled her until she awakened enough to realize she was in a boat. It creaked, but that was nothing compared to the noise of the night. Insects rubbed their wings like a stringed orchestra warming up to every music genre. Nocturnal birds hooted, screamed, and wheedled. Something large flew close by. *Bats*.

With a jolt, the reason for being in this strange environment brought her out of lingering sleepiness. Swallowing a stab of terror and gathering her senses, she kept her eyes closed so her captors wouldn't know she was awake. Her heart wrenched at the thought of Chad, who must be devastated. She wouldn't, couldn't think of her children's reactions to her plight. Emotion would break her.

She must survive and escape. Wherever she was, Azariah had given her the tools to evaluate it. OODA. Observe, Orient,

Decide, Act. She needed to focus, so she imagined a blank white canvas to add a plan onto.

Her captors must know that escape attempts would be futile from this boat, since no one had bothered to secure her. She vaguely recalled being on a plane, so she was a long way from South Carolina. Her abduction must be linked to the drug cartels that Wilfred was associating with. Was she somewhere in South America? *Have they also gone after Cole and Shannon? Please, God, let them be safe!*

The second O, her Orientation, was the most important step in this loop of information that would determine her decisions and actions. Outside of America, she was at a distinct disadvantage. Orientation was based on her genetic heritage, cultural traditions, and experiences. She'd have to ponder what attributes she could play up as a white American woman who'd grown up in the South in relatively privileged conditions, functioning under a conservative Christian worldview.

As a blonde, she was routinely underestimated and had learned early in life to exploit that useful fact to her own advantage. She'd have to operate at a faster tempo than her captors, but for that to happen, the Lord would have to throw them into her Orientation. She was out of her element in theirs. Being unpredictable was a characteristic she was known for back home, but here, she'd have a challenge generating the confusion and disorder that might give her an edge.

She would need a clarification of her captors' intentions before she could get to the D, Decide. Coming up with chaos later could force her opponent to over or under react, which would lead her to A, Act. Based on the limited information she had in her OODA loop at the moment, her action step was to be docile and cooperative. It would take restraint to master her defensive instincts.

The boat rocked and creaked. Caroline became aware of movement close by, then the sound of something sliding. She continued her game of possum and decided this emerging awareness was the best time to pray. Things could get busy soon, when they discovered she was awake.

Lord, you promised in scripture that there's nothing that can separate You from me. There is nowhere I can be in the universe that someone could hide me from You. But I'm being hidden from my family.

Caroline's throat grew tight with emotion and it hurt when she tried to swallow. *Give them peace! Please, I can't bear to think of how upset Chad and my babies must be, and Mama and Daddy, and Patrick and Marina, and everyone else in Painter Place. Camellia must be beside herself, trying to take care of the kids calmly when she's fearful of losing me and her sons. I can't even imagine what Phillip is going through. Please, influence the Painters not to blame the Gregorys.*

A hand on her shoulder made her start. A deep, hushed voice came near her ear. "Princess, are you awake yet?"

There was no hiding now, so she slowly turned her head toward the voice. Her neck was stiff and sore, and a groan of pain rasped in her throat. Someone had taken care to hang netting like a low tent over her body and the owner of the voice was lifting it. She opened her eyes and tried to focus them in the darkness as he reached to help lift her head.

"You'll have a headache, and your neck will hurt from being carried around. You were given a drug with temporary side effects, but I have a remedy that will help. You've been rescued, but we're being pursued, traveling downriver under cover of night to a village."

Something about the competent tone in his whisper and his genuine interest in her welfare put Caroline at ease. But why had he called her Princess?

She made out the shadowy silhouette of a tall, strong man with dark hair. He helped her sit up, and the first sledgehammer of pain took her breath away. She gasped and squeezed her eyes shut again, pressing her hands to her temples like a vise. For a few moments, searing pain was all that existed in her world.

The man made a clucking sound that reminded her of how Maggie Jane would react back home. She kept her voice in a whisper, rasping, "So this is like Alice in Wonderland? I get a drug to make me larger and one to make me small?"

He chuckled, kneeling in front of her with a thermos and gesturing for her to drink. He tore open the side of a bar-shaped package, handing it to her with two little lozenge-shaped pills. "It's refreshing to rescue a lady with a sense of humor," he whispered. "I had the camouflage duct tape ready if you were the hysterical girly type that would blow our cover. Here, get this down with a few bites of the protein. When you're finished, you can lie back, but keep your head elevated. I need to brief you on two things that can't wait. Do you feel well enough to focus?"

A wave of nausea passed while Caroline managed a mute nod and a glance around to see if he was serious about the duct tape. She gratefully took the dose of pain relief against a headache that would go down in history. With a moan, she trained her throbbing vision onto the man kneeling at her feet and found him looking intently into her face.

"On this mission to get you to safety, you're called the Princess. It protects your identity. Others on the main team have different identities. I'm the Panther, and that guy at the front of the boat with the oarsman, he's the Puma. But the king of the jungle 'round these parts is the Jaguar, and he's guarding the back in case we're followed."

The Panther tilted his head at a dark silhouette, barely discernable against an inky jungle. "The Jaguar isn't the man you once knew. He doesn't even remember being that person. If you try to engage him in recalling the past, it will put us all in grave danger. Follow his orders and don't interact with him. If anyone can get you out of here and back to your family, it's the Jaguar. Understand?"

Caroline stopped chewing and turned to sweep her eyes over the ominous silhouette, their last firewall in the back of the boat. Like the man in front of her now, he was tall and powerfully built, not someone to trifle with. In fact, something about the way he watched the darkness sent a chill over her.

She shuddered. The guy was lethal, she had no doubt, and he would do what was necessary and face any consequences later. Chewing the bit of protein bar and swallowing past her swollen, sore throat, her whisper squeaked. "I know him?"

"No. Not anymore. He has a new identity. And I've never seen him so surly about a mission, so keep your distance. Your husband knows you were rescued and we're on our way to a radio checkpoint where you might speak to him in a day or so."

She tore her eyes from the mysterious shadow at the back of the boat and tried to focus on the Panther. "When I was unconscious, I imagined hearing a familiar voice, and it made me feel safe. I don't remember who it was."

His tight smile came and went in a flash, framed by at least a day's worth of shadowy beard stubble. "The Jaguar's voice hasn't changed. But remember what I said. He's not who you think."

He gestured for her to drink more from the thermos. "It's important to hydrate, since we can't move fast if you're fatigued. You'll have privacy for toilet breaks, so keep drinking water to flush out your body from the drug they gave you. Pursuers forced us to detour from your first bus stop, so you're stuck with taking the long way home."

Wincing in pain again, she whispered, "It will take some getting used to being called the Princess." Her vision blurred, and she vigorously rubbed her forehead. "Are there 'shrieking eels' in the water to force me to stay in this boat? The 'cliffs of insanity' can't be far away."

With a soft snort of appreciation for her references to the Princess Bride movie, the Panther replied, "That's baby stuff compared to what's ahead of us."

"Who's after me, and why?"

The Panther shifted to a more comfortable crouch in front of her. "You were in the wrong car, Princess, that's all. They wanted Phil Gregory. It's complicated."

She looked down to see she was wearing her own sapphire blue cotton sweater, washed-out Calvin Klein jeans, and heavy Timberland boots she packed for comfort and a sure footing on Charleston's rough pavers. But she muffled a cry of dismay when she saw that her engagement and wedding rings were missing. Her hand shot up to her earlobe to feel for the sapphire and diamond settings that were still there.

"They took my wedding rings. Where am I, and what day is it?" she whispered weakly.

The Panther got up to settle himself against the side of the boat. "You're in a rain forest near the equator, on Thursday evening. All else is classified information. The less you know, the better."

On Friday morning, almost every man in Phillip Gregory's office gaped at the dark-haired woman who stood at the door with an attentive security guard. More than one may have described her as pretty, if it had crossed their minds. The two females on the team rolled their eyes at one another above their computer screens. Voluptuous in a skirt and sweater designed to allure, the newcomer used her low, sultry Spanish accent to present herself as a representative from another agency, sent to aid in negotiations.

The Weaver looked up from the monitor where he was analyzing information with a team member. He barely nodded to his assistant, who went to check the credentials she offered in a hand poised strategically over generous cleavage. Her blood-red nails were crisp against the white knit sweater stretched to her curves. The assistant flicked the badge from her hand without taking her up on the view, studying the information before holding it out to his boss.

The Weaver narrowed his eyes, turning the badge over, judging the weight of it. Handing it back to his assistant, he dismissed the woman curtly by telling her she could remain downstairs in the lobby as an aide for running errands and providing meals. Looking back down over his team member's shoulder to the computer, he focused again on the information.

The newcomer's pout prompted audible sighs from other men around the room. She announced to the director that although her agency expected her professional expertise to be used to a different advantage, she would help in any way until they recognized her value to the team.

Weaver didn't disguise his annoyance at this second interruption. Glaring, he addressed his assistant in a steely voice. "Pass along the errand and meal schedule to Isabelle, then give her a separate radio frequency to receive requests on. She'll need some essentials, like an unmarked note pad and pen. She's not likely to have thought of packing anything so practical. Then, have her escorted to a seat in the break room."

At a sharp tap of a file folder on his shoulder, Chad turned to meet his dad's scowl. He flushed. He'd been soaking in the alluring curves of Isabelle's form-fitting skirt. The only thing worse than his dad catching him in the act was if his father-in-law Andy Painter had been there.

Feigning interest in the contents of the file folder as his hot face cooled, he overheard the assistant's instructions to Isabelle for benign tasks. She wasn't at all his type.

He drew a sharp breath. *What?* Where did that come from? He flushed again. He didn't have a "type," he had a wife!

This vamp in his dad's office was exciting, but not just because of her teasing eyes and her siren sex appeal. This woman was irresistibly dangerous.

Unbidden, a scene like a movie with her and some faceless man began to play out in his head. He quickly slammed a door in his mind to stop it but didn't think before glancing back up.

He was startled to meet her dark eyes. Out of all the other men in the office, she'd been waiting for him, luring him like a target.

A target? This woman knew who he was!

Her dark eyes blazed triumphantly. Shaken, he broke his gaze, looking back down at the file in his hands. The whole room had hushed, watching him interact with Isabelle. What kind of man must they think he was? His wife might be dead in a jungle while he sat ogling a tigress.

The Weaver snapped at the guard in a steely voice, "Escort her out of this office immediately!"

Chad got permission to drive through heavy security from Global's tower down Main Street to the causeway bridge, leaving Azariah to analyze what he saw going on with the rescue operation for Caroline. He needed fresh air after his spectacular crash and burn in front of his dad and Weaver's team. The Spanish woman was somewhere in the building, and he was on edge at the thought of running into her at any moment.

He slid his sparkling blue sports car out of the ground level garage past reporters who braved the chilly, blustery day with a chance of some breakthrough in the kidnapping case. They shouted questions at the Porsche, wanting to know his state of mind about his wife's abduction. His chest tightened so much that he wondered what a heart attack felt like.

Once past them, he gasped for air and hit a button to change the radio station. He couldn't endure a commercial about romantic cruises to South America right now.

It was the music that snagged him. Images of Isabelle flashed through his mind. No matter that the song was about a drag race and a car named Panama Express, or that Eddie Van Halen's revving Lamborghini engine was in it—the lyrics still took his mind to a place where the dark-haired woman was slowly reaching for him across the console, her smile full of promise. She didn't pout at not getting her way this time. She expected to have what she came for, and she wanted it from him.

A vehement shake of his head fended off the invitation in her eyes and full red lips. Chad fought the impulse to change the channel again, for he liked the rocking beat of the music, and it had never been a problem before. He had disciplined himself early on to control his imagination, the same as flipping a switch.

While his hands turned the Porsche onto the causeway bridge, a sudden thought made him sit up straighter with a white-knuckled grip on the gray leather steering wheel. He'd always compared his own red Lamborghini with Caroline. The car was his graduation trophy for waiting four years in college to come home to court her. What if he had envisioned Isabelle's confident advances in it, soiling what belonged entirely to his lifelong love?

With a growl of resignation, he pushed the button to select the pre-set family-friendly Whitehaven station that he and the Young Guns owned. Journey's soothing lyrics flowed out. "When you love a woman, you know she's standin' by your side, a joy that lasts forever..."

That's what Caroline was. Joy. And it was a whole different thing from the sleazy turn his thoughts had taken with Isabelle. What had popped into his mind had nothing to do with love and everything to do with power.

A wave of doubt nearly bowled him over. Was he having a middle-age crisis or some deeper problem that was just starting to surface?

Out of nowhere, a long-buried memory popped into his mind. There was that time just before he left for college when he'd almost compromised, but he told himself it was only to mark his territory, like those jaguars in the books he'd just read with the kids. He was moody about his impending departure when a group of friends enjoyed a late afternoon and evening on Wyeth Painter's boat, the *Artistic License*. It was a lot of fun, fishing, swimming, playing music, and having a picnic on a small isolated island. He kept feeling pangs of homesickness, knowing how much he'd miss it all.

Caroline had worn a modest bathing suit under a tank and cutoff jeans, not trying to entice him into things he shouldn't be thinking about. But he let himself think about it anyway, and her brother Patrick had noticed Chad's lingering looks, especially when she shed the tank and shorts for swimming.

The memory of that day was interrupted when the Atlantic Ocean sparkled ahead, blinding him before he flipped down the sun visor. He eased his Porsche past the security station on Pavilion Way with a nod to the guard, and his mind slipped back in time again as he passed the Big House to turn right onto South Castaway to get home.

He remembered the close darkness of the garage as if it was yesterday. After everyone unpacked the boat, Patrick had carried things inside, expecting Caroline to follow him after saying goodbye to friends. Chad rarely had a chance for a moment alone with her, and he felt a heady surge of power. He knew her heart, and she would respond to a certain look from him to stay a few risky minutes when friends left. Exchanged glances that afternoon had told him she'd picked up on his mood like an antenna. He placed himself close to her whenever he could, craving those distracted, wandering glances from her when he'd taken off his shirt to swim.

Sure, the other girls tried to get his attention. He was used to it. The look in their eyes roaming over him made him feel defensive, almost violated. Chad had always been exclusive to only one girl, and she would be the only one who ever touched him. She was the only one with too much dignity to chase him, the only one who always tried not to look.

The only one out of his reach.

He'd waved from the shadowy background to Caroline's best friend as Carly got in her car under the driveway spotlight. Watching Caroline's silhouette, the familiar, longing ache for her had washed over him, and he mulled over the repercussions of pushing the rules. If he weren't going away, he could ask her dad if he could court her. Without that, touching and making promises was out of bounds. Both their families trusted him not to cross any lines, and he couldn't ask Caroline to deceive her parents.

Chad remembered drawing in a quick breath as she turned toward the garage under the raised foundation of the house. The moment was surreal as her hair gleamed with moonlight, swinging around her, falling down her sun-kissed shoulders and back to create one of the most romantic visions he'd ever imagined. He felt transported into one of his dreams of her.

Then his heart had twisted in a rousing rebellion. The Painter Place rules were too strict. Most teens dated any way they wanted to.

Throwing caution to the wind at the irresistible shy question in her eyes, he'd stepped over and grasped her around the waist, pulling her roughly into him. She gasped, stiff with surprise, but didn't push him away. He'd made a soft choking sound in his throat instead of words he wanted to say. Words asking her for a commitment to wait for him while he went off to college, that he'd always loved her, and he wanted to marry her. But a forbidden, possessive touch down her waist and hip would be enough to convey it without those words. It would be a silent commitment from him, and if she let it happen, she wouldn't see anyone else while he was off at college.

He'd mustered the courage to attempt his hasty plan, his hand at her waist just starting to inch down, when Patrick's icy voice from the stairs told Caroline her mom was asking for her. Caroline hadn't jerked away guiltily. She had waited on him to drop his arms from around her. Then she took a step back to put the expected respectable distance between them.

Her brother took deliberate steps down to confront them. Chad remembered saying in a reassuring tone, "I'm sorry, Care. This is all my fault—I lost my head. I'll handle it. Go on inside. Everything will be okay."

Reluctantly, Caroline turned and walked past Patrick, ignoring her brother's narrowed eyes and offering no excuses for her behavior. The screen door had barely banged shut when his friend reached him.

"Are you crazy?" he hissed, pushing Chad's shoulder. "What if my dad was here, checkin' to see where she was? She's only sixteen. That's underage for a lot more than just alcohol! Maybe we better leave for school sooner than we planned."

Chad had accepted the shove from his best friend. Patrick was right, and like him, he kept his voice low so no one could hear them through open windows. "I knew your dad wasn't here, and you know I wouldn't do anything illegal. On this island, it doesn't take much to be just across the line yet remarkably far from the goal."

Patrick had exaggerated a sigh of incredulity and run both hands through his hair in agitation. "Around these parts, my dad is the law, and in his version, what you just tried was illegal. He's like God. Your opinion doesn't negate his rules. Why risk it, Chad?"

His mouth dry, Chad wet his lips. "I want her to know my intentions are the forever kind. She's mine, now and always. Someday I'll make it official."

Patrick had snorted and resolutely planted both hands on his hips. "Okay, well, until then, here's what's official: don't touch her like that. You're playin' with fire, Chad. Exactly what response did you want from her? Which would've made you happy, that she pushed you away, or let you have your way? Which one would've disappointed you? Would things have become awkward between you two? Will you spend the next four years wonderin' if she allowed anyone else to touch what's yours?"

Chad had looked away, instinctively copying his friend's stance of hands on his hips. He didn't like those questions and hadn't thought that far ahead. But he was sure if he'd gotten by with it, he'd be the only one. "She wouldn't," he answered defiantly.

Patrick had pointed a finger at him. "If she'll be yours someday, I pray you're a better man by then. A Christian man trains to be the spiritual head of his house, not a guy who tempts his dream girl in a dark garage. My sister deserves better than this. People change, Chad, and if you fall for some fashion model or a famous starlet when you get away from here into the big wide world, I don't want my sister to feel dirtied and betrayed by my best friend. Here at Painter Place, a Gregory always works in the best interest of a Painter, and vice versa. Do we understand one another?"

His words had stung. "I'm sorry. It won't happen again."

"This isn't you, Chad. You thrive as the guy in the white hat, playin' by the rules, with a clean win and no speck of dust on your integrity. That's how you roll. Here at Painter Place, you and Caroline seem destined to be a couple, but life away from here is different. She doesn't comprehend your status out in a world that sees you through dollar signs and power-up buttons. You don't know who you'll be in that influence six months from now, or who she'll be without you around."

The memory of the specifics that night trailed away as Chad punched in the security code for the gate in his driveway, but the consuming love for Caroline that urged him to cross the line at eighteen was even deeper now they were married.

He parked in the garage under the house, then tugged the keys from the ignition and rested his forehead on his hands at the top of the steering wheel. He was grateful that his brother-in-law had come on the scene in the nick of time back then. God had reigned him in when he made a bad decision for himself and for Caroline. She hadn't known what he planned to do, and he hadn't known yet that he couldn't see her for four years. Regardless of her reaction if he'd made that move, it would have been one of the last interactions they had before she thought he'd left her in his past. He didn't want to imagine the pain he'd have inflicted on her.

Until today, he'd thought his distant teenage departure in wisdom was his only slip. Maybe he'd even patted himself on the back. Today, God had reminded him of how dangerous it was to feel comfortable in his pride.

Just thinking about Caroline was like a breath of fresh air. Chad never wanted her to know about what happened today at the office, and he didn't want the excitement Isabelle promised,.

He couldn't guess why he was so electrified by her. Long ago, he learned not to pursue fantasies, because people don't dream up the negative repercussions that accompany reality.

This was a spiritual attack. Sure, he admired beautiful or unusual women sometimes, but he never thought of them in any personal interaction.

Like Gran Vanna once said when he and Caroline were separated by the aftermath of Hurricane Hugo, being apart created a playground for the devil. He clenched his teeth. What if Caroline was struggling in her own devil's playground with forbidden thoughts about the Jaguar? He was a man she'd already imagined herself with when they were dating, trying on the idea that they might someday marry.

The Jaguar was captivated by her. Between the three of them, Satan and God would be awfully busy. Like the Bible said, looking with lust at someone else was cheating in your heart. Yet, a temptation in and of itself wasn't sin, only acting on it. Perhaps it boiled down to how far the look at someone went. He hadn't envisioned himself touching Isabelle and couldn't allow for Caroline imagining more from the Jaguar, either.

Sitting up, Chad tapped his fist against the steering wheel in frustration. Where was the point at which either he or his wife would cross the line?

Patrick looked askance at his brother-in-law while shells crunched under their running shoes. Chad would be open and talkative after he spent his tension physically, but Patrick was unsure how long that would take today. Straight blonde hair blew back off Chad's face, away from his tortured green eyes. His guard-trained German shepherd, Lancelot, ran alongside him as if this escapade, this moment, was all that mattered in his entire existence.

Patrick was getting over the initial shock of his sister's kidnapping. Now he was digging in for a long haul. She tried to prepare him for this, discussing a plan of action a few times when Chad wasn't around. He needed to be strong for his distraught parents, his wife, and best friend. It was a relief that his Uncle Wyeth and Aunt Chrissy were flying home today but Juliette and Cameron had been told to stay in Florida. They were on location filming a movie, and movie schedules wait on no one. There was nothing they could do here that would help Caroline, anyway. Juliette often checked in with Gran Vanna, concerned over how her aging mother was handling the stress.

Wyeth told the staff of Painter Gallery to close it for a few days due to the media presence and security in these uncertain times. It would be a financial hit he couldn't afford, for he and Caroline were still trying to recover from the expense of re-building after the hurricane. Perhaps publicity would boost sales for her upcoming birthday exhibition.

If she lives to have her birthday. If she ever comes home. Patrick squeezed his eyes shut at the thought of losing his little sister. She was the next generation heir to Painter Place, and Wyeth might not live long enough to complete training for little Noble.

Beside him, Chad was slowing down. Under the pier, he gasped for breath and leaned his forehead on an arm he braced on a piling. Then he turned to lean his back on the gray weather-beaten wood, sliding down to sit on the sand beside his panting dog.

Patrick saw what was coming. His best friend was like a tall ship off course in a maelstrom.

"There's no Painter Place for me without Caroline," Chad rasped. Then the sobs swept in like crashing waves to overtake him.

Part Two

Multiplayer Mode

Chapter Seven

Comfort and prosperity have never enriched the world
as much as adversity has.
-Billy Graham

A cacophony of whistles, warbles, squawks, chatters, and caws surrounded the rescue team on their trek along a river, just out of sight of any boats that might navigate the murky waters. Sometimes black caiman roared in a manner befitting their monstrous appearance, crawling out of the water with unnerving speed. The Puma told Caroline to climb a tree if they were in an ambush by one, so she glanced around to judge which trees would be the best for frantic climbers. Her eyes followed the trunks up to the tossing sea of green treetops that hid much of the sky, except along the river's edge.

The Jaguar had treated Caroline with distance and disdain for two days. Dismayed and dejected, she mutely obeyed his orders.

Yesterday, on the first morning after her rescue, she overheard him telling the Puma he needed to get her home before she broke a nail or got a blister. Seething, she pulled on her backpack for the trail, remembering all the years spent helping with scrubbing bathrooms, floors, and repairing cottages and campsites on the island so that artists, writers, and musicians could enjoy a retreat at Painter Place. Painter Place ran on her sweat, not on standing posed like a Barbie doll.

More team members showed up last night in a village they rested in. Now the group numbered six men and herself. She struggled to ignore her lingering headache and tension in her back from lugging the pack of her things. The team slowed their pace for her and arrived at a village later than they hoped.

Several women were grinding corn and another grain between two flat rocks. Others around the fire tended the cooking, making what looked like pancakes. Caroline inhaled the aroma appreciatively, her stomach rumbling in anticipation.

The sullen Jaguar barked curt orders to the team. Expecting him to ignore her again, Caroline let her eyes roam to scout out a seat somewhere, hoping he'd order her to plop down in it and stay out of his long sweaty hair.

"Princess!"

Caroline's head snapped around at the Jaguar's sharp, irritated treatment of her code name. "Yes, sir!" she barked back before she could catch her insulting tone.

He blinked, open-mouthed, so taken aback he forgot what he was saying. A muffled snort came from one of the new team members behind her. But the leader soon recovered his flinty look and attitude. "Do they teach any Spanish in Cotillion classes?"

She knew her neck would soon sport the telltale splotches of the angry heat rising toward her earlobes. She couldn't tell him that as Chris Shepherd, he used to teach her the Spanish he used on mission trips.

"*Un poco*. I can sing *Feliz Navidad*," she quipped disdainfully, and one team member guffawed while others turned chuckles into coughs. She added, "Oh, and I once learned from a matador how to say *Te quiero semipre*."

His eyes became hard, and the set of his mouth was as cruel as his statement. "The matador should've taught you something more useful than telling him you'd always love him. But I suppose that was useful in its own way, to get what he wanted from you."

She'd steeled herself against a demeaning response from him, but this was a ripping stab of shock in her heart. Chris Shepherd would never, ever have insulted her honor, nor would any well-bred gentleman.

Inwardly cut and bleeding, she tossed him a breezy laugh. "I hear they have adult Cotillion classes now for people who missed learning any manners. Be sure you catch the lessons on how to talk to a lady in polite society. You've spent too much time as a jungle animal."

Caroline turned, dismissing him with a carefree toss of her long ponytail. She announced to the Panther that she needed to eat and get some sleep.

Village leaders walked up to the Jaguar before he could hurl another scathing insult. While they conversed in rapid Spanish, the Panther led Caroline to a plump dark-haired woman who smiled and offered her a broad leaf that served as a plate. In the middle of it was a duet of the flat corn cakes, piled with something steaming inside them and rolled. A sauce was drizzled over them, and it smelled delicious, but she couldn't help wondering if the leaf had been washed of the insects that must have crawled over it. Perhaps they were part of the sauce.

The woman pointed to a flat stone as an invitation to sit down beside her while she worked, and the Panther re-joined the team. Another petite woman with beautiful deep chocolate eyes came to the fire, chattering companionably as she helped make up more of the leaf dishes for the rest of the team. Caroline assumed the food was safe if the Jaguar planned to have this. With a cautious peek into the baskets of food the women reached into, she saw vegetables and corn flour. She tasted a small bite, and the women clucked disapprovingly at her, making gestures that she needed to put more into her mouth.

Obediently chewing a larger bite, she earned their smiles and figured out they were advising her to pack on some weight if she wanted to keep her man. They inclined their heads to the Jaguar who overheard their Spanish and quickly glanced over to look at her.

She searched his green eyes for Chris Shepherd. The bite she was chewing stuck in her mouth and she looked down, feigning concentration on her food.

Night fell quickly in the jungle, without the twilight she loved at home. Small fires and lanterns around the village warded off wild animals and cast spooky shadows when the Panther led her to a rustic room sandwiched between two others. As he helped her pull off her gear, she groaned from the ache in her back. When she turned around to thank him, he whispered, "Princess, it's not personal. Nothing in this world matters more to him right now than for you to get out of here safely under his watch."

Caught off-guard, her hand clapped to her mouth. She squeezed her eyes shut against the sudden threat of tears, trying to ward off the memory of Chris Shepherd insinuating that she'd been used by a matador.

But it wasn't Chris. The Panther was dead on when he told her to beware of the Jaguar. "He's just testing what you're made of in the only way he knows how," whispered the Panther in a soothing tone. "You've no idea what we're up against."

She stiffened to hear the Jaguar's voice near the narrow doorway before the bulk of him filled it. The Panther beckoned her to come with him to the entrance, but she sniffed and looked away, crossing her arms, stubbornly rooted to the boards in the middle of the room. While she let her reddened eyes cool so the Jaguar wouldn't see how hurt she was, she noticed movements of fire-lit shapes and figures through gapping slits in what passed for walls.

Beside her, the Panther sighed with the patience of a parent dealing with a petulant child. He whispered, "Princess, there are some strangers in the village tonight who arrived before us, asking inconvenient questions about an American woman. They're staying overnight in a room next door, for no one travels in the jungle after dark. The villagers are loyal to us, using the Jaguar's alternate identity as an agent for an oil company who pays well for lodging and food when he passes through. To cover for you, he said he brought his wife along this time. He must sleep in here."

Caroline worked her mouth like a fish, trying to form words that tumbled helter-skelter though her mind. "Absolutely not!" she hissed. "Tell everyone we're fighting, and he's in the doghouse."

Unbinding her ponytail, she shook bits of the jungle out of it. A dark shape passed close to the wall, pausing a moment, and the Panther took her upper arm and whispered closer to her ear. "There are no dog houses here, Princess. Men don't get kicked out of their beds, and you'd be beaten for suggesting it."

She gasped, infuriated, jerking her head around to glare at the Jaguar. He was smirking in the doorway. *Smirking!* She pointed to a corner and whispered, "Then he sleeps over there!"

The Panther tried not to laugh outright. His tone was gentle again as he leaned to her ear. "No, he won't. Don't be tonight's entertainment in the village by forcing him to pretend to rough you up."

Twisting away, Caroline growled in her throat and gathered bundles of blonde hair into clawed fingers. Then she stood tall again and took several deep breaths, smoothing out her hair as if regaining her dignity. Turning back to them, she whispered, "I appreciate everything this team risks to protect me, but I loathe deception. I'd take my chances with honesty rather than pretend to be someone else, but your lives are in danger, too, so I'll endure this humiliation. Just get me back home."

In the dim glow of the flashlight in the room, she saw the team leader no longer wore a smirk. He turned and walked out. The Panther whispered, "Welcome to our world of covert operations, Princess, where honesty will get you killed. Remember, your movements are watched. Do nothing that gives away your true identity."

He patted her arm reassuringly as he turned to leave, meeting up with the returning Jaguar just outside the door. After another low-toned exchange between them, the Jaguar appeared, walked in, and put down the load in his arms. Crouching, he lit a lantern and scooped up what looked like homespun cushioned bed rolls. He smoothed them out on the wooden floorboards and set a folded blanket on top. Then he sorted out items from his backpack into a smaller one that he shouldered.

"I'll take you to a private spot to wash up and change. Bring what you need from your pack."

Seething, she followed his commanding stride. Just outside the door, he grabbed a jug of water, then led her to a dark clearing of closet-sized space in the jungle. He set down his automatic rifle and pack in the veils of leafy vines, but kept an alert look around. "There's a towel, toilet paper, and so on. I hired a village widow to wash your clothes and towel. She will dry them by the fire tonight, and we'll have them to pack in the morning."

He looked uncomfortable without his rifle and picked it back up. The vines separated them as he turned to walk a short distance away.

She eyed the fragile barrier of foliage in the eerie glow of the flashlight. Previous camping trips in her life told her what the hole dug into the ground with two boards over it were for. Despite her weariness, she rushed through a rugged sponge bath, then put on her only change of clothes.

Soon she peered through the vines to find the Jaguar's back and paused to consider his dark silhouette against the firelight in the village. Chris Shepherd sure had filled out.

She bit her lip, then said coldly, "I'm ready."

Impassively he turned back to her, gathering the empty water container and a tidy bundle of her laundry with the underthings buried inside. An old woman with a kind smile was waiting to take her clothes, saying something unintelligible to the Jaguar.

Stepping aside to let her pass through the doorway first, he followed and settled their things. She heard a scuffling sound along one wall and glanced at it. Soft light filtered through a few slits large enough for an eye to peek through, and she noticed a shadowy form blocking one slit. Someone was there. Unnerved, she turned to see if the Jaguar was alert to the situation.

Her heart leaped to her throat to meet the gaze she'd known for so many years. He extended his hand to her.

She hesitated, chaffing at being forced to act like a compliant wife for the audience at the wall. When she stepped forward and let him take her hand, he made a show of saying she should lie down and sleep while he went to bathe. His voice was loud enough to carry through the slits in the wall when he said he might hang out a bit with the guard.

With affection in his tone and manner, the Jaguar wished her goodnight and leaned down to brush his lips against her forehead. She stiffened while he whispered, "Lie down next to the front wall and get under the blanket. Turn off the flashlight. The spies are only a threat if they leave without being convinced. Relax and get all the sleep you can."

The hair on the Jaguar's neck stood on end, awakening him with a certainty that he was being watched. All his senses heightened like radar and he fingered the reassuring shape of the cool metal on his rifle beside him. Peeking through squinting slits in his eyelids and hoping they looked closed, he watched along the wall. After a few moments, he made out the sliding motion of a form against the wood slat.

The only other sounds were the jungle, Caroline's steady breathing, and the Puma's familiar footfall as he passed slowly on guard. Lantern and firelight outside filtered into the shadowy dark room to make motion barely discernable. The awkward goodnight he said to Caroline earlier had not been convincing for their audience, but he dreaded pushing her further now while they watched. He didn't trust his acting skills to pull off being a cowed American husband or pretending to manhandle her.

Indecisive, he prayed, begging the Lord to help the Princess remain calm and for the spies to be deceived. He pretended to stir and awaken, running his hands through his hair before turning over toward the sleeping form beside him. His heart pounded as he balanced his torso up on his elbow and forearm, picking up the edge of the homespun blanket and pulling it over himself. He leaned his face closer to the impossibly delicate curves of her ear, inhaling an alluring scent on her neck. "Stay calm, Princess. We're just acting."

She didn't respond. He hesitated, stretching his hand open under the blanket before closing it into a fist. Another shuffle of movement that seemed closer along the wall to his feet reminded him that someone watched him and the *gringa*. A married American heiress being rescued from a cartel would not be on intimate terms with her rescuer.

Stretching his hand open again, he touched the soft skin on the Princess' arm. He began his once-rehearsed warning near her ear, accidentally brushing it with his lips, then froze when she sighed and rolled back against his chest and thigh. His pulse spiked to outer space as he wondered what to do next. He longed for the power to suspend time as he etched every detail of this moment into his short list of memories. Then he swallowed back the unreasonable, forbidden attraction to her that had seized him the moment he rescued her from *Puña*.

A fierce protectiveness surged in his chest, clutching his breath away. Convincing their audience of spies behind the wall that Caroline was his wife was the best chance he had of keeping them from following the team in the morning. So he repeated the whispered warning into her ear. This time, she turned her face toward his with a contented little groan, lips parted as if expecting a kiss. His heart was in his throat as she settled groggily, warm and trusting.

Then, she flinched and tensed. He put his arm across her middle to hold her down, his palm flat on the bedroll, whispering in his most reassuring tone. "You know I won't hurt you, Princess. We're only acting, okay? Relax. Someone's spying again through the wall."

She faintly whimpered, pushing under the blanket at his hand. He tried to calm her by whispering more desperately, "Relax enough to convince them you're used to sleeping next to me and you can go back to sleep. That's all, you have my word."

He planned to keep her pinned at the waist with his arm under the blanket until she got used to the idea. But he could hear the rising alarm in another stifled whimper, then she turned to his ear, begging, "Please! I panic if someone holds me down against my will! Please, Jaguar, I can't do this your way!"

His heart wrenched and tears stung his eyes. He relaxed his arm and took her fighting hand reassuringly, pulling their clasped hands out from under the blanket. Then he rubbed the back of hers tenderly against his cheek on the side visible to the wall, as much to comfort her as for the staged intimacy. Hoping she felt safe now, he settled beside her, propping his head higher on his arm and a rolled pillow, resting their clasped hands together on her hip.

The Princess became less rigid with tension and her anxious breathing became steady again. He tried to imagine the view of the spies and figured they could only see the outline of the back of his head as he put his face closer to hers. With his hair hanging down and brushing the top of his shoulder, they couldn't tell that he wasn't kissing her when he whispered, "Just trust me."

Plantain was the main ingredient in breakfast, and Caroline's rescuers ate it with gusto. Suspicious, she tasted a bite while inspecting it for evidence of a rodent, reptile, or insect. The elderly woman who cooked it chattered something encouraging to her. She understood the woman's Spanish urging her to eat, and the words *illume* and *bonita,* which she recognized as "light" and "pretty." The old woman extended a withered but capable hand and timidly stroked Caroline's blonde ponytail.

She smiled back at the woman and grasped her gnarled hand in friendship, using her limited Spanish to convey gratitude for the food and the compliments. But when the Jaguar appeared a few feet away behind her new friend, the look in his green eyes jolted Caroline.

His steady gaze held her own before he turned back to preparations for the trail. Those eyes didn't light up with effervescent pleasure to see her like they once did. But she sensed Chris Shepherd at her side in the dark last night and wondered if it changed anything in their new relationship as a victim and rescuer. In her exhaustion, she had done as he asked—she trusted him. She soon fell asleep again after he awakened her to explain his attention. He was gone when the Panther came to get her this morning. It made her feel queasy to be a hot potato Chris was eager to toss off to someone else.

The peeping visitors left before dawn. The Jaguar acted uneasy and his team studied the tracks and direction of their exit path. She heard him confide in the Panther that he attempted to feign affection between them when he and the Princess were spied upon again during the night. The Panther turned to glance at her.

Caroline blushed. Turning to her backpack, she organized her roll of clean clothes, considering how absurd her dainty underthings must have looked to the kindly old woman who washed and dried them for her last night.

The team set out from the village. The Jaguar and the Puma sometimes hacked out a trail with machetes. Considering the power behind their efforts, she slipped into imagining what the Jaguar's arms and shoulders must be like under his loose shirt and a heavy backpack. There were a few small scars on his tanned face, neck, and hands now, only noticeable because she knew a time when they didn't exist.

She'd become less nervous about snakes and poison tree frogs, guessing that if there was anything threatening ahead of her, the Jaguar and Puma would take care of it. But since awakening in the boat after her rescue, she'd sensed an invisible menace in the jungle. This ever-present foreboding feeling kept her spirit alert, as if peace was being stalked by chaos.

The surly Jaguar had returned, nothing like the protective rescuer who caressed her hand and stayed close by her side last night. The Panther and one of the new team members asked for a break after looking back to consider how she held up, and he growled at the second request. She noticed the impatience in the jerk of his arm to set down his pack and remain alert with his rifle as he scanned the river's edge.

Caroline cringed inwardly and flushed outwardly, trying not to sound so out of breath. Tears stung her eyes at his inconsiderate rebuff, but a few blinks and a sniff put them under submission. He wasn't Chris Shepherd, and she wasn't a crybaby. Fatigue made her more emotional, that's all.

After the team rested with an energy bar and water from their canteens, the Jaguar raked his eyes over the two sitting nearest Caroline. But he never looked at her. He turned and picked up his pack, the signal for everyone to march again. It struck her he looked tired, too. He had little sleep last night, keeping so close to her as the spies watched them. Now he had to watch after her again and make life and death decisions for them all.

It didn't excuse the way he treated her. With an irritated huff, she shook her ponytail in case any tiny wildlife had hitched a ride. Looking around the jungle from the trail was a reprieve from the socially maladjusted Jaguar and the aches of a difficult trek.

She had never imagined there could be so many birds in so many colors and shapes, all with different songs and calls. There were indescribable hummingbirds. A profusion of varieties of mushrooms grew in all kinds of unexpected places, and fern fronds swayed sometimes as if they were legs on a centipede. The views were inspiring, and she longed to stop and sketch.

When they came to a bluff where they were vulnerable to attack from only one side, the Jaguar gave the signal to set up camp for the night. The men jumped into a quick routine, ignoring Caroline. Setting her pack down at a nearby tree, she stiffly stepped over to the considerate team member who had requested an extra break for her on the trail, asking how she could help him.

The Jaguar strode up. "There's no time to train the Princess to do anything—we're quicker without her." He gestured with his commanding attitude. "Just go sit by your things and I'll take you to wash up soon."

He spun on his boot heel dismissively and walked away. She stood staring at the sweat-dampened area of his shirt where he'd carried his heavy pack. This demeaning treatment was wearing her down. It was time to come to grips with the fact that it was not her old friend who was gouging her heart this way. He no longer existed.

She squirmed to get comfortable on the ground against the variegated gray bark of a gargantuan tree, muttering that her Gran Vanna always said a good attitude was something you could take with you anywhere. With a wry grin, she imagined the Jaguar coming face to face with her beloved grandmother. Attitude adjustments were one of her specialties.

The grin became a grimace as she gingerly stretched her aching legs out before her. At least she had no blisters. She had packed running shoes and worn sturdy Timberland boots with thick winter socks to Charleston, and someone had packed all the essential contents of her bags for her to have in the jungle.

As she rubbed aching muscles in her shoulders, she studied how the camp was being made and what she might do to help next time. Two men dug a latrine in some jungle growth that offered privacy, and another stood guard, watching the jungle. Someone was always armed and watching for attacks.

One man gathered the straightest of the limbs from off the ground. She thought the wood was kindling for a fire, but he piled some at four places, spreading them like a foundation for something else. He covered them with palm leaves and rolled thin mats over the top. The foundation in the center of the camp was wider than the others.

The Jaguar busied himself with a machete, chopping some wooden poles and setting them into the ground around the four piles. He draped mosquito netting and light tarps to cover the tops, glancing her way to see if she had done as she was told.

The Panther improvised a table on a log, where he set up radio equipment. Within minutes, a fire was crackling near the jungle to ward off animals and heat a meal.

The Jaguar slung his rifle over one shoulder and two thin towels over the other before he strode by Caroline and curtly ordered her to bring her things to wash up. She pulled her only change of clothes and a pretty designer bag of toiletries from her backpack, then scampered to follow him on a path down to the water.

He put the towels on a large rock, then handed her a small bar of soap that smelled like herbs. The scent would keep insects away, he explained. Then he scouted out the edge of the water to make sure there was no unwelcome wildlife, shed his boots, and waded in himself. A menacing-looking knife protruded from a band strapped to his muscular thigh, and he held the rifle alertly. Satisfied that all was well, he gestured with his head that she should get in. Then he turned his back.

Caroline laid her clean clothes on the rock and hesitantly stepped into the cool water, dressed in all but her shoes and carrying her socks. Grateful for a chance to bathe off the sweat from the warm day, she squatted on her heels underwater in the shallows and unfastened things as best as she could, washing her body and the clothes at the same time.

How long would she have to deal with having the privacy of a goldfish? She rushed to be done, for the thought of making the Jaguar wait stretched her nerves taunt. As she stood dripping in her clothes back on the bank, she asked, "Where can I change?"

He turned and walked toward her, scrutinizing her appearance. "If you want to bathe this way, fine, but it's unnecessary. You're free to come onto the beach to dress and tell me when to turn around again. None of the men will dare look this way or come down here when you're with me."

His lip curled cruelly as if he couldn't help his next taunt. "All you had on was your designer underwear when I rescued you, Princess, so you're not hiding much I haven't seen."

Caroline flushed while he snatched up her towel, clothes, and toiletry bag off the rock. She followed him to the jungle's edge, where he thrust her things into her arms and stepped a few feet in to scout out some safe space for her. "If you're so shy, you can change here."

Seething at his scathing attitude over her modesty and embarrassed at his revelation about her rescue, she sullenly entered the spot he showed her. Huffing her frustration, she used the thin towel and pulled dry clothes on, struggling with shaky hands on her jeans zipper. He could've told her all that, before she got in the water! Maybe he ran from cartels, guerrillas, and wild animals every day, but he knew very well she didn't.

With the back of her hand, she brushed away another stinging tear. He wanted to demoralize her, but why? Last night, he insulted her in the worst way by suggesting she had an affair with Alejandro, then a few hours later he had the audacity to hold her and beg her to trust that he was only keeping her safe.

Now, Chris Shepherd's evil twin was back again. Exactly who was the Jaguar? Compared to Chris, his character had taken a serious dive into a slimy mud hole.

She stomped past him, imagining he was smirking cruelly behind her. But he was impassive as he pointed to a limb to hang her wet clothes and towel on, close to camp out of reach of monkeys. He motioned for her to sit down on one of the big logs beside the fire, where her pack was moved. The welcome smells of food made her stomach rumble, and one of the team handed her a small metal plate with beef stew on it.

Two men followed the Jaguar down to the river. Caroline relaxed, relieved to be out from under his scorching scrutiny and his perverse pleasure in bossing her around.

Despite the anger simmering just under the surface of her raw emotions, she felt and smelled better after that bath and clean clothes. The stew was reconstituted, but she consumed it with unladylike enthusiasm, imagining her Gran Vanna's delicate frown at her manners.

She sampled the fruit gathered on the trail along the way, looking over the bluff into the west. There would be no magical twilight here. That was her favorite way to wind down from a day back home. Near the equator in a tropical climate, altitude determined the seasons and darkness fell quickly.

The Jaguar led his group back into camp, all of them shirtless above unbelted camouflage trousers and boots. His damp hair hung in dark, loose clumps. He surveyed the jungle before propping up his rifle to hang wet clothes on the tree limbs.

The smell of food beckoned, so he grabbed his dry tee shirt nearby and turned toward the log seat where he left the Princess. He froze, steeling himself from reacting when he caught her watching him. A somersault deep in his middle made him forget to breathe while he read the frank admiration in her eyes. Then she raised them to meet his, and a lingering few moments passed before she blushed and ducked away.

He felt as if her soft hand had rubbed lightly over him. There had only been appreciation in her scrutiny, not longing. But he'd take it—in fact, he suddenly craved it. His heart was racing while he pulled the tee shirt over his head and shoulders, strapped on his belt and knife, and picked up his rifle. A shake of his head helped him gather his wits and settle his hair into place to dry.

What he wouldn't give to know what she'd been thinking! But she was maddeningly mysterious, and he never felt comfortable around people like that. This woman was the deep water in a river. He couldn't read her so he couldn't trust her. She was at once both accessible and reserved, congenial yet aloof, and cool with the promise of heat. She was smart, logical, and resourceful, dynamite to destroy all the blonde jokes he ever heard. His gut told him she was withholding a lot from him, and he was dying to discover it all.

So far on this mission, he had relied on insults to assess how she might handle herself if her pursuers caught up with them. He learned she would not crumble into a hysterical heap. She was furious with him when she went to sleep last night, but when she awakened to find herself trapped in his embrace, she kept her head, controlling her panic until she could express it to him.

Even then, she did not throw herself at his mercy, but tested his word of honor. It was one thing to ask him not to pin her down, but if she was captured out here, the next guy was an attacker. She had a weakness. Too many to fight would hold her down against her will, so panic would obliterate any rational thinking to gain an advantage.

The Jaguar stepped over for a hearty plate of stew. From his seat on a log across from the Princess, he took a hungry bite, studying her as she looked off the bluff. The last rays of sunlight set her hair aglow as it dried into silky wisps that stirred languidly in a caressing breeze. He sniffed the fresh scent of the sea in something she combed through it after bathing. The glow reminded him of an aura or a halo, and he was seized with the desire to take her hair into his fingers.

His grip on his plate and a fork tightened. Beauty was merely a matter of taste, he knew that. It also comprised a total package of preferences in voice, mannerisms and personality. But as for his own taste, she was far and away the most beautiful woman he'd ever seen, in the most enticing package he'd ever encountered. He was shaken to his core the day he rescued her, before she ever opened those stunning blue eyes.

Her Southern heritage flowed unstaunched in her unhurried drawl, genteel mannerisms, courtesy, respectfulness, and aloof distance from anything distasteful. He chewed another bite without tasting it, overcome with a sudden longing to see her smile. It would change his life.

Quickly, the Jaguar looked down to his dinner. No, not that. He was unsure why, but he was certain it would be painful on too many levels. For the first time, he understood his effort to make certain she had no reason to smile. An image of his heel grinding an indescribably soft magnolia petal popped into his mind, evoking a flush of shame. This magnolia blossom couldn't be more out of place if she was in a sandstorm in the Sahara.

Rising, he left his log seat to clean up his plate and get on with the mission to get this maddening distraction out of his life. Slinging his ever-present rifle over his shoulder, he followed the Panther to the netting that shielded the radio. The Puma was one of two wet-haired, bathed guards who took their places at the edge of the camp, alert to any movement in the dense jungle.

After everyone had eaten by the campfire, the Jaguar's team turned its attention to tasks related to the camp. Caroline went to help the man who gathered the plates and canteens. Water had been boiled for twenty minutes to clean the dishes and to re-fill the canteens. Behind her, she heard the Panther working with the radio, trying to reach someone he called the Weaver.

Suddenly, strong fingers curled around her arm, pulling her toward her assigned seat on the log. She tossed her head in defiance, dashed with hot humiliation that the Jaguar went so far to call her out in front of the team.

His tone was as stony as his face in the stark shadows of the firelight. He looked menacing with strands of long damp hair, and his strong squared jaw reminded her of Tarzan. He was civilized, and yet untamed, all at once. "We can't afford any mistakes," he growled.

Something between a thrill and a flash of fear ignited within her. But her indignation snuffed it out when he jeered, "Sit here and sketch in that expensive book of yours, Princess. I'm sure you don't do the dishes back in your castle."

So, he was the one who went through her bags to fill the backpack! He had scanned her sketchbook and thought it would be handy as a babysitting device. Unwittingly, he had jammed her last un-pushed button. The Panther's orders about pacifying the Jaguar were tossed into oblivion with her patience. She knew her eyes flashed because he blinked in surprise before she jerked her arm free, turning her back to march toward the dishes.

But he didn't accept her mutiny and delivered biting words as he reached out for her arm again. "On this mission, I'm in command, not you! Do as you're told, and we all might get to go home. If you can't keep up on the trail, just say so. I'll stop. Then the guys won't compete for their name on your dance card!"

Caroline's next move was a spin and a kick she practiced with Azariah and Chad. The Jaguar lay pinned against the mossy ground with her knee in his ribs and her forearm pressing across his neck. Her eyes blazed while a hiss came from between clenched pearly teeth. His astonished eyes were trapped by the fury in her sea-blue ones.

"Stop treatin' me like I'm somethin' you need to go scrape off your boots!" she shouted down at him, her hair brushing his cheekbone. The rowdy jungle hushed, listening. "I promise, I can make your life so miserable you'll be beggin' to have someone take me off your hands!"

"Caroline?" he managed to croak.

Abruptly, she stood up over him, still breathless from taking him down. He knew her!

Flustered and furious, she marched past the fire to the gaping Panther, who stopped his conversation with the Weaver in mid-sentence and left the radio on. She directed her voice in her most intimidating tone. "Weaver, do you hear me?"

Out of the corner of her eye, she saw the Puma rush to the Jaguar who was gasping and grabbing his head into his hands. Pain utterly consumed him.

She knit her brows in concern as the voice of an older man came back over the radio. "Affirmative."

"Forget the code talk!" she snapped. "I don't know your cool club lingo, so listen to me straight up. I want my bodyguard sent to wherever I am. I can't work with the Jaguar. He's officially fired. Don't even dream I have no authority to do that!" With a stamp of her foot, she ordered, "Make it happen, tonight!"

The Puma pulled the Jaguar to sit up, bending his knees. The Jaguar was oblivious to anything but pain, gripping his head while groans escaped from deep in his throat. The Puma injected something into his arm.

The Panther recovered and rushed back into his role in communicating for the team. "Weaver, this is the Panther. The Jaguar is down and mewing. Over."

"Roger that, Panther. Leave the radio on and see what you can do. I need the Princess. Over."

Chapter Eight

Being a princess isn't all it's cracked up to be.
-Princess Diana

Chad shot to his feet and took two exploratory steps closer to his dad's office desk before the Weaver held up a warning hand. Caroline's voice was furious, and she was bossing the Weaver like she was the one in charge of her rescue mission. Not only was she alive, she was throwing her weight around!

The Weaver looked as if he was considering whether to send him out of the room. "Please—let me talk to her," begged Chad from where he stood. "Anything you want, I can get it!"

"Princess, are you near the radio? Over," said the Weaver.

"Yes," came Caroline. "The Panther is with the Jaguar. I hope I didn't hurt him."

The Weaver raised an eyebrow at Chad. "Tell me what happened. Over."

"He's inexcusably rude and demeaning, and he pushed me too far tonight. When he grabbed my arm again to make me listen to more of his threats, I used some self-defense moves my bodyguard taught me and pinned him to the ground. I don't think he hit his head, but he seems to be in horrible pain."

"Affirmative. Ask the Panther if he's still mewing. Over."

"Mewing?"

"It's what we call it when he remembers something from his past. It strikes him down because of a serious head injury from a few years ago, causing intense, debilitating pain."

They listened as she got a response from the Panther. "He says negative, he has the situation under control."

"Princess, I can give you a few minutes with your husband while the Panther handles this. But every time we use a radio, we're risking exposure. Over."

The Weaver motioned to Chad, who pounced to get to the radio. "Caroline! Are you all right?"

Caroline's knees buckled before she caught herself by grabbing a tree trunk. *Home.* The voice she'd loved all her life, the deep, lazy drawl that sang oldies and love songs to her, but preferred rock-and-roll.

"Caroline?"

Her voice trembled as she fought not to break down. "I'm here." Then she choked on a sob and took a shaky breath. "I miss the sound of your voice. I'm exhausted and homesick. Are you and the kids okay?"

"We all miss you like crazy. And Granddad is touch and go in intensive care."

"What happened to him?"

Chad looked at Weaver, who nodded. "He watched you being taken in his place and had a serious heart attack. They said he only made it because your grandpa Tony arrived for the surgery. You need to get home, so he won't blame himself."

"Oh, Chad, how awful! Please, assure Grandad I'll be praying for his recovery and I love him dearly. I know there's been no mistake in God's eyes. Grandad couldn't have endured this run through the jungle. And Chad, our Rhett—he will need concrete assurances, some words. Tell him I've been hangin' on to a verse from Psalm 34:7 that says the angel of the LORD encamps around those who love and honor Him, and He rescues them."

Chad gulped. "I will. He's catchin' on that God still speaks to us through the Bible and in His work through His people. Little Savanna is fallin' asleep on my shoulder before I put her to bed, or else she cries for you and I can't bear it. The rest of the family is frightened. Care, are you savin' your heart for me?"

"Always—just like I promised. Are you're askin' 'cause you know who I'm with?"

"Yep. Don't forget who you are. Or who I am."

Caroline stifled a sob. "You're my forever love, Chad! But I sense danger everywhere, like a mist swallowing me. I can't see it, but I feel a depressing presence—demonic influences, like when the Bible talks about evil spiritual forces in principalities and powers. People are chasin' us to find me, and everyone carries machetes, military knives, assault rifles, and Glock 17s. It's hard to imagine I'll make it back home, and you're too young to be lonely."

"No!" shouted Chad, choking on the word and clenching a fist. "We've been through this, so don't mention it again! We're not like other people, Caroline. I made a promise, a commitment to you about Painter Place."

He stabbed the air with a pointed finger she couldn't see. "You listen to me! Get that sizzlin' sassiness back, like you had before you heard my voice. I'm not communicating with you if you're goin' to fall apart on me."

His voice broke and he struggled to continue hoarsely, "You do whatever it takes to get home to us, Caroline—whatever it takes, you understand me? You have skills. If they think takin' down the Jaguar is all you've got, they've seen nothing yet! I'll try to persuade them to move Azariah and some guy named Jack in there. Jack sent me your rings. The guys who took you left 'em like a calling card in the Mercedes."

The Panther came to stand beside Caroline, handing her some squares of toilet paper for a tissue. With a tremulous smile, she wiped her eyes, then her nose. "I'm so relieved about my rings! Chad, you know I'm not afraid of anything in the world except not seein' you and the kids again. Every time we get to talk might be our last, and today on the trail I remembered a secret I've never told you before. Want to hear it, so I have no regrets?"

Chad grinned. Even in a life-or-death situation, she knew how to entice him with her flair for the unexpected. "Keep it clean. We've got company."

"No way. They want somethin' raw. So here it is. When you're ready to swing a golf club, I adore that little wiggle you do. I never told you because if you knew, it would distract you and mess up your concentration. That's cheating."

Chad couldn't help it. He laughed outright, and it felt good. "Oh, yeah? You just sabotaged my game. When you get home, I'll take you to any course in the world you want to win at for the first and only time. And since you already know your golf wiggle brings me to my knees and you're all cool and focused anyway, I've got no comeback right now."

"Then I claim victory over the undefeatable Chad Gregory! Listen, uh, the Panther is here. I have to go."

"Wait! I know what you're doin', Care, distractin' me so I can endure this. But I need you to focus on yourself right now. Stay on top of things, but not on top of the Jaguar. Adjust his attitude like your Gran Vanna would, then work with him. You know my motto—only the best for my girl. He's the best. They say he breaks through that darkness down there. I'm waitin' for you and love you endlessly."

"Me too—endlessly. Take care of our babies."

"Weaver, this is the Panther. The Jaguar is calm now, but he recognized the Princess. Any orders? Over."

The Weaver sighed. "Affirmative. Remind him he's the Plumber. Radio me before taking down camp in the morning. Over."

Emotions roiled in every pacing step Caroline took on the outskirts of the camp at the bluff. The clamor of a jungle night reverberated from everywhere, jangling her nerves. She longed for the rhythmic beat of pounding surf as it massaged smooth sand, retreating, returning, reliable.

She crossed her arms to hug warmth against the chill of a breeze. One part of her wanted Chad by her side to face this, but she'd never want him here. He was right about how she'd broken upon hearing his voice. Becoming a soppy mess meant letting him down.

This Princess and Plumber code was no Mario game. She was cruelly plopped into a deadly nightmare where real people would die. Any chance of surviving meant working with the insufferable Jaguar.

The aching in her legs intensified, interrupting her train of thought. Absently, she balanced on one foot and rubbed a muscle. Looking out over the rippling moonlight on the dark water below, she spoke a prayer. "When Chris left, I questioned You about lettin' us waste precious time headin' nowhere. You gave me assurance that he was in Your hands, and nothin' was wasted."

She planted both feet and clamped a hand over her mouth to tame the sob that convulsed her torso, then prayed hoarsely, "Help me forgive him and follow his orders. Protect these men. Please, when I leave this earth, let it be in a way that doesn't involve guilt or blame for anyone!"

Drawing a ragged breath, she turned her hands and face up to the stars. Constellations were different here, a showcase over the Amazon instead of the Atlantic. There was something familiar about a grouping of five stars, but it eluded her as she continued her prayer. "Whatever happens here, Lord, make it all count for somethin' good, for Your glory. Amen."

Emotionally and physically spent, she pivoted toward camp and bumped hard into a shadowy silhouette behind her. Strong arms steadied her from staggering back to the edge of the bluff and pulled her tightly into the warmth of a body that smelled like the team's herbal soap.

Caroline instinctively mumbled an apology against clean cotton, scrambling through the sudden disarray of her mental cues for the proper response. She pulled back to a respectable distance as if they were dancing, since the Jaguar kept his hold on her arms. Even in the near darkness, she could see his eyes had changed when he looked at her.

"The moment I first saw you, I knew I'd have a problem in this mission, but I can't trust anyone else to get you out. I tried to build a shield against your memory and the strong emotions associated with it. You were upending my life, and I resented it. I'm sorry about how I've treated you and assure you we can work together. Don't fire me."

Strong emotions? Upending his life? Glancing at the black jungle and campfire, she tried to grasp whether this moment was real. She nodded mutely and met his eyes. He was waiting, so she stammered, "Okay."

As if walking in a dream, she let him lead her to a nearby fallen log, gritting her teeth at the squatting movement to sit on it. He plopped down cross-legged at an angle on the ground in front of her and pulled her legs into his lap as if he did it every day. She sat speechless when he started feeling through the leg of her jeans to exactly the right muscles, smoothing gentle strokes of pressure into them with strong fingers and the heel of his palm. If this was God's answer to the prayer for the strength to follow the Jaguar's orders, she loved the quick response.

He spoke quietly as he worked. "This will help keep your muscles from cramping while you sleep. The last checkpoint only stocked four net tents and blankets. There are seven of us now, and two at a time rotate as guards while one sleeps with the radio equipment. We'll change that up some tonight, because I'm now medicated and can't be trusted."

With a mischievous half-grin, he added, "Trusted to watch, that is. Every night we're not in a shelter, you must sleep beside me. I'm charged by the Weaver with protecting you as a last resort, in case danger gets past the other guards. It's called a 'den.'"

"Oh," was all Caroline could think of to say. She wondered how she'd have handled this news earlier if he had smirked and ordered her to lie down beside him in his tent. He deftly handled her other leg while they sat together under infinite starry heavens.

When he finished with his version of muscle therapy, he sighed and looked up at her. "Any better?"

"Like a miracle," she murmured, avoiding his eyes. "Thank you."

The Jaguar stood and helped her up, letting his hands slide down her arms like a fleeting caress. Instantly, she missed the warmth, so she hugged her arms across her chest and began walking toward the camp. He fell into step beside her, just as Chris Shepherd would have done.

After trips to the makeshift latrine and getting their packs to bunch into pillows, they wished the others goodnight. The Jaguar pulled up the edge of the netting for Caroline so she could crawl onto the mattress of wood sticks and palm leaves. As she settled, she couldn't help wondering if the insects that may lurk under it were as large as a Palmetto bug on the island back home. All the Painter and Gregory men were adept at cleaning Palmetto bugs out of sight of the women. She hoped the Jaguar would handle anything like it here.

At her side, the Jaguar settled with a grunt, shaping a pillow from a smaller pack he took out of the one he carried on the trail.

He positioned his rifle within reach. Spreading a thin blanket, he covered Caroline. The distance he kept from her left his arm and leg by the rifle exposed to the night air.

Caroline bit her lip, remembering when she camped in groups as a chaperone with Chris Shepherd on Dog's Head at Painter Place. Tonight, alert guards and other sleeping team members surrounded them. "Come on, get under cover."

The Jaguar inched closer to the Princess at her invitation, until their sleeves touched under the light blanket. Then he closed his eyes to the whine of cicadas, croaking frogs, hooting owls, and twittering bats. But the melody of the Southern accent beside him was the real music of the night.

"What does a jaguar sound like, if one was near us?" she asked. "Aren't they supposed to be the king of the cats down here, always prowlin'?"

He blew out a snort and grinned. "What, you researched that when you were buying a car, Princess?"

She giggled. "No, I'm into horses, not cats. First a vintage '65 Mustang and now a Ferrari, and I like lots of horses under the hood, though I try not to break the speed limit 'cause I can't get by with anything. The press would make sure every corner of the universe knew about it. My husband drives a 1985 red Lamborghini Countach on Sundays and special occasions, and a blue Porsche 944. But my kids like books about animals, and the big cats fascinate me. Some of them have blood-curdling cries."

"Not a Jaguar—he doesn't cry. He makes short, throaty grunts and rumbles. But he's the king around here, all right. He's such bad news that he hunts boa constrictors and does not need to hide when he takes a nap."

She shuddered, and he knew she'd conjured a mental image of one of the deadliest snakes around. The anaconda, or boa, got big enough to tip over canoes. That it was non-venomous made it no less a threat when it was crushing you to death.

"Is the boa a king around here?" she whispered.

"No, the bushmaster is."

He was struggling against the relaxing effect of the medication the Puma had forced on him when he mewed, and his voice sounded lazy in his own ears. She whispered. "I'm sorry if I'm annoying. Unless you're married, you're not used to female chatter while you're tryin' to go to sleep. But my husband and I talk a little at night. It's like wanderin' into dreams together."

The Jaguar made a breathy sound. "It's okay. I'd love to wander into a dream with you, if you promise not to behave yourself."

She gasped and lightly slapped his arm. He chuckled and said, "I'm not married, and I'm not likely ever to be, at least not while I'm under contract. This is no life to share with a woman, and she'd be prime bait for my many enemies, like you are, for your husband. Frankly, it would be hard to meet my type down here, anyway."

"What's your type?"

He turned his face to observe her profile against the embers of the fire. "Statuesque *gringas* with silky straight long blonde hair, eyes that take me sailing on an endless blue sea, and a smile that leaves me breathless. Southern manners and accent seal the deal."

She turned her head toward him, and they peered through the darkness at one another. Her voice was soft when she said, "There are plenty like that where I come from. Maybe when this is all over, you should move back to a South that's north of here."

"Move back? I used to live there?"

Now she turned to look up. "Ummm...I messed up. I'm not supposed to engage you about the past. Thank you for risking so much for me, and for helping with my leg muscles. Goodnight, Jaguar."

Like her, he turned his face to the netting and tarp sheltering them and whispered goodnight. Wandering into dreams with her gave him a rare sense of happiness, and it swelled inside him as he drifted.

The Jaguar's last thought of the day left an upturned corner on his lips in the dark. *Please, Princess, forget you're not at home once you're asleep.*

Chapter Nine

I have but one candle of life to burn,
and I would rather burn it out
in a land filled with darkness
than in a land flooded with light.
-John Keith Falconer

A pink-edged horizon promised even more beauty as a reward for patience, so Caroline struggled to keep her anxious spirit still as she watched the sunrise from a seat on the bluff. Behind her was the camp and beyond it, a dark, mysterious, threatening tangle of vegetation. *If only the way home wasn't through there.*

The Jaguar, Panther, and Puma were conferring in low tones about the weather report and the route the Weaver had planned for them. She overheard some latitude and longitude numbers, but they meant nothing to her.

"Chad, I love and miss you," she whispered to the streaks of color in the sunrise.

It was Sunday morning. Normally, there would be a mad rush in her home while she and Chad got themselves and three children fed and dressed for church. No matter how they planned the night before, some gremlin often popped out of hiding to stir havoc into their schedule, and Chad had resolved not to let his angst ruin their family's peace at worship.

She doubted the Weaver would let them go off the island today. As the head of the family and the island, Uncle Wyeth would host family services in the Big House. A wave of homesickness crashed over her heart as she imagined the old French Colonial mansion throbbing with the Painter and Gregory families. Maggie

Jane would be, and it made Caroline smile to know she'd be praying scripture back to the Lord like He'd never heard it before. She might even invite her prayer warrior friends, and if God had an all-star team, they were on it.

The Jaguar came up from behind Caroline and sat down. While she dabbed at her tear-dampened face with her sleeve, he squinted into the sunrise. Then he opened a small book and handed it to her. "When I watch the skies, I like to think of this verse."

She sniffed and turned damp lashes down to Psalm 65:8 in the New International Version, then read out loud. "They who dwell in the ends of the earth stand in awe of your signs; You make the dawn and the sunset shout for joy." She closed her eyes, mulling over the words, imagining shouts of joy in the sky. "It's beautiful."

They watched light peek bashfully over the horizon. The Jaguar kept his voice soft as they sat together in the hushed beauty. "It reminds me of Romans 1:19-21. God reveals Himself to every living soul through creation, and they have no excuse for not believing in Him."

"You always liked that passage." Caroline glanced away. "Do you remember much of what you once knew about your faith?"

He studied her face before looking back into the blush of dawn. "Yes. At first, it was unsettling. My father, people around the compound—they were surprised at things that just poured out of me. I praise God for that. In every mission, He lets me know I'm useful to His purposes in this world, but He's mum about why it took my near-death and a remarkable rescue to get me here."

With a flick of his hand, he drew back a light brown wave in his hair to reveal a vicious scar on his scalp. "As you can see, if you wanted to joke about me being brain-damaged, you'd have a point."

She winced. "They told you how it happened, and when?"

"Yes, once they realized it may take years for me to remember, if ever. They protected me for a while to evaluate my recovery and keep me calm but didn't want to build a long-term relationship based on deception. I was with a mission team doing rescue work on the island of Montserrat after Hurricane Hugo, September 19, 1989. Later, my biological family was told of my status, and they support what I'm doing. They want me to remember them first instead of jarring me by showing up. If I don't remember, I'll try to meet them someday anyway—when I'm not doing this anymore. I'd served in South America somewhere and was fluent in the language, and my parents are moving around as missionaries."

Caroline stared at the sunrise, recalling the day she was in France and got the news of his apparent death, over a phone call with her sister. "That same hurricane destroyed almost everything on the island I live on. Two days after your injury, only a bare shelter of our battered three-hundred-year-old home remained of it all. A few of us became trapped there during the storm as we tried to evacuate, and I gave birth to my twins that night. For a while, I grieved and begged God to help me understand why He had to do things that way."

He grimaced. "So, God used the same storm to send us both searching for meaning in His ways. Did you find yours?"

"Every time I think He's answered my questions as I can comprehend this side of heaven, He reveals something new. The answers lie in layers that get peeled back, like an onion. I have pangs of nostalgia, but I've grown to appreciate the new start He forced on us."

Behind them, the Panther announced they needed to eat and get on the trail. The Jaguar rose, took his backpack Bible from her, and offered his hand to help her up. "If childbirth is as bad as they make it look in the movies and you delivered twins in a hurricane, get us out of this mess."

She brushed off her jeans and looked up to his lopsided grin. "It's infinitely worse than the movies, and I didn't look a bit glamorous."

Her breakfast of de-boned fish were caught and cooked while she watched the sunrise. The Panther came to sit beside her, speaking between bites while the Jaguar sat across from them and chewed nonchalantly. "Princess, do you know how to use a gun?"

"Sure. My daddy started me out with a .22 for all the fundamentals and moved me up. I have a big brother and tried to stay on his level just to irk him."

The Panther exchanged a surprised glance with the Jaguar before he reached for a holster beside his pack and handed it to her. "Wear a knife, too. We noticed you carry a tactical pen, and last night, you used some self-defense skills. Where did you learn that takedown move?"

"From my live-in bodyguard. Azariah has been with us five years now, since we got a threatening kidnapping note. I don't know if he taught me standard stuff or not—he was once Mossad."

The Panther coughed before he and Jaguar exchanged glances again. "Uh, that's overkill for a personal bodyguard, don't you think? Your family's been threatened before?"

Caroline nodded through her last bite of fish, then set her plate down. "Good thing we had him in France, too. Someone tried to take the twins and shot at Chad." She reached down and touched the tongue of her boot. "Azariah didn't like me going out of town without him, so before I left, he tucked some things away. My shoelaces are made of para cord and I have a razor blade, a handcuff key—you know, stuff like that, tucked into the tongue of my boots and shoes. I don't do that around the kids. I'm paranoid that they'll find the blade and get hurt."

The Jaguar grinned and shook his head in admiration. The Panther cleared his throat and said, "Good to know you can escape being bound. Where we'll be traveling in the jungle, a blonde white woman—a *gringa*—is a rare prize. We'll help you disguise yourself with a hat, and at the next shelter, we should have some unflattering camouflage for you to put on. I don't want to frighten you, but you must comprehend how important this is: pretend to be the Jaguar's wife again. Facing a fight with him will carry some weight when men are deciding how badly they want to have you."

"Have me?" Caroline's voice was small.

His look was sympathetic but solemn. "It is imperative that you follow the Jaguar's hint if he handles you in a familiar way. He tells me you kept your head in an emergency that night in the village. You aren't likely to understand his conversation with whoever we meet, so trust his actions. We both saw you in a movie once, the one with that matador, and you followed his lead. You might save your life by being so convincing, understand?"

Her mind raced. The Jaguar had known about Alejandro when he made the insulting comment in the village that hurt her so much. Or did he connect the dots last night after he mewed?

Unsettled, Caroline nodded. The Panther helped her with the Glock pistol and a holster at her back, then the knife strap and sheath. When he left her to pack for the trail, the Jaguar came over with her dried clothes from the tree limb.

"Trust me?" he teased with a half-smile.

She tried to hide how anxious she'd become at the Panther's instructions and her need to carry weapons. Snatching her change of clothes from his hands, she folded them tightly, rolling intimate items inside. "Chad knows about this?"

"Yes. I get a den, a mate, and your husband's permission to take any actions I deem necessary. No repercussions."

Caroline half-snorted and she tried to keep her voice light, but her hand trembled as the stuffed clothes into her bag. "Chad doesn't make deals like that. Somebody else did it, like the Weaver. How often does this happen, and how far does it go?"

He pulled on his backpack, settling it on his shoulders. "You'll be my first time, but don't worry, I'm a quick learner. At least one of us knows what they're doing."

With a swift jerk of her head, she met the twinkle in his eyes. Chris Shepherd would never have spoken so suggestively, and his evil twin unnerved her. He reached out to help her adjust the pack over her arms and back, lingering with an unnecessary touch on her shoulders. Caroline flinched and almost pulled away, then realized this was a test to see if she'd been listening.

He warned, "You can't do that, understand? This isn't America. And don't use that reflex you sprang last night to put me on my back again. If you forget and end up on top of me, just act like that's part of how we—interact—and turn it into, well, something more. Use your imagination. If you resist or don't act naturally about us, they'll pick up on it. Just close your eyes and pretend I'm your husband, if you're forced to kiss me. It's up to you to convince our enemies, so you'll want to be with your husband again. If they get past me and the team and you survive a gang of guerillas, you may not."

A sharp look up told her he was unwavering and deadly serious. She struggled to catch her breath. "A gang?"

"This is your new reality. I mean it, Princess. You won't be cheating on your husband if you act with me. You'll be saving what's his."

"But I can't just *imagine* kissing Chad instead of you! It wouldn't be the same. He's the only man I've ever kissed, and our first was our wedding day. I teased him about wanting a dangerous kiss, but I was referring to it leading to—"

She shrugged and looked down, ending her sentence lamely. "You know, something more."

He snorted, handing her a faded olive-green crushable hat with a brim wide enough to keep off the sun and cover the back of her hair. "Danger is something else in this jungle. Pray you never face what a truly dangerous kiss is, Darlin'. I'm just the Plumber, you're the Princess. But drastic times call for drastic measures. Do you have any of those magic pins women carry that will hold your crowning glory under this?"

"The outside zipper of my pack. Do you mind?"

She sorted through the items in his hand from the unzipped pocket and pinned up her hair while he put the other things back. "When you say I'm the Princess and you're the Plumber, are you referring to Mario and the video games?"

"Sure. The Weaver must have a good reason for making it the new code. It worked as a trigger to help me stay focused, so he knows something I don't. You play?"

She hesitated, looking down. "I used to."

He led her and the team to form on the trail. "We're heading to a village to rent a cart as a disguise. We should get to a shelter before nightfall and we'll try to make radio and video contact with the Weaver. It will rain tomorrow, so we'll lose some time hunkering down."

Chad didn't want to be in the Big House this morning for a family worship service and lunch. He wanted to be alone. Maggie Jane's tea had helped him sleep better, but now his mind kept replaying the radio contact with Caroline last night. She knew how difficult her abduction was for him, and how dire the future of Painter Place and Gregory Global.

He looked around now as if shaking a daydream. Little Savanna sat primly with Patrick's daughter Summer Painter, both holding dolls dressed in their Sunday best with an open illustrated children's Bible in front of them. They pretended to tell their dolls a hilarious version of the story in the bright picture. The twins sat with their cousins—Patrick's sons, Noble and Beau, and Christian, Marina and Danny Mitchell's son. Their daughter TJ sat on her great-grandmother Savanna's lap.

His heart ached now with missing his younger brother Cole, and he wondered how long he and his family would have to stay in London handling the bulk of the company's unrelenting affairs. Clients were being great about delaying their business with Phillip, Justin, and Chad right now, watching the news sympathetically. Flowers, cards, letters, and gifts were pouring in, handled by the overwhelmed publicity team.

The Sunday morning gathering began with simple praise songs the children asked for and they sang whole heartedly. But Chad watched the twins become subdued again afterwards. His heart melted at Rhett's haunted expression, and he left the group of boys to come sit on Chad's lap, burying his face in his dad's sweater. Predictably, Rayce tagged along. Not to be outdone by her big brothers, Savanna squeezed her doll against the lacy bodice of her dress and climbed up beside them all.

Chad tried to wrap his arms around all three, so no one got left out, then realized everyone had turned to look at them. He bit his lip at the stricken expression on Caroline's mother's face. Pity and sympathy were things he liked to give to others but chafed against them for himself.

Wyeth Painter stood and opened his Bible, reading a passage from the book of Genesis that the kids could interact with. He talked about Joseph, who was sold by his jealous brothers and eventually thrown into prison when someone lied about him. But through it all, God was faithful and never let the bad things that happened to Joseph be wasted. Everyone in the prison respected his demeanor, righteousness, honesty, and wisdom. It seemed like he would never get out, but when the time was right, God delivered him by giving him the interpretation of some dreams. He was freed and set up in an important position over the country, saving people from starvation during a famine. Joseph later told his brothers that while God did allow the evil in life to happen to him, he used it for a greater good, to save many lives.

Chad's kids sat quietly with him like they did in church. Rhett put his hand around Chad's neck to pull him down a little so he could whisper in his ear. "Daddy, I'm goin' to pray that God does somethin' good for other people with the bad thing that happened to Mama. And for the good guys who are helpin' her."

Rayce nodded enthusiastically, overhearing his brother's whisper and pulling Chad's head closer to claim his other ear. "And maybe God will let Mama tell someone their dream, so they can be ready for the bad things."

Savanna whispered, "And the jungle animals, Rhett. Somethin' good happens, 'k?"

Chapter Ten

No one lights a lamp and puts it
in the cellar or under a basket,
but on a lampstand,
so that those who come in may see its light.
-Luke 11:33

The Jaguar and the Panther hacked a trail with a machete when they had to. Two scouts flanked them, just out of sight. Sometimes, the Jaguar would halt, waiting, observing, and consulting the compass on his watch. Swinging locks of light brown hair tapped against his neck and squared jaw when he turned his head. He was the strong, silent type now, all business and narrowly focused.

Something slithered through the underbrush about fifteen feet ahead, and Caroline considered shinning up the tree beside her. The Puma came up to whisper close to the brim of her hat.

"No worries. The wildlife doesn't want to encounter us. A small group of natives you won't see are following us, staying clear of the scouts. They're friendly, just curious. They hate the guerillas and melt into the jungle if they come around."

"You mean human guerillas, right? Like guerilla warfare. The animal gorillas only live in central Africa?"

The Puma's delighted grin was instantaneous. "No worries, Princess. The guerilla factions here act like big apes, but there are no animal gorillas around. Politics in—" He broke off. "That is to say, the politics here are extremely complicated. It's difficult to tell who the bad guys are."

The Jaguar cleared his throat, and the Puma glanced at him. He lost his grin and sobered, stepping back to scan through the green foliage of ferns and elephant ears as tall as a man.

Caroline tensed to find the Jaguar staring at her, remembering his accusation about being a distraction for his team. She mentally chided herself, but his expression softened. With a tug at the side of his mouth like an attempt to smile, he winked at her before turning his back and surveying the woods before them.

Her eyes shot wide with disbelief, and a vague stir in her heart warned her the Jaguar had been right to keep a distance between them before. The wink was blatantly Chris Shepherd—*her* Chris Shepherd. Her knees felt like jelly at a rush of—what?

She squirmed under her backpack at the rekindling of her affinity with Chris, a bond of friendship that she shared with only a tight circle of people. But there was a satisfying gulf between her love for Chad and the nostalgia for Chris' friendship on a bar graph comparison she concocted in her mind. Looking at the jungle ahead helped distract her from the unsettled ebb and flow in her emotions. Had her kidnappers not pursued the Jaguar when he rescued her, she would be home, out of his life. She may never have awakened to find him alive. Now he and his team were stuck and in peril because of her.

Caroline found it difficult to measure time in the rainforest, since the green canopy overhead seldom let the sun's position peek through. Trudging along with the team, she breathed the sultry but clean, sweet-smelling air. She jumped once at the sudden raucous scream of a macaw close by and ducked a short time later until she located an angry monkey who chattered at them. She wondered if monkeys would drop onto humans, and whether they'd bite.

During breaks, the Jaguar allowed her to take some photos of scenic views or animals. He was adamant about approving each one, even monitoring the number left on the roll of film, but he pointed out birds, lizards, and other small animals that her children would love.

The oppressive sense of dark spirits in the woods was lighter today and dissipated when the slightest breeze carried wisps of distant voices raised in joyful abandon. As the team drew closer, their feet found an oxcart rutted road that led to huts with steep thatched roofs under the shade of enormous mango trees. The singing came from the largest structure, a roof on an open frame with no walls. Under it, the village inhabitants gathered, clapping and lifting upraised hands.

A short, barrel-chested, dark-haired man who was leading the group in worship noticed the team and waved his arms. The Jaguar's scouts came in from different locations. Since Caroline was not fluent in Spanish and had no wish to offend the customs of the villagers, she shyly tagged along in the background.

The jovial leader met them with open arms, and Caroline knew enough bits of Spanish to understand the quick greeting. "*El Jaguar, mi amigo, que tal?*" She noted the way the man pronounced the Jaguar's name "haguar," called him his friend, and asked what was happening. She realized the Jaguar was known and popular here, just as he was in the village the team sheltered with two evenings before.

Some children shouted for the Jaguar, Panther, and Puma, pantomiming big cat hunting movements and giggling. The leader carried on a rapid-fire conversation with the Jaguar and led them up front to sit on crude benches. Then he smiled and squatted in front of Caroline.

His accent was thick, but he spoke in English. "I'm a wandering pastor to friendly villages. I was imprisoned in a guerrilla camp with an American missionary who taught me English. His hope and joy won me to the Lord. When an enemy faction group attacked us, he was killed in crossfire, but I kept his Bible and was freed by the other group. I carry on the missionary's work here. God has given me a big love for these villages, and even for the guerrillas that were cruel to me."

The pastor gestured with open arms, holding the stained, tattered black Bible in his hands. Caroline wondered if the dark blotches on the cover were in fact the blood of the missionary who had owned it. He smiled. "I already preached from scripture this morning and we prayed, testified, and sang praises. Our service is ending so I can travel in daylight to the next village. Perhaps you and *El Jaguar* will lead us in a song as a benediction?"

Stunned, Caroline opened her mouth to object, her blue eyes wide as she peered from under her hat brim at the Jaguar. But to her dismay, he rushed to agree.

While the pastor addressed the villagers, and she sat wondering if this was really happening to her, the Jaguar whispered, "They have extended an honor to us, Princess. It would be rude to decline. Anyway, a woman here would never openly refuse a man's authority, so you have to obey me." He nudged her with his elbow and winked for the second time that day. "If you can't carry a tune, it doesn't matter here. They like simple stuff and want me to play his guitar. Do you know an old campfire youth group song called 'Pass It On'?"

She gripped the edge of the bench and nodded. *Does he unconsciously associate that song with me, or does he sing it because they like it?*

The pastor handed him a battered guitar leaning on an overturned crate labeled for medical supplies. While the pastor addressed the villagers, she caught the word *Pasar*, which Chris had once taught her was the Spanish interpretation for "Pass it On."

The Jaguar adjusted the strap for his height and casually slung the instrument over his shoulders as if he did it every day. He flashed an encouraging smile at Caroline and began warm-up strumming to adjust the tuning to his range. It was a routine she'd seen him do a thousand times, and her heart felt like it would pound out of her chest.

She wondered if he still had the wide vocal range of a baritone to tenor. As an artist, she always wanted to associate his voice with a color, and never could decide on just one. Closing her eyes, she pictured a campfire at Dogs Head back home. Then she opened them to meet his, watching for his signal to start.

"It only takes a spark to get a fire going,
And soon all those around can warm up to its glowing.
That's how it is with God's love,
Once you've experienced it.
You want to sing,
It's fresh like spring,
You want to pass it on."

His voice was richer after ten years and they harmonized beautifully. People were humming to the music now, swaying and reaching to the sky. With her elbows by her sides, Caroline held her palms up in a gesture of praise, hands open to what God wanted to give or take away. Chad taught her to live like that.

As she and the Jaguar reached the last couple of lines and repeated them, some villagers sang along in English.

"I'll shout it from the mountaintops!
I want my world to know
The Lord of love has come to me!
I want to pass it on..."

The pastor gestured for the duet to repeat the song. Caroline's heart surged as she turned her face to the Jaguar. She stopped singing at what was once his solo and sang a background echo instead. Surprise flickered in his gaze and he recovered to add more flourish to his part. When they came to her own solo, he remembered to drop out, then they harmonized the ending. The crowd looked skyward with joy.

With a full heart at how her coerced participation was a blessing, Caroline blushed and moved a step back, conflicted, now comprehending a much bigger picture. God's gift to her was to be a gift to them.

This is what Chris left me for. It's his ministry, his mission field. This is his destiny.

The Jaguar pulled the guitar over his head and the pastor closed the service with a hand on their shoulders, praying in Spanish. Caroline understood "illume" and "con Dios" to mean "shine" and "with God." Her spirit was moved by words she didn't understand while the pastor prayed, and she decided to live in each passing moment. If she found herself in this dark place, she had a purpose to fulfill. What was it that the slain missionary Jim Elliot once said? *Wherever you are, be all there.*

When the prayer was over, she opened her eyes to see the Jaguar watching her, perceiving that something was happening. With a quizzical tilt of his head, he waited. But she had no way yet to express what had changed.

Native faces with warm smiles and jumbled Spanish reached out with tentative touches on her arms, and she tried to breathe through her mouth sometimes to avoid crinkling her nose at odors. One white-haired woman tucked in a few wayward strands of blonde hair under her hat, a momentary alarm in her dark eyes.

The pastor and the Jaguar made an arrangement about the team borrowing a goat-drawn cart. Both declined any offerings of food from the villagers, insisting they were late for their next stop. Men armed with spears escorted the pastor in the direction he was traveling.

About a mile out of the village down the oxcart path, the Jaguar stopped his team to break for lunch by the road. He scanned the contents of the borrowed cart with one hand and held his food in the other. He shifted his rifle on his shoulder and pulled a drab tan shirt from a bundle.

The frets on the old guitar flashed in a ray of light that pierced the jungle canopy. He covered it and stepped up to pat the goat companionably. Then he swallowed a long drink from his canteen and came to sit down beside Caroline on a fallen log that had been checked for vicious insects and snakes.

"You were a trooper back there," he said. "It'll keep that village a safe stop for my team." He glanced at the cart as if gathering a thought, then turned back to face her. "It's obvious we've done that song together before."

"Oh—yes," she replied lamely. If only he remembered who he once was, there'd be so much to say.

The silence stretched awkwardly, punctuated by intermittent chatters, caws, whistles, and screeches from up in the safe havens of the gargantuan trees. "Put this on," he ordered, handing her the shirt from the cart. "We have a few hours before we get to the safe shelter, but since we had to disguise ourselves with the cart and stick to the road, we're likely to meet travelers. Rain's coming. I have a working pass badge for an oil company on a research assignment here, and you're my wife, remember? I'll talk about you being homesick for our kids—just use yours. What are their names?"

"My twins are Rhett and Rayce, and they're five years old. My daughter is Savanna Caroline, and she's three, almost four."

"Okay. We're from Houston, Texas. Let's use your middle name for your identity, and our last name is something you can remember. You tell me."

"Oh—well," she hesitated. Her life might depend on remembering this name. She could make it easy without it sounding suspicious.

"We have the pastor's cart. The word 'pastor' means 'shepherd,' so let's go with that. I'm Amanda Shepherd. What's your first name?"

"Wow! Quick thinking. Okay, Christian is my adopted first name, let's use that. I'm Christian Shepherd. That should be—"

The Jaguar stopped, startled. Her hand flew to her mouth, and she squeezed her eyes shut.

He put a hand under her chin to make her look at him. She saw it in his eyes. He was teetering on the edge of something familiar, but he wasn't holding his head in pain this time. He almost whispered, but his tone brooked no argument. "What's my name?"

They sat staring at one another, a tear escaping down her cheek. As tears welled in his eyes, threatening to spill over, she drank in the rare sight of something she'd forgotten. His eyes seemed to change color when he cried.

She gulped and rasped, "Christopher Shepherd—Chris. It means 'Christ-bearer.'"

The other team members had been standing spellbound, but when the Jaguar seemed to fight for breath at her answer, the Panther stepped forward. The Jaguar waved him off and wiped his eyes. Slowly, he rose, resting hands on his hips and looking skyward. His Adam's apple bobbed a few times, then he reached into his pocket for a band to pull his hair back into a short ponytail. He squatted down in front of his pack and fished out a crushable hat. Jerking the zipper closed, he looked at Caroline. The Jaguar was composed and resolute, as if nothing had happened.

"Okay, now it's easy. I'll be Chris Shepherd, you're my wife Amanda, and we have three kids named Rhett, Rayce, and Savanna

Caroline. The Panther and Puma are our hired guides and we're on our way to the next village. Put your hair up tighter under your hat."

His gruff role as the no-nonsense Jaguar was back. He rose and held out his hand to pull her up. Shy again with uncertainty, she avoided his eyes, buttoning the borrowed shirt on over her sweater for a shapeless effect.

He hesitated as if he wanted to say more. Then, he turned to hurry in front of the cart.

Chapter Eleven

I ain't afraid to love a man.
I ain't afraid to shoot him, either.
—Annie Oakley

It was strange to be at the offices of Gregory Global on a Sunday, but then, there was nothing routine about Chad Gregory's life anymore. It all changed in a seismic shift that left his world askew last Tuesday, like the earthquake on the other side of the globe. As far as he could tell, his wife was no safer or closer to coming home than after her abduction on Wednesday. Her descriptions of the deadly environment that entrapped her were haunting him.

Chad groaned when he thought of the Spanish siren that would hunt him down the moment he arrived in the building. He'd begun referring to Isabelle as Jezebel and confided in Azariah that she was a tricky personal problem he needed to avoid. His bodyguard understood, for Chad read the guy's tension and shifting looks when he realized his eyes were lingering on places he shouldn't have on his mind.

Jezebel was an expert at getting into Chad's line of sight. She adapted to his moves, craftily overcoming her banishment six floors down. She often got close enough to brush against her target, capitalizing on his awareness of her.

The woman was a trap, all the warnings in Proverbs rolled into one. His frustration grew, and he was confused at what was happening. He'd heard guys talk about struggling with their worst temptations when they were exhausted, emotional, or needing affirmation. It wasn't about love.

Love was Caroline. And there was nothing he wanted he didn't already have with her.

Isabelle came around the corner with a notepad, pen, and head-turning high heels. Her face lit up and that wanton smile spread with fascinating slowness, suggesting things he immediately slammed the door on. He looked past her and kept his purposeful stride.

"Chad, I'm taking orders for dinner here tonight. Would you like to see the menu?" she purred.

"*Mr. Gregory* and I will take whatever the Weaver's having," came Azariah's curt answer as he tossed it over his shoulder, emphasizing her mistake in addressing his employer by his first name. They continued to the offices on the seventh floor, and Chad glanced around to detect the new hidden security cameras the Weaver set up. A video feed would be installed in time for the Jaguar's team when they radioed in tonight, and thinking of seeing Caroline sent his heart rate up.

Chad marched into his dad's office, almost used to seeing it set up as an intelligence hub. The Weaver was bent over a computer screen with narrowed eyes, conferring with a team member. Fading traces of a Carolina blue sky hung above Painter Place, and he wandered over to look out the wall of windows. His prayer on last Tuesday morning popped into his mind, words that reflected a time when he was satisfied, happy, and deeply thankful. His prayer thanked God for the time of peace in his life since Hugo. He had asked for help to recall that blessing when the next inevitable dark valley had to be endured. Now he picked up where he left off. *God, I know You'll honor my prayer. You knew that valley was hours away.*

The Weaver came to gaze out the window. "If the team is on schedule, they're settling into a safe house. It's a shack hidden under camouflage netting. We'll work out the video kinks when things are up and running. Perhaps we can have a long-distance party tomorrow with your kids. When your dad gets here, I have a briefing about the status of the demands from *Temoso*. They discovered that *Puña* wanted to one-up them by hitting Global for ransom and nabbed Caroline, then lost her. Their *capo* wants both ransoms now, and revenge. The cartel is searching for her and promising there will be blood."

Chad pressed the heels of his palms into his forehead. Weaver crossed his arms over his chest. "I'm having some food and supplies brought in. The deliveries will arrive all at once so we can clear them with security. Can I borrow your bodyguard downstairs for the checkpoints?"

With a weary sigh, Chad turned to go sit on the sofa. "Sure, if he's willing."

Azariah followed Weaver and two of the three other men out of the office, leaving the video technician who showed every sign of suffering a long day. He huffed about some glitch in the video feed, mumbling that he needed to go adjust a power source on another floor.

Leaned his head back on the sofa cushion, Chad closed his eyes, sorting through Weaver's update. The ever-changing scenario Caroline was tangled with was maddening! Now she was in even more danger, pursued by both rival drug cartels competing to be the ones to gain a prized ransom. They'd stop at nothing to one-up each other and kill the Jaguar's men if they found she was with him. The rescue team's evasive moves still put her smack in the web of ruthless guerilla factions who thrived on kidnapping people, and all he might get for a ransom was a shell of his damaged wife. She was safer with the cartels, but that would only happen over the Jaguar's dead body.

Sudden weight on his lap made his eyes fly open. Knees pinned his forearms to the leather. Isabelle straddled him and she took his face into her hands, pushing her bright painted mouth roughly into his. Shocked, Chad jerked his face away for only a slide of her lips, but the assaulting skewed kiss seemed endless. He was at once pulling back from her mouth and struggling to push up and away with his body and arms, but she had the advantage of all her weight pressing him into the depth of the cushions. Feeling a rising panic, trapped in a hard-to-explain position at her mercy, he couldn't decide if it was a situation that called for injuring her, which would happen if he could muster enough force to send her back into the coffee table.

"Stop struggling!" she commanded in her sultry, heavy accent, and he froze in confusion. "This is a quick invitation to my room downstairs tonight, after the briefing, when there's more time. Your bodyguard is not invited, so find something for him to do. We both know what's been on your mind as you've watched me the past few days, and believe me, I crave you, too. There are no men like you where I come from, *mi hombre guapo.*"

Every desire she'd stirred within his imagination vanished. Just as he expected, reality was unlike wondering. Even the alluring scent of her repulsed him now. She laughed as he grunted in renewed protest, rocking enough weight from his legs to gather strength and push her away. She used some crude descriptive terms about playing rough, pushing back against him, then found her balance before hitting the low table at the back of her knees. The momentum forced her to sit down hard on top of the file folders scattered there. Her enticing high heels teetered drunkenly on the shaken tabletop.

With a hiss, she curled long nails around the hidden handle of a flashing blade, and Chad instinctively lunged out of the way toward the dark sky view from the windows. Dread seized him and his stomach lurched. If she'd pulled that out while she had him pinned, both he and the sofa would now be a bloody mess.

She arched her brows provocatively as he wiped her kiss off with the back of his hand. He felt a bit of her lipstick smear but dared not look away from those flashing black eyes to see if he'd gotten it all off. Sizing him up, she rose to her bare feet and took menacing steps toward him. "If this is a refusal of my invitation to act on the desire I've been watching in your eyes, we must settle this here, lover-boy. Pity we couldn't satisfy your curiosity before our negotiations."

Chad gulped and backed up to distract her from Azariah's stealthy cat-like entrance into the room. "Put me in touch with your boss right now. I'm in the mood to negotiate."

Isabelle caught Azariah's reflection in the glass, spinning around with a vicious swipe of the blade to fend him off. He had to twist back to avoid it. She ran, and when he jumped at her, she seemed to somersault out of his grasp across the floor to the door.

But two men coming from the elevator rushed to disarm her in the hall. Chad ran to the door, fearful for his bodyguard after noticing the slit of cut fabric on his sleeve.

"Chad!"

He spun back around to the office, flying to the video screen where he drank in the sight of Caroline. With a gulp, he fought to slow down his panting breaths and racing heart.

"Caroline! You're okay!"

"And you almost aren't!"

Being surprised seemed to be the rule of the evening, and a deep breath helped steady him. "Yeah, I just had a close call when I was alone. The guards checked in supplies downstairs and the video guy went out to check a camera."

"I saw the whole thing, beginning with you and a woman on the sofa. You didn't deny her claims about how you'd been watching her with something on your mind. Did she get the wrong message from you, Chad?"

Now he understood the look on her face, and he reached up to wipe at the smear of red lipstick with the back of his hand, just in case there was more. Behind Caroline stood a well-built man, his thigh to chest visible on the screen, and the man rested a strong, comforting hand on her shoulder. *The Jaguar!*

"She kept all the guys' heads turned on purpose, a plant in here for information—a distraction."

"Okay. So, you weren't the only one, and she got the right message from you?"

Speechless, Chad scrambled for an honest answer. He'd think of a million ways he should've handled this later. His heart broke as Caroline covered her mouth with her hand and jumped up from her chair, grasping her stomach with the other hand as if she would be sick. She ignored his pleas to let him explain.

With a cavalier attitude, the Jaguar replaced her on the screen. "She's outside, sobbing. Don't worry, a guard is with her until I get the honor. Uh, I'm sure she meant to tell you she's glad you're safe. So, you like our South American women? To each his own. I was just telling Caroline last night in our den that my type is a statuesque *gringa* with long blonde hair, with a graceful Southern accent and manners."

Fierce possessiveness suffocated Chad. "This isn't my fault! I was careful to stay away, and you'd better do the same with my wife. Get her back in here!"

The Jaguar smirked with a knowing look. "I believe you, Stud. Tell you what, I'll be fair and explain all this to her for you, from a guy's perspective. You know, how visually stimulated we are, and it means nothing. You just made my job here a lot easier, and I appreciate that. I didn't think she'd be able to convince a guerilla scout group she was mine. Now she can recall this scene with another woman all over you in your dad's office. Revenge can be the best motivator of all."

Chad slapped the top of the desk, searching for the right response, which came out with more of a growl than his voice. "I'll pay my own consequences, Tarzan. You just focus on your job and get her home where she belongs—to me."

"All in good time, Stud. If I'm alive in five more years, I can be finished here. I realized what I've been missing the other night when the Princess and I had to cuddle in a village where spies watched us. And lying beside me in camp last night, she invited me to come back to live in a South that's north of here. Maybe you'll mess up by then. I'll be watching."

The Weaver and others were pouring into the room as the Jaguar began standing up. Chad shouted at him, "You'll never be more than the consolation prize. Get my wife back in here!"

He fumed while the Jaguar staggered, holding his head and knocking the chair over. A tall man with black hair tried to help him.

"Panther, I need a report! Over." Weaver shot Chad a warning look before he concentrated on the screen, rolling up his shirt sleeves.

"I need Caroline back on there!" Chad demanded. "She saw Isabelle attack me, and she's upset. Let me explain!"

He listened to the interchange with the Panther and Weaver. The Jaguar was mewing again, and Chad was to blame. But the Jaguar was quick to recover from the disabling pain this time, and he responded to Weaver's curt demand for an explanation for his behavior.

"Gregory needed a wake-up call. His wife watched another woman wallowing all over him and almost witnessed his murder tonight. How would I get her out of here then? I'm no grief counselor! Now I'm in the picture, so he has a new reason to stay alive and think with something higher than his zipper."

"Why, you—" Chad hissed on his way back to the screen. But his dad rushed into the room in alarm, catching his arm. Chad didn't pull away, but otherwise ignored Phillip and directed his protest to Weaver, stabbing a finger at the screen.

"The Jaguar had better get his priorities straight! He's distracted by her, and when something goes wrong because he's a lovesick kitty cat, he better die in his failure, 'cause I'll find him!"

With a sarcastic laugh, the Jaguar retorted, "Yeah, movie star, you come find me. You're fish bait down here in my world! That'll get you out of the picture for sure, and I can't think of anything I'd like better than letting the Princess make a house cat outta me."

A collective gasp filled the room. Chad opened his mouth for a furious retort, but Azariah put his bulk between him and the screen. "There's trouble enough for one day," his bodyguard said in a steely voice. "Let's do this our way."

Chad's jaw worked in fury as he let Azariah lead him back from the Weaver's team. The Panther had no success getting Caroline to come in, so the Jaguar left the chair and went out the door.

Disheveled and tense, the Panther briefed the Weaver on the events of the day, and that the Jaguar had learned his previous name. They armed the Princess with a Glock 17 and knife to defend herself as a last resort.

Behind him, Chad saw Caroline come in with her hand on the Jaguar's arm, and he imagined them cuddled as the Jaguar had claimed. The team leader was courteous in holding the chair for her, then positioned himself behind it, confident and in charge.

Chad wondered if the guy was showing off his muscles to their best effect when he crossed his arms. The Jaguar's physical posturing made a statement. He could take care of Caroline or take care of Chad.

The Weaver explained to her the security situation, taking the blame for lack of protection for her husband. He asked her if the situation they discussed last night had improved. Her voice was calm, but her swollen eyes were red-rimmed. She looked weary, distant, and sad.

"I can work with the Jaguar. We sang together today at a village worship service. It was a good day, until this screen popped on. Your lax security wasn't the real problem with my husband."

Weaver pursed his lips. "Noted. However, there's already too much distance between you, without adding a quarrel. Will you give him a chance to explain and apologize?"

Caroline blew out a breath and looked away while the Weaver gestured to Chad to come over. Chad gushed to the screen, "No excuses, Care. I'm at your mercy. I can't get through this if I have to fight you along with the bad guys."

Crossing her arms, she glowered back at him. "The Jaguar explained how it is with men. It sounds like somethin' Patrick tried to tell me once, but I thought you were different. We'll talk about this, but not in front of the team. How are the kids?"

Chad wanted to put this behind them, not leave a contentious wedge in their relationship while she spent so much time close to the Jaguar. His sigh was heavy with disappointment, and he ran a hand absently back through his hair. She was right, of course. This was a private matter.

"The kids are fine, but they miss you. We went to the Big House for home church today. They'll love hearing that you sang in the jungle. What song was it?"

She turned a thoughtful gaze into the distance. "I don't know if I've taught them this one. Remember 'Pass It On?' The Jaguar played guitar. He told me I had to sing along with him because refusing would be rude in this culture, but as I saw what a blessing it was to the villagers, I remembered that verse in John 3:30, about how God must increase, and I must decrease. Like the steeple of a church. It points heavenward, and the closer you get to heaven, the smaller you become. I'm goin' to embrace God's purpose in why I'm here and live each moment."

Softly, Chad responded, "That's just what I'd expect from you. Shine on, Care. But never stop lovin' me."

Her tears broke afresh for a moment. "Never. Don't forget."

"Never could."

The Panther put his hand on her crossed arms and whispered they had to save the battery on the radio. Chad sniffed and rushed to ask, "Mrs. Gregory, will you go out on a date with me tomorrow?"

Caroline's swollen eyes held his so long that he wondered if she'd embarrass him by refusing. With a solemn expression, she said, "If I can wear camouflage."

He burst out laughing. "Babe, you don't belong in camouflage, surrounded by animals."

The Jaguar's arms tensed, and he re-crossed them behind her. Chad felt a heady surge of triumph as he continued, "You belong in gorgeous dresses designed by Chrissy and Juliette Painter, dancin' at the Pavilion and the mansion ball room. I'll bring one."

He said a quick goodbye but stayed in her range of sight when the Weaver took over. They set up a time to talk to the children the next morning, and a flexible time for a possible "date" that evening. Then the screen went black.

Phillip Gregory simmered until the Weaver signed off with the Panther, then he dropped the suave demeanor he'd worn for Caroline's sake. He was beside himself in anger over the security breach and the assault on his son. The Weaver was calm and apologetic, offering no excuses and nothing to fight back about.

Global's leader was grim when he, Chad, and Azariah left the nerve center to go home. Once they were in the hallway, he curtly asked Chad to go into his office for a private discussion.

Chad cringed inwardly. It was time to face the music for losing his self-control. Under Phillip Gregory's iconic self-assurance was a man who'd trained himself to be that way, and he'd always made it clear that he expected the same from his sons.

Azariah shot Chad a sympathetic look and closed the door to wait outside. Phillip gestured to his son to sit. He went to Chad's bookcase, running a finger over a collection of literary classics and South Carolina history as he searched for something else. He found a slim volume and sat down, leafing through the pages before passing the open book to Chad. He pointed to a paragraph.

"You were brought up on principles like this. Now, you're raising your own boys on them. If only I could pull what I've learned out of my mind and put it into yours!" He touched his fingertips to the strands of gray at his temples, as if grasping for a way to accomplish that feat.

Chad looked at the page and solemnly read out loud into the room. "What is life without honor? Degradation is worse than death. Stonewall Jackson."

"You're the shining star of what Global is about, Chad. But you've got the same problem I struggle with, self-control for the ones we love. Nothing makes me lose it like what happened to you tonight. You were almost murdered, right there in my office!"

Chad studied the desperate expression on his dad's face. Emotional outbursts from him were rare, and he wasn't finished yet. "I've never been so messed up as I was when you were stranded at Painter Place during Hugo."

Phillip held up four fingers with an outstretched arm. "Your life's been threatened four times, Chad, and that's just the ones I know about!" He clasped both hands together now, resting them between his knees. "I can relate to how desperate you feel about Caroline. But the world's watchin' you, son. You're not just anybody, and you don't have the luxury of anonymity. Envy the men who go to work for someone else and go home and forget it. You're the guy whose downfall will cost those men their good jobs."

He pushed back graying hair from both temples. "You're faced with this trial way too young, and I can't do it for you. It's yours to model, your experience to learn from. You've got more potential than any Gregory ever, and that's just the guy who has the farthest to fall. Problem is, you'll take your reputation and your family down with you."

Chad grimaced. He'd been miserable before he came tonight and wouldn't leave with any relief.

But his dad didn't let up. "In this moment in your life, Chad, in the history of Global, in the history of Painter Place and Whitehaven, your character is being shaped and you're revealing if you're a man of God, or your own man. I've always hated that song about looking back on life and bragging that you did it your way. Your actions are being recorded out there, son. Men of God can be righteously angry, and I don't blame you for callin' out the Jaguar. He deserved it. But do it coolly—not as a hot-head. Remember the quote by Thomas Jefferson that I used to nag you with?"

Chad repeated the memorized words. "Nothing gives one person so much advantage over another as to remain always cool and unruffled under all circumstances."

"The Jaguar's the one who's following that maxim, not you. He's pegged you, Chad, gamblin' that you'd react to your competitive instinct and rise to any challenge if you knew he wanted Caroline. Using your jealousy, he set you up to be calculated and deliberate about surviving, if only to spite him. If there's any of Chris Shepherd left in this guy, he downplayed what happened between you and Isabelle when he talked to Caroline.

Not for your sake, but to spare her feelings. That's why she came back in and gave you a chance."

"I thought you said you never really knew him?"

"I didn't, he wasn't home much. But I had my reasons for watchin' 'im. The day his dad came as our new pastor, Chris came from college to be presented as part of the family. He couldn't resist Caroline from the instant he saw her in the choir, though it was clear he tried. He couldn't avoid all the whispers about you, and he watched Derrick demand every minute with her when he was home. After struggling so long to keep her at arm's length, I don't know what made him ask Andy to court her right before he graduated college."

Phillip tapped his fingertips together, staring off into the night, gathering his thoughts. Chad recognized the absent-minded habit that calmed his dad down, and he waited for more insight into Caroline's relationship with Chris Shepherd.

"For two summers, Caroline and Chris did some ministry together on the island. That song they performed today was always a favorite at Dogs Head camp-outs and youth gatherings. Cole's heard them sing it often. The Weaver switched their mission code to the Princess and the Plumber to see if it would trigger the Jaguar to know his role in protecting her, because they played Mario video games with the youth at church for outreach parties. The kids wanted them to be a couple, so he told them he was just the Plumber, protecting her from Bowser, but never being her Prince. He used to say that's the way spiritual gifts work. We all have a unique part to play in the big plan, and no one else can do it. He encouraged them to be content with their own role and to have faith that their impact makes a difference."

Chad sat back against the cushions with dawning understanding. "How did she respond the first time he couldn't take his eyes off her during the church service?"

Phillip sighed and clasped his hands. "She was—affected—by him. They were always easy and comfortable around one another. But I never saw her light up around him or Derrick like she does with you. I never thought it would come to anything, and neither did Andy. We didn't get it, that she's a survivor, that she'd lost hope and set herself free from you to move on. It seemed better to let everything play out by your arrival back home."

"My gut says he's never gotten over her. Now what, I'm supposed to feel sorry for the guy? He was openly insulting and demeaning me in front of everyone!"

"I don't have the answers, Chad. I'm just begging that you watch how you direct the testosterone-laced volleys between you two. Act cool under fire, even if you're fakin' it. Weaver's team is biased toward the Jaguar and they are forming their opinions of us. Don't let them wonder if your wife might leave you for him."

Chapter Twelve

Wherever we are,
it is but a stage on the way to somewhere else,
and whatever we do, however well we do it,
it is only a preparation
to do something else that shall be different.
-Robert Louis Stevenson

The Princess reverted to the role of a silent tagalong who awakened a few days ago to find herself in the middle of a desperate rescue attempt. She sat on a log as far as she could get from the men, wiping falling tears and moodily sketching in her book.

The team cast uneasy glances at the tragic figure. They whispered about being convicted and confused. Raking your eyes over a beautiful woman and letting your mind wander meant nothing, did it? Yet a common mental dalliance had almost gotten the Prince killed.

Attempts at conversation without the Princess lagged. Since her rescue, her disarming sweetness and unpretentious manner had drawn them like the light and warmth of a hearth fire. Finally, their emotionally charged silence broke when someone asked the Jaguar to play the guitar.

He rose to get the scarred old instrument from the goat cart, then he settled near the Princess. He pulled the threadbare embroidered guitar strap over his shoulders and spoke softly when he asked her, "May I see what you're drawing?"

She shrugged and held the book out. The others came to see, turning the book at different angles to the firelight. The pages were filled with things from the camp on the bluff the previous evening, the animals and plant life on the trail, and the village worship service. They laughed at some poses that depicted the personality of the goat.

Over the light graphite sketches, she covered the lines with expressive, confident strokes of ink. Each page was signed at the bottom with "Caroline A. Painter" and the date.

When they joked that her signature claimed she was a painter, she explained that her middle initial was a statement about her heritage. She was a "Carolina" Painter from a long line of artists who settled on her island in South Carolina over three hundred years ago, before the Carolinas were split into North and South.

When they wondered if she would frame the pages, she shook her head, saying that they were unfinished steps to composing a painting, or references for future poses and ideas. Her sketchbooks were thoughts, records, and plans. One team member asked why she didn't save time by using photos.

"Because if I can't draw my subject, nothing magical will happen to make it right on the canvas with paint. I study things for an artistic interpretation, to see and interact with them in my own way. I also solve problems in the sketch before making mistakes and losing my way in the painting."

Much to the team's relief, talking about art brought the Princess out of the shell she'd withdrawn to after the radio contact with her husband. "A true artist composes a scene on their own as part of the way you judge their ability. Though our photos can be used as part of the process, we'd be cheating if we copied someone else's images for a competition. In a good photograph, the composition has already happened, making it the creative vision of the one who shot the scene. That counts more than the ability to paint it. Composition is vital to the skills of an artist, something a judge will weigh in an exhibition, and something the collectors of my work expect to be solely my own. They pay for my vision, investing in it, hoping the value of my work will increase."

"You must make big bucks as an artist," ventured the Puma. "What do you like to paint most?"

"People don't value creativity with their wallets these days. They gush over your 'gift' or 'calling,' but only a few comprehend worth in it. Many will say it is only paper or canvas and some paint, so why does it cost so much? They think a professional artist's painting is child's play, easy, fun—not a skill labored over in years of hard work."

She paused and shrugged. "Those who most appreciate art have tried it themselves or watched the process. My uncle is well-known, and his work is valuable in today's markets, but it can take years for the right person to come along to buy a painting. He teaches and speaks at events to earn enough to keep painting. We run the Painter Gallery and sell older paintings and prints from previous generations of artists in my family. But we had to build new facilities after a hurricane destroyed ours, and we haven't earned back enough to pay for it yet. Every month, we sweat about covering the bills."

Looking off into the darkness, she said, "I like to paint coastal scenes and sea birds, Southern subjects like verandas and rocking chairs or porch swings, and some scenes from traveling. My family has property in England called Seamure, and I enjoy painting there, too."

The Puma grinned. "I assumed artists liked to do portraits and considered nudes to be an intellectual pursuit that the general population was too crude to appreciate."

The Jaguar snorted. With a one-sided smile, the Princess replied, "I include people in some of my scenes, but I'm not a portrait artist. People are demanding and complicated. I try to depict the quiet solitude of places to escape from a noisy, demanding world."

She stared into the flames as they began to burn low. "I never do nudes and won't show in an exhibition that includes them. They're an oddity that distracts from the other paintings hanging nearby. Even a child knows by instinct that it's not appropriate. People don't sit around like that—it's a contrived setting, and there are laws against public nudity. It offends people. Anyway, God's very clear in scripture about His view of that issue. Other artists have argued with me that if there's a God and He created people with nothing on, then we should relish the beauty of the human form. But they twisted the Genesis account and didn't consult the rest of the Bible for context."

She paused when the Jaguar stopped the soft strumming on the guitar to listen. Seeing that they all stared and waited, she continued. "Adam and Eve's choice to sin changed everything. They lost their privilege of walking with God in Eden, so perhaps they missed the covering of light that shines over those who spend time with Him. Whatever was lost about their appearance, it was dramatically different if it made them so afraid. It was also unacceptable to God, who killed the first animal to cover them with its skin. It was a picture of the Lamb to be slain to cover their sin, when Christ came to the world for that purpose and died. If God Himself thought the only two people in the world needed to be clothed, then you can bet it's important. The rest of scripture always associates nudity with shame, except for marriage. When the sinless environment of heaven is mentioned, as in Revelation—I think it's in 1:13 and 19:14—we're all wearing white robes to signify innocence."

She ducked her face back down to her book in a rare moment of being self-conscious. "Anyway, I know sitting and sketching looks like an idle fancy, but it's an integral part of my work, not a pleasant pass-time. I practice and create my own library of images."

The Jaguar said, "I'm sorry I insulted you about wasting time in your sketchbook, so you'd stay out of our way last night. Of all people, I should know it takes a lot of practice and work to excel at something, just like playing this old guitar."

He started strumming softly again. "I was thinking, the tribe that's been following us in the jungle would probably appreciate those drawings of their world, if you could part with them. Like a goodwill gesture, a gift."

She peered uncertainly into the depths of the jungle. He waited, idly strumming a haunting melody she'd never heard.

"I've signed and dated the drawings. What if the men looking for me finds one?"

"The guerillas on all sides mostly leave the indigenous villages and people groups alone."

The Princess bit her lip, then carefully tore recent drawings from the sketchbook while the Jaguar pulled the guitar over his head and leaned it against the log. He asked a guard about borrowing his night vision goggles and took her hand to lead her yards deeper into the jungle.

They found the enormous stump of an ancient tree and she laid the papers there. He blinked at the one on top. It was not among the ones she'd shown him earlier. The drawing was a roadside view of a rough homemade sign which proclaimed, "Jesus Saves." At the bottom of the page, she'd written the Spanish words for "shine, and pass it on."

"I know this sign."

"Yes. And when I passed it on the road a few days ago, I thought of you." She laid her hand on top of the drawing and closed her eyes, though she hardly needed to in such darkness. "Jesus, my work is always for Your glory. Amen."

The Jaguar quickly covered her hand with his and bowed his head. "Lord, I know You're working in the tribe who is watching us. I praise You for including the Princess in reaching out to them and ask Your blessing on her offering. Amen."

He gripped her hand firmly. She waited in the dark, discerning his shadowy outline and listening to his breathing. After some hesitation, he seemed to change his mind about saying more. He led her back to camp and returned the goggles to the night watch.

The Princess sat back down with her sketchbook and the Jaguar settled near her again with the guitar. One of his team requested his favorite song, and the Jaguar joked that he'd forgotten it since last week. The man grinned and spoke to the Princess. "He humors me. I enjoy wallowing in my sad memories. Do you like Gordon Lightfoot?"

The tune was rising from the guitar strings into the night air, so she didn't need to ask which song. The team around the fireside sang the haunting melody. "In a castle dark, or a fortress strong, with chains upon my feet..."

The Jaguar's fingers coaxed music from the well-traveled, often-handled old instrument. His rich voice sang the words about never being set free. After the last notes, the man who requested it met her eyes over the dying campfire flames and she said, "I hope you'll sing happier songs soon."

Another teammate asked for his favorite song. He told the Princess he was married before joining the team, but he wasn't good with the words women like to hear. "It's hard for my wife, not knowing if I'll come home from a mission. She needs a lot of assurances about my feelings for her. It is good that *El Jaguar* and the other big *gatos* on this team have no attachments, you know?"

The Jaguar grunted and strummed, then sang, "I know it's kinda late, hope I didn't wake you..."

They joined in with the lyrics about having to say "I love you" in a song. But afterwards, they were melancholy, staring quietly into glowing embers and unearthing memories stirred by the two songs. The Jaguar strummed aimless chords. The Panther came out of the cabin to lean on the doorframe.

Suddenly, the Jaguar launched into bold riffs from "Sunshine of Your Love." The Princess caught her breath. She turned her startled eyes to his and found him waiting for her reaction.

"Tell me why I thought of that song just now. It's about you."

His commanding tone brooked no backing away. As they'd done earlier that day, the Panther and other men waited as the Princess swallowed hard. "Just sing what comes to mind."

He kept his eyes locked on hers and sang, "I'll be with you darlin' soon, I'll be with you when the stars start fallin'." He pressed his hand on the vibrating strings to stop the sound. "What does it mean?"

"I don't know what Clapton meant when he wrote it," the Princess began. She cleared her throat. "That's the thing with song lyrics, they're often vague and could mean lots of things. Maybe it's only about the stars fading and disappearing in the sunshine of a new day. But in the Bible, falling stars signal something dreadful. That part always tripped you up. You associated it with bein' the Plumber."

"The—Plumber? You mean, Mario?" Incredulity gave way to a dawning understanding across his features and his voice almost squeaked. "You—you're the Princess?"

She gasped and covered her face. "I can't do this tonight," she whispered pitifully into her empty hands, then she rose and wiped away fresh tears. Her voice caught when she announced she was going to bed.

The Jaguar put down the guitar and picked up his rifle to guard her trip to the latrine. The other men raised eyebrows at one another. They'd eavesdropped on something intimate and immensely interesting, and the last thing they wanted was a cliffhanger.

When she went inside the cabin and settled into a cot, the Jaguar stepped closer until he loomed over her. He kept his voice low, for her ears only. "I'm sorry. I'm pushing too hard. Have sweet dreams, Princess."

She pulled her blanket higher and turned to face the rough gray boards of the outer wall. Her voice was small and weary. "I understand you don't know what to say, and appreciate the sentiment, but sweet dreams aren't likely. I'm unraveling and the only safe place to fall apart is in my dreams."

He hesitated, ready to pull a makeshift curtain hung for her privacy. Outside the hut, the guard was changing. He was up for his shift. "When I get back in, I'll be right here beside you. If the stars start fallin' in your dreams, I wanna be there. Wake me."

In the murky edges of light around the outside of the cabin, the Jaguar stood with rifle poised to lift at any threat. The Panther moved close enough that their shoulders touched. He whispered, "The Weaver contacted me again in the cabin right before I came out. He's deeply upset about what happened to the Prince and asked how the Princess was doing. My gut tells me you're not the only one with a personal investment in this mission."

On Monday morning, Chad's children sat in front of a video monitor to interact with their mother for the first time in five days. Caroline's parents and Chad's mother were in the background. Little Savanna squirmed restlessly in a child-sized chair and chirped proudly, "My mommy's goin' ta be on TV."

Chad knelt behind his daughter, helping her sit still by encircling his arm like a seat belt and kissing her gleaming blonde hair just above a sparkling little blue bow. "So are you, sweetie, and you look beautiful. She'll see you on her TV."

And she'll see me. The thought made his heart jump, for the mirror told him this disaster in his life had aged him. He didn't have the muscular bulk and strength of the man her old boyfriend had become, but he made sure he looked his best in a sweater she gave him for Christmas a few weeks ago. It was the purple tones of twilight, and she said it set off his blonde hair and green eyes. He was courting his wife again, and he had to come out ahead of the Jaguar.

The Panther's face appeared, solemn and ready for business. His deep voice resonated smoothly from the radio and the screen speaker. "Weaver, this is the Panther. Do you read me? Over."

"Roger, loud and clear. We're ready for the Princess."

Savanna twisted to ask her dad excitedly if they could see the Princess. He whispered that the Princess was her mama, and she grinned in delight and bewilderment, asking if the Big House was her castle. Then Caroline replaced the Panther, and Savanna pointed. "Mama! I see Mama!"

The twins slid up to the edge of their seats, riveted to the screen. Chad heard family members behind him as they reacted to seeing Caroline. Her face had lost some of its softness with weight loss, and a sad, hollowed look settled about her eyes.

But she lit up when she saw the children. They all blurted out greetings, and Chad sniffed and covered his emotions by reminding his kids to take turns speaking because they only had a few minutes. They had to save the batteries in the jungle, just like their own radios.

"You look too beautiful to be on a jungle adventure," he said to the screen. "We dressed up for you. Your mom helped Savanna with her hairstyle."

"Everyone looks wonderful!" she responded. Then she told the twins she had some words for them today. "When you get home, ask Daddy to help you look up Nahum 1:7. It says, 'The Lord is good, a stronghold in the day of trouble; and He knows those who trust in Him.'"

Rhett furrowed his little blonde brows in concentration, mulling over the words. Rayce announced that they would and said they sang about her when they watched a video. Savanna jumped in to trill that they wanted to sing it with her.

"It's the one Fievel and his sister sing, Mama, with the big moon in the sky! Mimi Melia said it can be about mommies, too." The sibling trio looked at each other to start, then enthusiastically belted out some rehearsed lines to "Somewhere Out There." Caroline joined them to sing about looking at the same moon as someone you love, wondering where they were, and hoping on a star to be together again someday.

"That was beautiful!" encouraged their mother, clapping. "I can tell you love me so much, and you know I love you, too. I think of you all the time."

"Mama, what's that noise?" asked Rhett. "Is that what a jungle sounds like?"

"The jungle has many sounds. Today, the rain is crashing against more leaves than you can imagine. There are animals making noises in the daytime and different animals in the night. But this is my first day hearing rain, and animals seem to be quiet while they wait on it to stop."

"Did you draw some animals?" asked Rayce.

"Yes, I did last night, but then the man in charge here told me about how the friendly tribe watching us in the jungle would like to have my drawings of their world. We took my pictures out to leave them in the darkness. I also left them an image of something from my home, and we prayed for them with our hands on the drawings.

I'll create some more just for you. I think you'd like the goat that pulls the cart for us."

Savanna asked if the goat had a name, and Caroline said she didn't know. Rhett jumped in next. "Mama, do you think it would be okay if we meet that man in charge? Or some of the good guys? Why do they call one of them a panther?"

Caroline's gesture to the team stirred movement around her while Savanna said she'd seen a pink panther on cartoons. The Weaver said three men in the group were named for fierce jungle cats because they couldn't use their real names over the radio.

A swarthy, strong man came up to the screen first, looking very militaristic in camouflage. He bent to the camera with a boyish grin, greeting them and saying his name was Carlos. He told them two of the other guys were outside standing guard in the rain. Then two more men came to crowd him out, announcing that they were the Puma and the Panther.

Savanna giggled while the twins waved. But all the men made way for another who pulled up a chair beside their mother. He leaned in close to her, oozing confidence and wearing an olive t-shirt like the one she had on. It stretched over his muscles. He didn't play around like the other men had, but the corners of his mouth curled in a small smile. "Hi, I'm the Jaguar. Your mom told me about you, and it's nice to meet you. Have you heard about jaguars?"

Chad heard the gasps of family members behind him as they reacted to the change in Chris Shepherd. The twins were riveted and merely nodded at first. Then Rhett replied, "My dad, he said they're the king of the jungle. Like the lion is, in Africa. They're extremely dangerous."

Chad and the Jaguar locked eyes. Chad's knuckles turned white in his grip on Savanna's chair.

The Jaguar lazily turned back to the twins. "Your dad's right. But jaguars don't roar like lions. The Puma, the Panther, Carlos, and I work for the Weaver, and two other men are outside guarding us all. The Weaver figures out what he wants us to do next and we follow his plan, like game pieces on a board. In a few minutes, we will plan the next moves to bring your mom home. But things don't always happen like we want them to, and in those times, we're like real cats—we walk alone."

While Chad and the Jaguar stared at one another again, Savanna interjected in a wheedling tone, "Mama, just tell all the cats you're our princess and theirs is in another castle. I want you to come home now, k?"

She reached toward the screen, pulling against her dad's arms. Caroline impulsively put her fingertips to the bottom of the screen and blinked back tears.

Chad chafed when the Jaguar draped his arm around her chair to comfort her. They looked great together in that untamed setting, and it made Chad's blood boil. He let go of Savanna, but Rhett reached the screen first, touching it to connect with his mother's hand.

With tears standing in eyes like so much like hers, Rhett bravely stated, "Mama, Savanna doesn't understand. We'll try to explain it to her."

"I want to be home more than anything, Rhett. Thank you for takin' good care of your little sister. Has Daddy helped you find the words in the Bible about bein' glad during all the things that happen to us, even the bad ones, because somehow God's doin' good things?"

"We'll look it up when we go home," Rayce pitched in. "Uncle Wyeth said bad things happened to Joseph, too. Rhett told us to pray for God to do good things there and Savanna says we need to pray for Him to do good things for the jungle animals, too."

Weaver signaled Chad, so he reached in, moving a chair aside to kneel close behind the kids. Sniffles filled the room behind him. "Care, we have to go. You can wave at everyone in the background. They miss you and wanted to see you're okay. We all love you."

"Can I just have a few seconds with my mom?" There was a pitiful break in Caroline's voice.

Her parents jumped forward and Chad gently pulled Valerie in front of him, where she knelt before the screen and reached out with her hand to join their fingers. "Don't worry about anything here, baby. Take care of yourself."

"Mama, no matter what happens, don't let anyone blame Global. It's my children's heritage, their future, and I want it for them. I chose this. Promise me." Caroline's voice trembled and her eyes swam.

Chad could hardly breathe. He heard his dad stifle a choking sob.

"I promise," Valerie answered. "But I sense a mood in you that I refuse to accept. It's not who you are. This isn't over. Fight, Caroline! Fight! Jaguar?"

The Jaguar calmly leaned closer to the screen. "Yes, ma'am."

"The stars are fallin'."

Their gaze was steady, loaded with a passing message. "I read you loud and clear, Mrs. Painter."

Chapter Thirteen

The counsel of the Lord stands forever,
the plans of His heart to all generations.
-Psalm 33:11 HCSB

The pouring rain created a never-ending clamor that was nothing like the soothing rhythmic surf on a South Carolina seashore. Caroline curled up in her cot, pulled the oiled tarp that served as a privacy curtain, and sobbed with abandon. Her spirits crashed like the raindrops on the leaves. She ached all over with loving her children and the reality that she may never see or hold them again. Their sweet voices replayed in her mind, singing about her when the same moon hung over them all. In silent prayers, she begged God that they never learn of anything dreadful happening to her. Better to die from a gunshot and get it over with, like Wilfred.

When emotional exhaustion calmed her, she rolled over to face the drape. She had no will or energy to rise, and a distant murmur of voices was all she heard. She drifted off into a welcome deep slumber of nothingness.

The aroma of a cooked meal awakened her, and the roaring rain had slackened off. Her cot creaked as she sat up, groggily running her fingers through her long hair to untangle it.

There was a brisk rap on the wall nearby, followed by a voice she knew well. "Princess?"

Caroline cleared her throat and reached to pull back the curtain before the Jaguar took over the process. He offered her a steaming plate, a cloth for a napkin, and an aluminum cup. She couldn't help smiling at someone's attempt to cheer her. A brilliant purple jungle flower stuck through a cord braided of vines that encircled the cup and formed a crude bow under the blossom.

Her voice was husky. "Oh—that's so kind. Thank you." Leaning back to rest against the wall, she settled the meal in her lap while the Jaguar pulled up a stool.

"The tribe liked your gift. They left you fish, greens, and fruit," he told her with a nod at her plate. "Let's say a blessing, then dig in, while it's hot."

After a brief prayer, he said, "You're bound to be starving, and I'm sure you've cried out every bit of water in your body. Everyone at home is concerned that you've lost weight. We need to boost you to health in case the weather clears enough to move tomorrow."

Then he smiled crookedly and rolled his eyes. "I've got your mom on my back now. Didn't see that coming, or expect her to know Weaver's code."

"Not much escapes my mom," Caroline answered. She drank half her water before taking a bite of fish. "Did you already eat yours?"

He flashed a boyish grin. "They didn't leave me any, and it's too wet to hunt. I heated an MRE like the other guys and had some plantain. I'm stuck inside today, medicated again. At least I got in a long nap."

Caroline stopped in mid-bite to watch his face, then slowly chewed and swallowed. "You were mewing while I slept? I suppose you never used to be in pain until I came along."

He laughed now, a hearty, cheerful, relaxed Chris Shepherd sound. With a pang, she realized how much she missed it.

"There are just too many tempting ways to respond to that," he said. "Let's stick with an admission that I know myself better than I used to."

Caroline ate while he chuckled and looked down at his hands. Gravely, she said, "I may get you killed, you know. From mewing at a critical moment or just from being with me."

He leaned forward, clasping his hands together between his knees. "I'm immortal until I've accomplished what God sent me for. He holds my time in His hands, and nothing can take me until then. I settled that a long time ago."

They shared a look of understanding before she drank more of her water. He studied his palms while she took her last bites, and she suspected he wanted to ask her something. What memories had returned to him while she cried and slept?

Setting her empty plate aside, she reached for his hands. She sighed, imagining an early summer day almost ten years ago, on a path around the old Painter Place chapel that no longer existed. With a faint smile, she posed his hands in the way he'd held her own when he broke the news that he was leaving.

"Long ago, you held my hands just like this and told me you had to follow a call to far away, dangerous places. You knew I was hurt and disappointed. It was a courageous, noble thing to do. I looked down at these strong, capable hands, and I knew in an instant they would do amazing things. Not famous things, but things that really matter, where no one sees. Things only God could lead you to. He had a plan you and I couldn't dream up."

He looked up from their clasped hands to her eyes, tears standing in his, changing to a brighter color under his thick lashes for the second time in as many days. "That can't be true. I'd never, ever have left you, for any reason."

She gulped. "Oh, but you did. You had to fulfill your destiny—to become *El Jaguar*."

Her pronunciation was like the villagers when she spoke his name, the *j* sounding like an *h*. "You knew back then what you were meant for, and said you'd never be the same if you didn't do it. I wish I'd had a glimpse that day of who you are now. But discovering what God did in your life is an incredible gift for me, however this all ends."

Caroline looked at his hands again, noting the scars that had not been there ten years ago. His were work-roughed hands that wielded a machete and a machine gun. They rubbed sore leg muscles to ease her pain or placed them on her drawings in a prayer.

"These same hands that coax the sweetest sounds imaginable from an old guitar are the ones that used to reach for mine. These hands also used to handle a little steel cross you kept in your pocket. Sometimes, when you were struggling with whether a choice that seemed gray was black or white, you'd take it out and work it into your palm."

She looked up to find him staring at her with an expression she couldn't read. Reluctantly, he pulled a hand away and reached into his pocket, holding out metal that he placed squarely in her palm. He murmured, "It was all I had besides an ID card the day the Panther and Puma rescued me. I've never asked to see the card."

With a smile that dripped memories, she turned the familiar cross over in her hand several times. "It's more timeworn than ever, just like we are." She handed it back. "The Walkman and cassette in my things—did you leave them when you rescued me?"

"No, we placed them in a secret drop off point with other evidence. They'll be at the Chavarria compound for the Weaver. Your backpack had to be as light as possible."

"I'd like to give you the music. The band is a Christian rock group, and the song I like most is 'Light a Candle.' It reminds me of your calling."

"My calling—sometimes, I forget to think of my life that way. Thank you, I look forward to hearing the music, and it's humbling to know you think of my work a ministry. I'm not worthy of such high esteem. And it means a lot to me you shared something so important about the guy you knew." He paused and looked back down at his hands, touching fingertips together. "Just don't make the mistake of assuming you know the Jaguar."

After a few silent moments, he reached for her cup and plate. "I'll get you more to drink."

"You don't have to do things for me like I'm fragile. But if there's some warm water around, I'd like to clean myself up."

"You are fragile right now, Princess. You're too proud to admit it, but your mom and everyone else can see you're teetering on the edge. Besides, after this adventure, I may never get to do anything for you again."

"Then, if we're stuck inside and you can't be on guard, will you play the guitar for me? Let's see if you know some other songs you used to play."

Phillip Gregory paced his home office with the phone receiver to his ear, listening to his mother's update on his dad's condition. Her soft, lazy Charleston accent was sloughing away a barrier that held back his emotions.

A full-time nurse was with his dad around the clock, and Caroline's grandparents, Dr. Tony Rush and his wife Audrey, were staying as houseguests during his recovery. It was just as well that his dad was forbidden to walk upstairs, since he could no longer bear to step out onto the veranda. Maybe he never could, without that horrifying memory of seeing Caroline kidnapped. It wouldn't surprise Phillip if his parents put the home on Church Street up for sale.

He asked his mother if his dad was up to talking for a few minutes. At the sound of his voice, Phillip's eyes stung, and he leaned on his desk to steady himself through the expected pleasantries.

"I heard from Justin a little while ago," his dad said. "Sounds like business hasn't taken a hit over the past few days. You must be so proud of Cole and how he's stepped up. He's a crackerjack dealing with the London group."

"Don't worry about Global. But as for Cole, you bet I'm proud. He's smart enough to learn from his mistakes."

"And from his big brother."

With a shaky sigh, Phillip swiped his knuckles over his eyes. "Yeah, he idolizes his big brother all right. He listens to Chad when he won't listen to me. Dad, I—I had to talk to Chad last night. His runaway emotions and lack of sleep are combustible. Pray for him."

"Tell me what happened."

Phillip didn't want to unload on his dad, not in his fragile condition. But he needed to talk about the agent who infiltrated the Weaver's team, the confrontation between Chad and the Jaguar, his concern that Chad would make a public mistake, and about his own fears of damaged relationships with Wyeth and the Painters.

His dad listened and let Phillip calm down before he responded. "The priority right now is for you to spill your guts to Wyeth. Let him know you can't bear another rift between you two like the one after he learned what you and Andy kept from him while Chad went to college. Wyeth is ferociously loyal and expects the same from those closest to him. His dad's not around anymore, but I know what Noble Painter would say better than anyone but Savanna. Noble foresaw the possibility of something like this. You get Wyeth on a conference call with me if you two think it would help. Get this all aired out now and stand together if the unthinkable happens."

After a drawn-out sigh over the phone line, he addressed the problem with his grandson. "As for Chad, you handled it well. He'll listen to you, Phillip. That Gregory shepherding instinct, the fierce jealousy to protect people and places we love, harnessing it to make a secure place for them, is a trait I missed gettin' the full blessing of. I had to work too hard to live up to the Gregory reputation. Little wonder I wore my heart out. I was glad to see it turn up again in you. That's when Global thrives, you know, like when you came on board after college. Chad one-upped us all because he's you, Camellia, and his granddad Montgomery through her, wrapped in one amazing package. You comprehend what drives 'im better than anyone. I'm glad you admitted your weakness. He needs to remember you have one. You're an intimidating force, Phillip, and while he needs the security right now of knowin' you're bigger than life, he also needs to know you understand his fear."

Phillip expelled a frustrated groan. "Dad, I'm not bigger than life! It's an illusion, a facade I've created based on livin' up to you and the Gregory legends. What if I've just propped up my weak character all these years by imitating other men's wisdom, actin' like it's who I am in my head and heart? I'm so mixed up right now! I don't even know who I am or what I want anymore, except one thing—that this never happened."

He paused, pacing while he searched for the right words. "All this could have been avoided if I'd just held my temper with Wilfred Rothschild, years ago. Dad, if this all goes wrong, Caroline's blood is ultimately on my hands! You'll see it when you get the records of what Wilfred's been up to since then. The King's Road project I launched for Global after college, my first big one, he was competin' for it, remember? He never forgot how I won the investors, after someone brought up his drinkin' habit and I contrasted Global's no-alcohol, no-drugs, no-adultery policies, emphasizing that we stay soberly focused on our clients' interests. After that, he lived his whole life to make mine miserable! Do you have any idea how much money I've poured into security over his threats?"

Phillip made an expansive gesture to the ceiling, his voice raised and vehement, but his dad calmly responded. "He failed, son. His whole life was a failure, but for one thing—God used his pitiful attempts to hurt us as blessings that grew our faith and strength. That security expense, it provided an income for those who chose that career. It's not wasted, Phillip. Can you honestly say you'd rather never have known Azariah? You can't control men with evil hearts, like Wilfred. Recall where you were when he was executed in a filthy warehouse. That's what he hated more than you. He never had the joy and peace you have, since it isn't found in business and success."

The memory of the cozy time spent with his family warmed Phillip. He remembered the happiness spilling over in Chad's demeanor the next morning before they went to the office. Wilfred was dead when Phillip and his sons were hit with the damage he'd set into motion to destroy them.

Over the years, Phillip looked for opportunities to diffuse the situation with Wilfred. But it was business suicide to be associated with the guy, and he rebuffed Phillip's invitation to meet at his Global office in London. He was so toxic Phillip couldn't have lunch with him in public without an association to suspicious activity, and he knew this whole affair with Wilfred's execution would be nastier for Global if they had been seen together.

His dad interrupted his train of thought about what he might have done differently. "Phillip, listen carefully to me, son. Your life, what people think of you, it's not an illusion. Phillip Chadwick Gregory Jr. truly *is* bigger than life. I know, because I'm comparin' your character to the many thousands of people I've met or been around, read about in history, or seen in the news. The men you imitated because you admired them, they were worth it. The

Gregory standard has always been built on modeling the characters of men who were bigger than life. We're ultimately supposed to imitate Christ, and there's nothin' higher than that. When our hearts belong to Him, His spirit shows us His ways being lived out and spoken of, in other men. As sheep, we recognize the voice of our Shepherd, and we follow."

Phillip stared out at the distant horizon of the Atlantic, too choked up to speak. He felt like a boy again, soothed by his father's wisdom and encouragement.

"Son, men write about you that way, too. They quote you, set you up as a model. They want you to run for office. I understand that it's scary. Sometimes, when the world expects so much, you wish they'd just let you be an ordinary guy, let you crash. But you're not an ordinary man, not by a long shot. You're Phillip Gregory, and your heart and mind are the stuff of all those famous quotes and maxims. You've become what you filled your life with. Your list of shortcomings really is short, though your need for a Savior is as great as any man's. Thank God for the chance to be an example of whatever good He can bring from your trials."

The Gregory family patriarch handed his phone to Tony Rush, who sat by his rented hospital bed in a recliner. Tony set the receiver back into its cradle and leaned forward, his elbows on his knees, hands clasped and watching Phil's face expectantly.

Ben Grayson came over to the bed, fist under his chin and elbow on his crossed arm. "You didn't tell Phillip that I was here, or your plan."

"I think it's best to just send you and Jack up there. He's in a personal crisis, and he's worried about Chad. It's not a time to tell him I've created an A-team that I'm sendin' his way."

Ben scowled. "Is Chad in trouble?"

"Yes, a Spanish senorita wiggled her hips into his imagination, and it turned out she's with one of the feuding cartels. She tried to seduce him and carve him up if he didn't supply the information she was sent to get. A video screen came to life and Caroline saw things she'll never be able to forget. Can you call Jack in?"

Ben's brows shot up and he let out a long whistle, but he didn't need to get Jack. The bodyguard stepped through the door, his eyes meeting Ben's for a look of comradery.

Phil asked, "Jack, did you resign from your company yet?"

"You're my new employer, sir."

"Is it the money, or my housekeeper?"

"Both. And because I can't live with what happened to your grandson's wife right under my nose. I'm better at my job than that."

Propped up in his hospital bed, the Gregory family patriarch studied the two men before him. "Ben, when you pick up the agent you sent for at the airport, head straight to Whitehaven. Phillip will fight this. He might lose his son's wife, so he won't want to risk his daughter's husband. He's blamin' himself for startin' this revenge war that Rothschild has undertaken for over three decades. Global needs to step in as part of the solution. Get Azariah to plead your case. Phillip thinks the world of 'im."

He turned to Jack. "I have confidence in you, but I have reservations based on what we talked about. Promise me you've given it some thought and won't turn your back."

"I'm still thinking, Mr. Gregory."

"Well, I can't ask for more than that. Now, Tony and I want to send you and Ben off with a blessing." He stretched out his arms, gesturing for the other three men to surround his bed and join hands while he and Tony prayed with them.

As they made their way out of the house, Ben asked, "What's he askin' you not to turn your back on?"

"God."

Ben stopped dead in his tracks on the stone pavers in the driveway. He looked up to the cobalt blue winter sky, hands on his hips. "You're kiddin' me, right?"

Jack wasn't certain if Ben was talking to God or him, so he didn't answer. Ben narrowed his brown eyes. "Here's the deal. You get yourself straight on the way, or all you get outta this is a little vacation in Whitehaven. The scenery is great, even in January. I'm not takin' an unsaved man on a high-risk, unofficial, unauthorized mission to a lawless hotbed of paramilitary groups, guerillas, and drug cartels. Not only do I need my entire team to be guided by the same Spirit, I'm not goin' to choose lesser roles for you to keep you from death to a very certain judgement. You don't have to believe in hell for it to exist, Jack, or to take up residence there, and like Hotel California, you can never leave. Do we understand one another?"

Ben spun on his heel dismissively, but Jack reached out to catch his jacket sleeve. "Ben, I just need to mull over what I heard Mr. Gregory talking about with his son on the phone, and what he and his wife and Dr. Rush have been talking to me about. I'm not—I'm not far away."

"Then start runnin' in the right direction. You've got less than twenty-four hours, Jack."

Caroline washed up behind her privacy curtain. Her sweater was wrinkled, her jeans were loose, and everything smelled like herbal soap and needed fabric softener. Embers in a small stove kept the humidity down in the shelter for the hanging clothes to dry. Under the jungle canopy on a cloudy day, there was too little light for putting on makeup. She did the best she could by a window and lamplight with a small mirror. It would be a bad hair day, so she gave hers a twist that sent it in a flirty tumble over her left shoulder, pinning a spot over the nape of her neck to keep it all to one side.

If her date on the monitor with Chad was the last time he saw her alive, she wanted it to be as pleasant a memory as possible. Jealousy tempted her to make him pay for his distraction with the Spanish woman. But she knew he was in agony over her circumstances and humiliated by what had happened last night.

The guard shift changed, and the men took off wet clothes and boots under a porch roof near a cooking fire. Caroline smelled food as she packed away her toiletry bag and travel sized makeup. The Puma came in, his wet hair plastered to his head, and brought her a plate of meat, flat bread, and instant tea.

She hesitated. "I don't want to sound ungrateful, but this isn't a reptile or anything, right? I draw the line at insects, snakes, amphibians, and stuff like that."

The Puma laughed. "We hoard those delicacies for ourselves and don't serve 'stuff like that' to royalty, Princess. This is a mammal but not a rodent. Don't worry, it tastes like chicken. The flour for the bread came out of the pastor's supplies in the cart."

Caroline didn't mean to wrinkle her nose at a swallow of the tea but noted he had turned his back to unzip a pocket in his backpack. She was expressing her gratitude for the meal when he faced her again and handed her a slim bar-shaped package with some wear and tear on the golden paper wrapper.

"Take it. I hear chocolate does magic things for a woman, and you could use some magic today. I hope you're feeling better."

With her eyes alight, she gasped at discovering it was a bar of dark chocolate. Her spontaneous hug spun him around as if they were dancing. He chuckled and gave her an awkward pat on her back. "There, there, now! You're splashing magic all over me, for sure. That's a good sign, right? Eat your dinner while it's hot and we'll trip the light fantastic later. You choose the song."

She pulled away, beaming. "I don't know how to thank you!"

The Jaguar stepped through the open door and stopped in his tracks at the sight of the chocolate celebration dance. The Puma's foolish grin was contagious for the others as they came in to sit down with a plate.

After dinner together, the team settled down comfortably and wrapped their hands around warm cups of coffee and tea. The Jaguar reached under his cot to uncover a guitar case in a protective wrapping. He worked the fasteners to open it while the Puma grabbed the pastor's old guitar and began tuning it. Soon, they were both strumming.

An off-duty team member reclined with feet up in his cot. Carlos sat cross-legged on a tarp spread on the plank floor, his arms braced on his legs with his mug in front of him. Caroline sat at a small table with her sketchbook and a lantern. She nibbled half the chocolate and re-wrapped it tightly, securing it with a hair elastic to keep out insects.

With an exaggerated sigh, Caroline stared out the window into the dreary view. "We're not in a country where natives believe in zombies, are we?" she ventured.

Carlos erupted in laughter, rolling over on the floor. Puma grinned and the other guard chuckled in delight, making zombie faces.

She shrugged with a small smile. "Just tell me what supernatural stuff I need to beware of out there. I feel it, and it's not flesh and blood."

The Jaguar strummed a much nicer guitar than the pastor's battered one. His eyes were lively and crinkled at the corners when they met hers. "No zombies, Princess, but you're right. These people are in tune to the spiritual world. They pay attention to their visions and dreams. Be ready for anything."

"We could tell you stories that would disturb you for days, but they're classified," Carlos added. "You can't let something slip if you never heard it. If reporters knew, they'd be down here creating chaos worse than any supernatural event."

She sighed, a dark look crossing her face before she turned back to the window and stared with unseeing eyes. "Yeah, well, that's something I know a lot about."

The Jaguar stopped strumming a few moments as he and the others watched her. She offered no explanation, and the silence stretched out until it became awkward.

Carlos ventured, "This place feels a little haunted to you, Princess? Has this jungle spooked you, got you shaking in those running shoes?"

The corner of her mouth quirked as she stared into the gloomy rain. "Yeah, you could say that, if I believed in ghosts. My family has a restored old estate in England called Seamure Manor, with some detached castle ruins on the grounds. Legends claim them to be haunted, but they don't feel evil, like this jungle does. Hauntings aren't people returning from the dead. They're demonic infestations in a place."

The Jaguar studied her. Carlos watched the Jaguar's face and said, "It's killin' you, and you're not getting a better chance. Ask her your other theological stuff, like, what she believes about alien encounters."

Caroline turned to meet the leader's eyes, unwavering in her quiet response. "I believe that's demonic activity, too. Belief in other worlds requires evolution. I trust in God's creation account, not men's fantasies. His account fits the scientific evidence."

Carlos clapped, and the Puma whistled in appreciation, teasing that the Jaguar had met his match. The Puma grinned and played some chords. The Jaguar picked out harmony, and Carlos turned his thighs into drums to keep the beat. They sang, "Quivers down

my backbone, I've got the shakes down the knee bone, Yeah havin'
tremors in the thigh bone..."

Good-naturedly accepting their teasing, Caroline sang with
them. "Shakin' all over."

When they finished, the Jaguar studied her and said, "Guys, I
think what the Princess was asking about was more like this." He
started strumming a tune about running through the jungle, and
the Puma joined in with the pastor's old guitar. He sang, "Thought
it was a nightmare..."

The others joined in with relish. "Don't go walkin' slow, the
devil's on the loose."

When the song was over, the Jaguar said, "Some of the
brightest songs come out of the darkest places, Princess."

She sighed and gazed out the window again. He absently
played bits of the lines he'd played last night, with the words that
Valerie Painter mentioned about the stars falling.

"If you're having a Clapton moment, let's play this," Puma
suggested. He started toying with the notes.

Carlos gulped his coffee and sneered. "You know he doesn't
like that one!"

"It's not for him, it's for me," retorted the Puma. "You got the
sappy sad one you wanted last night."

Caroline turned to watch the struggle on the Jaguar's face. "He
loves the tune. It's the story behind it that bothers him."

The men stared at her in surprise. The Jaguar hesitated a
moment, but kept his gaze on the strings, strumming random
chords. Carlos asked Caroline what the song was about.

"They say it's inspired by a romantic Persian love poem that
Clapton was once given, about a man who fell hopelessly in love
with an unavailable woman named Layla. And then, there are also
the rumors that the story touched him so much because of his

unrequited love for his Beatles friend George Harrison's wife, but you know how rumors are."

The men were relishing her startling revelations about their leader and looked to him for confirmation. When he didn't negate her announcement, Carlos whistled softly, "Oh, man, I get it, that must be the part about giving Layla consolation when her old man let her down."

Puma sang the next words, about being a fool who fell in love, and the Jaguar strummed with him. Everyone joined the Puma to sing about Layla turning the singer's entire world upside down, then they belted out their favorite part, the chorus.

When it was over, the Jaguar began his random strumming again. "The Princess wants to request some songs to test me. What's first?"

"What about an easy one, 'Raindrops Keep Falling on My Head'? We used to brighten dreary days like this one with its hopeful message."

He tried it out, and Puma added his part. They all sang the encouraging words about how they couldn't stop the rain by complaining but wouldn't let the blues defeat them. The next song she asked for was his youth campfire version of 'Spirit in the Sky.' The Jaguar and Puma worked to coordinate two parts, then the group was clapping and singing.

Carlos and the Puma bantered about what song should come next. The Jaguar disengaged from them into his own world as he played the light, beautiful melody he'd been working on the night before, building on it by trying some new notes.

With a half-smile, Caroline ventured, "You're composing a song. It's farther along today than when you started, last night around the fire."

He glanced up in surprise, then looked back down at the instrument. She ventured, "It's exquisite—not at all like a pop, rock, or folk song. What inspired it, and will it have lyrics?"

The Jaguar picked out a few more notes, and Caroline wondered if he would answer. Finally, he met her eyes and replied, "It's called *Para Amanda*, which means 'For Amanda.' It's a love song, inspired by Amanda Shepherd. The lyrics are private."

Caroline dropped her eyes and swallowed, recalling the trail yesterday and their jungle identities. *Okay, now it's easy. I'll be Chris Shepherd, you're my wife Amanda.*

She blinked with a start as the radio sputtered on. "Panther, this is the Weaver. Acknowledge."

The Puma jumped up and laid the pastor's guitar on his cot. The Jaguar reached the communication equipment first. "Weaver, this is the Jaguar, and you're loud and clear. The Panther's on shift. Do I bring him in? Over."

They waited for some lag time in the response. "Affirmative, Jaguar. We've got some work to do. The team will move tomorrow, rain or shine. Over."

The Jaguar made a gesture to Carlos, who sprang to the door to replace the Panther. "Affirmative. Over."

"Report the status of the team and the Princess. Then we'll let her visit with her husband while the Panther gets dry. Over."

The Jaguar hesitated. "The Princess had a rough time for a few hours after radio contact and took a long nap. We're serenading her and feeding her well. Puma even hunted her dinner and beat his chest like the big monkey he is, then he baked her some bread and gave her chocolate."

He hesitated as if he didn't want to add the next statement to his report. "I've had a rough afternoon, too. I should be ready for the next shift. The team is soaked through, but safe. Over."

"Affirmative. You understood Mrs. Valerie Painter's code. Is it the source of your rough time? Over."

The Jaguar leaned back in his chair, annoyed. "Affirmative to the code, negative to the problem. Over."

"Identify when you discovered the key to the code. Over."

"Around the campfire last night—in a song. Over."

Caroline came to stand behind him and the Puma, catching her breath when she saw her husband sitting down in front of the screen. "Jaguar, this is Chad Gregory, ready to pick up my wife for a date and requesting that she be solo on screen. Over."

The Jaguar raised one brow at the respectful tone. "Granted. Over."

Chad was still wearing the sweater she'd given him. His smile was timid as he watched Caroline settle into the chair, then his deep Southern drawl flowed from the speaker. "It can't be normal to look so gorgeous in a shack deep in a jungle. Take it easy on the fellas down there. It's obvious that they have a crush on you, and they may decide there's no hurry in gettin' you home."

He held up a red rose boutonniere and used it to point behind him, where a peacock-inspired evening gown lay draped over a chair. An old tuxedo with his white jacket and black trousers peeked out from behind it. "I told you I'd bring you somethin' to wear. I'll never forget the night you wrapped me around your little finger in this, on a yacht in Mevagissey, where you publicly presented me with your first masterpiece. You wore this dress again the night you pinned me against the garden wall and told me you love me for the first time."

Tears made her eyes shine. With a sniff and a wry smile, she said, "You creatively contrived for me to have it on the night you set me up to tell you I love you, so you'd win a race with my brother. And you were the heartthrob with an attitude that arrived in that tux to rescue me from reporters and scandal. While the other women were swooning and fanning, you marched up and brushed a kiss on my cheek, whispering that someday you'd kiss me the way you'd always dreamed of. It was a knockout punch."

He laughed, at ease again. "Good thing I saved the real knock-out punch. I almost used it on Wilfred."

They both sobered at the thought of their now-deceased, self-proclaimed enemy. Chad drew a deep breath and exhaled. "Caroline, when you promised that night to see only me, you'd been through a rough week. You told me you said a final goodbye to Chris through that painting of the cliffs, and you told me the story behind the painting you gave me, *Tall Ships and Sunflowers*. Remember?"

He pulled over a chair with her painting propped on the seat, and she nodded. She was being set up, she knew, but Chad excelled at this. He'd win, but then he'd make sure she did, too.

"Yes," she answered slowly, replaying memories. "So much had changed in only a few days. Chis had left me, you had come home to me, then I met Baker. After you saw that photo of me with him in the news, you sent me the vase with sunflowers to remind me of home—a place where you'd fit in, but Baker never would. Your note with the flowers had a verse from the song you requested for our first dance a few days before, asking me to save my heart for you. Nothing could have been more fitting to say, or more poetic. My room at the inn had the ship in a bottle, which reminded me of your collection. The sunflowers, the vase, and the ship in a bottle were like you and me, growing up at Painter Place. It came to me that like the old things, in a new setting, we could be together in a new way, adjusting our relationship to who we'd become."

"It was a profound insight, Care, and it has come to define our life together. We desperately needed it after Hugo took the island, and now, no matter what, we'll adjust to bein' together here in a new way again. I'm still like that tall ship in a bottle, always sailin' off to adventure and discovery in that infinite blue sea in your eyes—but never leaving. I'll be here, even if your head gets turned down there. We've been together too long for a distraction to come between us. No matter what happens, I'm never lettin' go. Never."

Caroline turned to the wall of the cabin and bit her trembling lip. He waited. She sighed and looked back at him. "I've changed, and I have some things to say when we're alone."

"I know. I meant it last night when I said I'm at your mercy."

"When that photo came out in London of you and the model and I faced what I thought it meant, I was glad for an excuse to cut you out of my life, once and for all. Lovin' you made my life complicated."

His grin was spontaneous. "Yeah, well, birds of a feather, right? I'm often told I should've married an ordinary woman so my life wouldn't be so complicated. But I don't want an ordinary life, Care! I want an extraordinary one, and that's what I have with you—what we have together. You know it's true."

Chad held out the red rosebud, still wearing the grin. "Remember the night you came back with my family after the reception on the yacht, and I asked you to sleep with this under your pillow, so you'd dream of me? I don't think you have the luxury of pillows where you are now, but I'm askin' you to pretend you have it under your head when you sleep tonight."

At a signal from the Weaver, and his face became serious again. He leaned forward and touched the bottom of the screen with the hand he wore his wedding band on. She reached out, but a chill passed through her at the look in his eyes.

"Care, rest as much as you can. Stay alert and follow your intuition if the Jaguar is down. Be ready to use all the things you've learned from Azariah. You're armed now. Do whatever you have to do."

Caroline heard the Panther moving behind her to take over. "I don't want to go yet," she whispered in a strangled voice, tears stinging her eyes. "Right now, with you, it's easy to pretend this isn't real."

"I know, babe. But the team has to plan to get you all back home. Remember, we will adjust, after all this is over. Together, we can handle anything. I love you, endlessly. Save your heart for me."

His voice broke, and he closed his eyes, fingertips still touching hers over the distance. "Lord, I trust You to take care of her as only You can. Amen."

They both pulled back from the screen with yearning, tear-filled eyes while the Weaver, Panther, and Puma gathered. Caroline stepped out of the way, covering her trembling mouth with her hands, but her eyes locked on her connection with home.

The Jaguar paused to stand just behind her shoulder. He whispered into her ear, "The guy he mentioned—Chris. That was me, right? I was part of your story."

She nodded, giving up her view of the screen where Weaver was in charge and her husband was out of sight. Whispering back, she forgot not to remind the Jaguar of his past. "Chad saw you break up with me. He'd just gotten home and didn't know about you, then stayed at the top of the road to watch me cry by the pier in the middle of the night. The trip to Mevagissey two days later was how my parents got me off the island to sort out my emotions. He had to go to London for an emergency, and we both got caught in some—newsworthy activity."

"Where's the painting he mentioned, the one you said goodbye to me in?"

Startled, she looked at his scowl. "Well—uh, I met a British rock singer, and he bought one almost like it the night before. The painting fascinated my uncle, and he asked me to paint another version, as a demo for his video in the harbor. But I'd painted the first one while I was emotional about a newspaper photo of Chad and a fashion model, and the only way to duplicate the style was to become upset again. So, I thought about saying goodbye to you and letting go. The publicity brought the second painting into the news. Bids poured in to buy it, because of the rock singer's popularity, not any skill on my part. It's called *Sea Cliffs*. My uncle asked Chad to deal with the bids, so he and his brother, a fan of Baker's, worked to get a ridiculous price from a collector in London. It was a great career boost for me, because that sale placed all my work at a higher level in value."

She couldn't read the expression on the Jaguar's face. With a sad nod, he walked over to join the Weaver.

Chapter Fourteen

I have a very strict gun control policy:
if there's a gun around, I want to be in control of it.
- Clint Eastwood

The Jaguar grunted, jerking the tie-down strap on a cover over the goat cart. Only the jungle canopy veiled the team from an unknown observer in a chopper flying low overhead. Traveling on the muddy ox-cart track was slowing the team down to a crawl, and he'd much rather be tramping the jungle, like three other members of his team.

Under their feet, the ground vibrated with the thundering machinery over their heads. The goat was no stranger to gunfire, but the chopper made him jittery, so the Panther comforted him by holding his halter, giving him a treat, and whispering into his ear. With a long stride, the Jaguar placed himself beside the Princess. She leaned against the cart, closed her eyes, and covered her ears. Those blue windows into her soul had the shades pulled now, but last night, he saw them swimming in tears. He still hadn't gotten over it.

After the radio session with the Weaver, the Princess had tried to hide how upset she was by going outside on the small porch of the cabin. The Jaguar followed and wheedled her into confessing the trouble. She admitted being glad for the chance to see the Prince but couldn't forget the Spanish woman or her lipstick on him from the night before, or the woman's triumphant confidence about what he was thinking when he'd been watching her. Worst of all, the Princess couldn't stop wondering what the Prince had imagined that included the woman.

Her distress had the whole team convicted about their thought life now. It was an eye-opening insight for them to know women didn't experience the same things in the same way a man did. Women could see a guy without his shirt and forget about it, but a man seeing a girl in a bikini re-played in his mind for days.

When the blades slicing the sky overhead became a distant nuisance, he guided the goat back to the track. Then the rumble of a jeep engine made his stomach lurch. Apparently, they hadn't been the only ones waiting out the chopper, and there was no time to take cover again.

A surreptitious glance at the Princess told him she was alert but calm, with no telltale traces of fear. A possessive wave tightened in his chest at her quiet confidence in the team—in him. He scanned the countless layers of leaves and their shadowy depths. His guards had switched on body cameras by now, setting up to function as snipers. The friendly tribe continued to follow, but the only help he might get from them was if his team was left for dead.

Mud coated the approaching rugged vehicle, hiding any markings that might have helped identify it. The driver blocked the goat cart, and three men in sludge-spattered camouflage had weapons ready as they warily stepped out.

The Jaguar analyzed everything, eliminating groups on his mental checklist at lightning speed. Three against him, the Panther, and the Puma was too easy, but now the Princess was in the line of fire.

He smiled, deceptively alert. His M16 rifle felt good at his side, an extension of himself. The driver of the jeep returned his smile, with respectful greetings.

"*Aqui no pasa nada,*" the Jaguar replied as a common way of saying nothing was happening. Cautiously, the armed men stalked around the cart, sizing up the Panther and Puma, while the driver and the Jaguar carried on a casual conversation about the challenges of traveling in the mud.

Other than a startled blink, the Jaguar hoped he gave nothing away when the Princess walked over to him. The armed guards raised their weapons. In response, the Panther and Puma acted as one to level a dead aim at the men's heads.

But she charmed them all with an exaggerated Southern accent, complaining about the conditions of her journey. Seemingly oblivious to the silent standoff, the Princess set her hands on the hips of her borrowed, baggy green camouflage trousers in her sassiest pose. "You don't know how lucky you are to have a jeep! I'm ready to shoot this goat and have him for dinner tonight. We'd be faster if we hitched my husband to this stupid old cart."

With a bemused expression, the driver told the Jaguar in Spanish that though his English wasn't good, it sounded like his wife called him a goat. The Jaguar's hearty laugh was genuine, and he translated to correct the misunderstanding. Pretending to let the guy in on a joke at her expense, he said in Spanish that she couldn't toast bread, let alone cook a goat.

He made a low growl in his throat and reached out to pull her into him, kissing the long column of her bare neck and playfully pretending to bite it. The Princess clucked with a shake of her head and pushed half-heartedly at him, addressing the other man when she said her husband even acted like a goat, always nibbling at her.

With a raucous laugh, the driver muttered, "American!" He told the Jaguar that men in his country knew how to deal with cheeky women, and he deserved what she dished out if he didn't beat her now and then. With a gesture to the armed men, they lowered their weapons and tramped in muddy boots toward the jeep.

Tires spattered more of the soggy path onto the poor goat and the cart as the vehicle crept past down the trail. The Jaguar didn't let the Princess go when she tried to step back. He trapped her eyes with an intensity that made her wait on his murmur. "Don't pull away until they're out of sight. You were amazing, by the way."

"Thank you. Was that the dangerous kiss you warned me about? Maybe the goat will come in handy for you to get some practice."

His gusty laughter rang against the trees, but he lowered his voice to respond. "No. I'm saving that one for a worst-case scenario, because you won't allow me to repeat it."

"You wouldn't, if it came down to it, you know."

He lost the grin, narrowed his eyes, and added an edge to his retort. "Oh, yes I would. You keep assuming I'm somebody else. This isn't your world, Princess. You've landed in my world, where you'd better act like your life depends on that kiss and tell your husband to get over it. There's a price for protecting what belongs to the Prince."

Annoyed now, he dropped his arms from her waist and re-set his focus. The Panther shot him a warning look and pointed to his own shirt as the team set off again. He was on camera with his guys in the trees.

It was an effort to shake off the interaction with the Princess and get the team back on mission. He glanced sidelong at her as they trudged forward, his lips still tingling from his electric kiss on the indescribable softness of her neck, holding her tight so the baggy camouflage was irrelevant against him...

No. He stopped short and turned from the place his mind was taking him. She belonged to the Prince. With a swipe of his hand over his sweaty brow, he reset his focus on the next village where they would drop off the goat cart for the pastor. The day was wearing long, and they were near to a campsite of hidden Land

Rovers. If they could avoid detection from the air, vehicles were a faster and safer way to get out of the jungle.

When the goat bleated in protest at being unable to graze at a specimen it spied, he signaled the guards in the woods to converge behind the cover of a stand of huge tree trunks. The Puma suddenly jerked the Princess' arm away from where she was about to lean against the rough bark, encircling her waist with his other arm to steady her. He tipped his dark head to the tree.

She gasped at the mesmerizing, excruciatingly slow slither of a serpent as thick as her arm, then shuddered and buried her face into his shirt. Over her head, he looked at the Panther and Jaguar and raised his eyebrows up and down with a satisfied smile.

"The Weaver got the camera transmission," reported a teammate when he reached them. "They're enlarging the images to identify those uniforms. Since they aren't advertising who they are in that jalopy, he suspects they represent another intelligence group, maybe even one we're working with. That's why we got past without a cart inspection. Princess, your husband said to tell you he knows that scene was difficult, but Juliette and Cameron would be proud, and to sterilize your neck before it's his turn."

Carlos spurted out the last bite he'd taken. The Princess grinned, explaining that her aunt Juliette Painter was an actress and her uncle a director.

The Jaguar narrowed his eyes at the coded message intended for him. He lifted his canteen, swigging down some water as if putting out a fire. The guy had been brilliant last night with the Princess, using her own insight about changes in their relationship to promise her security. This Prince was the jealous type, but it was also clear that the guy thrived on competition.

The Jaguar planned to give him some. No harm would come to their marriage. He might even help it.

As for the Princess, had she used her acting skills to help the team, or to irk the Prince? She was maddeningly mysterious, a trait that made him uncomfortable. He watched her re-pin tresses of hair up into her hat. It was such an innocent, feminine thing to do. No, she couldn't have planned revenge, because she had no idea that he would reach for her and kiss her neck like that. He was as surprised as she was at his spontaneous improvisation.

Hearing a message from her husband revived the Princess more than the food and rest. She rose and looked over at him with an expectant smile, ready to hit the cart path again. Ready to get home.

He let the pang of loneliness strike like a snakebite as he gave the cart a final tie-down check. Then he braced himself to survive the venom.

There was no way to avoid the uniformed men in the next village. By the time Carlos radioed a warning from his hiding place in the jungle, the goat cart was seen. So, the Jaguar, Panther, and Puma marched their little procession into town, reviewing worst-case scenario strategies among themselves.

Wary guards copied the relaxed demeanor of the group they watched approaching on the path. The Jaguar greeted them in Spanish with, "*Hermano, como esta?*"

The Panther blocked the path of the goat who was content to stop and munch tasty leaves on a tree branch. Guards questioned their business and destination, so the Jaguar asked if he could reach into his pocket for identification.

While one man trained his weapon on him, the other took the offered information, looking it over and handing it back. The Jaguar noticed that the guard hadn't read or understood the

English on the badge but recognized the symbol for the oil
company.

The guards looked the Princess up and down, then walked
around the cart. Unintimidated, the Puma and Panther stood ready
to fire if anyone twitched. Two more uniformed men wandered
from the dark interior of a hut up to the edge of the cart path, one
laughing and sharing his thoughts in Spanish about the availability
of a woman guarded by so few men.

The Jaguar interjected with a sharp tone, snapping that he
understood their language and to watch their conversation about
his wife. The man studied him closely and sneered, leaning his
AK47 rifle against a nearby stump. Then his companion raised his
rifle to aim at the Jaguar, who was quicker to aim back in response.

As the only man now without a gun threatening him, the
fourth man stepped toward the Princess with a menacing chuckle.
But an unexpected, well-placed kick of her mud-caked boot sent
him staggering back while she reached for the Glock 17. Planting
her feet, she readied in a shooting stance that told them all she
knew how to use it, and she was aiming at the man's head.

His black eyes stared in disbelief. The Jaguar warned the guards
in Spanish that he'd never bring his wife to such a dangerous place
without training her in self-defense. None of them would walk
away if they started shooting.

A man whose rifle targeted the Jaguar's heart snarled and
ordered the other to get his weapon from the stump. But when
the man moved to obey, the Princess barked, "No!" She shot the
ground at his feet, spraying dirt and stones. He jumped back, then
froze with raised hands.

The clear leader of the group informed the Jaguar that his men
were looking for an American woman. The team could pass if he
could prove this one was his wife.

With his rifle trained on the head of the shorter man, the Jaguar laughed scornfully, asking in Spanish what one woman could possibly do in this jungle to be such a threat to four men. He demanded to know what impotent boss they worked for and then started an insulting rant, threatening to bring down the wrath of the big oil company he represented onto their heads if anything happened to his wife.

A flush of fury washed over the leader's face and he made a grinding sound in his throat. He benefited from the big oil companies that poured money into infrastructure in his country. But the woman's insult to his guard could never pass without some show of authority over her. He barked at the Jaguar to prove the woman was his wife and get out of his way. Waving him over to the cart with the end of his rifle, he shouted that otherwise they'd see who claimed the gangly *gringa*. He spat on the ground, sealing his insult for the Jaguar's taste in women.

The Jaguar pretended to weigh whether to demand satisfaction over the affront to his wife before taking cautious steps backwards toward the cart where the Princess kept a vigil with a menacing look. He suspected that her shoulders and arm muscles were screaming from holding a pistol on the man in front of her, yet she looked like a force to be reckoned with.

"Princess," he called, his rifle still aimed at the man with one trained on him. "I've been ordered to prove you're my wife or there will be a showdown, in which the last man standing gets the prize."

The man with hands raised in the air saw an advantage when she blinked and gulped. He dove for his rifle in the stump's direction, taking a hit through the fleshy part of his arm with a shot fired from the Glock 17. Her next shot immediately knocked his rifle out of reach and sent splinters flying from the stump.

Wild-eyed, the would-be attacker screamed in pain and a furious torrent of Spanish curses directed at her. Villagers cried out and scurried behind whatever shelter they could find.

"Yeah, well, sorry, buddy, *no habla Español!*" she shouted back at him in her Southern drawl, emphasizing the last three words in her most insulting tone. "I've got five more shots and I'm good at this. Make my day!"

If he could've collapsed onto the ground laughing, the Jaguar would have. As things stood, he nearly choked instead. If they lived through this, it would be an epic scene to watch from his sniper's camera later.

But right now, their lives depended on his acting skills. He blew out a breath and bit his lip, calculating his next move. His snipers in the jungle were targeting the man with the rifle aimed at him, so he shouldered his own as if in reluctant surrender, backing up to the Princess and extending his arm in front of her like an order not to shoot—on her part or theirs. He reached her side and found she'd only slightly lowered the Glock, keeping a poison stare on her groaning, bleeding attacker.

In Spanish, the Jaguar asked the leader if his wife's marksmanship convinced him she couldn't possibly be the American woman he sought. The man sniffed and insisted he had a job to do and a report to make. He was searching for the wife of a very wealthy man who'd pay an enormous ransom to get her back.

Lowering his rifle, the leader yelled irritably at the wounded man to stop moaning like a baby. It was shameful to be bested by a woman—a skinny American! He spat contemptuously into the dirt at his feet.

The Jaguar's stomach fluttered as he stood beside the Princess. He'd hoped it wouldn't come to this—and dreamed it would. He was fleetingly aware of smelling like a blend of the goat and a sweaty farm hand; he was filthy with spattered muck, and his lunch must still be on his breath.

She turned to fling her arms around his neck and her face into his sweaty shirt, pressing his backpack into the cart as he grunted in surprise. The goat bleated in a protest through a mouthful of leaves but remained where he stood.

The Princess' deodorant had also given up for the day, but the vague muskiness that mixed into the herbal-soap scented camouflage she wore stirred a distinctively masculine reaction inside him that was nothing close to revulsion. He tried to calm his racing heart and re-gain his wits by taking the pistol from her hand. Then he made a show of sliding it leisurely against her body and down into her holster.

It was a nice touch. He was glad he'd seen it in a movie.

She pulled her face back from his chest to look up at him. Then it happened. That smile. The one that promised something fun would happen. He waited breathlessly for her next move.

The Princess pressed her lips to the hollow spot on his neck and he quivered. Fighting for presence of mind, he reached up to put one hand on the back of her hat, pretending he was forcing her face to him, but intending to keep her hair covered. He warmed to his role in convincing the guard, pulling her tightly into himself as he had for the men in the jeep. He closed his eyes and shut out everything but her, memorizing the gift of the stolen moment and whispering something forbidden into her ear.

The Panther reported brusquely that they could go now. The Princess pulled back and half smiled as she whispered, "I win. For all your bluster, you couldn't bring yourself to do this. You're givin' me a terrible reputation."

He retorted in a fierce whisper, "You didn't warn me you were a cross between Annie Oakley and Princess Diana! Then you pulled out the real weapon, that world-conquering smile. I'm still armed with my greatest resource, a dangerous kiss. Pray we don't need it. I was serious when I warned that you won't let me repeat it."

"But I kept you from havin' to use it!" She wrapped an arm around his waist, snuggling up to him as they faced the glowering man who was letting them go.

The man jerked his head to point up the road and ordered them out of the village. The Jaguar nodded to him and said, "Gracias." He kept his arm around her shoulders to pull her along with him, muttering, "And I really mean that, buddy."

Out of sight of the guards and with a small plane droning in the distance somewhere, the Jaguar took his arm from around the Princess and ordered the team to duck the cart under cover. The Puma asked, "Was there an alternate plan for the pastor to find this cart if we couldn't leave it in that village? Wild animals will kill the goat if we abandon it."

"Just do what they do in stories—you know, for mules or whatever," Caroline suggested. "Dangle something on a stick to hang out of reach in front of it in the morning and send it down the path back to the village, while we go the other way. Maybe it will stay on the path after the treat and someone will stop it at the village."

Looking around at one another, the team struggled not to laugh outright. "Okay, well, it's truly a blonde idea, but it's better than anything I've got," said the Jaguar, grunting at her playful punch in his ribs. "We'll pin a note on the cover of the cart to say it belongs to the pastor. If the men from the cartel confiscate it, we'll buy him a new one."

The air overhead was quiet again, so he pulled on his pack and signaled the team to get back in place. He turned to the Princess and said, "We've all got to get some rest by sleeping in the Rovers. No one moves here at night. We'd raise suspicion if we tried."

The bedraggled team hiked until the Panther signaled toward a massive tree. They turned off, careful to disguise signs they'd disturbed the roadside. When they reached a clearing, they scouted it out and pulled back netting that looked like leaves.

Three rugged, intimidating, customized green Land Rovers emerged, like specialized military equipment magically rising from hedges. Two men guarded the perimeter while Carlos helped unload boxes of things out of the back of the Rovers. With hoods raised, the men installed some things at lightning speed and did some test starts, ensuring the engines ran. Then they unpacked the old guitar and a few items belonging to the team from the mission pastor's cart, tying the goat in a guarded spot where it could rest in safety and nibble foliage.

Chapter Fifteen

He has made everything appropriate in its time.
He has also put eternity in their hearts,
but man cannot discover
the work God has done from beginning to end.
Ecclesiastes 3:11

Night would fall within the hour, but with a narrow stream close by and only a skeleton camp to set up, the Jaguar's team could bathe and eat before then. He took the Princess to the water first, checking to see if it was free of piranha and snakes. She found a spot to sit on smooth rocks with the water up to her shoulders, scrubbing mud from herself and the borrowed shirt and trousers. The Jaguar scouted a private place for her to change out of the dripping clothes, then he scraped the dried mud off her boots while he cleaned his own.

"Now it's my turn," he announced when she finished combing her wet hair. He extended his arm to give her his rifle.

She glanced in the camp's direction before reaching for the weapon. "You'd trust me to watch over you?"

"You watched over both of us today," he answered, then showed her how to handle the rifle. "Only pull this trigger if you absolutely have to. The sound may carry into the village. We don't want to draw any more attention to your Dirty Harry skills tonight unless you're defending me. I'll leave it up to you about keeping your back turned when I get in the water. We're a man and wife now, Mrs. Shepherd."

Her outcry at his audacity came with a shove. Caught off guard and tumbling into the stream, he retaliated by rushing to unbutton his camouflage shirt. "You got me wet before I had my soap. Now you have to bring it to me—better be faster than I am!"

Groaning in exasperation, she raced to pitch him his soap. But he already had his tee shirt off and was tossing his belt onto the bank by his boots. With a quick spin on her heel, she set her focus on their surroundings. In a twist of roles, his life now depended on her alertness. Surveying the jungle, she held the rifle the way he and the team did.

Her neck tingled from his warm breath, giving her a start. "Caroline, was it always so easy like this with us?"

The jungle sounds around them filled up the time as she hesitated. "Yes. When you left, you said it best. We were good at bein' friends."

"That's not all I said. I stated for the record that you were the only woman I'd ever loved, and I didn't know how to stop thinking of you as my girl."

Caroline's hand clamped over her mouth. Tears stung her eyes while she reeled at hearing Chris Shepherd repeat the parting words that had once hurt her so much. She lowered the rifle, and he rested his chin on her shoulder companionably.

She managed a hoarse whisper. "This is silly. I don't know what's wrong with me. It's been such a long day."

"I know what's wrong with you. We're getting closer and there's something about us you never got over. What is it?"

Now, she squeaked, "I was so sure you were safe! You, the preacher's kid. But in the end, you were the most dangerous one! The strong, silent type, clean-cut, dependable, unassuming. I thought what I saw was what I got with Chris Shepherd. You wouldn't leave me, like I thought Chad did."

His deep groan made her shoulder tickle under his chin. "I've been remembering little things. It's humiliating to know I just showed up and pulled the rug right out from under you, leaving you aching and bewildered. Then I had the audacity to claim to love you! That's why you don't trust me to get you outta here. Your mom was right—the stars are falling, and I used to stumble around in a song to say I'd be there for you. But you know the truth. In the end, all you really have is God and your wits."

She wiped her eyes. "What's past is past. We're both different now."

They heard voices on the trail coming from the camp. He took a quick step back and pulled a fresh tee shirt over his head, then raked his fingers through his hair and shook it out again as the others arrived. She handed his rifle back to him and went to get her clean, wet clothes from a tree branch.

The short walk back into camp was a silent one, and they heard the Panther on the radio with Weaver before they reached the clearing. He was curt and tense as he gestured to the Jaguar to join him.

Carlos flashed an impish grin and motioned Caroline over for food. "Finally! Some decent company!" he proclaimed as he tended a burning white substance with an MRE over it. Then he tilted his head at a stump nearby. "More of the beef stew tonight. Sorry, no time to hunt and I'm not sure that stream has any fish big enough to eat. But we have some fruit, and I swiped the last packet of instant cocoa for you. You earned it today."

She took the warm meal. "You're such a blessing, Carlos. What are you burning?"

"C4."

Wide-eyed, she jumped back with both hands on her dinner. He laughed in delight. "You know what that is? I'm impressed, *Señora*. It's rare for a beauty to have brains. In fact, many men would rather they didn't. Around here, it's inconvenient. Don't worry, I'm an explosives expert and C4 is harmless, this way."

Caroline settled guardedly on the edge of the stump, eyeing the C4. Carlos had a captive audience as he flattened a ball of the putty. When his own meal heated in a flash of flame, he sat down beside her and dug in with a hearty appetite.

"My bodyguard taught me a lot of things," she said, glancing again at the white rectangle. "I don't remember him sayin' he heated food with this stuff."

The Jaguar came to settle beside her. "Your bodyguard—you have a good relationship with him."

"Yeah. He's like family. His name is Azariah, after one of Daniel's friends in the Bible. You know, the ones who faced the fiery furnace rather than bow to a false god."

Rowdy calls rang out from animals in the darkening jungle and blended into the team's small talk while they ate. After they cleared things away and brushed their teeth to settle in for the night, the Jaguar picked up the pastor's guitar and began tuning it. Soon, he warmed up by strumming notes from the new song he was composing.

The Panther's face was solemn. The lantern's light reflected in his brown eyes when he looked up at Caroline and said, "We have something of a ritual, Princess. On the nights when we know we're facing the biggest risks before escaping, we have a favorite song. Tonight, we have a guitar to play along."

Caroline locked her eyes with his, then she cleared her throat. "Is that what Weaver said? Things are worse?"

He glanced at the Jaguar for his nod before he answered. "Yes, but there's nothing to be done for now. We should get some rest."

The chords of an old hymn from the strings of the battered guitar made her think of the little Painter Place chapel with stained glass windows, now swept away in the hurricane. And yet, the song had never seemed more fitting than it was here, in the wild tangle of jungle around her. She swayed to the music, joining the team to sing the words.

Closing her eyes, she tried to memorize the harmony that arose from the camp to the stars like the wafting aroma of an offering. Some voices raised tonight might be silent in this world in the morning.

An overwhelming wave of bittersweet joy swept over her. She never wanted to forget this moment. The only way out of this dark place might be to enter heaven, but if that was the Lord's will at least she was with friends willing to give their lives to save hers.

"Some bright morning when this life is over, I'll fly away

To a land on God's celestial shore, I'll fly away

I'll fly away, oh glory, I'll fly away

When I die, hallelujah by and by, I'll fly away

Just a few more weary days and then, I'll fly away

To that land where joy will never end, I'll fly away."

When the Jaguar stopped strumming, he pointed upwards. "Princess, now that it's dark and we're not under the jungle canopy, look overhead. See those five stars right there?"

She scanned the velvety sapphire sky, then gasped. "The Southern Cross!"

Chad had shown it to her in books and told the twins about it on nights when they got the telescope out to see the constellations. He told them he'd try to take them somewhere in the world where they could see it in the sky.

She stared overhead, enchanted. In such a desperate moment, she had the gift of being in that "somewhere" in the world to see it. In her mind, she heard her children's voices from yesterday morning, singing to her. *Somewhere, out there...*

The Jaguar rose to pack the pastor's guitar away. He suggested she get her sketchbook and draw a view of the Southern Cross for him. Carlos reached for her pack so she could get her supplies, asking for a drawing, too

As she created quick sketches of the constellation, Carlos and the Puma took guard duty so the other guards could eat. They chewed while watching over her shoulder. She used the unsharpened end of a pencil to preserve a white spot for each star, then slanted another one on the long side of the soft graphite to create a dark sky. They watched as she smudged to blend the darkness with a small stick-like roll of paper.

At the bottom, she wrote, "Jesus Saves." Under those words, she continued, "Illume—spreading light. *Pasar*. Caroline A. Painter, USA, 1995."

Her eyes danced in lantern light when she looked up at the Jaguar. "Are the natives still here? I'd like to leave them this. Perhaps a missionary will translate it for them."

The Jaguar shot a glance in the jungle, knowing the tribe surrounded them like apparitions. She carefully tore the pages out, and he used her pen to print *Jesus Salva* under her words. Then he grabbed some night vision goggles and led her into the obscurity of the jungle's edge.

Raucous choruses of amphibians and the weird crick sounds of twittering bats were louder now. An owl hooted overhead to another, who answered from several trees away. When the Jaguar found a log, he pulled off the goggles while she laid the drawing on it. She spread her fingers out over the smooth paper, and he covered her hand with his before he prayed out loud.

"Lord, the stars can only be seen in the darkness, much like the assurances You send us in our worst times. Caroline filled these pages with messages about light—the only light that ultimately matters. We know You reveal yourself to every person who has ever lived, even in places unreached by printed scripture. There is no excuse for not believing in You, as the book of Romans says.

In the first chapter of John, we see that awareness of Your light is in all mankind. In Ecclesiastes 3:11, we're told that You've put the knowledge of eternity in man's heart. We know You've been working in the hearts of many in this tribe, and we ask now that they'll come to know You. Thank You for letting Caroline be a part of it. I know she's not—"

The Jaguar's voice broke off. He sniffed and took a deep breath. "She's not here because of drug cartels. She's here because of something no evil can overcome. I beg You to shelter her with Your hand and get her back home unharmed. Amen."

The Princess whispered, "Amen." She tried to pull her hand from his, but he pressed down.

"Remember when we watched the sunrise two days ago? God placed signs in the night skies, too, like that cross. He's reminding you He's always here, Princess. It may feel like the stars are falling, but He's not, and He never will."

"I know. But He also provided you, and you sensed that someday you'd be the one He used to rescue me."

"I warned you not to assume I'm Chris Shepherd. Now, I'm Christian Chavarria, and the Jaguar. I'm—dangerous. When forced to, I will kill, and you may have to live with seeing me do it before this is over. The well-bred young lady I left behind would never be with a guy like me. Your daddy would have been out on the lawn with a shotgun if I'd dared come by to pick you up. I've been remembering how you were too good to be real, way out of Chris Shepherd's league. He wasn't the worst you could do but was certainly nothing special. He was background. You took the spotlight."

She reached for the outline of camp light on his face. Pushing a drying wave of hair back behind his ear, she kept her voice library low. "You're underestimating him and overestimating me. Here, in your territory, you're the one in the spotlight. Women where I come from would need medical attention if you passed them, and if they were here in my place, they wouldn't want to go home. Maybe you believe you left Chris behind when you moved on to your destiny, but I see him. He's the core of the Jaguar. I moved on to my destiny, too. I'm not that naïve, starry-eyed young lady in your memories. Back then, I'd never have believed I'd give up my dreams of a quiet life to become surrounded by bodyguards, threats, news reporters, and ransom demands."

"I know this much about Chris Shepherd: he never got over walking away, living with never knowing what might've been."

She pressed her fingertips firmly over his lips. "Don't do this! It will separate us, and such regret on his part would always have held him back. If that's true, he needed that bonk on the head. God deserves our utmost, not grudging discipleship. There's no question about what might've been. It doesn't exist. Even if we pretend Chad had chosen someone else, and I was free, and that Chris refused a clear calling and put me in God's place, do you honestly think I'd have been enough to satisfy that calling in your soul? And do you imagine I'd have considered marrying a man who couldn't be my spiritual leader because he was running from the Lord? Jonah was sent by God to soak in saltwater in a big fish until he regained his senses. I don't know what God would've done with Chris about his rebellion, but it couldn't be fulfillment or happiness! And I'd never have agreed to be a part of it."

The Jaguar groaned and brought his free hand up to hers on his mouth, pulling it back enough to plant a gentle kiss her palm before bringing their joined hands down to rest on his knee. Encouraged by the quiver that affected her, he rushed to say, "I understand. But let me say this, because you deserve to know in case tomorrow brings the worst. Last night, I remembered something I used to pray for. All I ever wanted for myself was you, but I had to live with a 'no' from God. Everything you've said is true about not being meant to be a married couple, but you can't say He didn't mean for us to be here together, right now. It's a miracle you're with me again."

They heard the radio crackle on in the camp. He sighed, then kept her hands clasped in his as he pulled her up. "Come on, I'll settle you in the back of the Land Rover and take first watch. Go to sleep with your weapons at hand, ready to be on your feet. The most danger will be at first light, and I'll be beside you then."

Chapter Sixteen

We are pressured in every way but not crushed;
we are perplexed, but not in despair;
persecuted, but not abandoned; we are
struck down, but not destroyed.
-2 Corinthians 4:8,9 HCSB

Phillip Gregory sat at one end of the conference room table and rubbed his forehead as if a headache was coming on. A solemn group had gathered there, made up of the Weaver and his assistant, and Chad, Azariah, his son-in-law Ben Grayson, the bodyguard called Jack, who had been with his dad when Caroline was taken, and a lady named Nadia.

In a low, throaty voice, Nadia had described herself to Phillip and the Weaver as an evangelical Christian, born to a Jewish mother and Russian father who settled in Israel. She never married and was an independent agent like Azariah. Ben confirmed to the Weaver that Jack had recently—on the way to Whitehaven, in fact—met his requirement to travel with the team.

Phillip listened with growing anxiety as Ben, Azariah, the Weaver, and Weaver's assistant hashed through scenarios and locations that could enable them to help the Jaguar's team. The logistics were becoming a technical blur.

In frustration, Phillip stood up, sending his chair rolling back on the casters. A few long strides placed him before a window, from which he stared into the twilight.

An abrupt silence filled the room. The seconds ticked by before Phillip turned to look at the others, hands on the hips of his tailored khakis. "Painter Place will change forever if Caroline doesn't come back. The dearest relationships in my life will be damaged. It's torture to think of it, so adding the possibility that Ben won't return makes this unthinkable. You can't seriously believe you'll convince me to agree to this! How could my son or daughter, or my grandchildren, or my best friend, ever feel the same about me if somethin' goes wrong?"

He looked around at their silent faces, slowly shaking his head. "My dad and Justin may approve of this private rescue mission, but I'm the one with everything to lose. God has always made a way before. There has to be a way!"

Ben stood slowly, pushing his chair back and coming to stand in front of his father-in-law. He spoke in a low, calm tone, but it was full of assurance. "God has made a way, Phillip. I'm here with a way. You won't be able to live with yourself if you don't send us, and I can't live with wondering if I might have changed an outcome. You knew I'd often face danger in my line of work, but you let me marry your daughter, anyway. You think it's a coincidence that I can do this? There are no coincidences with Christians, Phillip, you once told me that yourself. Providing you with this team is how God made a way."

Chad's blue Porsche purred past the barriers behind which haggard reporters camped. Elated photographers rushed for their cameras when they saw his dad in the passenger seat. Catching the father-son duo together was a paparazzi goldmine, and the best photos would make the news the following morning.

He groaned out loud and kept an expressionless face like his dad's until they were past the camp of news vans. Phillip said dryly, "I suppose tomorrow's headlines will be creative titles like, 'Chad Gregory Takes Charge After Father Collapses,' or, 'Which Face is the Future of Global if Tragedy Strikes?'"

Chad snorted, glancing at his dad and noting how haggard he looked. More gray marked his hair, and wrinkles Chad didn't remember were etched into his face. "More likely, they'll say, 'Phillip Gregory Ages Twenty Years Coping with Cartel Kidnapping.'"

He warmed to see his dad smile, however brief. It was a good thing Caroline's Uncle Wyeth and Aunt Chrissy would wait as dinner guests at the Gregory's home. Wyeth's presence was just what his dad needed right now.

A week of existing within a nightmare had taken its toll on Chad, and he wondered how he'd sit up long enough to eat. An old photo of himself as a toddler flashed into his mind, with his face in his dinner. He'd conked out after a day playing with Patrick.

Setting down his briefcase on a bench, he mused that his mom should be able to catch the same shot tonight. His tossed keys clattered on a marble-topped table by the entry door from the garage, and he trudged into the family room after his dad.

He smiled to see his children stretched out on their stomachs by the fireplace. They were fed, bathed, and in pajamas as they read a book about colors with Wyeth. Transparent page overlays that seemed to mix colors before their eyes fascinated them, and Rhett kept lifting some to investigate how it was accomplished.

Encircled with his mom's welcoming arms, Chad whispered his gratitude for getting the kids ready for the night. Then the housekeeper took his face into her hands to study him shrewdly. Scowling, she pronounced her verdict he was exhausted and needed to go to bed.

With a grin, Chad promised to obey if she'd feed him first. He'd even submit to letting her cut up each bite, like when he was a little boy. When the food was on the table, they all clasped hands while Wyeth said the blessing. Chad grinned to see that the housekeeper had cut up his seasoned steak into bite-sized chunks, and he speared one with his fork and put it into his mouth, almost too tired for the effort it took to chew.

His dad seemed to struggle for the energy to enjoy his meal, too. Keeping his voice out of range from his grandchildren's hearing, he began a brief update for Wyeth about the latest happenings at Global.

The children chattered in the family room about a puzzle they were playing with. Chad smiled to hear Rayce echoing Rhett's explanation for Savanna about why the bus full of tourists on a puzzle shape wouldn't float across an ocean in another puzzle, even if some miracle made it fit.

He yawned, then snapped his head up at something Wyeth said. "I know this is tearin' you apart, Phillip, but somethin' will happen any time now. She needs Azariah and Ben there. As the Weaver said, there'll be blood."

As a shiver ran along his spine, Chad watched his dad's blue eyes look up sharply while he swallowed the bite of potato he was chewing and set down his fork. Wyeth winced under Phillip's scrutiny and toyed with the smiley shape of a lemon slice beside his last asparagus spear. "What I mean is, this has gone on far too long. It's time for somethin' to break."

Phillip stared at him, waiting. Wyeth exaggerated a deep sigh of resignation and dabbed his mouth with a soft cloth napkin, then patted it back into his lap before he faced his lifelong best friend. Everyone at the table sat frozen while something invisible passed between the two men. Chad knew what was happening. He'd often experienced it with Caroline. The Painter intuition was something to take seriously.

"Get some sleep as soon as dinner's over," Wyeth said. "You look terrible."

Avoiding his eyes, Wyeth turned his attention back to his meal. Phillip studied him a few more moments, then turned to his son.

With a slight nod, Chad acknowledged that he understood. Something big was about to happen. And it would be violent.

Rhett's radio crackled with the Weaver's voice. "This is the Weaver reporting to the Gregory twins from your dad's office. Acknowledge."

The twins gasped and made a dash to pick up the radio from where they'd left it on the hearth. Savanna Caroline placed both hands over her mouth in a promise to be quiet so they could hear, and Rhett held the radio between himself and his brother. He pressed a button. "You're loud and clear. Rhett and Rayce Gregory here, ready for today's report."

"Over!" blurted Rayce.

"Your mama and the goat got very muddy today, but they're both safe in camp with the Big Cats. I have some words for you tonight. I saw the Bible verse on your dad's desk calendar. Do you want to hear something God wants us to know about animals? Over."

Rayce looked at his brother, who nodded. He answered, "Roger that, Weaver. Over."

"In Psalm fifty, verses ten and eleven, the Bible says, '... every animal of the forest is Mine, the cattle on a thousand hills. I know every bird of the mountains, and the creatures of the field are Mine.' Rhett and Rayce, do you copy?"

Rhett tilted his head, considering. "Ummm—copy that, Weaver. My mamma—she's in a forest, and those animals are scary. They hurt other animals and people. If they're God's animals, why doesn't He stop them?"

"Yeah. Over!" blurted Rayce.

The Weaver didn't hide his deep sigh over the radio. "Remember, when God first created the world, it was perfect, right? No animals or people hurt others. But when Adam and Eve chose to sin, rather than trust God, the world became broken.

Justice has a price that someone must pay. As the Judge, God had to allow a curse of death on the earth, though He offered mercy, too. His animals changed, but He can still command them when He wants to accomplish something that glorifies Him. Sometimes, He did that in the Bible. Over."

Chad was confident he wasn't kidding himself about Caroline's romantic interactions with the Jaguar. It was a performance, a way to get home. She didn't touch the guy the way she touched Chad.

But the Jaguar wasn't acting. No way.

He narrowed his eyes, knowing it would take some creativity to top that suggestive stunt the guy pulled by sliding the pistol along her curves. Had the Jaguar seen that done somewhere, or was it some fantasy he dreamed up in their little jungle dens at night?

Chad's jaw worked as that little pass repeated over and over in his mind. If it stirred him, he could imagine what it did to the Jaguar.

On Caroline's part, she'd been a boss with the Glock, easily besting her would-be attacker. An unexpected thrill surged through him and made him catch his breath. Few men had a woman like that.

After a quick shower in case he had to leave for the office in the middle of the night, Chad prayed with the kids before tucking the boys into their beds. Bleary-eyed, he tried to persuade his daughter to sleep in her bedroom, singing along to her current favorite tunes. He left her surrounded by an army of dolls and stuffed animals in the nightlight's illumination.

Leaving his daughter's door open, he plopped onto the sofa cushions to see if she'd sleep. He drifted off before awakening to her sweet voice singing, "Somewhere, out there, 'neath the pale moonlight..." She trailed off into whimpering that made his own eyes swim in tears. Soon she was sobbing pitifully.

Longing for the energy he had ten years ago, he willed himself to go comfort her, muttering that his dad had been right. He should have had his children when he was younger.

Padding in bare feet past her dresser, he reached toward a little white crocheted puppy tissue box cover made by Natalie. It lay on its back as if wriggling on the floor, and he pulled several pink tissues out of its uplifted tummy to wipe her eyes and nose. He put his arms under the pretty bundle in bunny pajamas and carried her to a recliner to fall asleep on his shoulder.

With her head tucked near his chin, he weakly sang the song his nephew Noble used to like so much, calming her with quiet words about a lion sleeping tonight. She rubbed her eyes, hiccupped, and asked what lions dream about.

Soon, he could get her back to her own bed. But he fell asleep along with her, imagining what might fill a lion's dreams.

The Panther and Jaguar left their posts to a fresh guard shift, stopping by the makeshift latrine, washing up their hands and faces, then draining their canteens. All radio equipment was packed into the Panther's Land Rover. The team could bolt away in an instant.

The Jaguar stretched out his leg and shoulder muscles, then shut his eyes as he leaned back against the middle Rover. He worked on calming down so he could rest for a few hours. Sliding his back down against the window and door to sit on the ground, rifle across his lap, he whispered prayers.

"I know I have to give her back. The Prince started asking You for her long before You let me replace him, before I understood that I couldn't stay, and she couldn't leave. But she was in my life for a reason, and here she is—I'm a stand-in for her prince again.

I'm like one of those knights in stories who chooses a lady as his ideal, no matter if she's single or married, wearing a token like her scarf around his arm in battle. He was her 'champion,' and consummation of their relationship wasn't what drove him to pay honor to her. It was her respect, her admiration."

He stopped, his throat tight, despairing at the mental image of her handsome prince. *Stop comparing yourself to him—you're not competing. She's his. Game over.*

Massaging fingertips into his forehead, he expected the dreaded, disabling pain that memories brought. It didn't come but remembering was more a curse than a blessing. Better that she'd remained that elusive girl who flitted past in his dreams occasionally, the one he recognized in an instant when he saw her at the *Puña* shelter.

Rising to his feet, he surveyed the Rovers and his men again. He felt overwhelmed at having the responsibility for their survival—for her survival. "Lord," he whispered, "You read my heart, my very soul. You know I don't care what happens to me. But I care about what happens to her. She doesn't belong here. I beg You, get her home unharmed."

Uneasy, he knit his brows while scanning the perimeter of the clearing. At the open back gate of his long Rover, he lifted the mosquito netting. With a stealthy slide into it beside the Princess, he noted the layer of foam wasn't a mattress by any stretch of the imagination. But she hadn't complained. She never complained about any of their primitive conditions. The only thing she'd had a problem with was his rough treatment early on, and she'd taken care of that when she had enough and knocked him down.

He tried to stifle a grunt, positioning his rifle along the length of his leg, pointing out to the jungle. Then he gently slid the Princess' arm over to her side, freezing when she stirred and moved it across her waist.

Once she settled, he rested his head against a rolled towel. But his thoughts were busy strategizing over all the what ifs that the coming dawn would bring. For the first time since he'd accepted a mission for the Weaver, he felt fear.

Huffing in frustration, he turned onto his side with a soft bump against the Princess. He re-adjusted the blanket over her arm, and she grasped his hand and turned to her side, settling them over her heart.

His own heart thudded at least triple time. He waited to see if she'd realize what she'd done. His arm muscles were straining, and he needed sleep to face impending danger in the morning. Inching closer, he risked worse danger if she awakened and found him this way. Propping his other arm behind his head, he relaxed, his chest against her back and his knee curved into hers.

He was crossing a line. There'd be a personal price to pay later. But he was living for the moment and later didn't exist yet. In fact, later may be nothing more than dawn's coming light.

A tangle of vegetation concealed a dozen heads of dark hair huddled in a circle, their owners carrying folded pages of paper pulled from skin pouches strung across their bodies. The leader reminded them that the gift left in the jungle tonight proved that the Shining Woman was spreading the same light the stars witnessed to overhead. He made a sign of a cross with his arms. It was the shape of the sign the missionary evangelist had tried to explain to them. He said the symbols written at the bottom of the paper were languages he once learned in a village school when guerillas dragged him from the forest tribe. The message told them to pass on the light of those stars, the light of the God who created them.

Scouts reported that there were aggressive men in uniforms coming, all chasing the Shining Woman. It was too dangerous for the small tribe to engage them to help the man they knew as the Jaguar, for his enemies would seek their village and wipe out the women, children, and elders as punishment. Their tribe would cease to exist.

A man beside the leader suggested that if the evangelist who visited the tribe with medicine was right about the God-Friend called Jesus, who saves a man's spirit from the evil one, then Jesus had the power to protect the Shining Woman. He suggested that they test the one who put the cross sign in the sky by appealing to Him. If Jesus saved the woman, they and their families would believe and serve this Creator God.

But another blurted that if they did not believe the obvious message to begin with, there was no reason for this Jesus Saves Spirit to listen to them, or answer. He might even be angry that they dared to test Him. What if He sent a plague to punish them? They already knew He existed. He was the Spirit that the dark spirits warned the old shaman not to talk to.

The whites of dark eyes widened, and murmurs spread among the group. Their leader responded that there was no reason for Jesus Saves to be angry with them. They didn't ask for anything for themselves. They should appeal to Him to raise up help from the jungle He'd created to save His servant, the Shining Woman, because they wished her well but could not raise their spears.

With nods all around, the tribesmen agreed this seemed right to them. Their concern for the welfare of the Shining Woman would please Jesus Saves. Some suggested asking Him to raise up the most fearsome animals of the jungle, the jaguars and bushmasters, to rescue her. There was a flurry of nods and affirmative grunts at the prospect of having an undeniable sign of supernatural power.

The leader gestured for silence and said they would each take a turn asking on their knees, as the evangelist did. Then the scouts would rush to tell the forest tribesmen on the far side to do the same. He dropped to his knees first and began, his voice quiet but his body animated with emotion and hands toward the stars.

Chad barely roused from sleep when Savanna stirred in his arms, shifting her position to turn her face toward the room. She rested it again on his chest with a little sigh that tugged his heart, and he knew she'd never even opened her eyes. He could feel a cooling wet spot on his shirt where she'd drooled. It crossed his mind that he should take her to her bed and go to his own, but the gentle tendrils of the netherworld of sleep tugged him back under with the wonderful promise of peace.

"The snakes and the jaguars won't hurt Mommy," Savanna mumbled in her sleep.

Chad's eyes flew open. He resisted sitting straight up, not wanting to wake his daughter. There was enough dim moonlight through the windows for his eyes to adjust to seeing her blonde head. "You're dreaming of snakes and jaguars, sweetie?" he whispered.

Savanna stretched out an arm to touch his. She grasped his sleeve in little fingers as if to hold on to him, then relaxed it again. Finally, she mumbled again. "No, Daddy. They came for the bad men."

Wide awake, he tried to process the incredulity of what he'd just heard. Heart pounding, he gently carried her to her room and laid her on her bed, then tucked her in. He backed out into the hall again, then dashed to the master bathroom, freshening up at lightning speed and jerking a clean shirt out from under the dry-cleaner's wrap in the closet. He pulled his arms through the crisp sleeves as he slid his feet into shoes, then ran through the wide double doors to the main part of the house where his parents lived.

He was not startled to meet his dad in the shadowy hallway. Like Chad, he hurriedly fumbled with the buttons on a clean shirt. They walked as one with the same height and stride.

"Wyeth called?"

"Yep. How did you find out?"

Chad's hand trembled as he tried to button his cuff. "Savanna was sleepin' on my chest and woke me, talkin' in her sleep. She said the snakes and jaguars wouldn't hurt her mommy. I asked if she was dreamin' of the animals, and she said no, it was real, but they were after the bad guys."

Phillip drew in his breath, then stopped whispering to use his normal voice. "Wyeth said he fell asleep prayin' in the library at the Big House. He awakened, thinkin' vicious snakes and jaguars surrounded him, but he didn't fear them. Get Azariah! I'll wake up Ben. Your mom's dressing, then she'll watch the kids and call Sandy and your grandparents."

"I'm not waitin' for Azariah. He can ride with Ben. Are you with me?"

Azariah bolted around a corner into the living room, adjusting a heavy gray leather jacket he'd thrown on over an unbuttoned shirt. Ben rushed in, smoothing back his ruffled short hair. "Weaver just called. He wants the team. The Jaguar's surrounded and the cartels are closin' in."

The Jaguar awakened with hair standing up on his neck. For the span of a few breaths, he trained all his senses toward the jungle night that enveloped the camp. The nocturnal wildlife was too quiet.

The Princess no longer clasped his hand over her heart. It was on his rifle, where he'd have naturally placed it on a mission. He was on his back now, and she snuggled into his side, her face against his shoulder.

For a moment, he backed away from the urgency of his instincts, relishing an intimacy he would miss for the rest of his life. Then he realized his life was likely to end in a matter of minutes, anyway. He whispered, "Princess, I've got to check the camp. Stay here."

She stirred and muttered lazily, "The jaguar told me he wouldn't hurt us."

He tensed and peered through the shadows at her face. "What jaguar?"

She moistened her lips and nudged her nose into his upper arm. "The one with the snakes."

Obviously, she was dreaming. A stab of pain in his head sent him into oblivion. *No, not now, please, God! Not now, they need me!*

For the team's protection, he touched the camera on his shirt to turn it on, a signal when he was mewing so the Weaver would know if a mission was compromised. Then he pressed viciously against his old head wound. The seconds passed, as did the pain. Dazed, but regaining his senses, he groped about for a memory he abandoned when the pain as all that existed.

Listen to her. That was it. He remembered other times, in a far-away place...

Moonglow outlined the peaceful repose of the Princess, absurd considering the stalking enemy surrounding her like a dragnet. He was reluctant to frighten her. "Tell me the dream."

She didn't respond, so he raised the hand of the arm she snuggled into, bending his elbow to touch her hair. Her eyes opened, and she blinked sleepily before pulling back from his arm, listening in confusion at his urgent low tone asking about the dream.

Her eyes searched his eyes in the soft moonlight. Still bewildered, she asked how he knew she had a dream.

"You spoke of jaguars and snakes in your sleep. You used to be very—intuitive. Did you have a dream, or do you have one of those feelings?"

The Princess rose to her elbow and her eyes darted around for her Glock holster and knife sheath. Alarmed, he sat up to help her strap on her weapons. "They're coming!" she exclaimed as he helped her with a buckle.

Unnerved, he asked, "Who's coming?"

"I don't know who, but it's real! Something *extreme* is about to happen. Look!" she hissed, showing him the gooseflesh on her arm. "It's more than human. This is spiritual warfare. I warned you something dark is stalking me in this jungle. I'm seized with a wrenching urgency. Don't shoot the jaguars, pumas, panthers, snakes, or any other animals, understand? I mean it! Only shoot the men shootin' at you."

Her eyes were like cold steel in the moonlight, fearless and resolute. When he hesitated to marvel at them, she leaned forward and insisted, "Tell the team! Now!"

"Stay in here. The windows are bulletproofed."

But the Princess shook her head and kept the tone of authority in her voice. "No way. This is about me! I must be part of it for this to matter. You're outnumbered, it's dark, and I'm a great shot. Give me some rounds of ammo. Should I get under the Rover?"

With a quick move he turned off his camera. She secured her hair in a side ponytail, ready for business, and noticed his expression. "Please, Chris—Jaguar—we must hurry! I know this sounds absurd, but it's not just a feeling. Make fun of me later if this comes to nothing."

Grasping his arm, she added, "Be careful. You're one of the best friends I've ever had, and I can't live with you coming to harm because of me. I grieved over your death once in my life already."

"And you'll always be one of the best friends I'll ever have, Caroline," he blurted, pulling her into a tight hug. "Just in case, I want you to know that I'd do it all over again. I've loved and admired you since the day I met you."

He sniffed and blinked rapidly. "Let's go. Don't give away your position by shooting unless it's necessary. If the team's all down, try to spot a cartel group and ask to surrender to their leader. Under no circumstances can you leave this clearing with guerillas."

Chapter Seventeen

There are only two ways to live your life.
One is as though nothing is a miracle.
The other is as though everything is a miracle.
-Albert Einstein

Patrick's taillights were only yards ahead of Chad on the moonlit island road, barely taking the turn at the Big House onto Pavilion Way. Tires on his blue Corvette squealed just before Chad's did. Ben followed with his team in a Jeep, and Wyeth Painter pulled out of the driveway behind him with his wife Chrissy, his mother Savanna, and Caroline's parents.

Chad continued to race across the causeway bridge onto the mainland in Whitehaven behind Caroline's brother. Downtown was deserted except for the Global Tower on Main Street. Patrick was arguing with security guards to let him pass when Chad jerked his car into park and opened his door, standing up and shouting an order for them to do it immediately.

He glanced back and groaned. Vans with sleepy reporters were opening sliding doors to investigate. Another car pulled in behind Wyeth, and the convoy poured into the parking garage under the tower before exploding with people rushing to the employee elevator. Ben's team ran to the service elevator on the other side and were soon behind the sliding stainless steel doors.

Pastor Payne's car had been the last one in. He trotted up to the group and shook the men's hands, nodding at Gran Vanna and Chrissy before hugging Valerie. "I woke up with an urgency to be here for you. Just tell me if I can help or where I can wait, that's all I ask."

"You can wait with us," answered Chrissy with a grateful touch on his shoulder.

Chad blurted to Patrick, "How did you find out?"

"Noble had a dream. But you know how he is, and I couldn't rest 'til I found out for myself if there was a connection."

"A dream about snakes and jaguars?"

"Yeah! How d'you know?"

"Savanna. She was cryin' for Caroline again, so I let her fall asleep with me in the recliner. She awakened enough to say the snakes and jaguars wouldn't hurt her mommy. I asked if she was dreamin' of them, and she said no, they were there for the bad guys."

Patrick grabbed Chad's arm. "What?"

"She's the next one. I told you there'd be a Gregory artist when we mixed the bloodlines. She's got the Painter intuition."

Clutching Chad's bicep, Patrick whistled. "So maybe Caroline had the dream, too, and warned the Jaguar in time!"

They didn't wait for the elevator doors to slide fully open before piling inside, and Valerie Painter held her hands over her trembling lips on the way up to the seventh floor. Her husband put a reassuring arm around her, rubbing her upper arm. But his face told its own tale of fear and helplessness.

When the doors opened, the man Chad thought of as Weaver's shadow came up to them with a solemn expression to say the Weaver was in the conference room briefing Ben's team. They were about to jet to a specialized helicopter that would get them to the Chavarria compound.

Phillip covered his face with his hands and shook his head as if refusing. Chad put an arm around him, squeezing his shoulders as the Weaver came out and stepped down the hall toward them. But he slowed at the sight of Savanna Painter and Chrissy. He studied them, then nodded politely before acknowledging Valerie and shaking hands with the men. "I'm sorry to have this pleasure under such dire circumstances. I'm called the Weaver, and I wanted to meet you before I get involved in the situation in the nerve center. From my heart, I want you to understand that I'm merely a man, just a tool. God is the one in charge of the outcome of this mission."

He fixed an understanding gaze on Phillip Gregory, then excused himself to go back to the conference room. His solemn assistant gave the family instructions about non-interference and where to wait for updates, but Ben's team interrupted as they poured into the hall, fielding goodbyes as they made their way to the elevator.

Phillip squeezed his eyes tight as he clutched Ben and said a brief prayer over him. The other men joined him, touching Ben's jacket and praying in turn. When they released him, Ben turned a stern look to Chad. "Joey can't know about this until it's over. I mean it."

Chad bit his lips together and nodded, then joined his dad, grabbing Azariah's arm to pray over him. Tears trailed unchecked down Chad's face as he pointed at Ben and Azariah. He choked out, "Come back home to us, and bring her with you!"

When the special team was out, a female member of the Weaver's group kindly led the tearful, anxious group to the conference room, where fresh coffee was brewing. Other refreshments they recognized from the local bakery and specialty shops were out on a side table. She distracted them with compliments about the Southern food in the little town, asking what their favorites were.

Wyeth's mobile phone rang. Pulling it from a clip on his belt to check the number, he sighed before he answered. They could all hear the alarm in Maggie Jane's voice as she demanded to know why he neglected to call. She was waiting to hear from him after awakening in a panic to pray for Caroline.

He glanced at the others and went to stand in the hall, explaining where he was and why. He had no details yet to call her about. But Maggie Jane didn't let him off the hook.

"Tell me this much—why am I prayin' 'bout animals?"

Wyeth blinked. "I never mentioned animals."

"No, sir, you didn't, but you know what I'm talkin' 'bout."

Now he chuckled, ruffling his graying brown hair in resignation. "I only know they won't hurt Caroline, but they will hurt someone else. Noble and Savanna Caroline had a similar dream."

"You remember Ezekiel 39:17-20? I just looked it up. God uses animals if it suits His purpose. All creation is under His command. I'm callin' the gals in my circle now. We got a strategy room of our own, ya know."

"This one's called a nerve center. Bye, Maggie Jane. You're one of the best things that ever happened to my family, to Painter Place—to Caroline." His voice choked over his niece's name. He swallowed and added hoarsely, "She adores you."

"You're all the blessin' o' my life, and my sweet Caroline is a special joy. It ain't been the same without her. I fight for my own, ya know that. Let's spiff up our Ephesians Six armor and join the battle in the dark."

"It's an honor to fight with the best, Maggie Jane! I'll call when I know anything."

Caroline's brother Patrick was startled at seeing Phillip Gregory's office transformed into a hive of activity with impressive technology. Careful to stay out of the way, he wandered over to look out the wall of glass into the peaceful night sky over Painter

Place. Chad came up beside him with a manila folder from which he slid out a photo. Patrick grabbed it from his friend's hand and gawked as he studied the Jaguar.

"Just so you won't be shocked when the monitors come on," Chad muttered.

"Now I get it—the jealousy. But I stand on what I said. Man, he'd be a good ally to have, in case this ever happens to one of us again. I say let's all hold hands and sing 'Kum By Ya.'"

Chad snarled, "Right, and Natalie's stunt man would come in mighty handy, too! You plan to hold his hand and sing?"

They turned as Chad's mother hurried into the room and locked arms with her husband, explaining to him that Lisa, the pastor's wife, had insisted on staying with the kids so Camellia could be there. Phillip relaxed noticeably, and the team turned to admire her. There was a magnetic presence about Camellia Heyward Gregory that drew attention whenever she walked into a room, and she looked beautifully put together in the middle of the night.

At her first sight of the Weaver, Camellia whispered something to Phillip. He blinked and tilted his head to fix a quizzical gaze into her eyes. She raised a delicate brow and nodded.

While Phillip observed Weaver's profile, she curled a manicured finger to Chad to come over, where she waited with an embrace. She murmured up to his ear that everything was in God's hands, and He could be trusted with the outcome.

Chad felt himself melt into the arms that always provided comfort and security, wishing she'd been able to be here more often during this whole ordeal. Then the monitor screens around the room burst into life with views from various body cameras worn by the Weaver's team in the jungle, and Chad reached for the photo Patrick held. He passed it to his mother and watched her study it while he followed Patrick to the screens. Then he found her eyes again, knowing they would be full of gentle understanding.

Weaver dominated the room with his usual air of command and energy, analyzing everything at once. One team member made an urgent gesture and called him to look at a monitor view he was re-playing. Caroline's voice warned, "They're coming!"

His skin tingled as the hair on his neck and arms rose. His heart was in this throat even before he heard her caution the Jaguar that something "extreme" was about to happen and not to shoot animals. He heard her claim that this was about her, that she had to participate for it to matter. She had armed herself to join the team.

Chad was shaking by the time he got as close as he dared to the monitor, peering round the technician's head. The camera went dark to the image of Caroline putting her hair out of her way as if preparing to fight.

"What happened? Why can't we see her?" His dad and Patrick crowded around.

Weaver didn't look at him but responded, "The Jaguar's camera was only on because he was mewing. It's a safety procedure in case the Panther needs to take charge. But he turned it off. This is a re-play."

The screen came to life again with the views from the leader's chest as he relayed Caroline's bizarre orders to the team. His camera recorded the men looking at him as if he'd lost his mind.

The Jaguar had taken Caroline seriously! Patrick gave Chad's arm a light slap, muttering, "He remembers. That's why he mewed. Now he trusts her enough to put his life on the line."

Shouts in Spanish punctuated the night view portrayed on the monitor, and Chad's heart felt like a slingshot out of his chest. The cameras revealed the team diving to the ground and rolling into firing position with M-16s.

Where was his wife?

The Jaguar's Land Rover was sandwiched between the other two and offered the most protection for the Princess. He'd left her gathering cover for a bunker underneath it. The vehicles were only used by the team for refuge as a last resort so they wouldn't sustain damage beyond the ability to escape, but sheltering a rescued hostage changed the rules.

He crawled on his stomach to peer under the row of tires to look for her, but shots broke out in the jungle and he froze until he knew which direction to aim into. It was insane to do this at night, killing one another in friendly fire! Rival cartels were wasting men's lives in this ludicrous attack to get the prize first.

Terrified, the goat broke free of a tether and bolted back toward the cart path. The Puma hissed for the Jaguar's attention, gesturing for him to listen before pointing to the goat's route. Jeep engines rumbled nearby.

With a desperate groan, the Jaguar pointed at the camera on his chest. The Puma nodded vigorously, gesturing up to his earpiece and making a hand sign that Weaver understood their dire situation. Both ducked their heads when shots hit close by.

The Jaguar resumed his crawl to check on the Princess. A stray shot sang over him and thumped into a tree trunk, sending splinters flying. Voices hailed from all directions and another shot sank into a tree above Carlos, then another past the Panther. On the ground of the clearing, the team circled with their weapons aimed out on the perimeter.

The Jaguar aimed at a sudden burst of gunfire, but then realized he wasn't the target. He heard voices shouting all around him, and they became an unintelligible jumble to sort through while gunfire ensued. A shot hit something metallic, and he hoped it was a Rover instead of his men's equipment. His eyes darted around to account for everyone, recalling which had been on guard wearing bulletproof vests.

It was all he could do to stay down when he heard the Princess scream for him, a sound that cut to his soul and sent a shiver of dread over his whole body. She hadn't called for the name she'd always known him by, the one who'd walked away from her once, but the one he'd become.

Jaguar!

His jaw muscles clenched. He rolled to get to his knees, but a shot rang out near his shoulder and he dropped. Pulling himself to the side of a Rover for cover, he encountered a horrifying view. Three men were tugging the Princess into the dense blackness of the tree line. One had a bandaged arm. *The man from the village!*

With his rifle raised, he took a shot that might frighten the men to let her go so they could find cover. But they barely ducked at his effort. Her camouflage shirt was ripped and her ponytail ragged. Just before the darkness of the jungle swallowed her up, he caught his breath to see a dark stream of blood under her nose.

Silence fell all around. That desperate scream had alerted everyone on all sides that the Princess, the ultimate prize tonight, was in trouble. But who had her?

"I'll cover you!" shouted Carlos, who came under fire for revealing his position. He retaliated and hit his mark. One less gun threatened the mission.

The Jaguar prayed incoherently as he made his way on his belly to the jungle. A burst of bullets at his side sprayed dirt onto him, and he gauged the trajectory to shoot back. One less gun threatened his mission.

Terrified cries of *"jaguar"* rang out in the jungle, as well as and the hair-raising screams of pumas. Then a giant bushmaster slithered past, only inches from his arm. Fascinated at the rippling marked scales and his proximity to the deadliest snake in the

Amazon, he froze. It was much longer than he was tall. But the monstrous viper ignored him, making a beeline into the forest.

A nightmare became a reality for Caroline. She was taller than two of her three attackers, but they were stocky. In desperation, she had stabbed the fourth one when he tried to keep her from getting under the Rover, and recalling the sensation of sinking that blade had made her feel sick. The odious attacker had crawled off to get himself away from gunfire.

Despite her fanatical struggle to fight back, the others stripped her of the Glock 17 and holster before dragging her to the jungle's edge. The man she wounded in the village was still strong with one arm. Perhaps this group had been under orders to look for an American woman, but they were not taking her to a drug lord for ransom. Their leering eyes and the crude way they handled her differed from the men who kidnapped her. She guessed these attackers were guerillas. They had no complex chess-board plans, only a foul, immediate one that would leave her used and dead here on the jungle floor.

Cold metal dug into her back from an attacker's ammo belt. Under a clamped hand that slipped on her blood and stank of cigarettes and urine, she tried to scream for the Jaguar. All she managed was a muffled wild sound. Gagging at the odor while being pulled into the brush, she tried to use her running shoes to bruise plants, leaving a trail of evidence. When they slowed down to avoid stumbling over a fallen log, she threw all her strength into an elbow jab that sent her captor doubling over in an outburst of pain.

"Jaguar!" she screamed, jerking free of cruel hands. She dove for the enveloping darkness, desperate to roll under cover or climb a tree. *Please, Lord, use the deafening gunfire to mask my movements.*

Wild to escape and choking back moans of panic that would betray her location, she crawled behind the trunk of a tree. Not far away, she heard a blood-curdling cry of horror. It was the voice of the attacker she elbowed in her escape, and she seized the Spanish word she understood: *serpiente!*

Was it the snake in her dream? The possibility boosted her courage, so she readied herself to run while waiting for machine gun fire to hide the pounding of her steps to another tree. She didn't know how to turn back to the clearing. All she could think to do was to get off the ground and hide above the heads of the two men searching for her.

But behind the next tree, there were no branches within her reach. "Please, there must be a way," she whispered as a fervent prayer. She sank down, her mind racing to discover any resources. She fingered the tongue of her shoe with a shaky hand, knowing she had the tiny escape tools hidden there. But none would serve as an effective weapon. There were sticks around her, but she could see no rocks.

Grasping the outline of a large stick in the darkness, it crumbled in her hand, rotted through. She shuddered at the moldy smell and the feel of the mushy wood in her sweaty palm. She brushed off her hand against her pants, not wanting to know what creatures she'd just disturbed in that decayed habitat and hoping their remains weren't stuck to her.

Gunfire and voices erupted from the distance, along with a shriek of the Spanish word "jaguar." Her teeth chattered. The screams were not from fear of the man Jaguar. The enemy was encountering the wild cats of the jungle.

Rising to plan another dash for cover, she cringed at an unearthly feline scream in the distance. Small bodies of animals rustled the underbrush as they fled in fear. She groped toward a stand of elephant ears that somehow appeared even blacker than the night.

Ducking behind another enormous tree trunk, she unwittingly disturbed some bats and clamped her hand over her mouth to stifle a cry. She didn't know if the salty taste on her lips was from sweat or the oozing blood from her nose, but she smeared it on what remained of her shirt. Her grimy fingers snagged the last dangling button, and it fell away. With shaking hands, she managed to tie the ends in front so it wouldn't catch on branches.

Sporadic automatic rifle fire ripped through the forest. Caroline knew she must regain control from her panic. Hugging her arms around herself to still the violent trembling inside her, she tried to take deep breaths and imagine what Azariah would do.

But as she looked around to steady herself by recalling the OODA loop, she became impossibly terrified. She was suffocating in shades of black, folds of ebony within ebony, unrelenting layers of darkness within darkness.

Now her breath came in gasps. If she ran, it could be straight into the hands of the men hunting her. Every step may lead away from the Jaguar. Was he still alive to help her?

She closed her eyes to prove to herself there was as much light behind her lids as when keeping them open. Darkness surrounded her like an entity with cruel hands, reaching out. She had the sensation of falling backwards into a never-ending night, and once again, she clamped her hand over her mouth to keep from screaming.

Unbidden, some memorized scripture from childhood days in Bible drills came to mind. Her leader had promised then that verses her group worked so hard to recite would return when they needed them. Gratefully, she whispered bits of what she recalled of Psalm 59, turning the scripture into a prayer. "Deliver me—deliver me from my enemies, my God; protect me from those who rise up against me."

She stopped, breathless, too distraught to recall more than parts of it, but latching onto two words for dear life. "Deliver me—deliver me! Save me from men of bloodshed who ambush me."

Snagging on the brink of something almost on her tongue, Caroline rubbed her forehead briskly. "Oh! I know! Powerful men attack me, but not because of anything I've done. Lord—I will sing praises, because God is my stronghold."

Now she turned from scripture to her own whispered plea. "Good or bad, no one can hide from You—not even here. You alone are faithful when men fail. See us through this!"

More rounds of gunfire and cries in Spanish punctured the blackness behind the elephant ear leaves where she was squatting down. Azariah's drilling instructions echoed in her mind. *Stay off the x. Always keep moving.*

Peering to discern some outline of a tree for her next hiding spot, she plunged into that horrible abyss of darkness. When she wrapped her fingers around the scratchy bark of the closest branch, it gave way with a loud snap. Dropping the dead, dry extension of the tree, she jumped to gain hold of another one, then she scrambled against the trunk to grip with her shoes.

She cried out at the lightening burst of pain in both ankles when meaty fingers dug into them. Frantic to pull free, she kicked, but another man joined the one who'd captured her, and they pulled her shoes off. The fabric ripped in her trousers and shirt as they used them to secure her. With a wail of despair, her fingers scraped from the branch and she slipped into their arms again.

Another foul-smelling hand bruised her lips against her teeth and muffled her sobs. She didn't understand the Spanish exchange rapidly going on between them, but she knew what the obscene gestures were all about. They seemed to agree she was too much trouble, and they'd gone far enough away from the clearing for what they had in mind.

One used a rifle butt to clear a spot on the ground at her bare feet, and Caroline groaned. *Please, Lord, not this way! Don't let my family find out it all ended this way. Please don't make Chad live with this!*

Surging in strength born in utter desperation, she fought wildly, freeing her teeth to bite the filthy hand over her mouth and kicking out at the man clearing the ground. If she could make them angry enough, perhaps they'd just shoot her and get it over with.

While one man cursed, nursing his hand and grabbing at her arm, the other yelled in pain at her kick and retaliated with a rough push on her shoulders. Her knees buckled to the ground where he pushed her back, forcing himself on top of her. She hammered his bandaged arm with her fists until his partner squatted above her head and pinned them to the jungle floor.

Panic consumed her. "Jaguar!" she tried to scream from under the weight of the man struggling to untie the knot she'd made in her shirt. He cut her call for help short when his hand came down toward her face and blinding lights flashed in her vision. Just before everything went mercifully black, she heard the breathy grunt of a large animal.

It was Camellia who calmed Chad enough to keep him from being expelled from the nerve center of the mission. She and Patrick stationed themselves between him and the monitors so he couldn't interfere. Patrick sometimes swatted at his own tears, but he grimly pinched his lips together to be silent.

Chad's mother kept a comforting hand on her son's arm. He eyed the screens over her shoulder, desperate for a view of his wife from the Jaguar's camera. His knees became jelly at the faint sound of her scream. He'd never dreamed a sound like that could come from her, and he wondered if he'd lost his mind.

His dad's office walls rang out with the sights and sounds of a horror movie. Playing out before his eyes was a bizarre ambush scene of huge menacing cats, the biggest snakes he'd ever seen, swooping bats, and glowing-eyed owls who badgered men shooting wildly at one another in the jungle.

He covered his face and shook his head to make sure he wasn't having a nightmare. Something Caroline sometimes said echoed in his mind. *Is this real?*

The Weaver's team was efficient and unwavering. One man exclaimed in surprise and the Weaver jogged over, asking for a playback. Chad couldn't see it—didn't want to. All he wanted was for the Jaguar to find Caroline before it was too late.

The Jaguar donned his night-vision goggles and dared to stand up to follow a trail of broken foliage. Nearby, a blood-curdling cry came from a man bitten by a snake. He hoped he moved that direction, then became certain of it when he almost tripped over a uniformed body. Peering around for disturbed ground, he plunged further into the wild tangle.

Familiar grunts alongside him made him fight the instinct to defend himself. Steeling his mind to ignore rules about what to do when stalked by a jaguar, he let the cat rush past, and only yards away, a soul-rending cry of his name was cut short by the sickening strike of a hand.

The Princess! His gut convulsed, and he charged like a madman toward the outlines of two men on the ground. His chest heaved while he paused long enough to raise his rifle and fire.

His target moved at the last instant, startled by the spring of the enormous spotted jaguar. The attacker was wounded by the rifle shot, but the wild animal's jaws had crushed the back of the skull of his partner and then opened the victim's throat.

The wounded man got to his knees by the time the cat dragged the dead man off the Princess. He raised his own rifle with a dead aim at the animal.

Reaching the scene, the Jaguar shouted and dove to cover the Princess before the rifle went off above him. His face jarred against the mossy ground, knocking off the night vision goggles. Sickening thuds told him the bullets found their mark in the cat, and he waited to be next.

But the massive animal was unstoppable. He felt it brush across his back as it sprang over him and onto the assailant. When the man's scream ended abruptly in a gurgle, the Jaguar realized he'd been holding his breath. He pulled his head up to gulp air and crouched on his hands and knees over the unconscious Princess. The cat stared at him with eerie golden eyes, pacing soundlessly around the couple.

He'd been taught never to look a jaguar in the eye, but he stared, mesmerized, while it came up to stand face to face. The blunted shape of the snout and a dark triangle of the nose was so close he felt its moist, warm breath. He wasn't afraid, only captivated by a powerful presence. The moments seemed to pass in a timeless, peaceful silence.

Only when it turned to lope gracefully back into the darkness did he hear once again the clamor of battling enemies in the night. His team would be under fire. He tried to take the arm of the Princess to pull her up, but his hands slipped.

"No, no, no!" He fought a rising panic as he inhaled the heavy odor of fresh blood and groped around for the missing goggles. He couldn't waste time searching. A desperate check for her pulse told him it was either weak, or his own was throbbing too much to judge. He'd never encountered so much blood on one person, and he couldn't tell where it was coming from.

Jerking his head around for a sense of direction, he guessed he was near the stream they bathed in before making camp. He swiftly fumbled with his shirt buttons so he could pull it off and wrap it around her, then he gauged a way to balance her weight to carry her to the stream. He tried to support her neck and hold on to her dead weight as he stumbled around to find a path, frantic that she may bleed to death.

With the sporadic sounds of violence punching holes in the velvety air of the jungle night, he found the stream and propped her on the bank. Jerking the camera from his shirt around her, he pushed the button and dropped it on the ground before tossing his boots. He ripped a bloody piece of fabric and held it on a stick in the water to make sure there were no piranha, then dropped it into the stream when there were no bites.

The Jaguar almost slid down the bank with the Princess in his arms, easing her into about two feet of the shallow black water and settling at a little waterfall dammed up by rocks. Panic overcame him at her unresponsiveness to the cool stream.

Her too large, borrowed trousers were in tatters, ripped by both the jungle and her attackers. The belt was lost and now water tugged at the remains as they floated away. But her underclothes were still intact, proving their foul plans for her had not been realized. He could see a little better now by the light of the moon and stars.

Swiftly, he ran his hand over her neck and other vital sites where she'd be bleeding so freely, but he found no open wound. Maybe the blood wasn't all hers! She could be soaked in the spurting blood of the man the wild jaguar had killed on top of her.

The thought of her being bathed in that evil blood brought a growl through his clenched teeth and made him desperate to scrub her. He ran his fingers deftly through her hair to clean out dark stains and tangled foliage, holding her in his lap where he sat in the flowing waterfall that was washing gore from them both.

Why wasn't the cool water awakening her? Something was wrong!

A sickening sound of violence had cut short her scream before the jaguar eliminated her attacker. Peering closer, he examined a swollen area near her temple. He reached for a snagged piece of her trousers to rip off a piece of fabric, then dabbed it over her face, focusing on the dried blood under her nose and around her mouth and teeth.

"Wake up, Princess!" he whispered fiercely, then realized he was sobbing. "Wake up!" he tried to repeat past his swollen throat. It was absurd, but a fairy tale came to his mind, of Sleeping Beauty being awakened with a kiss from a handsome prince.

If only her handsome prince was handy! But the Jaguar was alone, and he was just the Plumber.

"Wake up, Princess!" he rasped again, shaking her a little. Gunfire was spurting not too far away, and his rifle was on the bank. He glanced at flashes in the darkness, groping in his mind for what to do. It was impossible to carry her and defend her with his rifle at the same time.

He tried slapping gently at her face with a threatening tone. "You know that dangerous kiss I bragged about? You're gonna miss it if you don't wake up. I mean it, Caroline, I can do it this time! You'd better wake up!"

Watching for any sign of consciousness in the limp young woman in his lap, he supported her neck in his palm. Strands of her hair were helpless ribbons at the mercy of the black current of the stream, and her arm floated palm-up. He choked back a desperate sob while an image of stars streaking toward the earth filled his mind, leaving the heavens black and desolate.

The banshee-like scream of a puma came from closer than he wanted to guess, followed by horrified recognition from its victim. The Jaguar blinked to see that the stars and moonlight above weren't really falling, but playfully dancing their sparkling reflections along the length of the water.

Like her. She's like a star reflecting light in the darkness, elusive, and boldly defying it.

Bursts of gunfire in the jungle shot down his flight of fancy. With an agonizing groan and a deep, ragged breath, the Jaguar positioned the Princess, so he cradled her pale, clean face, gazing into it with every bit of love he could imagine feeling and willing her to open her eyes before he made his next move.

She couldn't die here in this demonic pit that seemed to be forsaken by God Himself! Tears rolled down his face as he turned it to heaven. *What were You thinking? She doesn't belong here!*

But he'd no sooner asked it than he faced a question himself. *Weren't you the one wishing you could keep her here?*

With a frustrated sob, he shut out the violence that ripped the air. Relaxing, he replaced reality with the melody of the song he'd been composing on the guitar, "For Amanda." He let the notes fade into the haunting, distant strains of a waltz somewhere in his memory, perhaps from a ball in a fairy tale movie. The magical, shimmering starlight on the little stream caressed the sleeping beauty in his arms.

He closed his eyes and emptied his heart into his first kiss. When she began responding, he realized he'd awakened his Princess.

Chad shot his fist into a punch in the air when the Jaguar's camera went black. The Weaver shot back with a warning look as he monitored all camera views and snapped orders.

Patrick pulled Chad aside, listening sympathetically to his friend's whispered but heated accusations about the Jaguar. "It's surreal, impossible! I just—I feel like I'm bein' tricked or manipulated!"

He was still uncertain of what he'd seen from the positions of the Jaguar's movements. But he knew this above all else, something that shook him to the core—a very real jaguar had helped the human one find Caroline—or her bloody body.

Closing his eyes, he pushed his palms into the sockets against the image of her lying molested and bloody on the ground, pinned by a man being mauled by a jaguar, and the golden eyes of the cat staring into the face of the Jaguar. Minutes passed as he kept a vigil on his Rolex, pacing through the chaotic maneuvers via the body cameras on the team.

A gasp from the technician at the monitor for the Panther's camera brought Chad and Patrick rushing over. The Jaguar emerged from the dark jungle tree line, his hair dripping and wet camouflage trousers clinging. An M16 was slung across his bare shoulder. The Princess filled his arms and clasped her own around his neck. Fearlessly, he stepped into the clearing like he owned it and set her on her feet.

The wet-headed Princess donned his dripping shirt just past her hips. She was barelegged, barefoot, and shivering as she leaned on him. An enormous jaguar followed right behind them.

Chad was torn between relief at seeing Caroline and his shock of heated jealousy at the possessive way her beefed-up former boyfriend handled her. Something was different about the Jaguar's demeanor. Something new had happened between them, he was certain of it.

A red flush crept up his neck. After this, would she always be disappointed in the man she had back at home?

From the stand of ebony trunks of towering trees, a native man with a regal demeanor seemed to materialize and walk boldly toward the couple. The perimeter of the clearing exploded into a staccato of exclamations of surprise that gave way to an unearthly silence as he stopped in front of the couple and slid a covering from his shoulders. It was a wrap that bore the red and black geometric pattern of his tribe. Speaking first to the Jaguar and inclining his head to relay the message to the Princess, he ceremonially knelt on one knee and offered it to her.

The Panther moved close to record the interaction from his camera for the Weaver. Caroline listened to the Jaguar's translation when the visitor spoke. With his help, she came down to one knee on the level of the chieftain, reaching out to accept the gift with trembling arms. She looked dazed, otherworldly, leaning into her rescuer for support as he squatted down to his knees with his arm steadying her. With a small smile, she nodded at the native tribesman in respect and gratitude.

The Jaguar pulled her up and the tribal leader rose, raising decorated arms overhead and pointing. He reached into a pouch around his waist and unfolded a paper, gesturing to the sky and his heart. Someone on the Weaver's team in the nerve center was quick to translate the words as the native chief's voice swelled through the clearing like a testimony to friend and foe alike. He proclaimed that Jesus Saves, and men should pass along His light. He referred to Caroline as The Shining Woman.

Chad's hand went over his mouth to check a sob, and he heard gasps and sniffles behind him. His dad had been right. This was bigger than they knew, something that could only happen in the hands of God.

On screen from the Panther's body camera, the Jaguar helped Caroline pull the covering around her shoulders for warmth and more modesty. The chieftain nodded his satisfied approval before he and the Jaguar made hand contact that indicated a bond. Then the chieftain bowed farewell to Caroline before turning to melt into the dense foliage.

Not even the insects and birds breached the hushed silence that reigned during this drama. The big spotted wildcat strolled behind, watchful as the Jaguar carried the Princess to the Land Rovers, and the team cautiously backed up to the vehicles with rifles aimed at the perimeter. An enormous panther and a cougar appeared from out of the tangle of jungle making menacing, eerie sounds as they stalked the tree line. The undergrowth in the clearing came to life with movement. Snakes!

"Weaver, I hope you're recording this," the Panther gulped toward the camera fastened to his shirt. "If we ever make it outta here, I have to see this again!"

The men packed into the Land Rovers to follow evacuation protocol. The Panther started his engine to lead the convoy, while the Jaguar ordered Carlos behind the wheel with himself and the dazed Princess in the back of the second one.

Her movements were robotic. The Jaguar had to lead her and help her settle until he could return. Then he pulled out dry clothes for himself, speedily changing out of sight at the Panther's door while conferring with him about the precarious route to the main road.

On the ground beside the Jaguar's Rover, the Puma found the Glock and holster the Princess had once been armed with. He checked it out and handed it to the Jaguar as the leader strapped on weapons and collected ammo. Armed to the teeth, the team was ready as the last Rover pulled up to protect the rear of the convoy.

Just as their headlights sliced the darkness, a figure with raised hands left the trees to stand in the path. The Panther slammed on the brakes to keep from running him over and the Puma opened the passenger door, his rifle aimed and ready, listening as the young man identified himself in English as "Romeo" and asked to speak to the Jaguar.

Recognizing the code name, the Puma briskly searched the man while the Panther radioed the Weaver and the Jaguar. They ordered the newcomer into the passenger seat of the Jaguar's Rover, where Carlos had the wheel.

The Rovers sped off with no shots fired. The surreal scene disappeared behind them, and each man wondered how long the wild animals would hold their adversaries at bay.

Chapter Eighteen

Memories were like sunshine.
They warmed you up and left a pleasant glow,
but you couldn't hold onto them.
-Clare Vanderpool

The young man who piled in beside Carlos grinned broadly and introduced himself in good English. Holding out his hand, he piped, "I'm Dominic Vega. Recently nicknamed Romeo, at your service!" He glanced back, then whistled. "Great! I'm in the same armored vehicle as the prize everyone's after. What's next, do we take on the shrieking eels from the *Princess Bride*? Better hand me a weapon!"

The Panther's voice barked over the radio. "Jaguar—Weaver wants your camera back on immediately! He's waiting for your report on the status of the Princess."

The Jaguar was settling in as well as he could over the rough terrain that bounced the Rover. With his back to the front two rows of seats, he aimed his face over his shoulder. "I'm a little busy! I'll update him when I can and tell him I'll have to find another camera. I must've left mine by the stream."

He twisted to pass an extra M16 to the front, groaning at a jolt of the Rover that slammed his ribs into the seat. "Romeo, I assume you know this isn't for cowboys. You shoot when I tell you to, *comprendo*? Shrieking eels are only dangerous if you're in the water!"

The Panther came back on. "Jaguar! Chad Gregory is unleashed. He wants to know how his wife is doing, why she's only wearing your shirt, why you aren't allowing him access to her, and what happened at the stream when you got rid of the camera."

The Jaguar turned his face to the radio on the front dash and exploded. "Tell them she wasn't dressed for a room full of men analyzing monitor screens, so I gave her some dignity. I'm working on that status! You can tell Golden Boy this isn't Global and I'm the one in charge down here. He waits, or he gets nothin' at all!"

As soon as he spit it out, the Jaguar wished he could take it back. Beside him, the Princess made a pitiful little cry of dismay and shook violently as she clamped her hands over her ears.

He swallowed a stab of fear. She would distance herself from him if he disrespected the man she loved. His jealousy of the Prince caused him to abuse his power over the situation and hurl insults. What tipped the guy off that something unusual happened in the stream?

Yet, if he were Gregory, he'd be desperate to know Caroline's condition, too. He'd be throwing his weight around, or even the closest object in the room, if it would help him find out. He ground his teeth at having to bow to the Prince, then turned around and changed his tone. "Cancel that transmission, Panther. Convey to the Prince that I understand his concern and will report as soon as I can correctly assess her condition. I need a little time to get his wife calmed down. She's my top priority."

He sighed and whispered, "I'm sorry, Princess. That was way outta line—off the whole map, in fact. I'm—I'm beyond upset and stunned at what just happened. I don't have my bearings back yet, and I lost my manners in the adrenaline rush. Please don't hold my disrespectful outburst against me."

She sat staring out the back window, shell-shocked. His heart sank, wondering if he'd just blown everything. Grabbing her backpack, he pulled her clothes, socks, and underthings out, the same ones he helped Juliet put on the Princess when he rescued her from the *Puña* kidnappers. His new memories would always include the sight of her in the lovely sapphire cotton sweater and baby blue designer jeans.

Holding them to her arm now, he gently asked if she could dress by herself. She looked up with a bewildered expression.

She didn't recognize him.

The Jaguar's unsteady heart jumped into his throat at this bruised look of an encounter with horror. As he'd feared, she was in shock.

In the vague mist of light reaching them from the Rover's front seat dashboard, his hands felt their way into her pack again for her toiletry bag. He groped for the shape of the wide-toothed comb and the spritzer bottle of something that smelled like a fresh ocean breeze as it untangled her hair.

She allowed him to pull her shoulders to lean back into his chest, resting her cheek against his clean shirt. When he'd figured out how to comb through her damp hair without tugging, he whispered conversationally, "You need to get dressed, okay, Princess? I want you to meet my dad. What would he think of me bringing home Lady Godiva, huh? All those lectures about loose women, down the drain."

The Princess didn't respond. When the comb glided effortlessly through his long strokes, he returned it to the pretty bag. "If I hold the tribal chief's gift up around you like a curtain, can you get your things on alone? No one can see into the Rover windows back here."

She stared at him a few moments. Something inside him somersaulted, changing him irreversibly. What was it about her eyes that made him feel like he'd wandered into infinity with her?

A darkening spot under her temple was emphasized against her deathly pallor in the faint glow of dashboard gauges. Her tragic, blank expression drove him to the edge of desperation. He had to get her back!

First, she needed to feel secure. Being in her own clothes would be a step in that direction. Careful not to make a move she might perceive as threatening, he positioned her so her back was to him. Whispering encouragement as if she was a child, he held the chief's handwoven stole up to the height of her shoulders.

Her movements quaked against the fabric, but otherwise they were robotic. She squeezed her eyes closed to avoid the darkness through the windows, and he grimaced. She had become afraid of the dark, unable to face the terror of a black jungle inhabited by unleashed demons. It might take another shock to rock her out of this, but he'd seen it happen plenty of times.

When he heard the zip of her jeans, he lowered the drape and grabbed up the wet things, stuffing them in a recess in the corner behind him. He'd make sure she never saw them again.

Her pale profile and the misery on her face moved him past pity into a rage. Overcome with feelings of protectiveness and compassion, he wrapped his arm around her, pulling her to him with a hoarse whisper. "Are you hurt anywhere?"

Her breath started coming in shuddering gasps, and long tremors shook her body. He'd expected this wrenching reaction to trauma and held her tight like a swaddled baby. She was out of control, and his heart fell into a thousand shards as he waited out her release from terrified stress. He whispered over and over that she was safe now. He stroked her hair or rubbed her back with rhythmic, repetitive motions to give her a sense of security. Time seemed to stand still while more stars streaked from outer space to crash into earth.

Above her head and out of her sight, he had his own mini mew, a few seconds of blinding pain. Squeezing his eyes shut, he pushed his scar into the headrest of the seat he was leaning on so he could leave his arms around her. Then one of her favorite hymns came to mind, and he knew music would help ground her. He started humming the haunting, melancholy, almost medieval-sounding melody of "What Wondrous Love Is This."

The Jaguar hummed the first two verses before her sobs ceased. She wasn't shuddering as often. Her breathing became steady.

He crooned the words of the third and fourth verses to her.

"To God and to the Lamb I will sing, I will sing

To God and to the Lamb, I will sing.

To God and to the Lamb, Who is the great 'I AM'

While millions join the theme, I will sing, I will sing

While millions join the theme, I will sing.

And when from death I'm free, I'll sing on, I'll sing on

And when from death I'm free, I'll sing on.

And when from death I'm free, I'll sing and joyful be

And through eternity, I'll sing on, I'll sing on,

And through eternity, I'll sing on."

"I want everyone to sing that hymn at my funeral," she whispered. "I hope they'll be glad for me and celebrate a life lived well, not a tragedy."

"No tragedies or funerals for you yet, Princess."

A hiccup escaped, and she clapped her hand to her mouth. "Pardon me," she whispered automatically, then tried to stifle a giggle.

He snickered, charmed by her genteel mannerisms, cupping her face to raise her head up and see if she was herself again. She hadn't lost the deep, soul-wounded look, but Caroline was back in there.

The length of their searching silence became littered with every emotion he had for her across his face, but in the end, he allowed only friendship to remain. He was being honest, just as he had been in the jungle when they left her drawings for the wandering tribe. If this mission had taught him anything, it was that a rare rapport had always been the core of their relationship. He now knew she had treasured and missed it. There was a time when she even considered settling for it rather than what she wanted with her prince, because it was that good.

To test whether she saw that he finally understood, he unbuttoned the lower part of his shirt, watching a flicker he couldn't read flash in her eyes. He never took his gaze from hers as he pulled up the freed shirt tail to wipe her wet face. "I'll take care of your tears, but I'm not wiping your nose," he teased with mock solemnity. "That's what husbands sign up for."

She chuckled, pulling back. In an instant, he missed her, but he tossed her a lopsided smile while reaching for the nearly depleted roll of toilet paper in her open pack so she could blow her nose.

There it was. It lit up his world. The one and only smile. But, like all incredible sensations, it was spectacularly fleeting. He wondered if her Prince was so used to being bathed in that smile that it wasn't all that special to him anymore.

With despair now dissipated, she tried to sit up and fluff the fringe of her bangs. "I've made a spectacle of myself. You're so much larger than life, so strong and in control, while I handle things like a girl."

He chortled and kept his voice low and soothing. "Now who's underestimating herself and overestimating me? I'm just blessed that I had the arms you could trust to crash in. Do you understand what I'm trying to say, Princess?"

Reading one another's eyes again, she nodded. Seeing relief there, he wondered how he could ache with loss and still feel a rush of joy all at once.

He dreaded his next words, but the Weaver was waiting. "I know it's too soon, but I have to give the Weaver a report. Do you remember anything about what happened tonight? Your husband needs assurance you're unhurt. I have the rescue on camera. A jaguar saved your life by killing the men who took you."

She winced and rubbed her forehead with both hands. "The same jaguar who guarded us out of the woods from the stream?"

"Yes."

"I remember that the four men from the village found me before I could get under the Rover. Three dragged me away." The wild look came back into her eyes as they darted to the dark window. "I can't—I don't want to remember."

She started gulping deep breaths and her hands flew to her throat. He recognized the onset of a panic attack and grasped her hands away with soothing whispers. "It's okay. You don't have to remember. I'll handle it."

Sending furtive glances around at the dark windows, the Princess clenched his hand with a death grip that made him wince. With his free hand, he groped around in the packs to find a body camera. Then he turned half around to the front with a grunt of frustration. "Carlos, can you get the Panther? I can't locate a camera and I'm climbing over the seat for the radio."

He squeezed her fingers reassuringly in his palm. "You're okay here. I'll be right back, I promise. You can lie down or keep hold of my hand."

She let go of his hand and leaned back on the packs against the seat. She blew her nose while Carlos hailed the Rover in front of them. The Jaguar climbed over the back seat and adjusted to the cramped position for a man his size.

Her hand was soon on his shoulder. "I can't—I can't close my eyes. Not without you!"

His heart surged with joy that she needed him but ached at the reason. He draped his arm back over the seat and gave her his most reassuring look as she latched onto it. "I've got you. I promise. But you may want to cover your ears."

Carlos handed the Jaguar the coiled cord to the dash radio as the Panther said, "Panther here. Is the drowned cat still hissing? Over."

The Jaguar inhaled the refreshing scent of Caroline's hair conditioner on his hand as he pushed a button and smirked. "Negative. Jaguars like to swim, remember? It's a great place to hunt for dinner. Over."

A guffaw blurted through the radio. The Jaguar said, "Report a minor mew to the doctor since leaving the clearing, no medication, still on duty. I owe you for being my buffering translator again. Time for me to study my manual on manners before my next radio transmission with the Prince. Offer an olive branch at the next stop. Over."

"Affirmative. I bit my lip to keep from saying it your way, but unlike you, I'd lose my job. Then where would I be? Few guys get to discover and train their own boss. The Puma and I have a vested interest in you, and our constant over-arching mission is to make you look great. Over."

Staring off into the night, the Jaguar envisioned the videos he'd seen of his rescue from a devastated island beach. The Panther and Puma had been underlings on an assignment, following a tip about a smuggled shipment disguised on a plane carrying hurricane relief aid workers. That tip never panned out, but they soon realized it was not the real mission.

The Jaguar was resurrected. They liked to say God arranged the misleading information, so they'd find him.

"Yeah, well, that makes no sense to me. In fact, it's downright crazy. I'm only thirty-three, don't even know who I am, and you trust me with your lives. Over."

The Panther's voice lost all traces of teasing. "In case you missed it, we're vindicated by tonight—the pinnacle of your career. You have no room for doubt or excuses anymore, Jaguar, and you must accept the mantle of a reluctant hero. This has just propelled you into mythological status, bigger than your dad or the Weaver ever were. The Puma and I believe you were saved for such a time as this, to quote the biblical expression. Forgive me if I overstep here, but I think you'd have wanted to survive Montserrat if only to have lived the past week. Over."

As he stared through the window into the night, the Jaguar snorted, wondering what could matter more than this mission for the rest of his life. "Affirmative. You got me. Over."

"Panther requests a private conversation at the next stop. Over."

The Jaguar pursed his lips. Time to stop the chit-chat like a bunch of girls at a sleepover. "Granted. Convey to Weaver that the Princess was in shock and had a crash landing, but she's calm and dry now. She's not emotionally capable of questioning. Assure him I tried, but she had a panic attack. Relay to the Prince his Princess is roughed up with some minor injuries we'll attend to when we have some light and a first aid kit. She needs attention for a blow to her cheek and temple that made her black out for quite a while, though it was a mercy. What belongs to the Prince still belongs to him."

He took a deep breath, playing out the rescue in his mind. "She was so slippery with blood that I couldn't carry her safely until I wrapped my shirt around her after the attack. Hers was torn too badly to stay on. I removed the camera so it wouldn't get lost in the stream, and now I can't get my hands on one until we stop. Over."

The convoy suddenly turned onto a smooth road where moonlight lit the ribbon of pavement into the unpredictable distance. He looked around for pursuing lights and movement, but only the third Rover's headlights were behind them. He checked on the Princess and whispered for her to sleep while she could. She obediently snuggled further down.

The Panther finally radioed back after reporting to the Weaver. "Roger. Identify the source of so much blood. Over."

The Jaguar pursed his lips, staring out into the darkness again. "The crushed skull and torn throat of her attacker. Over."

The Princess whimpered in despair. He rubbed her shoulder reassuringly while he waited on the Panther to confer with the Weaver.

"Roger. Report what happened to the assailants. Over."

The Princess moaned and let go of his arm to cover her ears. He kept a light touch on her shoulder, rubbing up and down with the back of his knuckles and trying to keep his voice directed away from her, low but clear. "The Princess says there were four at the Rover, the men from the nearby village who detained us earlier in the day. You have them on camera to identify. I don't know what happened to the fourth one, but I saw three dragging her to the jungle. One of the three attackers was killed by a giant bushmaster which I followed as I tracked her. Then a jaguar came to hunt with me, and I shot and wounded a second man, who had her forearms pinned beside her head. The jaguar killed the man on top of her—the same guy she shot earlier in the village. I covered her when I saw the wounded accomplice raise his rifle. He shot point blank at the jaguar, and I heard the animal take the bullets. It turned and leaped to his throat, brushing against my back. Over."

While he waited, Romeo looked back at him, shaking his head in wonder. "Your fate is sealed, man! The legend of the Jaguar just became a fact, with eyewitnesses from two cartels, guerillas they hired, at least one Amazon tribe, and who knows who else. When they tell how they watched a real jaguar, panther, puma, and even snakes and bats follow you, doing your killing for you, your job will be a breeze from now on. You must play video games or fall in love with a woman to get any challenges in your life."

The Jaguar smirked and sighed. *Done.*

He pushed away the memory of kissing his Princess and replaced it with images from Mario games, with a relentlessly bright, friendly tune accompanying the Plumber in his heroic efforts to rescue Princess Peach. He'd just heard the sound that accompanied a jump when the radio sparked to life again.

"Roger. Was it the same jaguar who circled and looked you in the eye on your camera? The Weaver wants confirmation that you realize the cat had no wounds or blood on him to collaborate your report of the two kills. Over."

"Affirmative. I have no explanation. After the cat looked at me, he went into the jungle as if pointing the way for me to the stream, and I followed. Once I discovered the Princess wasn't the source of the bleeding and she regained consciousness in the cool water, he appeared again to lead us out to the clearing. She was in shock, too unsteady to walk. But I didn't see the need to fear taking gunfire, and the Chief of the tribe didn't, either. He came out with a remarkable story and tribute to the Princess that would take too long to relay here, so that report will follow later. That's my story and I'm stickin' to it. Over."

He looked out into the darkness as he waited. The Weaver didn't doubt him. This wasn't the first time there was no logical explanation for sequences in missions. It was just the most bizarre one. He was being grilled for the classified records.

"Roger. Weaver wants an account of why you spent valuable time at the stream instead of rushing the Princess to the camp for medical help. Over."

The Jaguar hesitated, drumming his fingers on the seat. He brought his hand back to his mouth with the radio in it, inhaling the lingering fresh scent of Caroline's hair. "I heard an assailant hit her as she screamed for me, and she was unconscious moments later when I arrived on the scene. Her pulse was faint, and there was so much blood that I feared it was hers. The camp was taking fire, so

I couldn't carry her and defend her all at once. I decided the best emergency care was to wash her off and find the wound before she bled to death. Remind the Weaver that when I can't stick to his path, this cat walks alone. Over."

While vague enough for wiggle room, this report made enough sense of the facts that Weaver wouldn't question him. He'd also just reminded the Weaver that there were no repercussions. A little smile of deep satisfaction played on his mouth, a corner twitching with a treasured memory. It wouldn't be in his report.

"Copy that. Weaver is sending a special team to the compound to handle trouble over the Princess and Romeo and Juliet. Transmissions and ground sources report hasty movement in that direction. Your father is prepared, and the troops are en route. The Fly will divert from his mission for *Puña* and land with Juliet. Confirm that you understand the new plan. Over."

The Jaguar lost the contented smile and sat up, rigid. He locked eyes with Romeo, who turned back to him in excitement. "Affirmative. Who is the special team? Over."

He waited on the transmission lag, addressing a hopeful Romeo. "You know yourself that things go wrong. The Fly won't risk her life landing into a hotbed of conflict, but your father will kill her, and her's will aim for you. Here's where you prove yourself, Romeo. You betray us, and I promise you this will be another Shakespearean tragedy."

The Panther's voice broke in. "The special team is led by Ben Grayson, brother-in-law to the Princess, with classified credentials. Two others are former Mossad agents, her personal bodyguard and a female handpicked by Grayson. The fourth is an ex-Special Forces bodyguard who now works for the man she was mistaken for, the Prince's grandfather. Over."

The Jaguar mulled over these various backgrounds and considered how they'd mesh into a coherent unity. "Roger. Identify who's ultimately in charge of this motley crew. Over."

He waited and chewed his lip, scenarios playing through his head. *What a mess.*

"Jaguar, three agencies are involved. We're the fourth, and the special team is fifth, classified under the Weaver. Ben Grayson was never here. After the party we just walked out of, Weaver is approved by the agencies to call all the shots, meaning they are desperate now and in over their heads. Follow the standard protocol of authority. Over."

The Weaver, my dad, then me. But now Ben Grayson will be a wild card for the Prince's interests, and I've got what amounts to two more Gregory family members to protect.

"Roger that. Has the Weaver considered letting the cartels duel in their own O.K. Corral over Romeo and Juliet? He should send me to the hacienda with the Princess to keep her out of this family feud. She's got no business there. No one would know her location. Over."

He shifted to stretch long muscles, anxious to stay away from the Chavarria compound. The Panther's deep voice came back over the radio.

"Affirmative. It was considered, but Gregory wants his wife with her bodyguard and brother-in-law. Besides, the only way Weaver can coordinate Grayson's special team and all agencies on the ground is to focus on one location, at the compound. You've got Romeo, and the agency he's working with only fights where their asset is. Left on your own, you'd only have him and your exhausted team to fend off cartel members who hunt him. Over."

The Jaguar closed his eyes and scratched his forehead. *Touché, Prince. Separate me and Caroline with your strongmen, if you think she's tempted. If I thought for a second that she'd cheat on you, it would be a total turnoff. I want her fair and square, all mine, never to return to you. All it would take is for you to commit adultery or die, and neither option is a stretch. If you weren't scared out of your mind, you'd trust me to call the shots down here.*

With an exaggerated sigh of resignation, he spoke into the metal in his hand. "Roger that. Respectfully request reconsideration of the option and notification of any changes of heart. Over and out."

He handed the radio to the front, telling Carlos he would try to lie down and rest. Carlos lifted the metal radio case to his nose with the hand that wasn't on the wheel, inhaling the lingering scent of the Princess' hair. Romeo grabbed it from him, sniffing.

The Princess was asleep, physically and emotionally spent. The Jaguar didn't have to be strong for her now, so he put his head against the seat and let the full impact of what had happened sink in. Tidal waves of emotion crashed and ebbed inside him. Gratitude gushed from his heart and tears burned his eyes with silent thanks to God for sparing her the worst that could've happened.

He was overtired, thinking with his heart and instincts instead of logic, but he must sort some things out before he could rest. Squeezing his tear-dampened eyelashes tight, he prayed the first thing that came to his mind—that the consequences of his forbidden kiss in the stream only fell on him. He'd warned her he'd do it if it meant getting her home. It was reckless, but it was his last idea for how to awaken her. Sure, it sprang from fairy tales. But wasn't that irrelevant in a place where impossible things happened every day?

Two days into this mission to rescue the Princess, he weighed the risks to his heart. Then, he'd deliberately chosen to live every ephemeral second with her. There were only two outcomes for his emotions once she was gone, anyway. He chose the pain of bittersweet memories rather than the regret of missed opportunity.

Opening his eyes, he let his gaze roam over her in the dim glow from the gauges on the front dashboard. The Princess was much the same as his mind was allowing him to recall, only better with the passage of time. She'd grown womanly, with soft curves, despite the weight loss since her rescue. She'd be—almost thirty?

A deep ache he couldn't describe left him helpless. He longed for a way to bottle this peaceful, precious, elusive moment, along with so many other moments of powerful memories packed into the last week. Was it the aspect of living on the edge that made everything with Caroline so vivid, or was she this remarkable on an ordinary day on her island?

Perhaps he would take out bottled moments for a long time, wallowing in them the way his team members did in sad songs. He grinned ruefully. Maybe he'd have to sing a few country songs for a change, laments about heartbreak and the one that got away.

But no, that wouldn't work because he didn't touch alcohol, and country singers claimed the secret behind the best country and western songs was booze, broads, and blues. The people that hang out in Honky Tonks are lonely. To please them, the song had to make unhappy people keep crying. It had to make even the ones who don't drink buy a case of beer. Unfortunately, the pleasure in the song was its power to keep them trapped in a destructive cycle.

If there was anything he knew about life, it was that pain and loss were tools God used to help people mature and learn to trust Him. Running from problems and trying to numb the thinking process was not a step forward, and it could do a lot of damage where you were at.

He sighed, peering through the shadows over her sleeping face. The Princess wasn't just the wife of a wealthy man who didn't make idle threats. She was a mother to three impressive, adorable young children who needed her. She seemed to be a notable professional artist, though she may ride on the wings of her famous uncle for that honor. He'd have to look up her work when this mission was over. But one thing was certain, she was crucial to the island she would inherit someday. She had an important life a world away, a different mission field. She belonged there, but he didn't. He belonged here—for now.

This was God's will for him. Coveting another man's wife was not.

Romeo was right a little while ago, but he didn't know half. The tribal chief had revealed their prayers for the Princess—the Shining Woman—and in answering in such a miraculous way, God had proven and perhaps renewed his call to a young man named Chris Shepherd, now Christian Chavarria. The Jaguar.

A chosen wild jaguar in the Amazon had risen to an immediate call from his Creator to save the Princess, while the man known as the Jaguar, also called by his Creator, took over the human side of her rescue. He would become legendary, all right. There was no escape for him to another life for at least five more years, no way to ignore miracles—no way to run from God.

People in the States were always surprised and uncomfortable at the accounts of missionaries for whom miracles were a part of life in remote places. Perhaps only those in the jungle tonight would ever believe what happened to the Princess.

From his perspective, there was no greater miracle in this rescue mission than that he lived out a gripping prophetic situation he used to sing about while playing his guitar. It was something so classified that it would never be revealed to the world. It was something exclusively his own, something even the internationally proclaimed golden boy, Chad Gregory, didn't have.

But she'd never forget, and neither would the Jaguar. He'd been with Caroline Painter when the stars were falling.

Chapter Nineteen

Life is all memory except for the one present moment
that goes by so quick you can hardly catch it going.
-Tennessee Williams

Chad Gregory paced like a caged animal in front of the dark wall of windows in his office. Miraculously, his wife was safe. "That's all that matters," he muttered to himself.

He tried to relax with the view he'd loved all his life. A vast array of stars spanned the night sky over the Atlantic. But another sight muscled its way back into his mind's eye, taunting him like a bully. He pressed the heel of his palms into his eye sockets. He'd never be able to erase the memory of watching Caroline being hauled into a dark jungle, blood streaming from her nose, screaming for the Jaguar.

Even horrific things become part of the past. But he'd never be the same, and she certainly wouldn't. The Jaguar reported that Caroline was suffering from emotional shock. Would she need counseling?

The unfolding rescue and escape weren't the first miracles the Weaver's team had seen in the Jaguar's missions, but he could tell it was the big daddy of them all. The mighty Weaver himself had been so shaken that he had to turn and walk away with his face in his hands.

How he kept up with all the threads of this was beyond Chad. Little wonder he was the best in the world to weave the traps that catch the bad guys. He was brilliantly pulling the strands of a tapestry together, juggling competing agencies like an ambassador, designating what he couldn't handle to his assistant and team. Yet under all this pressure, Chad had never heard him use a curse word or let his temper explode. He could learn a lot about temperament from this man, but he didn't plan to tag along behind a guy that followed trouble on the scale of stuff in the Book of Revelation.

Too tense to stand still, Chad stretched both hands behind his neck. He longed to pray, but he couldn't sort the things flooding his mind. Out loud, he said, "You know my heart. Show me how to have Your mind, to be praying in Your will instead of my confusion."

A physical and mental fatigue washed over him, and he dropped his arms to cross them in front of himself. When he looked back at the expected view of the island, he found that he'd moved into enough light from the lamps to see himself and his office reflected in the window like a mirror.

Startled, he straightened his back and stood staring. Moments passed as he drank in the masculine décor of his workspace behind him, which exuded confidence and a sense of power. Then he isolated his silhouette against the space. As if analyzing a stranger, he noticed that despite losing a little weight the past few days, he still cut a fit profile many men would envy.

Backlit by the glow in the room, his facial features were subdued by soft shadows that hid details. He despised false modesty and never denied he was handsome. But he learned long ago to be nonchalant about his looks and live with both the perks and the adverse issues they brought into his life.

His eyes scanned the entirety of his reflected image again. Satisfaction and pride began swelling in his chest like a warm rush. He welcomed the renewed sense of worthiness. His self-respect was in tatters and his confidence battered. It would feel good to feel good again.

But in the next instant, he realized his looks were partly what had drawn Isabelle to lure him. And not just Isabelle, but other women whose attentions he'd deflected his whole life. They cared nothing for who he was inside. The attractive package and the chance for notoriety was all they desired.

As for the power represented in the Gregory Global office behind him, wasn't it also what had drawn the wrong attention to those who wanted to raid Global? His looks, his company, his whole identity was vulnerable, easily and irrevocably spoiled, and the shock of understanding left him trembling.

There was a knock on the office door and Patrick's muffled voice called from the other side. "Chad, we've got somethin' to eat. Open up, man."

Still shaken, Chad turned away from his reflection and went to the door. His pastor and brother-in-law stood waiting with two trays that emitted an enticing aroma he'd never been able to resist. He gestured to invite them in.

"I'm not goin' to ask whether you're okay," began Pastor Payne. "You're not. But I'm a good listener if you'd like to talk."

They settled the trays on a low sofa table, peeling back lids on containers of some homemade vegetable soup and the foil around some buttered and seasoned bread. Maggie Jane had sent a cousin over with the meal made for him and asked the security guards to bring it up.

Chad's eyes swam. He wiped them with the back of his hand. Since he was a boy, she'd known just the right time to come through with his favorite comfort food. Nobody made vegetable soup like Maggie Jane, not even when they used her basic recipe. Maybe her success was the love and prayers she put into it.

The pastor quickly asked the Lord to bless both the meal and the person who sent it. The three of them took exploratory sips of their broth to check the temperature, then dug in with soup spoons.

After making a groan of appreciation and swallowing a hearty bite of bread, Pastor Payne broke the comfortable silence. "I remember a dark stretch of hours about five years ago, when I prayed with your families at the Whitehaven shelter during the hurricane. What a night!"

He shook his head, looking off into the night sky through the windows and remembering. "I saw pity in some people's eyes, a look that said we were wastin' our breath. They'd written you off and given up hope, just goin' through the motions of prayin' with us."

Patrick grunted and wiped his mouth with a paper napkin. "We didn't know if we'd make it, either, but I had to believe God wouldn't wipe out my home, most of my family, and my best friends all in one fell swoop."

Pastor Payne looked each of them in the eye in turn. "Can you honestly say today that you're the worse for that experience?"

The young men were silent as they considered the question. Chad studied the grain pattern on the hardwood floor, hands clasped between his spread knees. "In some ways, I feel the worse for it. Like when I remember the happy memories of things that were destroyed, a lost era of innocence on the island, things I'll only be able to show my kids in old photos. The financial losses and new security limitations for visitors to Painter Place seem like such a waste. But other things came to light, too, treasures that would have remained buried. I admit, even as I suffered, my faith and resolve grew by leaps and bounds."

He sniffed and shook his head, leaning back in the sofa. "But that was a storm, Preacher, an impersonal force at work. Caroline's kidnapping was at the hands of evil men, old grudges, revenge, money, power, and corruption. How can we ever be better for this? And my marriage—how in the world will I repair the damage? For as long as I can remember, I resolved to be the perfect husband.

Caroline would have nothing to regret and a million things to be thankful for. But now I've created a sense of competition. She'll wonder how often I have other women on my mind, even when I'm with her, when I'm—holding her."

He looked away and swallowed before saying tightly, "Tonight, those men almost raped the love of my life. She'd have endured that horror knowin' that their thoughts were not so different from where I'd been with Isabelle. I just wouldn't have had to force my way."

His sentence shattered into empty hands that now covered his face. After a heavy silence, he heard Patrick's sniff. He lowered his hands when he heard his brother-in-law confessing to Pastor Payne that he'd gone through something similar with a glamorous vacationing customer. She noticed him in the Castaway, when she was there having dinner with the middle-aged boyfriend she was traveling with. She began dropping by alone to eat lunch while the man was fishing or golfing, suggesting places to meet alone.

Now he turned to Chad with a pained look and gulped. "What she did repelled me, but it was flattering to be chased. The things she wore, the teasing, it sent my mind to places it shouldn't have been. I was ashamed to confide in you or Joey. You've always been so committed, the guy who didn't slip. I wanted to measure up to you."

Chad blurted that it wasn't hard to measure up to a man who was now flat on his face, and that he was glad Patrick was spared the agony of having Natalie and others find out. At least fifteen people knew about Isabella, including Caroline.

Patrick admitted that watching Chad face the humiliation of being caught made him wonder if he had to tell Natalie, but he didn't want to hurt her and create suspicion or mistrust in their relationship.

Pastor Payne listened to their questions before discussing the line between a temptation and committing a sin. He talked about knowing the time to flee instead of sticking around to fight it. He opened the Bible on Chad's sofa table to point out some verses about overcoming moral struggles and failures, remaining righteous when a line in the sand seemed blurred, and never letting a weakness become exploited by their enemy.

"I've heard about times when you two were single and used to hold one another accountable for your thoughts and actions," the pastor said. "I know from men's Bible Study group meetings that both your dads taught you the verse about how iron sharpens iron, and you've watched them live it out together. As men, you understand what happens in your minds in a way that women can't."

He chuckled before sobering again. "Your wives are smarter than you, fellas, so never underestimate them. But they're wired to need security, and they have every right to expect it. You're the ones who asked them to give up every other man and make a life with you. Spare them hurtful specifics about temptations but be open to conviction from the Holy Spirit about when it's appropriate to confess struggles."

The Jaguar groggily awakened at the sensation of slowing down. He sighed in contentment, loathe to move. Every breath with the Princess was like sand through an hourglass, inevitably depleting to emptiness.

He braced her while the Rover pulled onto a trail off the main road. Barely discernable lashes fanned onto her face, stirring a new memory. This one was free of the blinding pain but was accompanied by a gripping sweetness. He remembered her face framed by indigo sky. Music floated from a distance as they strolled down a pier lined with colorful paper lanterns. The sound of endless pounding surf engulfed them, and the breeze was scented with salt air. Her home?

The rough terrain that the Rover was mastering also jarred her against him. Disoriented, she brought her hand up to the swollen red spot on her cheekbone.

The convoy slowed, then stopped. She needed help to slide to the back of the Rover where the Panther opened the door and reached into a compartment for a first aid kit. The Panther popped open the kit between himself and the Jaguar who deftly examined bruises and scratches on her ankles and feet. "Check on her cheek and temple and see if her eyes can follow your hand. I don't want her falling into the latrine."

The Panther cupped her face to study the bruise. She tried to follow his directions while cringing at the Jaguar's efforts to dab ointment on some scratches. He swiftly bandaged some spots and reached for his backpack, grabbing a pair of his thick socks and pulling them on her feet. He turned to address the Panther. "She'll need the extra cushion if we're forced to run through the jungle. Can she focus?"

"So far. Let's see what happens when she stands."

He watched the Jaguar lace her boots, then they both helped her up. She leaned on them. When she was steady, they guarded her to go into the area they designated for a latrine.

The rest of the team gathered with flashlights in a clearing just large enough for the vehicles and a shed they unveiled from camouflage netting. Some men were bleary-eyed. Soap and water splashed as everyone cleaned their faces and hands. Several balls of the C4 were ignited to heat coffee all around.

Caroline gritted her teeth as the Jaguar lifted her to sit in the Rover's open hatch, and Romeo asked permission to approach them. "My girlfriend's a nurse, like a physician's assistant, if her dad would let her work. She's taught me some things for when I'm out—uh, in the field."

He glanced at the Jaguar and a flash of understanding passed between them. He asked if he might check her shoulder, and with a few motions that made her bite her lip, he diagnosed strained muscles and bruised ribs.

The Jaguar asked her if there were any places covered by her clothes that needed attention before they could get her to a doctor, and she reported burning streaks on her back. He nimbly climbed in behind her, discreetly rolling up her sweater. The flashlight revealed some angry red scratches that never bled, and he took packets of ointment that Romeo tore open to swab on the wounds.

As he rolled down her sweater, he asked if she was allergic to any medications. She shrugged and shook her head. He crawled to sit beside her and cleaned off his hands with a disinfectant wipe, directing Romeo to hand him some packets from the kit. He studied them, then put them into her hand and told her to take one dose and keep the rest in her pocket. "This is what the Panther gave you for pain the first night you woke up with us, with some magic added to help relax those stiff muscles."

They waved off her efforts to thank them. She moved easier on her own to get coffee and a trail mix bar but wrinkled her nose at the dose of pain reliever. When the Jaguar turned his head, she only took one from the packet, washing down the half-dose before stashing the rest in her jeans pocket.

The Panther pulled the Jaguar to the side while he chugged his cup of coffee. The team gassed up the Land Rovers and re-stocked ammo in the back.

"I think the Weaver left the radio open because he wanted me to overhear something. He's closely connected to the Princess—not sure if it's with her family or through Global. He doesn't want her caught in the line of fire when we break through into the compound. But the agency aiding Romeo is all over Weaver to deliver him so they can leave. It's the only way he could keep command of the whole operation. I think he wants you to go rogue and keep her safe until the showdown is over." He shifted his weight and glanced at the efforts of the team. "Obviously, I never overheard his private conversation or told you this, and I'm not responsible for what you do with the information."

The Jaguar stared at him and let out a low whistle. Then a light came on in his eyes. "Wait—where's he retiring? Wasn't it a sleepy little Southern coastal town?"

"Yeah, in South Carolina. The briefing we got as we ran out the door was that the kidnapping victim was the wife of Chad Gregory of Gregory Global. Global's main headquarters is in Whitehaven, South Carolina."

The Jaguar joined him to repeat the name of the state in unison before he added, "So, do we hunker down here and hope the cartels miss clues on the road about the trail, or make a run for the hacienda?"

He waited for the Panther's answer as he checked his watch and looked for the Princess. She'd washed her face and brushed her teeth. A healthier color bloomed across her features and she brushed her hair before stashing items from freshening up into her nearly empty pack. She grimaced as she stretched stiff muscles, eyeing the dark perimeter of the clearing and keeping her distance from it.

The Panther kept his voice low. "This supply station is indefensible if they stumble onto us here. I recommend the hacienda when the cat walks alone. You have the authority for this, based on circumstances. Like perhaps, the injured condition of the Princess?"

The suggestion lingered in the air between them like a conspiracy. "I need to think it through."

"I'll check in with the base to let them know we've refueled and see if we can extend that olive branch to the Prince. Permission to speak freely?"

"I know what's on your mind."

"You and the Princess have something rare, something higher than romance. It takes a special man to bear being the champion who doesn't get the girl. This place would destroy her—it still might. In time, you'll mew with the memory of getting over her."

He lightly slapped his boss on the back and went to escort the Princess to the radio in his Land Rover. The Jaguar watched her face light up at the prospect of speaking to her Prince.

His friend was wrong about only one thing. He might mew and remember having peace in accepting God's will for his life, but not getting over Caroline Painter. It never happened.

Caroline pushed one of her sore shoulder muscles against the cool metal of the Land Rover's door, improvising the benefit of an ice pack. The Panther updated the Weaver, then told him the Jaguar wanted the Prince and Princess to have a minute to connect. Taking the radio in her hand, she waited for Chad's languid drawl.

"Hi, beautiful! I hear you're gettin' in touch with your wild side. Can you hang out with the monkeys a little longer?"

She took a haggard breath and quipped, "Yeah, uh—it's a zoo down here, all right."

He chuckled. "Are you savin' your heart for me?"

With her free hand, Caroline pushed her bangs off her forehead. The pain medicine kicked in with a rush, and this question was more complicated than it used to be. In fact, she didn't want to think about it.

"Just like I promised," she rasped from memory.

His exhale sounded breathy over the speaker. "Granddad called in the cavalry. Azariah and Ben are on their way, maybe in the sky over you by now. Look up."

Looking skyward, she winced from sore neck muscles, then gazed at the infinity of layer upon layer of stars. "You know what? I don't see them yet, but I see somethin' else. The Southern Cross."

"Seriously? Maybe we can see it together. I'm flyin' down to get you when the dust settles. You should be out of danger soon."

The night sky always made her feel tiny, insignificant, but never more so than now. How many people had looked up to the moon and the stars since Creation, wondering what difference it would make that they even existed? She was dust in the wind, destined to go unnoticed in the passage of time. Her chest tightened, and she gulped for a breath.

"Care?"

"I've learned not to look too far ahead," she managed in a strangled voice. A sudden spring of tears slipped down her cheeks. "I just make it to the next minute, then the next." She put a hand over her trembling lips.

"Little wonder, after what you've been through. Listen, Care, put the Jaguar on. You stay close so I can say goodbye, okay?"

The Jaguar was right behind her and took the radio from her hand. But he backed away to get out of earshot. "It's the Jaguar."

"Straight up, how is she? Over."

The Jaguar's jaw flexed, wondering if this unexpected conversation would become a confrontation. "Improving after an impressive meltdown, but she's still emotionally shaky. She was in shock and can't talk about what happened. We treated her for minor injuries from fighting back, like muscle strains, bruising, and scratches. A blow to her face knocked her out cold for a while and we're observing her. I just gave her a dose of pain reliever with some punch to it to make her more comfortable. She's now afraid of the dark, but we'll work on that. Over."

He glanced sidelong at the progress of the team's preparations for the next leg of their journey, waiting for a challenge in the Prince's deep voice and slow Southern accent.

"Roger. That new fear—you can cure it? Over."

"Roger that, given time and the right conditions. Over."

"We're runnin' outta time, and I don't like the conditions. But I'd appreciate her not comin' home with it. I know you'll do the best you can for her, and I know why. May I say goodbye now? Over."

The Jaguar didn't know how to respond, so he went to the Princess and handed her the radio, then turned to check on the status of the convoy. When he'd made the round, she'd finished her goodbye. He was all orders for her to be armed and made her put on a Kevlar vest. Being mindful of her injuries, he tried to hide how much he enjoyed helping her with the returned Glock, holster, and thigh strap for a new knife with a wicked blade.

"So, since I sank my other knife into a guerilla, I've graduated to a big girl knife now?" she quipped.

Startled, he looked up. "Is that what happened to the fourth man?"

She squeezed her eyes shut and nodded, then gulped a deep breath. Her eyes glistened with unshed tears when she turned them to him and tried to breathe normally.

He elected to go for humor. With a grim smile, he replied, "Yeah, you did well with the kindergarten knife we had for peeling fruit. With this new one, even if you stab like a girl, you'll do a man's work."

A spontaneous grin lit her face despite the subject, and he gave the knife strap a reassuring pat. Then he assisted her into the passenger seat of his Rover. Reaching for his M16, he settled it on her side at the console. "It's here in my reach, but you know how to use it if I'm—incapacitated. Don't hesitate."

He turned to tell Romeo to stuff extra rounds into his ammo vest and stationed him in the seat behind her. Carlos and another guard would get some sleep in the back of the last Rover, and the Panther would sleep as the Puma led the team in the first Rover.

While the convoy crawled through the black tunnel formed by the tree canopy over the trail, Caroline leaned in, putting a distance between herself and the fathomless darkness through the windows. The view ahead reminded her of a horror movie, where unsuspecting and amazingly helpless people followed an eerie path lined with grotesque trees that reached for them like menacing arms.

She lowered her gaze to the sanity of the glowing gauges on the dash, then became distracted by the muscles knotting in the Jaguar's arms as he wrestled the steering wheel to conquer the rough terrain. Her head felt light and tension in her muscles eased.

Once they pulled onto the smoother main road, the Jaguar reached into a slot in the door with his left hand and passed something over the console to her. She shot a surprised look up from the gift to his impish grin. "I hear this stimulates a remarkable recovery in women. Do you believe in magic?"

She examined the package in the soft light of the dashboard gauges. The brand markings were like the chocolate that the Puma had given her the day they were stranded in the cabin. She'd been too upset then to consider the wrapper, but this one was a clear yellow gold that reminded her of sunflowers. Elegant lettering officially proclaimed the word "Chavarria."

The logo was a stamp like an engraving. She squinted in the dimness to see that the image was a man harvesting a plant. Putting it up to her nose, she inhaled. Dark chocolate, her favorite! Not too sweet, with the caffeine boost she liked.

Amused, the gift-giver said, "Maybe you've mistaken that package for something they inhale down here. This drug works through your mouth. I'd offer sweet tea or lemonade and a pillowed porch swing, but they're a little scarce in a south that's south of Painter Place."

As if he was a testy child, she admonished him. "No one who's serious about chocolate would mess up the taste with another taste. Plain water lets you savor it."

She peeled back the end of the gold foil-lined package, breaking off two pieces to see the impression of feathery textures waving and an elegant embossed "C" in the middle of each square. "Wow, these are almost too beautiful to eat! But not quite."

She leaned over the console to the Jaguar with one square in her fingers, touching it to his lips as he drove. Surprised, he obediently opened his mouth and followed her instructions not to bite into it, just to let it melt. Then she offered the other square to Romeo, but he wouldn't accept unless she fed it to him, too. This brought the reminder that unlike the Jaguar, he didn't have to keep both hands on the steering wheel at a high rate of speed. He snorted and claimed that having hands on an M16 and watching out the windows left him in the same realm of helplessness.

This won him a bite after all, so Romeo leaned up close to Caroline's seat and she turned to put the square in his waiting mouth like a baby bird. Then she sat back with a contented sigh. With a pantomime of luxurious indulgence, she closed her eyes and put a square on her tongue.

"As a connoisseur, would you say it's pretty good?"

She groaned in rapture, but made the Jaguar wait for her verdict until it was totally melted, and she swallowed. Looking up to the headliner in the Rover, she exclaimed, "Divine! If I had better, I've forgotten it in this new experience."

He laughed outright. Romeo reached up to slap the Jaguar's shoulder. "Will you include her response in your product reviews?"

She turned to the driver in astonishment. "Chavarria—that's *you*?"

"My dad gave me the business last year when it was too much for him. I'll have something to do if I retire when my contract is up as the Jaguar, or if a serious injury prevents me from continuing the role. I don't get to spend much time with it yet."

"So, there's more where this came from?"

He grinned and glanced over at her. "Shall I send a case home with you?"

"Yes, since my birthday is next week, then ship more to Painter Place." She offered them each another artsy square, which they would only accept if she fed them like baby birds.

Avoiding the menacing night view outside her window, she returned to studying the Jaguar while the miles raced by. The glow from the Rover's dashboard exaggerated shadows on the planes of his face. She struggled to suppress a grin at how the teen girls in youth group would have reacted if he'd once looked as he did now, all filled in, his hair almost brushing his shoulders, his demeanor a titillating air of mystery and danger that put him in the realm of being unsafe. The girls would have twittered and gawked with their minds on something much different from his gospel message.

"You've always enjoyed wearing green, so you're at home here in jungle camouflage," she said. "But years ago, no matter the color of your shirt, you were often guarded by a little crocodile on your chest baring his teeth at me."

From the back seat, Romeo exploded in laughter and slapped his thigh. "The Jaguar was preppy? That's rich!"

The Jaguar chewed his lip but enjoyed her attention. He glanced over and quipped, "There's just something about a man who owns the source of the best chocolate in your universe, right?"

She exaggerated a sigh. "It's the little things."

He snorted at how she never missed a beat. She must have grown up with a brother. "Now I wish I hadn't let you get by with only a half-dose of that pain stuff. I'm keepin' you on it if it makes you let your hair down this much."

With a lofty sigh and a wave of her hand, she replied, "You've always asked me to wear my hair down."

Romeo chuckled. "You two have history—and chemistry. Why d'you ever dump 'im, Princess?"

"I didn't dump 'im. He dumped me."

Romeo sputtered various exclamations of disbelief while the Jaguar glowered at the road. "Did you love 'im?" Romeo blurted.

Caroline's smile evaporated. She turned away to stare into the first Land Rover's taillights. "That's—classified."

Everyone in the Rover jumped at the Puma's shout over the radio. "Jaguar! Jaguar, you read me? Weaver says company's comin' and it ain't the Welcome Wagon! Over."

The Jaguar hissed, looking in the rear-view mirror. "Romeo, who knows you're with me? I mean it, you lie to me and it's the last one you'll tell!"

Romeo sputtered. If this was his father's men, they were guessing. He would be missed after the escapade in the jungle, but it was too dark for them to know he wasn't lying somewhere with his throat opened by a cat or bleeding out from gunfire. "If it's my father, he's literally shooting in the dark. If he finds out Jadyn is arriving at the compound and thinks I've run off, he'll look for me there! Maybe this is *Puña*?"

"Who is Jadyn?" asked Caroline. She raised her hands in the air to keep them out of the Jaguar's way while he slid his hand over her Kevlar vested torso, testing her seat belt lock. Then he felt for his M16 as if it brought him comfort.

"Jadyn Rios. Her code name is Juliet!" Romeo exclaimed, nervously twisting to look out the back. "She's the daughter of the leader of the *Puña* cartel, and I'm Dominic Vega, the son of the *Temoso* cartel leader. We're trying to escape and be together. We became Christians and won't live this criminal life!"

Caroline grimaced with pain as she twisted to look him in the eye. "Did your dad send a vamp to Gregory Global to target my husband?"

Startled, he blinked his soft brown eyes. "All I know is they sent her out to discover what Jadyn's dad wanted with you. Sorry, but if she tried to seduce your husband, she always gets her man. Jadyn broke up with me several times over her."

"Did you deserve it?"

He looked away and huffed. "I don't know—maybe! But I never physically cheated. A man's not a man if he doesn't get a little sidetracked now and then. It's how we're wired. It means nothing."

"Yes, it does!" snapped the Jaguar as he grabbed the radio. "Roger that, Puma," he barked. "Romeo claims no knowledge of our pursuers but warns that *Temoso* might search for him since he was missing in the jungle dragnet. Tell Weaver I have confirmation that Isabelle was on assignment from *Temoso* to infiltrate Global to find out what *Puña* wants with Gregory's wife. I repeat, Gregory was a target! Dock all the radios and leave them on. Turn your cameras on. Over!"

"Jaguar, I've got headlights! Can't tell how many yet," shouted the driver behind them. The radio filled with gunfire that raked the vehicle even as he spoke, and Caroline thought of Carlos and the others in the first line of defense. She gasped when she felt herself sliding back...

"No, not again," she wailed into her hands. The Jaguar pressed her back to the seat with an arm like an iron bar while he floored the Rover. Shouts became a blur as she teetered on the edge of an emotional cliff, over which loomed some nameless something she couldn't face again. She gulped some deep breaths and clenched her fists. Her heart raced, pounding in her ears.

Please, Holy One, protect the men trying to rescue me! Help me stay calm. Give me strength to fight with them! Her prayers were an incoherent tumult in her mind as bullets struck their Rover. Her cry of dismay sounded pitiful in her own ears, embarrassing her. She wasn't like the cowering sissies she always complained about in the movies. She was Caroline Painter, descended from men and women who always faced dreadful trials with courage.

The words from Psalm 139:16 popped into her mind, memorized when she was a child. *And in Your book, they were written, the days fashioned for me, when as yet there were none of them.* Then she remembered the Jaguar's words in the cabin two days ago, telling her no one could kill him until it was his time in God's plan.

Sudden peace and resolve blanketed her spirit. If it was time for her to die, it would be a story of courage, a story worthy of re-telling when her children remembered.

Glaring lights in her mirror revealed that the last Rover in the convoy couldn't hold off both lanes. The Jaguar bellowed orders to the Puma to move over and let him pass with the two prizes, then he was to fall in beside the last Rover to block both lanes. Romeo and Jaguar were working on a plan for returning fire if the two Rovers behind were lost. She instinctively checked her weapon and asked if she should crawl in the back to help Romeo.

The Jaguar did a double take. "No! No, I need you up here to cover for me. Shoot out of your window."

"Jaguar, Jaguar! More lights are comin' up, too many, too many! I repeat, we can't hold them off back here!"

Bullets pelted the team like hail. Caroline's soul cried out in silent prayer. *Surround us with angel armor! A barrier, please, I beg You! Deliver us, Lord!*

"Roger that! Panther, tell Weaver the Hammer brothers are here and the Plumber is jumping down the pipe! I'm going in hot to the hacienda for cover in the jungle. Tell him to call ahead and evacuate the staff, have security on standby, and send me Grayson's team, *now*!"

"We've got one hit! One hit back here!" screamed the driver in the third Rover. "He can load for Carlos, but that's all I've got behind you!"

"Roger that, hold on, follow me!" shouted the Jaguar. He barked at Romeo to lower his window and brace himself to shoot through it in the turn, covering the last vehicle so they could make it in. Then he fought the wheel with a guttural roar to get through a sharp turn without rolling over. Caroline steadied herself with her arms and gritted her teeth at the jarring of her injuries, wishing she'd taken that whole dose of pain medicine. Romeo's M-16 rattled into the headlights past where Carlos was making a desperate hedge.

"Puma here! I'm right behind you, Jaguar, but there's no room to help Carlos! Panther's hittin' anyone hanging out the windows and counting 'em out loud like he's gonna carve notches in his rifle when this is over. Weaver's diverting Grayson's chopper. Over!"

"Jaguar, Jaguar! We've got mayhem back at the turn-off! Romeo scored in that turn and the road's blocked with wreckage. No tagalongs yet. I repeat, the Hammer Brothers did not make the pipe. Carlos wants to celebrate with fireworks. Over."

Caroline expelled a sigh of relief, but a glance at the Jaguar spiked her heart rate again. He hesitated unnaturally, then his hand went to his head. He clenched his teeth and squeezed his eyes shut in agony. She grabbed the steering wheel, expecting his other hand going to his head to stop the pain that would consume him.

The Jaguar instinctively put his foot on the brake twice, and as the vehicle slowed down, Romeo leaned over the console to help Caroline with a hand on the wheel. She directed her voice to the radio. "This is the Princess! I need the Puma. Over."

"Princess, Puma here. Is the Jaguar mewing? Over."

"Yes. We're steering for him..." She trailed off, open-mouthed. An enormous jaguar had just run past in front of them. "Puma, did you see that? We need to get out and follow him!"

Beside her, the Jaguar recovered enough to comprehend that he needed to keep his foot on the brake and stop the Rover.

Chapter Twenty

Christ wants not nibblers of the possible,
but grabbers of the impossible.
-C.T. Studd, Missionary

Azariah resisted looking at Nadia during the flight, but his instincts were like a radar trained on her. Her fine-boned yet capable hands thumbed through file folders from the Weaver. Occasionally she'd look up, tossing her head and staring far away before turning dark lashes back down to the pages. Sable bangs fell in a satiny sheen to obscure one eye, creating a mysterious profile that made his heart rate go up.

He'd been re-focusing too often lately and wondered if he was going through a late mid-life crisis. The woman who tried to seduce his boss had upended his own quiet, no-fly zones, places he once assumed would get no more traffic. That's how the enemy worked. Just when you got comfortable, patting yourself on the back for your strength to have that front covered forever, an unguarded moment could take you down.

But unlike Isabella, there was no hint of seduction in Nadia's movements, and he was finding her irresistible because she was safe. He'd begun taking little mental rabbit trails about what her story might be and about how many years the fine lines on her face were so gently hiding. Had she once had a husband and family, as he'd had a wife and children?

"You asked me to call you Azariah, is that correct?" She addressed him in an accent that dragged traces of Russian and Middle Eastern influences into her perfect, if formal, English.

He welcomed a legitimate chance to peer into those deep amber windows to her soul. "Yes, ma'am."

She flashed a pleased smile. "I see you've adapted to the Southern culture well. It is pleasant to hear respect in conversation."

"Southern culture suits me. Painter Place is my home now and I never plan to leave."

She searched his face, then looked down at a page in her hand. "I'd like to know more about the situation we're dropping in on. This—Jaguar—was once in a relationship with Caroline Painter Gregory, and the communications I've reviewed seem to show there's a, ah, I think you say, 'rekindling of the flame' on his part. Will this be a problem in her marriage?"

He worked on veiling a surge of fierce loyalty to Caroline, turning his curt answer to the window. "Absolutely not!"

After a pause, he turned back to see her pursing her lips. She ventured, "Her husband isn't entirely innocent in complicating matters. This is a perfect time to get back at him."

Azariah's expression mirrored his stern tone. "Chad Gregory's universe is his faith, his wife, his family, his home, and his company. He won't allow anything to destroy those foundations, not even a brief distraction Caroline might wander into, and she won't betray him. He'll never rest until he proves she's still first in his heart and mind."

Nadia raised a dark eyebrow. "Realistically, many couples wouldn't survive the circumstances of this whole ordeal. She hasn't our training to endure the trauma without permanent emotional baggage."

"She'll recover!" Azariah snapped ferociously. "People are always underestimating Caroline, and I've prepared both her and her husband for kidnapping situations." He jerked his head away, ending the discussion.

Ben made urgent gestures for them all to get their earphones. When Azariah picked up on the message through them, he grabbed the edge of his seat to keep from coming out of it. White-knuckled, he listened while Ben scrambled for another map. He impatiently acknowledged Nadia's hand on his arm, and she held one earpiece away to show she wanted to speak to him.

"You love her."

Azariah was in no mood to come up with an evasive response. "Yes! She offered me unconditional friendship soon after I took her on as a job. I fought not to get involved, but it's impossible with her, you'll see. She drew me out, showing me how to feel free to live like a regular person again. Now she's my family, and there's nothing I won't do to keep her safe."

The Jaguar's team tumbled out of bullet-scarred Land Rovers, racing to grab backpacks. Their leader was all orders now. "Park sideways, triple-deep, blocking the road. We're following the Princess. Her jaguar is waiting. I need Carlos!"

In the mad hustle to obey orders, the Puma made sure the bandage around the wounded guard's arm was tight before sending him to wait with Caroline, who fussed over him. "You're exhausted," she said, making him sip from his water bottle.

"The bullet's out now and hit nothing vital. Don't worry about me, Princess. Let me pound my chest and roar for you!" He did just that with his other fist, pantomiming a silent roar.

"You're just tryin' to take my mind off how brutally desperate this situation is."

"And you're too smart to fall for it. I can't be your dance partner now, like on your first jungle trail last week when you couldn't keep up. Seems like so long ago, doesn't it, Princess? Your enemies are still in hot pursuit, we're both hurt, the team is worn out, and our leader could be incapacitated by an old injury at any moment. Have I covered everything?"

She turned an apprehensive eye to the jungle's edge. "No, you left out that we're following a wild animal into the deepest dark imaginable."

Distant engines roared as the rest of the team gathered around. The Jaguar announced, "You're the new leader, Princess."

She turned wide eyes from him to the darkest spot in the tree line along the road. "It's just over there."

"We're with you."

She gulped and looked back up at him with a plea for help in her eyes. His Adam's apple bobbed before he set his jaw firmly. Seeing his resolve, she clenched her teeth to keep them from chattering and turned back to face the jungle's edge. The cat was waiting there, leading her into the blackest spot in the darkness, fearing nothing and having no enemies.

A slight breeze cooled the sheen of sweat on her brow. She began jogging as best she could manage in that direction, keeping the beam of her flashlight pointed to the ground in front of her. As if expecting her to panic at the path, the Jaguar grasped her hand just before the first step of faith into a veil of ebony. They took it together.

After a few yards into the dense foliage, moonbeams illuminated a small patch through an opening in the trees. Golden eyes stared at her, mesmerizing, ignoring the men behind her. She stared into them for a moment before they blinked and turned away with a deep throaty rumble. It wasn't a purr, but she felt fear fall away, and she increased her effort to hurry along.

Doors slammed and terse voices rose somewhere behind her. Suddenly, she reeled forward when an explosion rent the night and rocked the ground. The Jaguar reached out to keep her from falling and met the question in her eyes.

"Carlos rigged the Rovers to blow. No one will follow us for a while."

She gulped, peering back through tree limbs at slivered views of the distant flames. The shouting enemy voices had been silenced.

"It was the only way," the Jaguar said flatly.

To protect me, to protect Romeo, to save all of us, her mind finished for him. She squeezed the hand he'd steadied her with. "I understand. You did what you had to. I told you, I can handle seeing you kill someone. What I can't handle is seeing them kill you because of me."

Spinning on the heel of her worn Timberland boot with renewed urgency, she followed the trail of the jaguar who reappeared now and then with his rumble and breathy grunts. The wounded guard muffled groans a few times somewhere behind her.

She couldn't judge how long they labored through the foliage before she suddenly sensed a wall rising in front of her. Pulling back snarled vines, she took a tentative step into a closed, pitch blackness and froze.

The Jaguar touched her shoulder with reassurance, then stepped around her. Behind him, the Puma hissed to the Panther. "Did you know this was here?"

The team disappeared behind the drape of vines over a door-less threshold, replacing the hanging jungle cover. Their flashlights flitted over bullet-pocked walls and boarded-over windows.

"Something horrible happened here."

They all turned to the Princess at her ominous pronouncement. She'd taken but one reluctant step inside and seemed on the brink of bolting back out. Her hair was in disarray from branches whose fingers grasped vainly for her on the path. Her face looked young and vulnerable in the dim up-lit glow of flashlights, and the effect of the whole scene was on a par with being told a ghost story around a campfire.

Carlos shivered and passed a hand over his brow while the others turned uneasy looks at one another. Though time and the elements had taken their own toll on the unkempt building, the cruel scars of spent weapons were everywhere.

The Jaguar and Puma began a methodical investigation of the large room to see if it was free of animals and structurally safe to hide in. They stamped their boots on the remains of the floor to see if it would hold them. The other guards peeked through gaps in boarded windows for unwanted company outside.

With a sigh of resignation and then a moan of pain, the Princess stiffly tried to remove her backpack and couldn't. The Panther rushed to help her, his fingers raking away stray bits of foliage and sticks that clung to her hair, brushing off the shoulders of her sweater. He decided not to mention a few insects that hitchhiked on the fine cotton weave.

The Princess went to a dark stain on one wall. She stood stolidly with her small flashlight shining, studying the gouges in the wood. The Jaguar wandered over to join her.

"It's where my dad's wife was murdered."

The Panther came to stand in front of the dark-stained wall. "Chavarria never talks about it. He hates this place. Someone told me he thought no one would connect her and the hacienda to the Jaguar of those times. He assumed enemies would target the compound if they ever thought he had a family. But just in case, they tucked away their son in Cali in boarding school. There were guards stationed here, and many cocoa workers stayed overnight during harvest. One day, he was called out on a mission that lured him away from the area. The hacienda was attacked. Trusted guards tried to sneak his wife out under cover of the cocoa trees, planning to find refuge here in his foreman's headquarters. But the former Jaguar's enemies hunted them down and granted no mercy."

He turned sad brown eyes to the Jaguar. "Your father was a broken man, the old-timers say, but having their son to raise gave him a reason to keep living. Over time, and with the Weaver's aid, he made certain that everyone responsible came to justice. His son grew and replaced him as the next Jaguar. When he was killed in a mission, the Puma and I found you. You know the rest. Your father's grief was bearable because of his joy in nursing you back to health."

Turning to the Princess, the Panther explained, "God has kept a Jaguar here for decades now. We don't know for how long and don't question why."

She reached for the Jaguar's arm and her soft accent softened the otherwise cruel, desolate setting. "No wonder your father let the jungle swallow this place. He sounds like a fine man who has endured many trials by fire."

"You see now why I can't have a life like yours?" the Jaguar blurted, dragging his eyes from the dark stain and rubbing his face as if he could scour the scene from his memory.

Beside him, she grasped the body cam on his shirt and found the button to turn it off. With furtive glances at one another, the team followed her lead, turning their body cameras off and busying themselves with finding a place to rest. The Puma examined the wounded guard, who had sunk to the floor and propped against a wall.

Now the Princess wrapped her arms around her friend, who clutched her in desperation. He didn't realize his strength was hurting her injuries. She shifted and felt him shake, fighting not to make a sound. *After all, jaguars don't cry.*

"I'm not sorry you've come to this point," she whispered near his ear, pulling back the lock of sun-kissed brown hair that he grew long to hide his scar. Her eyes swam in tears of awe at who he was and at the price God's plan had cost him. "You know how people in scripture were entrusted with incredible, impossible, terrible tasks? This is greatness. This is what it means to be larger than life. Almost no one else can be trusted with so much."

He tried to suppress a sob, trapping it between her hair and his lips against it. She ran her palm back and forth over his shoulder to soothe him. "Don't you see what an honor it is to live your calling? It's lonely because it's lofty, high, far and away above what almost anyone can be. Remember that quote of Jim Elliot's you once taught me, something about how our own personal dreams are tawdry, not worthy of the aura of wonder we often surround them with, when compared with surrendering to God?"

Stroking his head with one hand and keeping the other around him, she whispered. "It's a gift just to know you, Jaguar. I hope you'll always be my friend."

He choked a whisper. "You're one of the few people who can understand, because you know what it's like. It's part of our bond."

She felt the familiar searing ache of collective memories, of times she had felt isolated, different, misunderstood, set on a pedestal, or slandered by those who couldn't grasp the things she could perceive. But she had her family and some friends to fall back on, and one who knew her like no other.

"Yes, I do, but God provided someone for me who understands and helps me get through it all. Chad is a lot like you—like both of us. God didn't leave you alone, either. Perhaps a woman can't survive here, but you have your father, this team, and many people who back you up."

A whimper escaped her at a shift of his arms on her ribs. "Can we find a place to sit down? I need to rest, 'cause I hike like a girl."

His chuckle rumbled against her, relieving his tension. He peered around in the near-darkness with red-rimmed eyes, then pulled her back toward the concealed doorway, away from the hated dark blood spot.

As the leader again, the Jaguar's voice was hoarse when he told the team, "Let's take whatever break we need outside now. Panther, set up the radio and see if Weaver's got the special team on the way."

Caroline tilted her head, listening. The jungle wasn't lively and raucous tonight. Perhaps the wildlife had run away to escape the faint biting odor of the three exploded Land Rovers. In the shadows, she could make out that Carlos, the Panther, and the wounded team member catnapped on tarps strewn around the floor. Puma, Romeo, and the other guard took advantage of sitting down while they peeked out of holes in the walls, though the married guard's eyes often went to the dark bloodstain on the wall. He'd been on edge ever since hearing about Chavarria's wife's murder, and it made her think of Chad.

Her husband was struggling to posture calmness in front of her, but she knew he was a wreck inside. Longing seared her heart. If only they could rewind their lives! But no, that had been a time of illusion, a time when they didn't grasp how perilous their safety was. They'd been joyously ignorant, living in a boat sailing in shimmering-scaled waters that obscured the treacherous monsters lurking below. When the boat got rammed and tipped over, they fell prey to the ever-present snapping jaws.

How could anything ever be the same after this? Would fear rule Painter Place and Gregory Global? And what about her marriage? Could she move past the seismic shock of a wrecking-ball to the walls of her heart when she realized Chad had entertained fantasies of another woman while his wife was facing a life or death situation? What kind of man did that?

Loneliness washed over her like a tide. Perhaps her destiny was to ride in that boat of illusion over treacherous waters, at the mercy of another monster to tip it over, never knowing serenity or happiness again.

She slid closer to the Jaguar. He'd stationed himself at the empty threshold, stretched on his stomach and elbows, keeping watch through a hole in the concealing vines.

Observing him, she decided that drawing was the therapy she needed to evade her gloominess. She pulled out her sketchbook and propped the flashlight. Looking up to consider her rescuer, she captured a pose of him. With a light pressure on her pencil, she wrote a note to the side of it. Touching his shoulder, she gestured to him to turn off his body camera.

Raising an eyebrow, he reached up to press the button, then looked around to be sure the other guards weren't watching. She slid the sketch to him and waited.

He grinned appreciatively at the portrait and squinted to read the message. With a wry smile, he whispered, "You're getting pretty bossy, Princess," he whispered.

She nonchalantly erased the message so no other eyes would ever read it. "I just wanted to tell you something in private," she whispered.

"Like that classified information you wouldn't divulge to Romeo earlier?" He scrutinized the darkness outside the door.

"No, not that. I want you to know the day Chris Shepherd told me he was leavin' for a dangerous place and not to wait for him, I had the sensation of all the time we'd spent together escaping like water out of my hands."

Startled, he jerked his head around to see her put down her pencil and cup her hands together. "I tried to hold on to it, but that's not a property of water. He had moved on, in the invisible, intangible ways of the heart and mind. My hands were empty, our relationship dripping to disappear into the sand, as things do when their time is over. I was part of his past, just a mark on the timeline of his life."

She watched the tears glisten in his eyes, reflected by the illumination from her flashlight, and imagined the color change she knew was there. Brushing away a tear of her own, she tried whispering past the lump in her throat. "Please, don't leave me empty-handed again, just a blip in your history. We have a different past to go forward from now. People change, emotions evolve from experiences. But you saved my life. Be respectful to Chad and he won't prevent a friendship between us. He trusts me. He never kept me and Derrick from each other, even though he was jealous."

The Jaguar wiped his eyes and sniffed. "Derrick?"

"Derrick Wallace, the basketball star—back in the States. Anyway, I spent a lot of time with him before and during my relationship with you. Now he's ecstatically married to a journalist, our official media liaison at Painter Place, and they have a little boy. Derrick is a business partner with Chad and my brother."

The Jaguar huffed and looked at her with narrowed eyes. His whisper was vehement. "Are you admitting that you ran around on me with some hotshot jock?"

"No!" She muffled a laugh. It was strange telling him his life story. She shouldn't talk about his past at all. "To Derrick, you were a buzzing sand gnat. He was on the scene as soon as Chad left Painter Place for college, planning to get settled in a career in the pros and come back for me. You and I spent time together as friends whenever you came home, but right before you left, you asked my dad if you could court me. He agreed but wasn't thrilled, and he asked me not to make any commitments to you without talkin' to him first. I didn't know he was waitin' on Chad to pass a test and come back and marry me."

"You said Chad was your first kiss. That means we never..."

"That's right, we never. We both pledged purity in our youth group, and a kiss that matters stirs things we couldn't satisfy. Our parents also taught us the Billy Graham rule, not to be alone together anywhere. That way, no one could gossip about us, and we could avoid the temptation to cross the boundaries."

He snorted. "I bet I struggled with that one. Hope you did, too."

The rhythmic throp-throp sound of rotor blades made them both look up to the dark roof beams. Caroline snapped her sketchbook closed as a sudden exchange of gunfire filled the air over the jungle canopy. "Ben and Azariah are here!" she exclaimed.

The Jaguar switched his body camera back on. His napping team members stirred, then groggily hustled to get their packs on and be ready to evacuate. The Panther fired up the radio to find out if the Weaver could tell him if a friend or foe was overhead.

"Wait, is that—thunder?" asked the Puma. The old building shuddered, and the sky flashed a brilliant burst of lightning. "Did the Weaver say anything about the weather radar?"

Carlos groaned. "The choppers can't meet us in a thunderstorm!"

The metallic clamor of dueling helicopters drew closer while the Panther struggled with interference in a partial transmission from the Weaver, who confirmed an electrical storm that had popped up on the radar. Ben's team discovered and reported the smoldering remnants of the Land Rovers from the air but picked up an aggressive chopper searching the exploded site.

"Grayson won't risk rappelling his team down and giving away our location," exclaimed the Puma. "There will be a fight up there.

If those choppers come down and break apart, we're sitting in a box of kindling!"

The timber of the shelter shook with violent cracking from the sky overhead. Caroline felt her bruised ribs rattle as she leaned against the wall to spy past the vines into the jungle, which didn't seem as dark as before. Perhaps this long night was finally over.

She gasped and sat up straight. The sleek, mysterious jaguar appeared out of nowhere, staring right at her through the tangled vines. Lightning made a spooky play of blue light around his spotted markings, but the cat didn't flinch at the bone-jarring storm. He took a few steps into the undergrowth, then waited.

The Jaguar shouted over the storm for the team to follow the Princess and the cat into the deafening darkness. They were barely away when an ominous clap of thunder ushered in an explosive lightning strike that threw them all to the quaking jungle floor. Dazed, they looked back to see the shelter was now a roaring bonfire whose flames licked the sky wickedly.

The Panther and Jaguar scrambled up to help the Princess, who struggled between them on her hands and knees. Dirt smudged her face and the wild tousle of her hair seemed to radiate from the flames behind her. Blue flickering lightning above created a bizarre contrast to outline her form.

The Jaguar stared at her as if memorizing the sight, then he switched off his body camera. He reached out, resting his fingertips along her cheek, his voice was full of awe as he said, "Shining Woman."

A gentle smile accompanied a far-away look in his eyes, then he moved his face close to her ear. "It's gettin' near dawn..." he sang. He pulled back to meet her bewildered eyes. "I'm here with you, Princess, like I always promised to be, when the stars are fallin.'"

The Panther nudged him, pointing to a leaning tree. Their enormous guide stretched its spotted coat out luxuriously, rubbing the sides of his face on the bark. "He's marking his territory, here on the plantation. I think he's staking a claim on us."

The cat rumbled. With a lithe leap back to the ground, he melted into the dark green leaves. The men looked in all directions to take in the fiery furnace of the abandoned building, the chopper chase, the lightning, and the cat's path, then gathered behind the Princess, ready to follow. At an encouraging nod from their leader, she took a limping step forward, but stifled a cry by clamping her hand over her mouth.

The Jaguar reached out to steady her and glanced at his watch. He growled and slapped his forehead, then grasped a bottle of water from the side of her pack.

Her fingers searched her jeans pocket for the pain pills. The Panther insisted she eat with a full dose of the medicine, so she chewed a mouthful of a protein bar while the Jaguar began pulling off her pack and a bulletproof vest. He snarled, "It's too long since she had a decent meal, and she shouldn't be on the run like this. She's hurt!"

"I'll carry her pack. It's almost empty," offered the Puma, stepping up to take it from the Jaguar. "She can lean on you and the Panther."

Romeo grabbed the Jaguar's pack, and Carlos shouldered the Panther's. Overhead, the sudden coughing of a chopper in distress startled them. Casting frantic looks around, not knowing which way to run, they found the jaguar. He waited, and the Jaguar and Panther caught Caroline under her arms and rushed her along between them. Failing engines roared and sputtered before another explosion toppled them to the ground again. Caroline's escorts banged into a tree to keep her from falling.

Looking in the distance to the third fireball she'd seen, Caroline screamed hysterically for Ben and Azariah, trying to run toward the crash. The Jaguar and Panther struggled not to injure her further while she strained to free herself. Imprisoned, she looked past them to the crash, wild-eyed. Then she startled them by going limp and wailing inconsolably.

Totally unnerved, the Panther let go of the Princess so the Jaguar could support her with both his arms. The others gathered protectively around her in the din of the crash, the storm, and the other chopper, assuring her that her friends were likely the victors in the air battle. Carlos pointed out the sound of the remaining one as it maneuvered to evade the lightning.

But then the other chopper dropped altitude. "That's what Grayson would do to rappel the team down," the Panther exclaimed.

"It's also what my dad's men would do," growled Romeo, his eyes wild with alarm when he turned them on the Jaguar. "We don't know for sure, and he's desperate. His men will stop at nothing to find Dominic Vega! I can never go back, understand? Never! I can't let Jadyn down, not when we're so close. If she gets away and I don't, we'll never be together. Please, we have to run!"

Chapter Twenty-One

*They received help against these enemies
because they cried out to God in battle,
and the Hagrites and all their allies were handed over to them.
He granted their request because they trusted in Him.*
1 Chronicles 5:20

Jadyn Rios' father, the *capo* of the *Puña* cartel, threatened to kill his own men. All plans to extract his daughter from the Chavarria compound had been foiled. Some had redeemed themselves by discovering that her forbidden boyfriend, Dominic Vega, may not be on the premises. Perhaps she had not bribed the new pilot to fly her here to meet him. She could have been abducted for leverage in case he got his hands on the Gregory woman again. The conniving plans that brewed in the pretty heads of females baffled him more than the plans of his enemies!

He had little patience for any woman except Jadyn's mother. She was a rare jewel. But marrying him had been her death sentence.

Trying to placate Rios to win his mercy, someone scrambled to find out why a group of his men had not arrived at the compound. He learned they were fighting past a wreckage of vehicles left by *Temoso*. Then he got ridiculous reports of how the Jaguar had escaped with the American woman by commanding animals. How dare his men make up such an outrageous story to cover their failure!

But hacked radio transmissions confirmed what his men were saying, and that *Temoso's capo* Vega was in a terror, trying to determine if his only living son was lost in the jungle or a prisoner of the Jaguar. Now Rios was forced to consider that if his men were lying, so were Vega's men, and they somehow came up with the same story. Unlikely! This was a trick rigged by the wily Jaguar to fool them all while he got away.

Rios pulled his thick, graying hair when the next radio report said chaos reigned on the road where *Temoso* vehicles took fire from *Puña* when they caught up with the Jaguar. Vega's tally of lost men was high, not only from *Puña* forces, but the deadly precision of the Jaguar's snipers. In desperation, he'd called in air support to determine what was going on, but who could give him reliable information from up in a chopper at night?

Puña's capo was fed up with confusion. Trusted employees were hard to come by in this business, and he was wasting his, accomplishing nothing but the obliteration of his organization. He bitterly regretted his decision to aggravate Vega by kidnapping the American. He decided it was time to get word to Vega that he wanted to arrange a meeting between them, one that would unite them against the Jaguar and the agencies that hunkered down in the fortress of the Chavarria compound. Communication would require radios, since any messenger would be shot on sight.

His *halcones* on the ground reported American CIA and DEA inside the compound, as well as British agents. It was an outpost of the Weaver's organization, and Rios made it a firm rule to avoid entanglements in that no-win situation at all costs—until now. If only he'd known there was a link, he'd never have taken the American woman. She might well bring down his empire.

The atmosphere in the Weaver's nerve center was as electric as the freak storm that popped up on the radar. Radios and cameras on the Jaguar's team were down, but Ben's voice burst through the speakers from the Weaver's helicopter. The abandoned shelter where the Jaguar's team had taken refuge had been struck by lightning and was now engulfed in flames.

Chad nearly collapsed before reaching out to prop himself against a bookcase. Patrick's knees gave way. He stumbled into a sofa where he covered his face in his hands and sobbed.

Ben shouted over the commotion surrounding him. "If they're followin' a jaguar as their last report claimed, the team was led away before the strike. I've altered the rescue plan..."

His voice dissolved into static.

Azariah and Nadia stayed in sight of the inferno that was once an old foreman's quarters, hiding behind stalwart tree trunks that were far enough away to escape charring. This frantic rescue attempt was now an investigation. Evidence of separate trails led into and away from the building, indicating the team had made it out.

Swiping sweat from his forehead with a trembling gloved hand, Azariah leaned back against the scratchy bark to collect himself. In an adrenaline rush to save Caroline, he'd shaken off the jarring effect to his joints from a rusty effort at rappelling to the ground. Now his body needed a break to recover.

He wasn't the man he used to be, and now Nadia would know it. Worse, she'd know he wasn't the ice man he once trained to be, either.

Nadia maneuvered behind foliage to thump her shoulder into his, leaning back and catching her breath. She had been limping since landing and scouting the situation, securing the area for Ben and Jack. Now, she moaned as she bent a knee and propped her boot against the tree trunk.

"Are you all right?"

"An ice pack should take care of it. It's not my age, it's the mileage."

Azariah grinned at her Indiana Jones line from *Raiders of the Lost Ark.* But he did a double take when he glanced over and encountered the effect of the fire reflecting on her face. Glorious rays radiated from the irises of her eyes, reminding him of sunbeams that lost their way and became trapped in there. Her coloring heightened with a soft rosy bloom, accented against her tousled short hair. He caught himself staring and broke away, a blush crawling up his neck like mercury in a thermometer.

Nadia used a tone of assurance that affected him like a touch. "She's safe with the Jaguar, I just know it. When Ben gets here, we'll find them."

He merely nodded, watching the silhouettes outlined by an eerie blue flash. They instantaneously raised automatic rifles at an unearthly scream that seemed to come from everywhere at once. "A jaguar?" he speculated, unnerved, goose fleshed, and watchful. He didn't look forward to the prospect of meeting up with anything that sounded like that, and he prayed it knew he was one of the good guys.

She stood ready at his shoulder, pointing behind their position. "No, a puma—a cougar, I believe they say in America. Jaguars don't cry or scream. They grunt."

"Been to the zoo recently?"

"I studied up on it en route here. This is perhaps the one place in the world I haven't been assigned before. I didn't imagine it would be easy to impress you."

He couldn't help glancing at her profile in surprise. It occurred to him that her homework en route probably included what she'd be able to find on him, too. Unless she had some deep mutual connections, it was scant little information. He'd made certain of that when he practically wiped his identity clean. Even the press couldn't figure out who the Gregorys' bodyguard really was. If she wanted to know him, she'd have to discover it first-hand.

The electricity in the turbulent atmosphere appeared in a frenzied dance along a giant tree nearby. A sudden whirlwind targeted them with smoke, causing Nadia to cough. Nudging her shoulder with his in a direction where the wind wasn't gusting, they inched away from the sheltering tree and behind others, working as a unit to keep both their backs covered. They stopped to look up when they heard the sputter of a chopper in distress.

Spectral light spawned by the wild electrical storm ignited the path of the jaguar. The cocoa bean trees were sheltered by a canopy of taller ones that waved tempestuously, like a sea heaving in a hurricane. The air felt alive, charged, dispersing the wafting odor of burning fuel from the downed helicopter. There was no way to know if they were being followed, but the second chopper was no longer risking the storm.

The Princess wore a shell-shocked expression, totally disengaged from everything except following the cat's trail, often stumbling between the Panther and Jaguar. Thunderclouds kept time shrouded in mystery.

Eventually, the hacienda came into view, and there was a welcoming shout from guards who recognized their boss. They ran forward into a practiced formation, rifles trained on the trees to cover the Jaguar's team into the clearing, but also wary of the presence of the biggest jaguar they'd ever seen. Their leader wearily warned them not to bother the cat or any animals that might emerge from the jungle into the plantation.

The Princess turned to the animal. Thunder and blustery wind snatched away her attempt at saying thank you, as if he understood English. Yet the jaguar blinked an unconcerned acknowledgment before melting like a liquid under the shelter of the raised porch.

The strong front doors at the top of the steps burst open to welcome the team. A guard rushed out to help them inside to the homey fragrance of steak, eggs, biscuits, and the crisp scent of citrus for breakfast.

Without a sound, the Princess collapsed, oblivious to the fact that the Jaguar's quick reflexes saved her from hitting the polished woodgrain of the plank floor.

Barely an hour after their boss made it with his team into the hacienda, the guards stationed on the covered porch warned the Panther of activity outside. Six people donning jungle camouflage were walking up, hands raised.

"Is the cat threatening them?" asked the Panther on his microphone, leaving his plate and jogging to the door. The rest of the team sprang up, still armed and rushing to position themselves at their own stations.

"Negative. I think one in the group is a female."

The Panther opened the heavy door, peering at the wraithlike figures emerging from the plantation cocoa trees. "Stay where you are and identify yourselves!" he shouted.

The figures froze, raising their hands higher. One of them responded in a rich, deep voice, "The Weaver sent us to relieve you and protect the Princess. I used his coordinates to find this place. You left a trail a child could follow. I expected more from a team with your reputation."

The Panther lowered his rifle at the slow Southern drawl and disarming manner but didn't gesture for the other guards to do the same. "The Weaver sent a team of four."

"Four of us were assigned to hit the ground, but extenuating circumstances demanded that I crash the chopper and bring the crew."

The Panther tried not to let his jaw drop and needed a few seconds to recover. His mind reeled with images of the chopper and dollar signs. "You—are you reporting that you dropped out and intentionally crashed the Weaver's specialized equipment?"

"Roger that. Now he knows the timed self-destruct option he installed works for the next one. I needed a diversion to get the cartel off your trail. Short-term, they'll wonder if you died in the building and we died in the crash. The storm stalled their investigation to find Romeo. By now, they know he's not with Chavarria at the compound to meet Juliet. If you lived where I come from, you'd offer us some food and rest before they get here."

The Panther considered this. The man ventured, "Look, your new yard cat is under your feet instead of at my throat. That proves I'm on the right side. By the way, do 'ya have to charge his batteries to keep his eyes glowin' like that?"

Controlling the urge to grin, the Panther curtly ordered the group to come forward, keeping their hands up. Thunder clapped and rumbled to create a mini earthquake that ran along the boards of the porch under his feet. When the newcomers stood on the bottom step, he looked in the leader's deep brown eyes, studying him for a betraying flinch. "What's your name?"

"I'm Ben Grayson, but I was never here," the man drawled with a smirk.

"Which one's Azariah?"

The biggest man in the group took a silent half-step forward. He wasn't what the Panther expected, with gray-sprinkled auburn hair plastered to his damp forehead. Eyes that missed nothing were set in a ruddy complexion. The two men sized one another up for a full minute before the Panther said, "You trained her well. Just thought you'd want to know that it counted for something."

The Israeli bodyguard's eyes conveyed a disarmed moment that wrung the Panther's heart. The man regained a mask of professionalism, and the Panther jerked his head to the door to invite them in. Posted guards watched the ominous tree line.

The interior of the hacienda was not what the newcomers expected, and they looked around in surprise to find it so tastefully and comfortably decorated. He saw admiration in their quick analysis of the displayed collections of antique swords and armor. When Ben didn't see his sister-in-law anywhere, he asked for her.

"The Princess collapsed when she walked in the door, unconscious again. The Jaguar and I practically had to carry her between us to follow the cat here, which is why our trail is so obvious. She's aware again and clear-headed, but exhausted, injured, and distraught after seeing the chopper crash. The Jaguar's guarding her in his room. I'll take you in."

He held out his hand to shake theirs, then acknowledged Nadia with a polite nod. "Would you mind looking after the Princess for a bit? The Jaguar will be the next one to collapse if he doesn't lie down. We need him rested to lower his risk of mewing."

She agreed and started to step forward, but caught her breath when the movement became a limp. She blushed and waved her hand that it was nothing, but Azariah took her elbow and asked for two ice packs.

The Puma said he'd bring them along, so the Panther led them down an airy hallway lined with beautiful paintings and wrought ironwork sconces. He addressed a young guard standing at the last door, armed to the teeth. "Romeo, this is the Weaver's special team. They'd like to let the Princess know they're okay."

The dark-haired young man with a friendly grin stuck out his hand, pumping each of theirs with enthusiasm. "You don't know how relieved we are! When that chopper crashed near us, it was all we could do to hold her back from running to help. She's not been herself ever since, and she's scaring us. I'm glad you took down the other guys."

"No, it was ours, all right. The other guys just didn't know we weren't in it."

Romeo's brows shot up and he whistled before muttering "Cha-ching!" like a cash register.

He moved to allow them to walk through the door into a spacious suite where the Jaguar occupied a chair pulled beside a huge bed. A plate of half-eaten food was in his hands. Caroline was lying back against plumped pillows with a man's shirt on and blankets pulled up. She spread her arms open, crying out their names, and Ben and Azariah rushed to her.

Caroline didn't seem to trust her own eyes, feeling over the men's arms. "I'm okay, now that I know you're alive! I'm just so tired," she assured them. "The team took great care of me. Are we safe yet?"

Azariah gripped her hand, rubbing the back of it as if he could infuse his strength into her. Ben answered, "I don't know, honey. They think we're dead. But Romeo's dad will want proof of where he is and who's responsible for what happened to him. When the sky calms down from this storm, I'll contact the Weaver. Don't you worry. You did your part, but you wore out your first batch of heroes. The second string is here so they can rest."

He reached out over her legs to shake the Jaguar's hand. "It's an honor to finally meet the mysterious Jaguar. Is she truly okay? She'd say that even if she was dyin', ya know."

"We think she's only exhausted and roughed up, but she needs to see a doctor at the compound as soon as possible," the Jaguar answered quietly. "That swollen area on her face worries me, and I don't like it that she lost consciousness again."

Ben scrutinized him. "You look like somethin' your new cat dragged in. Get some sleep and trust us to handle things for a while."

An hour passed before the storm subsided. In a bizarre contradiction of itself, the weather now hushed the world around the hacienda with a soft rainfall.

The Weaver's special jungle team was snoring in various places around the house, and their leader lay on the floor in the hallway outside the door of his room. The Weaver had assigned him a den with the Princess, and he wasn't off duty until there was no threat. The Panther slept on a sturdy gray sofa near the radio, his full height bringing his boots over the armrest.

Another hour passed in peace. The longer it rained, the more unlikely it was that there would be an attack on the hacienda. But Ben was eager for radio contact with the Weaver. He dreaded reporting that he destroyed the Weaver's special bird, the cost of which probably rivaled the economy of a third world country.

Ben also needed to report to Chad that Caroline was safe. Closing his tired eyes and rubbing his face, an image of his brother-in-law came to mind. Chad's existence was in a sky-high realm above the low-life cartels and men like Wilfred Rothschild. Working for his family's company, Chad nimbly avoided financial landmines and scouted investing gold mines as professionally as Ben handled surveillance and rescue. But the seedy, criminal side of life eluded him. Seeing it on the news and in movies was entirely different from comprehending how to deal with it.

Chad had self-defense skills, and he had shot an intruder in France five years ago. But he didn't fathom the evil heart behind the crime. The criminals here could kill without blinking an eye to ensure cocaine supplies flowed into the States, where it would destroy families and kids, then they'd take the money home at night as family men and saw no contradiction in it.

Ben had always been amused and impressed at how quick Chad was on his feet in the unusual situations Caroline landed in. She never had to look far for adventure! But now her life and the fate of Painter Place was on the line, which put the fate of Gregory Global on the line. Not only that, there was trouble between the two of them, and he doubted they'd ever had a real fight. Chad was the tempestuous one, but her wrath was the stuff of stories when someone pushed the wrong button. There was no question Chad had pushed one, and he hadn't paid for it yet.

Squirming, Ben remembered he had not been home since that incident between Chad and the female spy in Phillip's office, and he and Sandy made a point of never arguing or talking about matters that would distract him while he was on assignments. Maybe she would lack all curiosity about whether he could relate to her brother's stumble, but something told him she would explore that territory.

He reasoned it would be in his best interest to treat that possibility like any other mission—be prepared. Chad would have fared better if he'd seen the incident coming. Ben planned to practice some things to say that would take his wife Sandy on a rabbit trail that never led her back to a yes or no.

A chilling cry from outside made both him and Jack jump, and the Panther roused to see their startled reactions. He yawned. "Just a puma—a cougar, or mountain lion, I think you *gringos* call them. Usually, a male only makes that sound in a rivalry for a female, but we heard it a lot last night."

He peeked out the front window. "They can purr, too, which a jaguar or lion can't do. Looks like there's a panther with him. But panthers are only black jaguars or leopards, and they don't scream. The jaguar, he's the leader. We have three cats under the porch right now—just like a farm back home in America, right?"

Jack narrowed his eyes as he peered outside. "So, is that panther a leopard or a jaguar?"

"A jaguar. Leopards live in Africa. In the sunshine, you'd be able to see the darker spots under his coat. The pattern is what's

different. A jaguar has a spot somewhere in the middle of the larger
rosettes. Since I'm the back-up for our Jaguar with the team, I'm
the Panther. Basically, I'm the shadow of the Jaguar."

Jack and Ben jumped again when the Weaver's voice hailed
them through the radio. The Panther raked back his straight, dark
hair as he sprang up. The Weaver's voice was hoarse after a night of
commands. "Weaver, this is Grayson. Everyone is accounted for at
the hacienda. Over."

"Copy that. The bird is MIA. Did you ground it? Over."

"Roger. The bird is grounded. Permanently. Over." Ben glanced
at the Panther, whose expression said he didn't want to be him.

The Weaver's voice was weary and scratchy when he sighed and
responded. "Roger. Explain. Over."

"Jack and I will file a report, in his name, and he'll notify his
employer, Phil Gregory, in Charleston. I had to adjust the plan
when lightning struck the shelter, turning it into a beacon that gave
away the Jaguar's location. To buy them time, I created a diversion.
Both choppers were already damaged by heavy gunfire, so going
down was believable. The crew is safe, here with me. Over."

"Stay where you are. Things are winding down at the
compound, and I'll be on a plane soon to arrive later. The *capos* are
both dead. They met face to face to plan to work together, but a
nervous *Temoso Lugarteniente* mistook a clap of thunder for a shot
fired in betrayal. They all opened fire on one another. Watch for
leaderless *Sicarios* in your vicinity. They'll try to convince Romeo
to return. Convey my sympathies to Romeo until I arrive. Over."

Ben sat with a blank expression, too stunned at this turn of
events to respond. The Weaver said, "Grayson, do you copy? Over."

"Uh—yeah. Yes, sir, I copy. Will you want us to travel to the
compound? Over."

"Roger. You'll be notified when the area is secure. Update status
on the Princess. I'm flying down with the Prince. Over.

"Roger. She collapsed when she got inside, but she's sleeping now. She looks haggard and has a bruise from the hit she took in the jungle that knocked her out cold. The Jaguar says she needs medical attention at the compound. Over."

The hair-raising scream of the puma penetrated the room from just outside, and Ben turned to Jack's station at the window. Weaver's voice instantly dropped the weariness and demanded to know what was happening. Ben grabbed his rifle and kept the microphone on so he could respond hands-free. "Weaver, we've got three cats guarding the house from under the porch. The Puma just screamed, and we're investigating. Over."

"Explain the cats under the porch. Over."

Ben shouted back to the microphone as he and the Panther took shelter by windows. He risked peering out, listening to his guards reporting on walkie-talkies. "A jaguar led the Princess out of the abandoned building before lightning struck, to the hacienda. It was a rendezvous point for joining a panther and a puma. Over."

Ben watched the three cats pace menacingly. "Update that report, Weaver. The cats are out creating a no-pass zone. Over!"

The Panther shouted at the microphone before Weaver could respond. "Weaver, we've got a hostage situation here! My guards report that Temoso will kill Romeo's friend if he doesn't give himself up. Over."

By now, the Jaguar and the rest of his team were awake and running in to get an update, shaking off the lingering disadvantage of having too little sleep. They tucked in shirttails, turned on body cameras, and checked their weapons.

Beside the Jaguar, Romeo's head snapped up. He ran to the Panther's side, peeking out to see who the hostage was. "No!" he wailed.

Carlos took a quick position at Romeo's other side, sandwiching him between himself and the Panther. He was trapped.

The Jaguar snapped, "It doesn't matter who it is. You're not leaving this room!"

Weaver barked from the radio. "Jaguar, is the Princess with you? Over."

"Nadia is assigned to her, and the guards in the back are still at their stations. Over." The Jaguar ordered the team member with the wounded arm to go reinforce Nadia's watch and nodded his assent when he caught Azariah's eyes.

Then the leader turned his attention to the window. Threatening voices outside yelled their terms for the release of Dominic Vega.

It's not that Azariah didn't trust the skill of the wounded guard on the Jaguar's team, but his arm was in a sling. Not only that, this hostage situation could be a distraction while the back of the house fell under attack.

He left the threats and defensive positioning in the huge front room to follow the guard down the hallway. If Caroline and Nadia were in danger, he wanted to be there. He cuddled the cool hardness of his rifle in readiness—*for what*? Sweat beaded on his forehead and the hair on his neck stood up. *What is it, God? Show me...*

"Azariah, get Caroline!" The Jaguar's shouted order was accompanied by running boot steps, then gunfire erupted from both the front and back yards.

The guard in front of Azariah aimed toward the shutters, yelling for him to go. Azariah was almost to the Jaguar's bedroom door when he hit the floor. A small explosion rocked the front side of the hacienda.

He pushed forward to crawl to the next door, but a smaller explosion rocked the back of the house, near the outside corner he'd just come from. The structure groaned and splintered in protest, sending glass shattering and falling. The room to Caroline may already be open at the French doors.

Azariah groped for his rifle again while his vision swam. His ears rang as he looked back to see the Jaguar sprawled out on the hallway floor. The extra guard couldn't cover either of them, for he had been knocked back against the wall like a limp rag doll. Voices came from somewhere, but he couldn't distinguish words yet.

Crawling on his stomach toward the room door, he glanced back at clamor behind him. A shot from outside sent splinters flying from the doorframe. The Jaguar roused enough to roll on his side, firing into the room.

Making his way on his belly, Azariah barely saw through the smoky mist and scattered debris. It looked as if two men were jerking Nadia from the floor near the shutters and threatening her. Caroline's bare calf and foot were just disappearing under the high bed on his side. He crawled closer, then pulled his loaded Beretta 71 pistol from its holster.

Nudging Caroline's ankle, he made sure she understood that it was cocked as he pushed it under the bed skirt. He felt a twinge of anxiety at handing his weapon to her. A part of him was missing now. The pistol wasn't a dainty piece, but it was effective and accurate. She practiced with it sometimes and had the skill to bring anyone down if she needed to.

He peeked under the fabric and put his finger to his lips, narrowing his eyes at her sternly until she nodded. Rising cautiously to one knee behind the bed, he snaked the barrel of his rifle over the tangled blanket.

Nadia cried out in fury, freeing herself from one attacker and deftly sweeping her knife out of its sheath to bury it in his thigh. Her victim fell into broken debris, frantically trying to staunch his gushing blood. Another man jumped over the remains of broken glass and a splintered shutter to help disarm her, yelling and slapping her. She didn't answer, so he switched to broken English, demanding to know where the American woman and Dominic Vega were.

She pushed back into the attacker who held her, but he was stocky and regained his balance. That move earned her a knife at her throat. After warning her not to try anything else, he kissed the blade to her skin to draw a slim trickle of blood.

Azariah was ready to shoot, but Nadia remained in his line of fire. No one was standing still. He caught sight of a fourth man jogging through the yard toward the gaping hole to get into the room. Nadia's interrogator unwisely had his back to Azariah, but was right in front of her, threatening in his heavy accent. "If you don't cooperate, you'll never answer another question again. I'm asking for the last time. Where's the American *gringa*?"

"I'm right here."

The man spun on his heel with a wild shot at the bed. It narrowly missed Azariah, who never flinched as he pulled the trigger. But he knew that it was a shot upwards from the floor that kept the man from ever firing again. It was the familiar sound of his own Beretta.

A blur of golden-bronze and black streaked past outside the mangled shutters, and the fourth attacker screamed, *"El Jaguar!"* Those were his last words.

Nadia seized the distraction to disarm the man who held her, using his own weapon. By the time Azariah rushed to her aid, his rifle aimed, she stood over her moaning attacker, blood dripping from what looked like his hunting knife. Her chest was heaving, and she licked her dry lips. But the look in her eyes—how many times had he lived it, felt it?

The Jaguar burst through the door with frantic shouts for Caroline, blood and dust smeared over his camouflage shirt. Her answer was muffled from her hiding place under the bed. He nearly choked with relief and dropped to his knees to pull her legs, helping her back out while the buttons on his borrowed shirt made scratchy sounds on the polished hardwoods. She held out the gun to him as she sat up and quickly re-tied the string in the waistband of his borrowed gym shorts. Then he pulled her up, ignoring everyone while he wrapped his arms around her as if needing assurance that she was real.

Azariah turned to give them privacy, but the Jaguar's mood was contagious. He grasped Nadia into an unprofessional hug, and she responded with zeal. It didn't matter that she smeared enemy blood from her hand all over the back of his bulletproof vest and her own against the front.

The Jaguar found his voice and used it near Caroline's ear. "I had to keep *Temoso* from coming through the hall, but when I heard the shots, I thought they killed you! I'd never be able to live with losing you here in my house, my own room. You were my mission!"

"I couldn't let them murder Nadia," she rasped. "But I think—"

She clamped a hand over the quiver in her lips, bracing herself to utter the next words. Her eyes were full of pain when she met the Jaguar's, and she dropped her hand to her chest. "I think I killed the guy who shot at me. I've never killed anyone! Now he's in—now he has no more chances to be in heaven."

Nadia exchanged a lightning-fast look with Azariah and pulled away, kneeling to check the pulse of the man. "Azariah took him down with a clean shot, Caroline. I saw it. You hit him all right, like an ace, after that brilliant effort to distract him. God Himself is the one who decides every man's time to die. This criminal used up all his chances, like the thief on the cross who mocked Jesus."

The bodyguard knelt beside her to feel for surveillance equipment on the man's body and blurted, "That's right, Caroline. You saved the day, though, by getting his attention. I couldn't shoot with Nadia so close to him."

He tossed a small radio and other items onto the bed, then walked over to Caroline with open arms. The Jaguar was reluctant but sniffed and let her go to him, then picked up the Beretta and looked it over. He held it out to the bodyguard who holstered it as he stroked the back of Caroline's hair and soothed her as he spoke. "That was incredibly brave, Caroline. You disobeyed my orders to stay quiet, but you kept Nadia alive."

She shuddered, her face buried in his shoulder, so he communicated with the Jaguar over her head. The Jaguar's eyes locked on the bodyguard's, gesturing for clarification and getting a nod. He grimaced while Azariah said, "You're a great shot, Sugar, but Southern Belles aren't meant for such unpleasantness. I'm trained for this. Don't go taking credit and making me look bad. I don't want you to wonder about it anymore, you understand me?"

Part Three

Power Up

Chapter Twenty-Two

Our scars make us know that our past was for real.
-Jane Austin, Pride and Prejudice

Phillip Chadwick Gregory III carried himself with an assurance that had no trace of an attempt to impress. In fact, his manner said he couldn't care less about anyone's opinions of him. He'd own any room or situation he walked into, yet he was self-unaware and unpretentious.

Christian Chavarria liked him instantly.

When the Prince climbed athletically out of a helicopter at the airstrip in the compound, he carried himself like he was starring in this role in a movie. Christian remained quiet. Silence and distance between them seemed to suit the Prince just fine.

It was one thing to be impressed. It was another thing altogether to witness the man's reunion with the Princess. He slid her wedding band and a diamond engagement ring on her finger and kissed her like he'd never see her again. The look on her face as he stepped out of the chopper tugged out a frail tendril of a memory—a black and white newspaper photo, where she was looking up at a younger version of this Prince. The memory brought a fresh stab of hurt, and he heard his own voice in his mind saying to someone that this guy was the one, because she'd never looked at him like that.

She still didn't.

Weariness lined every face around a late dinner in the beautifully decorated dining hall in the Chavarria mansion. Chandeliers and candelabra illuminated a sumptuous meal served on elegant china, sparkling crystal, and silver. All discussions of the mission were taboo until the next morning.

Romeo and Juliet sat together, comforting one another by grasping hands, grieving both their fathers and the friends lost in the rival cartels' implosion over the last week. Their reunion was bittersweet when the bedraggled teams from the attacked Chavarria plantation arrived at the compound. A sobbing Juliet ran to meet Romeo, bemoaning their role in the loss of so many lives. He shushed her with assurances they'd done the right thing, come what may.

Juliet held on to the hope of her father's last words when he promised he'd asked for Christ's forgiveness. Romeo could only hope his own father found the same. His friend, held hostage at the plantation, was wounded in the skirmish with the hacienda guards and kept in bed tonight, but would accompany them in fleeing to a new life.

Christian was given a seat beside the Weaver and across from the Princess. She was beautiful tonight in clothes her husband brought, her hair styled and her makeup perfect. He tried to focus on his food, silent unless answering the Weaver or his father when they drew him into conversation. Likewise, she only spoke if asked something that required an answer.

Beside her, the Prince appeared to restrain himself from being overly attentive in the company of others. Since being reunited, she wasn't warm to him. She often looked around as if on guard for danger, but she sought no security or reassurance in the man beside her. Christian met the disturbed gaze of the Prince. Perhaps her husband didn't understand the lesson the Jaguar had learned out in the jungle.

The Princess knew men would fail her. She looked over their heads to a higher power.

In the interlude after dinner when tea and coffee were served in front of a cheerful fire, the Prince suggested that the Princess point out the Southern Cross for him from the patio outside. Her eyes darted warily as he led her out by the elbow, reminding her of the times they'd talked about seeing it together and that the twins would be excited about it when she returned home.

The stargazing was a good idea, for she seemed more at ease when they strolled back inside to enjoy a dessert. Christian was curious when the Prince left her talking with Nadia and Azariah while he went to speak to his brother-in-law, so he wandered over to pour himself a cup of hot tea on a cart behind them.

"Look at her, she acts like she's being stalked," the Prince said to Ben. "She barely ate, as if she might have to run before swallowing. As far as she's concerned, she's not out of this jungle yet, or ready to break away from dependence on the Jaguar."

Ben nodded. "Technically, she's right, Chad. Terrible things happened on the other side of the walls of the compound. This is the Jaguar's turf. He knows how to deal with it."

"Chavarria says it might be a good idea to keep her out in the open living area here on her first night back. He had all large plants removed before we arrived so she wouldn't think of the jungle. The fire in the hearth and space to see what's around her might project security. She won't relax in a strange room off somewhere in the dark, by ourselves. I'm goin' to suggest to her she rests tonight on my lap on the sofa, and we'll take things a day at a time. She sees me as another potential victim, not a protector, so Azariah and Nadia offered to stay over there in the chairs."

Christian's wounds from the explosion were trivial in the scheme of things, but they were bothering him. He said goodnight along with the others who left the great hall. It was a relief to be going to his own bed, safely tucked here in the compound, but he'd miss his den with the Princess. What would her Prince whisper about as they wandered off into dreams together again?

He expected the ache of separation as he drifted away into sleep. But he awakened in the first hours after midnight from a dream that men were coming for her, and he reached for a rifle that wasn't there. He threw off the sheet and sat up, massaging the tension from his temples. The crippling flash that had stricken him too often the past week made him press his palm into the scar on his head. He knew by now that it wouldn't help, but instinct made him react as if he could be master of the debilitating pain. Only a few seconds ticked past to endure it, but the ache it left in his heart lingered.

The inevitable price had to be paid for living every moment with the Princess, and this was only the first night. He rocked himself back and forth, hugging his arms around his bandaged ribs. His own voice, his words, were like an echo throwing itself against the walls of a canyon in his mind. He stared into the memory of her face, full of pain she never expected to encounter from him.

I wanted to have a life that included you ... now I see that I was running from what I was meant to be, and wanted you to run with me, away from what you are meant to be... running from what I was meant to be and wanted you to run with me...

The distant crashing of waves accompanied visions of palm trees that swayed around him, waving congenially as if there was no need to rush off. There were stained glass windows. *This week, I had no excuses and no room for doubt anymore. I know what I'm supposed to do, and I'll never be the same if I don't do it... Caroline, I can't take you where I'm going, and you can't wait for me to return.*

Heedless of the bandage on his ribs, he hugged himself tighter, as she had held him in the abandoned ruin on his cocoa plantation. But this time, he gave up the fight to be strong like a jaguar. There was no one to see. Swift tears were salty on his lips before he could keep them wiped away. Like the taste of a day in the surf.

I'm not sorry that you've come to this point, she had whispered. He squeezed his eyes tight and let a stab into his heart drill into an underground pool of bitterness. Some relief came as it drained and spread. Of course, she was glad he'd come to this point. She was the one who'd gotten what she'd always wanted! A girl like that always gets what she wants. What would she know about letting go of a dream, about sacrifice?

But then her stricken expression came into his mind again, full of disbelief that he was breaking off their courtship. He couldn't bear it, and he growled in his throat while he rubbed his eyes, trying to erase the sight forever. Another scene in the old foreman's quarters on the plantation replaced it, and her voice drowned out everything else again. *This is greatness—to be larger than life. Don't you see, that's what you were called to be? Our own personal dreams are tawdry, not worthy of the aura of wonder we surround them with, when compared with surrendering to God.*

He could sit like this no longer. Padding over a plush rug and onto hardwoods, he reached the French doors and rested his head against his forearm to watch the activity that accompanied a raid on the compound. Guards and repair crews scurried along the wall. The wild tangle of jungle lay beyond it, noisy, menacing and unsearchable. This is where surrender had led him.

Turning away, Christian paced the room before going to the door. He would rest easier if he saw the Princess he'd guarded with his life for a week.

His silent steps lead to the catwalk railing, and he grimaced at the aches and pains of a challenging mission while lowering himself to sit on the top step. Peering through the ornate wrought iron, he saw the Princess sleeping, her head on a small pillow in the Prince's lap. Her hair had come loose and spilled over him. She looked more like a dreaming fashion model than a wife and mother of three small children. Her husband had been right, of course. She didn't fit in here.

The Prince roused himself from nodding off, using one hand to massage his neck and rake back his hair. A flash of reflected firelight bounced from his platinum wedding band as he covered his yawn with a tanned hand. Gazing into the low flames, he no longer looked strong, confident, and in charge. He looked exhausted, young, vulnerable—scared.

It was time to stop acting like a peeping Tom. But Christian froze with his hand on the cool iron railing when he saw the glistening trail of a tear down the Prince's face. An instant bond with him made Christian's throat tighten and his red-rimmed eyes sting. Neither of them knew what tomorrow held, or next week, or next year.

They were about the same age. Maybe the Jaguar was the one who worked in the wild jungle half the time, but he knew the Prince's world was just as much a jungle. The Jaguar would be a miserable failure at the Prince's role, and as he'd told the Prince a few days ago, he'd be fish bait here where the Jaguars saved the day.

They were different, yet the same. They functioned in the places their talents and spiritual gifts were meant for. It was as it should be.

The Prince seemed to sense he was not alone. He wiped the tear away and glanced around. Ever so slowly, Christian—no, the Jaguar—rose to his feet, and the Prince looked up. For a long moment in which the Jaguar knew his face was being studied in the shadows, they acknowledged one another in silence.

Then something he couldn't have expected happened. The Prince mouthed the words *thank you*.

The busy physician in the compound gave Nadia the verdict: her rappelling days were over. His pronouncement was expected, and Nadia accepted it graciously. She wasn't as gracious about using the wood-carved cane he borrowed from Chavarria.

In a sterner tone, the physician ordered Caroline to rest. She inclined her head to a table where her sketchbook and a leather-bound volume of Kipling's *Jungle Book* rested.

The Jaguar peeked in to check on the ladies' reprieve in the sprawling room that served as a library and drawing room. He knew the doctor ordered Caroline to rest, but he found her walking leisurely over to investigate a painting that dominated the room.

She was dressed in a sophisticated pairing of black and white with a sweater and pants tailored to her best advantage. He couldn't help imagining another Princess, actress Grace Kelly, wearing this at a refreshing picnic luncheon in a gazebo by a sparkling lake. The lake would be somewhere in the world where there was no trouble, and an afternoon was something to savor, passing in slow motion.

Caroline's gleaming hair was styled in relaxed waves that almost reached the middle of her back, a style impossible to create on the run in a hostile jungle. This version of the Princess would take some getting used to, like seeing the winking chunk of a diamond on her ring finger and the ones that swayed from her earlobes.

She stopped under the enormous painting of a jaguar, transfixed. "I admire people who can paint like this," she said to Nadia. "I've always dreamed of being able to accomplish such a masterpiece. This jaguar looks like he could walk right into the room, yet the blurred edges of his form are painterly, as many of the trees are. My work is always a bit fanciful, impressionistic—more contemporary."

"I've seen your collection," Nadia replied. "You've developed your own voice, so you're unable to copy a subject. That's not how it gets processed in your creative lens. You see so much more than the shell of that jaguar. You get inside of him, you consider where he's been and where he's going, what a day in his life is like. Your painting expresses his essence. That's quite an accomplishment, and most would-be artists never reach it."

Caroline laughed, a musical sound that made the Jaguar's heart skip. "Nadia, have you been talking to my Uncle Wyeth about me?" She peered closer at the painting, searching for the artist's signature.

Christian checked the time on his watch and decided he had more fleeting moments to steal while she was in his life. Clearing his throat to announce his presence, he strolled in, relishing the warm smile that greeted him. He went to stand beside her, delivering a teasing comment in his most serious tone. "I'm serving notice that you've had your limit of beauty sleep. If you're not caught up yet, it's illegal in these parts to look any better."

Grinning, she bumped her shoulder into his shirt, meeting his eyes with camaraderie. "I slept fairly well, but not long enough. It will be awhile before I reach that illegal limit, and only the extra makeup is keeping that bruise around my temple from being shocking. You look great, too, exceptionally dashing in regular clothes. I hope you're obeying the doctor's orders."

"I'm properly bandaged, if that eases your mind. It seems neither of us are a good patient."

Caroline looked at Nadia for support as she protested, "But I've been resting! I just needed to stretch my legs and get a close look at this magnificent painting. Who's the artist?"

He pointed to the signature, camouflaged in the brush strokes of jungle growth. "His name runs up this tree to blend into the trunk, as a vine would do. Many years ago, the Weaver commissioned this as a gift to my dad, and he included instructions there was to be nothing in the scene that might distract viewers from being in the presence of the majestic jaguar." He sighed, his eyes roaming appreciatively over the expanse of the painting. "The deviation from the typical artist signature was a good call. His would've been a conversation-starter. The artist signed his work as 'Noble Painter.'"

Beside him, Caroline gasped, eyes wide and fixed on the name that skipped up the tree. Christian spoke haltingly, watching her reaction. "It's a clever play on words, a painter characterized by being noble."

"He was certainly that," Caroline said with a dreamy tone and expression. "Noble Painter was my grandfather. My Poppy Noble. I want to know more about this painting! Was it completed here, or shipped?"

Christian gulped, uncertain he believed the unlikely connection yet. "I'll ask my dad. This was the first thing I saw the day I awakened after almost dying in Montserrat. Can you imagine its impact? The painting, this room, all so foreign to me. I was in a hospital bed right over there, with my head wrapped and a nurse at my side. My dad—Chavarria—marched in here with love in his eyes and a cheerful voice. I didn't know him or this mansion, but I felt safe. The jungle outside wasn't strange to me, so I assumed I'd lived in it before."

With a reflective tone, Caroline said, "So, you opened your eyes with a clean slate and a vision of your destiny—your new life, your new home. The Lord always seems to show you who He wants you to be. You always land on your feet."

He crossed his arms over his chest and planted his boots farther apart, scowling at the painting and weighing her observation. "I never thought of it that way."

The stance he'd assumed was so Chris Shepherd that Caroline bit her lip. Days she'd spent in the jungle with him proved to be a monument to his calling. Her grandfather's painting on the wall was a reminder of her own path, and yet it blended both. Somehow, her Poppy Noble's work had ended up in a diabolical jungle as a statement about who Christian Chavarria was.

It was also a statement about where she belonged. "I wish I could go back to being who I was!" she blurted in a strangled voice.

Chad hesitated with a small tray of food from the kitchen, his bright greeting dying on his lips at hearing Caroline's heart-wrenching statement. Nadia rose, reaching for the carved cane borrowed from her host. "Just what we needed. Thank you, Mr. Gregory!"

Following her lead, he recovered and continued toward a buffet table. "Just call me Chad, so I won't look around for my father. I wanted to check on my wife before I join the Weaver in an excursion this afternoon."

Christian caught Chad's deliberate choice of the words "my wife," and the nuance in his tone. He checked his watch again and strode toward the carved double doors. "She just needs time to get past the jungle jitters. They are common after missions. It's a change to go back to the ordinary."

He hadn't meant to insinuate that Chad Gregory was ordinary, but once he saw the look on his face, he let it go unexplained. "If you'll excuse me, I'm on my way to a debriefing with the team."

The Weaver and the elder Chavarria interacted in a way that reminded Chad of Caroline's uncle, Wyeth Painter, and his father. They were as easy together as his twins Rhett and Rayce were. He'd seen the Weaver at work and could believe his reputation, but he was still getting used to envisioning Chavarria as a former Jaguar. He kept the build of a once-powerful man, but his role as host was so refined Chad couldn't imagine him on a mission, functioning as his son just had. It was also uncanny how much the current Jaguar favored him, as if he was his own blood.

Chad both anticipated and dreaded what he would encounter on this supervisory tour of the mission area. He and Ben had come along as liaisons of Gregory Global's interests concerning the kidnapping. The first site on the list was the clearing where the attack on Caroline occurred, and Chad had asked to land the chopper when they got there. After some private discussion, the Weaver and Chavarria agreed that there was time to check on how the investigation on the ground was progressing.

He grimly watched the monotony of endless green canopy as they flew over it, but his mind was mulling over something else. While Caroline had taken a shower that morning, he flipped through her sketchbook. The last one she finished snatched his breath away. On the ground, alert, with a rifle pointed out, lay an arresting pose of a man ready for danger. There was confidence in his bearing, strength in every underlying muscle and in his jawline.

Chad knew it was the Jaguar, and he was impressed by the imminent danger communicated in the lines. Caroline had been this close to whatever he faced to protect her.

Along the side of the page, he saw she had erased some writing.

He'd glanced up at the bathroom door to hear that the water was still running. Toying with his conscience, he wondered if she made one of her notes about a color, smell, sound, time, or feeling, then made a decision to erase it. But why would she do that? The only plausible reason was no one was ever supposed to see it. And that made him want to.

Reaching for her lightest pencil, he rubbed graphite on his fingertip, then smeared it over bruised indentations in the paper where the words had been. Dismayed, he stared at the spectral traces of her handwriting and caught his breath. *Turn off camera.*

At the sudden sound of the shower door opening, he had rushed to use a kneaded eraser to obliterate his graphite smudge and leave the page looking undisturbed. There were no other personal notes except the date, which placed the setting for the sketch as being the building struck by lightning.

The circling motion of the chopper jarred him back to the present. Miniscule figures below were combing through the clearing site where the Jaguar's team had been attacked. They radioed shocking news about the body count to the Weaver and Chavarria as they set the chopper down. Most had died by gunfire, some near to one another. But wild animals and snake bites killed many. The few rescued survivors were getting medical attention and being interrogated.

Investigators were on the scene where attackers had pulled Caroline into the jungle. "I want to see where it happened," Chad announced in his most authoritative tone. He knew he sounded just like his dad, and like him, he expected to get what he asked for.

The Weaver tried to dissuade him. But Chad was resolute. "This is for Caroline. I'll walk where she's been so she won't think only the Jaguar can comprehend the nightmare she endured. I can't be her bridge back to what's normal if I've never even seen where it happened."

He turned on his boot heel toward the jungle's edge. His brother-in-law stepped up beside him, with Weaver and Chavarria tagging along behind. The surrounding jungle rang out with the chatter, calls, and screams of rambunctious wildlife.

A gloved investigator handed the Weaver a knife in a clear bag with labels on it. A quick interchange revealed it was the one the

Panther armed the Princess with. It was found near the Jaguar's Land Rover and used to stab a man whose body had been identified from the videos of the village confrontation earlier that day.

"Was this the cause of death?" asked the Weaver curtly.

"No, sir, the cause of death is the venom of a snake bite. We'll confirm her prints on the handle. She sure is a fighter!"

The man's tone brimmed with admiration. Chad stopped with an alert look back, listening. The agent didn't know who he was and might give away something confidential. The investigator pointed his finger to tracks that bruised the ground. "Don't know who taught her this, but she dug in with her shoes to leave a clear trail and slow down her attackers. They had to stop and struggle with her. Without her efforts here, there's no doubt the outcome would have been much different."

Taking a few steps ahead, the investigator gestured toward the evidence of the Jaguar's crawling movements when he chased them. Lengths of string were pinned in trajectories from his trail, leading to the bodies of those killed when he'd rolled and returned fire into the trees.

Chad's spirit sank, his confidence waning in the Jaguar's stellar competence in the rising body count. He was no longer eager to face what lay ahead of him in this terrible place. Perhaps he'd be the one who needed counseling and treatment for trauma, for he'd never get over what Caroline had endured for the sake of a vile man's vendetta.

Ben, the Weaver and Chavarria led him into the dense foliage. He watched them scowl at colored tags marking things they understood about the trails, and they often squatted down to look closer. He steered clear of a body bag in which there was said to be a snake bitten attacker, but the others went closer and asked a few questions of the man taking measurements on the ground.

Chad brushed away sweat beading up on his forehead, then walked toward a handful of men who were exchanging information. Ben rushed up, gripping his arm at the same instant Chad froze in horror. Gagging, he turned from the grotesque view of two mangled bodies the wild jaguar had ripped the throats from. The stench of those remains made him reel, and Ben grasped his other shoulder to steady him.

This was where it happened. One of these men pinned her down, and another had knocked her out for being so much trouble and crying out. She'd been helpless to their intentions.

A wild sound rumbled from deep inside him, rising to his throat and erupting in an incoherent roar. He blindly tried to jerk free from Ben to go forward.

"You can't touch anything!" the Weaver was firm, but kind. "God's hand dealt them justice for eternity. There's nothing more you can do to make them pay."

A bloodstained, ripped shirt laid on the ground, the one Caroline had been wearing two nights ago. Nausea swept over Chad in waves, and he gulped deep breaths to keep down his lunch. Chavarria fished out a roll of mints from his pocket, handing him the package and explaining that he never came to an investigation without them.

The three men stood around Chad as if shielding him from the view. He dissolved the mint in his mouth and soon asked where the trail to the stream began.

"You've had enough," the Weaver replied solemnly. "There's nothing there. It's not a crime scene."

"That depends on your definition of a crime." He met Ben's eyes before directing his question at the Weaver. "Did you find the Jaguar's body cam?"

"On the bank, just as he reported."

"Show me the stream."

Chavarria and the Weaver exchanged a long look before the Weaver turned, following flagged markers of a trail of moss and decomposed plant matter. When they reached the banks of an unremarkable stream, Chad stepped around the scrapes of the Jaguar's boot marks, careful not to disturb anything. Gurgling water played over rocks and winked in reflected sunlight.

He closed his eyes, trying to imagine the scene that night, with moonbeams illuminating it through the break in the jungle canopy. He filled his lungs with the damp jungle scent that Caroline had been breathing for over a week. Then, he squatted down, eyeing the shallow pool and gentle waterfall formed from smooth rocks. This was where the Jaguar had awakened her. He'd been frantic, thinking she could die, yet still he shut off the camera rather than let it record his actions.

The guy had a great point about her modesty. But couldn't he have left it on one of those rocks for reporting sound and a view of the trail from the attack site?

Chad narrowed his eyes at the sight while his pulse throbbed. Something happened here that changed the Jaguar, he was sure of it. He'd seen it in his demeanor afterwards, and he knew the look. If he'd been in the Jaguar's place, what might he have done in private desperation under such extreme circumstances? What might he have done if he thought they wouldn't live through the ordeal? No repercussions, that was the condition the Jaguar demanded.

He rose slowly, turning a scenario over in his mind and hoping Caroline hadn't reciprocated or made any declarations. The answers he wanted were not here in the evidence. The Jaguar was too well trained for that. As for Caroline, she was in shock, so she wasn't a reliable source yet. But in time, and with enough distance, she might mention something he could use to piece this together.

Then a thought struck him. He ran his hand across his face. Maybe he was better off not knowing. Had she kissed the Jaguar, made rash declarations? That would explain the Jaguar's new demeanor.

As the Weaver's group climbed back into the chopper to continue their rounds, Chad felt the irreversible change that comes with a loss of innocence. His very soul felt raided. The scenes he had watched on the monitors in Whitehaven were now a stark reality, and all he could do was pray that this violating experience would help both him and Caroline heal from a dark valley in the shadow of death.

It wasn't long by air to find the exploded Rovers and the sooty ashes of the abandoned building amid scorched trees. Chad met his brother-in-law Ben's eyes and shook his head again at the incredulity of Caroline following a wild animal straight to the hidden structure. Not even the Jaguar had known it existed. But his report stated his belief that Caroline's forced trek into darkness and trust in the cat who had destroyed her attackers had gone a long way to resolving her sudden terror of the dark.

Ben explained to the Weaver and Chavarria what happened in the freak lightning storm. The Weaver's face was grim at the sight of the twisted remains of his helicopter. Chavarria asked if they could land on the scorched ground.

At the rock pilings of the foundation, Chad felt queasy again at the ashy smell. His wife missed the lightning strike by less than five minutes, and his first thought was that she might burn alive.

Chavarria stared at the sooty remains as if seeing something else. When he spoke, his voice was as distant as the look in his eyes. He talked of a day when he thought his family was safely pocketed out of reach from his enemies. His voice grew stronger as his story unfolded, and finally he was choking with unchecked emotions. They waited for him as he struggled to finish the account of finding his wife, brutally murdered, and he'd never been able to bring himself to tear the building down. Instead, he buried her and let the jungle have the place as a hidden monument to her memory, and as a reminder not to fall in love again.

The Weaver stood beside Chavarria during this unexpected memorial until his friend fell to his knees. Tears poured down his face before he, too, went to his knees, putting his arm around Chavarria's shoulders. Then the two white-haired men leaned on one another as they stiffly rose to their feet, and Chavarria said, "No matter what you do, my friend, only God can keep her safe."

He and the Weaver started walking back to the chopper, and Chad turned a quizzical look to Ben. "Who's he talking about?" he whispered.

Ben murmured, "You haven't guessed? A lot will change at Painter Place when we get back."

Wide-eyed, Chad belted himself into his seat and tapped his brother-in-law on the arm to get his attention. He mouthed a name. Ben nodded and clicked his belts in the next seat while the chopper's blades roared in the charred jungle surrounding them.

Back in the air with a bird's-eye view, Chad was intrigued by the cocoa plantation and asked Chavarria some questions about the next harvest. He had learned something about the business in Panama, helping an investor get through the days of conflict with Dictator Manuel Noriega and with *Operation Just Cause* over Christmas back in 1989. It was one of the fascinating jobs that helped him get past the grief and discouragement of the destruction of his home by Hurricane Hugo.

When Chavarria mentioned he gave the plantation to his son a year ago, Chad felt the proverbial pail of cold water drenching his ignited embers of interest. He had no plans to become business partners with the man who announced he was waiting on him to die or make a wrong move so he could have his wife. But even while the sizzling steam spiraled up from those embers, Chavarria fanned them again by pointing out the window, noting that his son would need help to recover from the setback of delays and damages. Chad's conscience whispered that Global was partially responsible for the Jaguar's heavy losses on the plantation.

His first glimpse of the house from the air spiked his pulse rate. Men scurried to clear away debris, and covered bodies lay along one tree line. He groaned. The destruction and death toll were mounting in the wake of Caroline's kidnapping.

The moment the Weaver and Chavarria stepped from the chopper, investigators rushed up with reports, tagging along as they all ducked under the rotating blades. Chad stopped in his tracks when the biggest wild cat he'd ever seen stretched from under what remained of the front porch with a lazy blink of huge eyes. Two more stepped out to look at them as if analyzing whether they were friend or foe.

A chill went down Chad's spine. If they attacked only a gun could stop the takedown. He caught himself checking for his as Chavarria addressed the cats. "If you wish to remain here, you're welcome, but we must build you some different accommodations. That porch is unstable."

Whether this jaguar was the answer to the tribe's prayer in defending Caroline or not, Chad couldn't tell. It had the same golden-green eyes and the same spots. The cat acknowledged Chavarria's conversational tone with a throaty, gravelly grumble, and slowly stepped over to the group. His sleek companions followed at leisure. The panther looked like the cast shadow of the jaguar, but the tawny mountain lion was smaller.

In an unconcerned tone, Chavarria told the men to stand still. "They're just curious, not hungry. This is likely the same jaguar that saved the Princess, which isn't impossible if he ran as the crow flies that night. The Rovers had to wander the only roads we have here. But this jaguar wasn't limited to running, of course, in supernatural circumstances. After all, in Acts 8, verses 39 and 40 in the Bible, Phillip baptized the Ethiopian, then disappeared when he was snatched away by the Lord, finding himself in Azotus, where he began preaching."

The jaguar's responding rumble was followed by one from his dark companion. "Gentlemen, this panther is a jaguar, as you can see from the markings on his coat in the sunshine. On our team, the Panther is the Jaguar's shadow, second in command. The puma may be smaller than they are, but he means business. If you ever hear him cry out to intimidate a rival, you'll never forget it."

With one giant paw poised in the air as if he hadn't made up his mind where to go next, the jaguar looked from Chavarria to Chad, who struggled to swallow a lump in his throat. This was a fresh new perspective for him on the Bible's account of Daniel in the lions' den. Things ended well for Daniel, but the same lions who were meek with him had ripped apart his enemies. King Darius acknowledged afterwards that God did exist and had saved Daniel, much like the proclamation of the tribal chief here who presented his woven mantle to The Shining Woman.

The cat came to Chad, who felt eerily like he was watching in slow motion. It sniffed around his shirt, then shoved the black triangle of his nose firmly against the palm of his hand. Finally, he turned to make his way to the porch.

"He smells your wife," explained Chavarria, his voice low. "You must have held her today."

Chad wiped his palm against his khakis and tried to wet his lips to reply, but his mouth was too dry. Chavarria beckoned the group with a gesture, leading them around to the back of the house where debris was being piled farther from the structure. Most of the hacienda was now open to the elements, and he climbed on stacked cement blocks and pointed inside a large room. "The master bedroom," he announced, shaking his head sadly, then he glanced out at Ben. "This is where she killed him?"

Ben shot an alarmed look over at Chad, then turned to the Weaver. "Is this for the record?"

The Weaver twisted from his waist to look around. None of the investigators or cleaning crew were close enough to hear. "No. Off the record."

Ben climbed up into the room beside Chavarria and pointed out positions as he described them. "Azariah crawled in under cover of the confusion created by the explosions. The bed was high from the floor and Nadia ordered Caroline to hide under it. Azariah saw her taking shelter there and slid his pistol to her to use as a last resort. He positioned himself as a sniper but had no clean shot that wouldn't hit Nadia."

He moved and gestured to another spot. "An attacker over here demanded to know where Caroline was, threatening to kill Nadia if she didn't cooperate, drawing blood with a blade against Nadia's neck. Caroline took his threat seriously and pointed the gun up at him, announcing that she was right there. He shot at the bed toward her voice, almost hitting Azariah. For all she knew, Azariah was down. She took the attacker out just before Azariah did."

While Chad stood gaping at the scene, Ben addressed him. "In the official account, Azariah took down the attacker and Caroline helped with a nearly simultaneous shot. She was upset that she may have killed the man, and after all she'd been through, he and Nadia didn't think she should live with it, even in the assurance of self-defense. It's enough for her to know she has it in her to do it. The Jaguar agrees with them."

Chad inhaled the wafting putrid odors of blood, corpses, and scorched building materials. His stomach lurched. Spinning away from the room to run to a pile of charred and mangled debris from the hacienda, he threw up the water and remains of the last mint he'd had. Like his experience in the men's room at Global on the day he learned Caroline was in danger of gang rape, his stomach kept trying to expel nothingness, as if purging him of an awakening to an evil that had utterly changed his view of the world.

He heard Chavarria's commanding voice behind him, asking someone to bring water and a towel. But his mind reeled from his wrenching emotions. He re-lived the moments in darkness when he fought an intruder in France and shot the man's gun arm. In his mind, he heard his dad's advice when he was a teen, hitting targets at the range. If he ever had to shoot, go for the way the attacker is armed, like his gun or knife hand. *If that fails, do whatever it takes in the name of self-protection, but you'll live with it the rest of your life. Taking a life will change you in a way you can't fathom until it's done, and you'll always wonder if there'd been another way. Make sure you're in the right, because a Gregory going on trial for a manslaughter charge would mar the reputation of the company.*

Bent with hands on his knees, Chad gasped ragged breaths that seemed to calm the heaving. *Caroline protected her friends and herself by taking a life. She knew Azariah couldn't shoot from his vantage point without harming Nadia. She didn't know if he'd been hit by gunfire and therefore unable to defend her and Nadia. So, she made a decision that changed all other outcomes. This is classified information, but if the world finds out, there'll be speculation, investigation, and acts of revenge. Nadia and Azariah understood all this. Azariah had to take the credit.*

Beside him, Ben waved the Weaver and Chavarria away. Chad straightened to see if his stomach would stay where it belonged, and Ben stuck out a hand with a water bottle and a small towel. It embarrassed Chad when his arm trembled, but he reached for them and swished out his mouth several times with the water before spitting it out.

He turned to face the exploded wall of the room again. "How am I supposed to hide this from her?"

Ben crossed his arms. "You promised your dad you'd represent Global's interests here if he'd let you come down in his place. If it weren't for me and Azariah bein' here to protect you, you'd be back in Whitehaven watchin' the dust settling on your desk. You'd know only what the report said, because Phillip wouldn't have told you. This is what it is to be a Gregory, the one who takes the helm of the business, protecting Global's confidences. Can you grasp now that your dad went out on a limb to let you do this? You know why he took the risk? 'Cause it could be you next time. He and Wyeth were once on a short list for kidnapping, and you'd better get your head on straight about who you are, Chad. Caroline has been through enough and didn't ask for any of this!"

"She knows," moaned Chad to the sky. "She's just goin' along with this to avoid facin' it."

"This stuff happens way too fast for someone with no training to comprehend it. Azariah wasn't exactly dishonest with her, because the shots could be considered simultaneous. He says he heard his Beretta as he fired. If it makes it any easier, remember that he killed the guy, too."

Chad wiped beading sweat from his forehead with the towel. Ben tried another tactic. "It's mind-blowing, Chad, what happened when Wilfred Rothschild set all this into motion, chuckling at the trouble he would cause for Global. His plot grew, pickin' up speed like a snowball, and God allowed Caroline to be rolled over and trapped in its path. What men meant for evil, God meant for good."

Turning, Chad stared at the ravaged remains of the hacienda. Ben became animated now. "Only in the Lord's hands could a young American woman from a lazy coastal town obliterate the two most powerful drug empires in South America. They imploded, Chad—that's never happened! To put it in Global's language, she was the 'catalyst for a dramatic economic downturn in the cocaine market.' Not only is that good news for the citizens of Columbia, and kids in America who end up snortin' this stuff, but the Jaguar's report claims there's a wandering tribe in the Amazon who claims to follow the Lord now, testifying to other tribes. The chieftain said his people saw a sign from God in answer to their prayers for the Shining Woman. They had the faith to pray for somethin' as childlike as the behavior of the animals. Those men who attacked Caroline in the clearing did so against their own rules of engagement in a dark jungle, like the true accounts in the Bible, when enemies destroyed one another. When she was defenseless, God sent confusion among her attackers and guardian animals to save her. You know anybody else with a testimony like that?"

Chad's children's voices filled his mind, sitting in his lap at the Big House last Sunday. Rhett had whispered, *Daddy, I'm goin' to pray that God does somethin' good about the bad guys who took Mama, and for the good guys who are helpin' her.* Then Rayce had tickled his ear with a breathy response. *And maybe God will let Mama tell someone a dream, so they can be ready for the bad things.* And beautiful little Savanna chimed in, *And the jungle animals, Rhett. Somethin' good, 'k?*

With a near-sob and a sniff, Chad bit his lips together, looking out into the distant cocoa trees with stinging eyes. The Jaguar's team and Caroline were just ordinary people in the hands of an extraordinary God. But the experience had changed everything for her, including the core of who she was. It was now clear to him what the Jaguar had meant in the drawing room earlier today. Even if her world became ordinary again, Caroline never would be.

Chapter Twenty-Three

You get bad breaks from good shots;
you get good breaks from bad shots –
but you have to play the ball where it lies.
-Bobby Jones, Golf Champion

Cheerful sunbeams played on the windowpanes, splashing prism rainbows into the room where the Princess and Nadia relaxed. After another debriefing, the Jaguar's team stopped by to inhabit the peaceful setting, looking like any American group of friends in jeans and polo shirts. They teased about their bandaged injuries and told her to bring her frying pan and parasol next time she dropped in.

Appreciating the references to the favored weapons of the Princess in the Mario video games, she teased back, admonishing them to refresh their training to be better prepared for BoBombers and *El Diablo*. After more light-hearted banter, the Jaguar, Panther, and Puma asked her to join them for a short stroll to tour the compound.

The Spanish mansion was magnificent with tiles and ornate ironwork balconies. Well-kept gardens showcased a riot of brilliant flowers that nodded in their beds. Sculpted ornamental pines rose as focal points to balance the pathways. The men enjoyed identifying plants for her until Carlos called out to the Panther and Puma from an open door along a terrace, leaving the Jaguar to complete the tour. But some mechanics carrying tools from the garage building waved, shouting, "*El Jaguar, que tal?*"

At once, the Princess spied something in the open garage behind the mechanics. The Jaguar waved back to the men while she exclaimed, "It can't be!"

He tagged along to see where she went with such determination. She grabbed the drape that partially concealed an old sports car that should have rested in peace. He watched her face, hardly daring to breathe, unsure what came next. Open-mouthed, he grappled to find the right question to ask while she ran her hand over the 1967 Triumph Spitfire Mark II. Then she opened the protesting passenger door and gingerly settled her sore body into the cracked old leather on the seat.

"You know this car?" It was a lame observation, but it was out before he realized it.

She laughed, a happy melody that seemed to warm everything around them. "Yes, of course. Don't you?"

"No. It's a piece of junk. My father bought it for me to restore during my recovery the first months I came here. He found out I understood something about cars. Soon I was too busy training to be the Jaguar to work with it."

"He really loves you. I see it in the soft way he looks at you and the proud way he talks about you. Your father found Chris Shepherd's car and got it here. It was running when you left, but you and your biological dad were always working on it. It was his, once."

The Jaguar trailed a hand along the faded paint, then opened the creaking door on the driver's side. He favored his ribs as he settled in, then he gripped the steering wheel and looked ahead. "That's why it feels so familiar. You dated me in this thing? Were you embarrassed?"

She huffed and slapped a reprimand at his arm. "I'm not a snob! Besides, it looked nice enough then, and you kept it spotless."

Now he grinned. "Okay, so I'm the snob, then. Come on, let me show you why." He got out and came to her door, which opened with squeaking protest. Then he pulled the cover from the next vehicle, relishing her astonishment while he folded it back to reveal a sparkling yellow hood.

"A Lotus Esprit!" she exclaimed.

"James Bond's '77 version, the one that turns into a submarine in *The Spy Who Loved Me,* wasn't in my budget. But this is a '94, one of the first to have power steering." He opened the door and gestured for her to get in. She admired the dashboard as he slid behind the wheel. "What do you think?"

"I love it! It looks like you, or at least, the Jaguar you. Not to be confused with Chris Shepherd." She turned a wistful look back over at the old Triumph.

"Princess."

Her gleaming hair swayed with the turn of her head. He savored her smile as she waited expectantly.

"I don't think we'll have another chance for a private moment before you leave tomorrow. There's so much to say."

A pounding a concussion of air against the bay doors overhead announced the imminent arrival of Chavarria's helicopter. A team gathered outside, ready to re-fuel and perform maintenance.

The Jaguar ignored them to look at her as if she was a rain cloud after a long drought. "I meant what I whispered in your ear at the last village, against the goat cart. Nothing will ever change that. But I understand what you've been trying to tell me, and it's okay. I'll make friends with the Prince. He's everything I'd expect you to want, and everything you should have. I liked him from the moment he arrived yesterday."

Her sigh was as soft as her gaze. "Then you're making this misadventure count for something good, for the rest of my life."

Men's voices rose from outside the garage. In resignation, the Jaguar opened his door and came around to open hers. Then they walked toward the paved area to greet the passengers. The Prince stopped short, then recovered, stepping over to take her arm possessively and brush a kiss on her forehead. "Hello, beautiful. You must be feelin' better."

"The team and I wanted the Princess to see that not everything in this country is uncivilized," the Jaguar said, putting out his hand. "She got a tour of the gardens, then saw something inside the garage."

The Prince shook the Jaguar's hand briefly, then looked in the direction he indicated. A flash in his eyes said he remembered this car and he walked toward it.

Conflicted emotions crossed the Princess's face, so the Jaguar winked and turned to follow the Prince. He could see the Prince liked cars and knew something about them. But the tension in his jaw as he looked inside this one communicated that he was likely imagining his wife in it, with another guy.

The Prince dragged his eyes from the passenger seat to where a convertible top should've been attached. "Take the time to restore it, if that interests you," he said brusquely. "It's an unusual car. When it's finished, it could be worth something."

"Speaking of an unusual car, you should sit inside this one!" The Princess now stood by the yellow Lotus and beamed her special smile toward her husband, who relaxed as if stretching out in warm sunshine. A compelling lilt in her voice promised a pleasant surprise, so the Jaguar followed her lead, urging the Prince to get behind the wheel.

He wandered over to the sports car and whistled in admiration, running a finger ever so lightly over the spoiler as he talked specifications with the Jaguar. He slid inside, settling into the driver's seat, hands on the wheel. The Jaguar kept up a steady stream of conversation about the Lotus, lamenting being unable to go out with him for a spin. He crossed his arms and leaned casually on the front panel, pausing rather than prattling on.

Soon, the Prince looked up, his cool green eyes meeting the Jaguar's warm ones. "Maybe I can drive it the next time I'm down here, on business."

The Jaguar blinked, shifting his back jeans pockets slightly against the sports car. "Business?"

"I've wanted to invest in a small organic cocoa plantation ever since I helped a client through the turmoil in Panama. When I visited yours today, I felt a strong connection to it. Let's discuss what it would take for me to give Caroline a share of the place as a gift for her thirtieth birthday next week."

The Princess gasped out loud. The Jaguar's Adam's apple bobbed. "You felt a strong connection, you say?"

The Prince nodded. He kept a cool gaze on the Jaguar's face.

He knows the truth about what happened in the plantation, the Jaguar realized. They now shared a bond they'd resolved to keep from the Princess, in her personal best interest and in the interest of Gregory Global.

Uncrossing his arms, he stood up and held out his hand. "I'll talk to my other partners, the Panther and Puma, then we'll discuss it after dinner. She loves the product, and we want her to go home with more than nightmares."

The Prince got out of the Lotus and shook the Jaguar's hand. The Princess rushed up to hug him, and he kept her pulled close as they all walked to the house together to go clean up before dinner.

Chad closed the guest bedroom door and instantly dropped the cool act. Reaching for Caroline, his voice was gruff when he blurted, "I saw everything. The clearing, the stream, the exploded

Land Rovers, the ashes of the building where Chavarria's wife was murdered, the chopper crash, the jaguar, the plantation house. It's a miracle you made it through this. I had watched some of it on the cameras, real time, so it felt like I was re-living the terror of losing you."

He squeezed his eyes shut against the replay of what he'd seen in the jungle. "The jaguar who killed your attackers knows your scent. He smelled you on me. He's real, about the size of Shelly's old Volkswagen, and he's sticking around the plantation. I don't think I believed in him, until that moment he nudged my hand with that gigantic black nose."

Caroline started to tremble in his arms. Her pent-up sobs burst through the dam that had held them in check, and he stood there, rocking her back and forth, as much to comfort himself as to soothe her. He hadn't seen her this way since the day she saw what Hurricane Hugo had done to her demolished home. When her knees seemed to buckle, he led her to the bed to lie down.

Now he understood why she hadn't felt close to him since he'd arrived. Then, he could not relate to what she'd been through, and she couldn't describe it. Nobody could. She could only break down after he saw where she'd been. His mind was still reeling, and he'd never forget the stench of corpses and scorched buildings.

After some time, the looming darkness outside told him they were expected downstairs. He glanced at the face of his Rolex and saw he could still freshen up. Caroline had stopped crying and rested in his arms. "Do you feel up to going down for dinner?" he asked with gentle strokes down her arm.

She sniffed. "It would be impolite not to. Can we make it?"

"Yeah, we have about half an hour until we need to leave the room. I've got to shower that jungle off me."

She raised herself on her elbow, bringing one finger over the carved bone buttons of his shirt up to where it opened at his neck, tracing the hollow spot she loved while he gulped in surprise. Then she turned to get off the bed, and he touched her arm to stop her. "Care, it's hard for me to think of you in that car, imagining yourself with him, the way we are."

She clasped his hand and kissed it. "I imagined you first, Chad. That was a long time ago, when I thought you left me behind for a better future. You've always been my destiny. Being the Jaguar is his."

He reluctantly let go of her hand as she pulled away to go to the closet. If he had his way, they'd stay right here, enveloped in the closest moments they'd had since he arrived. She was acting more like herself now. Maybe he could get her to come up here to sleep tonight, instead of remaining by the fire.

Soft acoustic guitar music seemed to come from speakers everywhere, creating a relaxed, romantic mood in the soft light and rich décor of the Spanish mansion. Dinner was excellent, but Caroline missed seeing Dominic Vega and Jadyn Rios at the table. The couple and their wounded friend had been secretly whisked away by the Fly that morning.

Since Caroline and Nadia were the only females at the table, most of the conversation included romping stories of misadventure between the Panther, Puma, Carlos, Ben and Jack. She'd be seeing more of Jack in Charleston, where he now worked for Phil Gregory. Was it only a little over a week since she asked him if there was a Jill in his life?

Ben directed a few questions at the Jaguar's team about their last mission, which roused teasing stories about the adjustments made when having a woman along. They laughed at her question about zombies on a dark, rainy day, and Carlos said they'd sung along with the guitar music to ward off the gloom, just like primitive villagers did. The Puma embellished tales of the Princess as she ducked under trees alive with monkeys, birds, reptiles, and insects.

As the staff served dessert, Carlos chuckled over the Princess' unexpected revelations about the Jaguar's quirks. The Jaguar, now as Christian Chavarria, shifted his position in an elegant dining chair, his silver fork poised in the air as he met Caroline's eyes across the table.

She felt Chad stiffen beside her, so she looked down quickly at her plate. The vague throbbing in her temple had returned, and the other bruises were aching, reminding her she'd forgotten to take her latest scheduled dose of the pain reliever the doctor had given her. Reaching for the crystal glass of citrus-spiked water near her plate, she was surprised to see it tremble in her hand.

She felt light-headed and carefully set the glass back down. The Panther's voice sounded like it came from far away as he told the account of the Jaguar suggesting to the Princess to put her sketches out for the wandering tribe as a gift. It turned out to be a fateful turning point in a raging spiritual battle in the jungle and played a role in her subsequent rescue.

Caroline shut her eyes, transported back to the log seat by the quiet campfire, surrounded by a close darkness and the humid promise of rainfall. Then she caught her breath, for the searing pain she'd felt in her heart that night stabbed her afresh. An image of Chad and Isabelle flashed across her mind.

Chad reached for her hand under the table, but she jerked hers away, using it to stroke back her hair from the cold sweat forming on her forehead. The room was spinning all around as he urgently whispered her name. Her eyes fluttered open to focus on something fixed.

She latched onto the first thing she saw across the table. The familiar green gaze of the Jaguar held rays of color that had always reminded her of a palm frond.

He rose abruptly, alarmed, his chair falling back in slow motion. His mouth moved as he called out to Chad, but she never heard his words.

She sank into a million hues of green in the gathering darkness of the jungle.

Caroline became aware of the kindly doctor's voice urging her response, assuring her she was fine. She had fainted, and the doctor clucked reprovingly at her neglect to rest and take her medication. Since he could not trust her to follow his prescription, he turned over her medication schedule to her husband and had just given her something to make her sleep a while.

She peeked at him from under heavy eyelids, mumbling a weak protest that people in this jungle had an obsession with drugs. He chuckled, then said in his upbeat manner that he understood her avoidance and nothing he gave her would cause any lasting harm. She would feel much better in the morning.

Within the comforting embrace of the softness supporting her, she slipped into the lush green surroundings from which there seemed to be no escape. Life sprang up everywhere her eyes fell, growing wild and unchecked. Curious creatures called out to her in their unique voices. Then the Jaguar appeared, hacking a trail for her with a machete. His camouflage shirt was wet with sweat under a heavy pack of supplies to accommodate her. He turned back, and a long brown strand of hair parted like a curtain, showing off the jaw of a man not to be trifled with.

The Jaguar winked and assured her she would make it through this. His mouth formed the words, "Trust me?" She almost nodded that she did, then stopped.

Suddenly, she was surrounded by villagers who praised God with unabashed abandon, singing "Pass It On." Her heart swelled to bursting with love, which inspired tears that ran down her face. But she became confused, because a gentle unseen hand wiped them away, kissed her forehead, and smoothed her hair.

Later, she blinked a few times, comprehending by the glow of firelight that she was in a spacious room in the still hush of night. With this sense of security, she closed her eyes again, returning to sit by the campfires where the Jaguar's team cooked food and boiled water to sterilize it. She smiled at their banter, then the Jaguar sang softly to her in the richness of his unmatched voice. His face was younger against the evening sky and inky silhouettes of palm trees. A long-ago, sweet warmth crept into her heart at the way he looked at her. They were in a safe place, a simple place, sitting on the beach at Dog's Head, back at home.

Home. A gentle surf swished, erasing the edges of reality. She stretched out on wooden boards that still retained the warmth of a summer day, lying on the pier as twilight blanketed the island. Her heart leaped with joy, for Chad was sprawled out beside her on a beach towel. When twilight passed quietly into a lofty realm of starlight, she knew he would identify the summer constellations. Like the captain of the tall ships he loved, he'd search for the North Star. *A star to guide your ship's course by...*

Chad. She tried to reach out for him beside her, but her hand seemed to be held down. She fought a rising panic and made her way to the surface of consciousness, gasping for breath. Close at hand, the rustling sound of old leather faded as Chad put his hand on her shoulder. "Hey there, beautiful. I'm right here."

She relaxed at the sound of the deep, slow Southern drawl she loved. Home!

Her hand was still restrained as she tried to touch him, and she groaned in anxiety. Beside her, he got down on one knee and pulled out a blanket tucked tightly under her arm. Instantly, she opened her eyes to see him and gripped his shoulder in desperation. In her dream, he looked so young. When did he become so tired and tense?

"I couldn't reach you," she mumbled, letting a tear roll and fall to the sofa rather than take her hand from him to catch it. "Don't let go of me!" Her weak whisper trailed away as he struggled against the beckoning promise of peaceful sleep.

His reassuring smile didn't drive away the haunting sadness in his eyes. She felt him lift her to make a place to sit on the sofa, laying her pillow in his lap. Then he stroked her arm lightly.

"I've got you, Babe, and I'm never lettin' go," he whispered. "Never."

Her heart was tuned to his voice like a homing beacon. As everything faded past her control, she had never felt more secure.

Chapter Twenty-Four

I was born when you kissed me.
I died when you left me.
I lived a few weeks while you loved me.
-Humphrey Bogart

Christian Chavarria waited for Caroline Painter Gregory and her husband to say their goodbyes at the airport and board the Weaver's private jet. As far as he was concerned, the Jaguar's mission ended only when he escorted his Princess to that plane and said goodbye with words he'd rehearsed during the night.

Dragging back a lock of hair from where it blew onto his cheek, Christian stopped short on the instinct to touch his scar. Last night, he'd paced and prayed outside the drawing room where she slept. The Lord knew his every thought, every feeling, every desire. Sometimes on dark nights around the campfire, he and the team strayed into a gray area in discussions about when a passing temptation and action became sin. But he crossed the gray area on this mission. He needed forgiveness, from the One who made the rules.

He spread his feet and crossed his arms over his chest, watching the Princess thank his father for the hospitality. She would never be the same. Nobody knew that better than he did. Those closest to her would notice she never laughed as easily anymore or shared their definition of a dire situation. She might even need counseling. But she was going to be okay, back in a South that was north of here.

Who could have imagined that guarding a momentous secret from her would become a shared bond to build a bridge to Chad

Gregory? Their exchanged apologies for mishandled communications was a relief to him he saw mirrored in the other man's eyes. Moving forward, Gregory would handle the business side of his wife's share in the plantation. Perhaps he wanted a measure of control over any exploitation of her ordeal on site, or maybe he wanted personal access to the Jaguar and his team. Maybe investing in the plantation was Chad Gregory's way of showing gratitude for saving his wife, and by extension, Gregory Global.

All Christian knew for a fact was that Chad Gregory had a stellar reputation for shrewd business deals. He was counting on Christian's pride to ensure Caroline's success as a partner. The plantation was bound to recover and thrive.

Something else came with Caroline's birthday gift of stock in his cocoa plantation. It was almost breathtaking in its brilliance, and Christian would always admire Chad Gregory for his insight. *He's not allowing me to be a forbidden topic between them, a question mark to intrigue her imagination, a memory to escape to when she's upset with him. He's risking competition so he'll stay at the top of his game—always the winner, always undefeated.*

The Prince was suddenly in front of him, eye to eye, a weighty expression of gratitude in his strong handshake. He said he'd be in touch soon. Those cool green eyes were like the shadow side of a leaf, yet the sentiment in them was sincere.

He told Caroline he needed to go check with Azariah about arrangements for security when they landed, so he'd wait on her at the stairs to the plane. He brushed a kiss on her cheek and walked away with that signature confident stride.

Christian clenched his jaw and had to resist a snort of admiration. The guy used one effortless gesture to proclaim he had no competition, giving his wife privacy to say anything she wanted, to a man whose friendship was important to her. He'd also handed

Christian the privacy to do the right thing or reduce himself to a fool.

No matter. The gesture was a gift from a guy who made sure if you lost to him, you still won something.

The Princess had a healthier pallor this morning, but her smile wasn't the one that took his breath away. It conveyed her struggle with a bittersweet goodbye, and it spurred him to help by starting first.

"Mission accomplished," he began. "I've escorted you to the plane back home, with my sincere apologies that this is not a *gringa*-friendly environment. I wish you hadn't been terrified and hurt. But I wouldn't have missed knowing you, Shining Woman, or seeing God's hand in those miracles. This has been a turning point in my life."

"Like I told you in the old foreman's quarters, I'm not sorry, either. I'd never in a million years have chosen to discover you again under these circumstances, but since it was God's way, I'm just glad we are safe now it's over. Not all stories have a happy ending in a cursed world. I'm at peace about our friendship now, after so many years, and I hope you feel the same. I'm privileged to know you, Jaguar. It's not every day an island girl like me gets rescued by a legendary hero."

His attempt at a laugh was more like he'd muffled a cough, but there was mirth in the crinkles around his eyes. "Yeah, well, a good thing my calling finally counted for something. It cost me everything."

Now his voice broke, and he swiped his hand over his face, embarrassed. She reached out to touch his arm, as if unable to resist a connection with him. "Not everything. You still have that famous dangerous first kiss to use wisely."

He blinked and looked out at the airstrip hanger, composing his face to give nothing away. She didn't remember. Perhaps she never would. But if she did, his response at this moment would matter a great deal.

He locked eyes with hers with an intensity he wanted her to memorize. "Legendary heroes come with legendary love stories. That kiss was always reserved for the love of my life."

Impulsively, he scooped her into a hug, as platonic as he could muster, then put a respectable distance between them. "You got that birthday box of chocolate to last you until I can send some to a South that's north of here?" he asked thickly.

Her eyes sparkled with tears she blinked away. She swallowed the lump in her throat. "Yeah. Thanks for making thirty years taste so good."

"Nobody wears those years better. Let me know how the jungle in your camera turns out."

"That's kind of you to say to an aging woman. And the kids will love the photos. I'm sendin' a surprise here soon for you and the guys, for your new front porch when it's rebuilt. You know, somethin' to remember me by."

He bit his lips together to master the tremble, then quipped, "You really think we'd ever forget?"

Then she smiled, and his world was full of sunbeams streaking through the clouds. "I love y'all, too. That's how we say it in a South that's north of here."

She took small steps backwards to the plane, long blonde strands of lustrous silk blowing in a gentle jungle breeze across her shoulders, and the smile transformed into the one he craved, the one that would hurt in the sweetest way imaginable every time he remembered it.

An entourage of vehicles snaked through traffic in downtown Charleston, South Carolina. Caroline warmed to the views of sprawling Southern charm, shielded behind the bullet-proof windows of a limousine, sandwiched protectively between Chad and Ben as the security escort turned toward Church Street. She gushed with relief to see ladies skillfully weaving sweetgrass baskets at the Market. Tourists clad in jackets and sweaters were snapping photos, checking maps, or licking candy and ice cream cones. Shoppers from off the cruise ships toted colorful bags branded with shop logos and stuffed with souvenirs to give the less fortunate who were stuck back at home.

At the sight of The Bend, she made white-knuckled fists in her lap. But residents were waving at one another, stopping to chit-chat, walking dogs, and jogging. There was no hint of danger in the last rays of sunlight on the historic street.

Chad grasped her hand, forcing it open to entwine into his. His smile was reassuring as they passed through the open driveway gate and he massaged around her diamond and wedding band as if to point out to her she had them back. His grandfather had vowed that the wrecked Mercedes would never pull into his drive again. But his sister Sandy's car waited beside his dad's Maserati Spyder. His Heyward grandparents would arrive for dinner, then the group would rest from their flight here tonight. Caroline's parents were preparing a homecoming celebration for her arrival back at the island tomorrow.

Azariah, Ben, and Jack got out of the car and efficiently scanned the area, though it had already been cleared by other officers before their arrival. They surrounded Chad and Caroline to usher them up the piazza, but when Caroline heard her children's voices shouting to someone that their mama was back, she made a cry and bolted toward the door. The twins had it open just in time for her to burst through and gather them around in the foyer. They pulled her to the floor to be their size, giggling and talking all at once. There was no way to make sense of the jumble, so she didn't even try. It was enough to touch them, hug them, and exchange kisses.

Rhett's expression grew solemn as he studied the swollen bruising under his mother's makeup. Savanna had a purple bruise on her knee she wanted to show and tell about, but her mother could only make out that Lancelot was involved. The German Shepherd was allowed inside for the reunion, and he strained forward at hearing his name. A sidelong look at Chad made him settle again. Rhett and Rayce gushed reports on all they'd learned about jungle animals. Their little sister announced that she'd faithfully sung the Fievel song every night, the one about seeing the same moon her mommy did.

The children were reluctant to free their mother when everyone else came to hug her. Lancelot whimpered and groaned as if in agony, turning pleading eyes to Chad, who smiled and gave him a nod. The dog stepped over to where Caroline was wrapped in Camellia's arms and gave her thigh a gentle nudge, respectfully requesting his turn. His patience was rewarded with a hug as she sat down on the floor to cuddle with him.

Chad complained with mock sternness about all the roughhousing, warning that he didn't want to endure another frightening collapse like the night before. She grinned up at him over Lancelot's soft ears, thanking him for taking such good care of her. This earned her an intimate look, and a murmured, "I love you."

The watchful dog was put out on the piazza and the children were served an early meal so they could play with Ben and Sandy's son, their cousin Joshua. Once the Heyward grandparents arrived, it was time for the adults to have dinner, and the conversation turned to the reception Caroline had missed in their home. Stirred by the breaking news of her ordeal and the state of emergency to find her in Charleston that evening, every anxious guest attended while a trusted friend hosted the event, for the Heywards were at the hospital with Lucinda Gregory. Some guests were distraught and in tears at both her abduction and Phil Gregory's heart attack and surgery. They held a prayer vigil for her, Phil, and the mission trip they were trying to raise money for. Every single painting sold, raising more than expected to fund a small building to function as a church and school in South America.

Ben teased that he was glad Caroline was home in time for him to relax and enjoy the Super Bowl. She quipped that she'd just sleep through that and be rested for the real excitement, the upcoming Daytona race. This led to a lively discussion of predictions about the winners and superstars involved in each sport while they all settled down to dinner.

Phil Gregory had Caroline seated next to him at the head of the table. As the patriarch of the family, he said the blessing, and easy conversation was accompanied by clinking silverware on china.

Sitting with her family was so normal, so safe. With a look around, Caroline felt a pang of something she couldn't describe, and she sighed. Phil reached over to cover her hand on the gleaming wood tabletop, keeping his voice low. "I read the reports about what happened. It should have been me. You didn't deserve what you went through."

Caroline gripped his hand reassuringly. The sparkle in her eyes matched the lilt in her voice when she leaned toward him and said, "I deserved it. I chose it, when I married into the Gregory family. You know, the whole 'for better or for worse' thing. No one really knows what they're gettin' into on their wedding day, do they?"

Phil searched her face and chuckled. "Then promise me you'll be all right."

She knew the flicker of pain got away from her before she could hide it. But she recovered with a one-sided smile. "I'll promise, if you won't rush me."

He sighed, winking as he renewed the strength of his grip. "I have to rush you, sweetheart. I don't know how much time I have left, and I won't be content until you are."

"Then pray for me, so it won't take too long."

"I started prayin' for you before you were ever born, Caroline, and as you grew up, I joined Noble in praying you'd marry my grandson. There's no better match in the universe. Rest assured, I'll pray for you until the day I die."

Beside her, Chad had turned from his conversation with Ben about football and draped his arm around the back of her chair. He brushed a quick kiss against her temple before picking up his glass to sip from. Across the table, Phillip's watchful blue eyes ensnared hers, calculating her reaction. *Phillip wonders if I needed that reminder from his dad. He wonders what impact Christian Chavarria has had on my marriage, and how much damage was done by Chad's attraction to the sizzling Isabelle.*

And if he wondered, so did other family members. She tore away from her father-in-law's gaze and conjured a smile for the elder Gregory. "I'll always treasure the gift of your prayers. God has honored them. I have the man of my dreams, and your prayers and hard work have made Gregory Global part of our children's heritage."

The deep lines across his forehead eased. She turned and caught the expression on Camellia's face. It conveyed that no matter how true all this was, she knew Chad didn't have a clean slate with Caroline yet.

Wyeth Painter tried to appear relaxed in front of his guest tonight, putting down his empty teacup on a low carved table and settling his arm around his wife. He was glad for the legacy represented in the massive library in his unique French Colonial mansion, on an island that had been in his family for over three hundred years. He instinctively wanted to prove his worthiness as the husband of the woman beside him on the comfortable sofa. Chrissy still carried herself with the fluid movements of the model she'd once been, and she was beautiful in a sapphire blue dress that would be elegant at a formal dinner party yet understated enough for hosting a sophisticated dinner guest in the mansion.

His mother had spent a lifetime earning an unrivaled reputation as an outstanding hostess. In her nearby wing chair, she was impeccable, so stylish that those who didn't know her age would guess she was at least a decade younger. Her hair was white now but swept away from her face in a contemporary hairstyle of layered waves that softened the lines there. Wyeth could imagine nothing that would dent his mother's genteel demeanor. Her voice and manners were as elegant as the antique silver teapot she served her guests from.

The Weaver had been a charming and interesting dinner guest, carrying on conversations as if he inhabited drawing rooms more often than the nerve centers where he brought down dangerous criminals. If it was the first time they'd ever met, he'd never have guessed this was the same man who brilliantly handled Caroline's rescue, or that surveillance, espionage, kidnapping, murder, and mayhem was his life and business.

But they had met once before, years ago, watching one another across the Thames in London. Wyeth had been so disturbed by their encounter it was a long time before he accepted it. Then, at Gregory Global on the night they gathered for the showdown in the jungle, his startled eyes locked with the Weaver's again, this time with an understanding. And now, the shadowy man on a nearby yacht so long ago was a guest at Painter Place.

When they retired to the library for a dainty dessert, Wyeth awaited the climax of the evening. Weaver had used up all the usual compliments about the décor and rare collections on display. Soon, he would reveal the reason for the request to visit.

Wyeth was certain this man was trained to cloak telltale body language, like the squirm in his leather chair. Then the Weaver cleared his throat, admitting that while getting to know them was an honor and a delight, he had another reason for requesting an informal gathering.

"I wanted to share something personal with you. I'm retiring, just down the road in a house I have on the waterfront. Oh, I'll still own the business, but my long-time assistant will step into my role." Pointing up at his white hair, he smirked. "He'll look like this soon enough."

Savanna Painter's response dripped with an irresistible invitation to divulge his plans. "What a surprise! I hope we'll be seein' a lot of you, then. Whatever will an accomplished, well-traveled man like yourself find to do in this sleepy town?"

He blushed, then flashed a smile at Wyeth. "Well, I might give Wyeth a run for his money against the *Artistic License*. I'm bidding on a boat used out here at the pier about ten years back, when they filmed *Sea Spy*."

They all laughed at Wyeth's groan, and the Weaver met Savanna's brown eyes with a hopeful spark in his own. "I'm also planning to write a spy novel series based on some of my true adventures, which everyone will think is fiction. I'll need some coaching and would love to consult the Author Extraordinaire at Painter Place. That must sound mighty presumptuous, Mrs. Savanna, but..."

His voice trailed off, and they waited while he seemed to gather courage. "I hope to spend time here on the island, anyway. You see, I'm Chrissy's father."

The crackle of the fire was the only sound for what seemed like a long time. Finally, the man with eyes that concealed a million stories had revealed himself to his daughter. Wyeth rubbed his wife's shoulder as she sat still, lips parted, staring at the Weaver.

"What's your real name?" she asked softly.

"David Weaver. When I started my career, the agency that employed me decided no one would dream I'd use my real name, which was common enough. When it morphed into a nickname based on my skill at weaving traps in the intelligence world, we built my reputation on it. I disguised myself as your mother's friend from work, with a short beard and fake glasses, and came around sometimes while you were growing up. I couldn't resist seeing you in person and could carry no photos out in the field. Monica and I communicated often through the office, and we met about a dozen times a year. If I wasn't in the country, she'd travel on what you thought were business trips. The housekeeper, your nannies, and almost anyone we allowed around you were in place to keep you and your mom safe."

Wyeth cleared his throat. "Were you and Chrissy's mom ever married?"

Weaver drew a long breath, staring into the fire. He began a story of meeting Monica Carnet, Chrissy's mother. Whenever he was in town the first year in his career, he kept running into a beautiful co-worker in the agency who worked under tight security, handling sensitive information. He was strongly attracted to her but had no family ties by the time he graduated a military academy and wasn't looking for a relationship.

He arrived back in town from a mission one weekend and headed to a party to celebrate a co-worker's promotion. It was unexpected to see Monica there, and what the guys all said about her not being the partying type was clear enough at the gathering. She was classy and uncomfortable with the sloppy manners of most of the conversations. More than once, he saw her wince during a conversation before she maneuvered away. And more than once, he'd caught her glancing at him.

After struggling all evening to resist her, he broke his own rules about drinking. It was a misguided effort to relax. Other men without his dedication to bachelorhood were vying for her attentions, and he wasn't the only one coping with the strain by having a drink. She was grimacing over the taste of sips from her champagne glass.

The last straw for the Weaver was when a dashing and arrogant analyst suggested Monica go somewhere private with him to talk. She replied it was getting late and she should go home. He laughed, almost spilling his drink on her blouse as he leaned in close and announced they were finally on the same page. Taking her home was exactly what he had in mind.

The Weaver walked over to pretend she promised him a dance and that he could escort her home. She acted out her part in what he saw as a rescue mission, and the end of the evening was that they drank too much and went too far. When he took her home, his self-discipline was back in one of the empty glasses at the party. He begged to come in, explaining he was reluctant to leave so soon and confessing he'd been wanting to ask her out. They planned a dinner date the next evening.

Heady with champagne, she confessed going to the party for a chance to meet him outside of work. He promised she was the only woman who could make him forget bachelorhood and there was no reason they shouldn't start their future together that night. Neither of them had been with anyone before and had no plan for protecting against a pregnancy.

"I didn't lie to get my way—I was obsessed with Monica, consumed with a feeling that we were meant to be together and that we didn't have much time. When we woke up the next morning, she was embarrassed, full of regret, sobbing, and she ordered me to leave. Now that I was sober, my heart ached more than my head. I knew I'd trampled a rose as if it was a weed, but I didn't understand how to comfort her. What could I say now to earn her trust? I was in the business of making people safe, yet she hadn't been safe with me. I'd taken advantage of her. In a panic, I went to her phone to see the number, jotted it down on my hand with an ink pen, and promised I'd be calling when she had time to calm down. I was jealous of the other men at the party and considered her mine."

But when the Weaver returned home and showered, he got orders to leave the country on a mission. She wouldn't answer her phone, and he had no time to go by her house. Frightened that she might refuse to see him again and desperate that she not believe she'd been used, he penned a quick note explaining his orders and had a trusted friend deliver it, along with a bouquet of roses, while he rushed to board his plane.

About seven weeks later, he rushed from his flight home to the office to invite her to dinner. His heart soared when the elevator he was on opened at a floor where she and her boss stepped in. She flushed and gave him a startled look, penning something in her notebook before continuing to brief her boss on a report. He relished in hearing her voice and brushed into her on his way out. In that contact, she discreetly passed him a folded note. That's how he learned she was pregnant and had become a Christian. She offered to let him stay in touch with their child.

"I had to find an empty room in the building to gather my wits," Weaver said. "I was reeling, shocked. Back in those days, it was humiliating for a woman like her to be an unwed mother. By the time I left that room, I knew I'd give up my career rather than desert her. She'd never get rid of me."

She agreed to meet him at a coffee shop. He begged her to marry him right away, before he was sent on another mission. But she said two wrongs wouldn't make a right. A Christian couldn't be yoked with an unbeliever. He grew up being taken to Sunday School and church sometimes, but now, he searched for how to believe as Monica did. She had something much more than an acknowledgement that God existed as the Author of morality, which he conceded. He saw her whenever he could, and Chrissy was born soon after he'd prayed for salvation and married her mother in a private ceremony at the hospital.

"For public records, we kept your name under Monica's maiden name, though she wore my wedding band. By then, I had many enemies. Monica knew the business and understood what she was getting into. Neighbors would always gossip because we'd never have a normal relationship."

Through the agency, she usually knew where he was, and even worked to gather intelligence for many of his missions. The mutual decision to keep their marriage from their daughter, Chrissy, was agonizing. But every communication outside the office was a risk, and even inside, his mission could be in the hands of a mole.

When he was undercover with the elder Chavarria in 1959, a sniper killed Monica as she left home for work. He suspected an inside leak and left the agency. Almost crazy with grief and with the killer on the loose, not knowing if Chrissy was the next target, he decided it was too dangerous to reveal the truth to his daughter in what was the most traumatic time in her life. He surrounded her with layers of security she'd been unaware of, and he'd coped with his own grief by immersing himself in pursuing the trail of the killer while it was hot.

Chrissy seemed to be recovering and would graduate from private school, but he knew she was compromised. So, he worked to guide her to security in a setting she dreamed of, living near the sea. Once he narrowed down a goal to provide for her, he arranged an opportunity that took her to London for a modeling assignment. He set up a way for her to meet Wyeth Painter, hoping for a relationship to develop, and kept track of her ever since. Though he had found and eliminated his wife's killer, he became more convinced than ever that he couldn't put his daughter at risk by revealing who he was.

The Weaver paused, wet his lips, and gazed into the fire with regret. Then he turned back to Chrissy. "I wrote a letter to you every year on your birthday, beginning with the day you were born. They're in a safe deposit box for you, along with this account I'm sharing tonight. I don't expect you to act as if we have anything between us. Right or wrong, I used my talents for what I thought was a bigger picture than being a daddy. Saving the world was more important to me than my personal life, and Monica was the only exception. But unless you tell me to stay away, I want to live out what little time I have left in a place near you. I'm past the years the Bible says are allotted to a man, which is a miracle in my profession. Perhaps Christ kept me going for this time when your family needed my connections to rescue Caroline. But in choosing selfishly once again, I'm putting you in danger. I have someone to watch over you in the mansion. You've met Nadia. Promise me you'll think about it."

When she didn't respond, he looked at Wyeth. "You knew the night we met in London that I would only bring danger and chaos to Painter Place. I was unsure you would overcome your responsibility of the island to allow Chrissy a place on it. Your father Noble and I had an agreement, and only upon my death was he free to reveal it. He went home to heaven first, but he had a premonition that his family would need the help I could supply."

Wyeth was taken aback. He'd always sensed his father wanted to share something with him. He glanced at his mother, but her eyes only held the misty look reserved for memories of Noble.

Chrissy's father watched Wyeth's expression and said, "You're bewildered that I arranged your marriage to Chrissy. I was raw from heartbreak over Monica's murder, and if my daughter became a mother, she'd never get over it if her children were endangered or killed because of me. I also arranged for you to meet Dante Kent after some undercover work that led me to believe he was the steward of the Painter holdings at Seamure, which finally came to light without my interference during Hurricane Hugo. A painting you've never seen hangs in the Chavarria compound, one of your father's masterpieces, and I commissioned it to get to know him after business dealings with Phil Gregory in Global. That's information for another evening. Chrissy will need your attention tonight, and she's what's important."

He rose to his feet and nodded in respect to Savanna while she, Chrissy, and Wyeth stood. "I don't know how to express a gracious goodnight after unloading so much on you and your family, ma'am. My daughter has the best mother-in-law God ever dreamed up, I made sure of that decades ago. Of all the beauties that grace Painter Place, you're the crowning jewel. I'm certain you'll handle this in the perceptive wisdom you're renowned for. May I call you tomorrow, to check on Chrissy?"

Savanna replied that she looked forward to hearing from him and appreciated both his candor and compliments. Still off-kilter, Wyeth accepted his new father-in-law's handshake. Then the old man shifted his attention to Chrissy, who hadn't spoken since asking his real name.

His nod was polite, but hopefulness dissolved into disappointment in his eyes when she didn't offer a goodnight. He turned toward the wooden double doors of the library and took a step.

Chrissy matched his step and reached for his hand. "I'm uncertain how to feel about all this, but thank you for explaining. It's a relief to know I was loved. I thought I was past needing that from a father."

The Weaver sandwiched her hand with his other one, tanned wrinkles and veins testifying to his years. "Your mom and I, we made a mistake, but I'll never be sorry God worked through it to create you. Who knows if she'd have become a believer without help from a trusted friend when she learned she was pregnant? Would I have sought God, so she'd marry me? Maybe we made another mistake trying to protect you until you were eighteen, when you could understand how important it was not to let anyone know whose daughter you were. A wrong word innocently spoken to teachers or friends could have betrayed all three of us. But Monica was murdered before we could tell you, Chrissy, and I panicked, terrified of losing you, too. I couldn't rest until I brought her murderer to justice. I wasn't a mature Christian, and I spent months in the field without a way to attend church, hiding with hardly a suitcase to carry a Bible in. But I knew enough to put you in the arms of a godly Christian man who would give you the love you needed and a safe home. I have to believe a merciful God brought good out of my mistakes."

Chapter Twenty-Five

No man ever steps into the same river twice—
for it is not the same river,
and he is not the same man.
-Heraclitus of Ephesus,
Roman philosopher

A wind speed of about seven knots played with Caroline's unbound hair. She ran her fingers idly along the smooth white railing of the veranda at the Big House, looking out to sea at crests breaking on large wavelets, contemplating all the colors of blue, white, beige, gray, gold, orange, and the dark greens of moss-draped live oaks, waving palms, and oleander. Breezes nudged leaves and grass into perpetual motion, and the winter's bright red and pink blooming camellias created a riot of cheerful color.

It was a gorgeous winter day of legendary blue skies and fifty-nine degrees of warmth. She couldn't get enough of gazing around her island since coming home and had arrived early for lunch with Gran Vanna to spend a few minutes alone with this view.

How had Poppy Noble captured the infinite nuances of green in the jaguar painting hanging in Chavarria's drawing room? His life had been here, looking daily at the seascape she now enjoyed. She didn't yet know the story about his experience in the jungle, and could not comprehend the link between his magnificent painting and how she came to know it existed.

The double front doors opened, and she glanced back over her shoulder. Her grandmother and Aunt Chrissy came to surround her protectively. These days, everyone did that. Gran Vanna hooked her arm around Caroline's waist and squeezed into her shoulder. "My grandma used to say, 'Penny for your thoughts.'"

"Oh, yeah? Well, my grandma says the same thing," Caroline responded, touching her head against Gran Vanna's. "But save your pennies for a rainy day. You can know my mind by looking around and wondering how Poppy Noble would describe this view, or Uncle Wyeth."

"Oh, child, don't you understand how unique your vision is? You have a perspective your grandpa and uncle can't match. And you're much more mysterious, you know. You hold some things too close. Be free, little one."

Caroline turned a faraway look back out to the beach and seascape. "I don't mean to be aloof, as some call me. I just feel things that go so deep that I can't express them in a way most people could understand. But I have this to say today—I won't be using much green in my paintings for a very long time."

Chrissy burst out in a hearty laugh, leaning forward against the railing, and Maggie Jane opened the door behind them. "Have mercy! You pretty jewels are gonna catch a chill. Get on in here, lunch is pipin' hot and in want of someone to gobble it up."

She snatched Caroline's arm as if she was in charge of her, shooed the other two over the threshold first, and followed close behind, like a sheep dog rounding up the herd. On the way in, she examined Caroline with questions about her healing injuries. Caroline assured her she was almost herself again except for some fading bruises and tiredness every afternoon. But she evaded Maggie Jane's probing look into her eyes.

Chrissy leaned in to hug her and kiss her cheek at the foot of the rotunda staircase, saying goodbye before heading to the Gallery to organize Caroline's birthday exhibition. Maggie Jane went to the kitchen to make a special dessert for dinner.

Caroline followed Gran Vanna up the massive staircase to the cozy sitting room that always made her feel as if she'd stepped into a fairy tale cottage. Floor-to-ceiling shutters were painted sky blue and folded like accordions to open the expanse of a view of the marsh and Dog's Head at the northern tip of the island. The aged leather spine of a book was lying open on a crocheted cotton afghan strewn across the antique sofa, as if waiting so the adventure could resume.

A mosaic-inlaid ironwork patio table was set for two in front of the wall of windows to the panoramic view. Charmingly mismatched but coordinating place settings graced it, and a low fire crackled a warm welcome in the hearth. She knew what would be served today: Maggie Jane's famous chicken and dumplings, Caroline's all-time favorite comfort food.

After Gran Vanna said the blessing for the meal, Caroline spread an embroidered napkin in her lap and asked if the table was new. Her grandmother confirmed that it was a find from her recent treasure hunt with friends in a coastal antique shop. "Your Poppy Noble never tired of stargazing over the ocean, remember? This design, with the waves on the shoreline and the sprinkling of stars above, it reminded me of him. He'd like this table. As I stood there in the shop considering how it would look after cleaning it up, it occurred to me that life is like a mosaic. It's beautiful from a distance, but when you get close, you see that everything in it is broken and mended back together. Those dark shapes had sharp edges, and on their own, they're ugly, like our problems, or bad things that happen to us. But the artist saw them as a background that sets off the pretty pieces. We appreciate the picture, but we accept that the dark ones are part of the whole effect."

Caroline chewed a mouthful of her dumplings, recognizing this familiar tactic. Gran Vanna was painting a word picture to communicate a life truth. It was her subtle way of comfort or counsel. Caroline sipped sweet tea with lemon before she took the bait. "Are you sayin' that even the good things in life are broken?"

Gran Vanna swallowed her dainty bite. "Everything in this world is broken, child. This is not our real home. The original creation was cursed because the God-given gift of independence was abused, and people still haven't figured out that choices are never made in anonymity. The ripple effect of a bad choice breaks a lot of things, including hearts. But the ensuing darkness reveals that goodness is still at work in the world, carried out by broken people. We want time to stand still so we can hang on to those pretty tiles. But then we'd be stuck there, unable to become whole, to experience the richness that makes the pretty tiles matter, to tell the story anyone finds worthwhile. The pretty pieces get whisked away with the tick of a second-hand, don't they? God's taking the entire mix and creating somethin' wonderful from them—the light and the dark, the pain and the joy, the agony and the ecstasy. It all counts for somethin' in the mosaic of life."

Caroline fell silent and thoughtful as they continued enjoying the savory meal. By the time the shell design on the plate under her dessert was showing, she felt languid. It became difficult to focus on contributing to her grandmother's conversation. A glance down at the empty dish brought to her mind the MREs she'd been so grateful for in the jungle. She suddenly recalled the plate the Jaguar had brought her in the cabin shelter when she was emotionally wrung out. She'd ached from missing her children, wondering what would become of them if she was killed. She'd ached from what she saw on the security monitor between Chad and Isabelle. But the Jaguar's team pulled together a special meal from the gifts the tribe left, and it was only one of the kind gestures they offered in comfort.

The sound of rain splattering on countless leaves filled her mind, a backdrop for snatches of conversation. The Jaguar sat beside her bed, medicated from mewing and not fit for guard duty. She heard her own voice saying, *I suppose you never used to be in pain until I came along*, then heard his cheerful Chris Shepherd laugh. *There are just too many tempting ways to respond to that. Let's stick with an admission that I know myself better than I used to.*

I could get you killed you know...

I'm immortal until I've accomplished what God sent me for. God holds my time in His hands, and nothing can take me until then...

... You were called to an absolutely awesome destiny—to become El Jaguar...

She missed the Jaguar. Or did she miss Christian Chavarria, or Chris Shepherd? How would she know? For if she'd learned anything, it was the Jaguar wasn't created in Montserrat in a tragedy. He'd been groomed for his role since birth, and he took the first step to his destiny right here on the island almost ten years ago, at the old chapel.

She turned to the view out the window. An impressive obelisk monument stood on the site, replacing the historic chapel structure when it was swept into the sea by Hurricane Hugo. The words of Sir Francis Drake's prayer were emblazoned on one side, originally penned in 1577. They were among Chad's life-words, but so universal and timeless that they fit all courageous men who sought to do good in a broken world. Words like, *Disturb us, Lord... when our dreams have come true because we dreamed too little... to dare more boldly, to venture on wider seas... where losing sight of land, we shall find the stars...*

She longed for a few minutes again with the Jaguar, the Panther, the Puma, Carlos—the whole team. She wished she knew how to contact Romeo and see if he and Jadyn had married yet. Even a phone call would do, if she dared, but she wasn't sure what was appropriate between herself and male friends after they saved your life. Passing her hand over her forehead, she brushed her bangs aside, turning from the island view back into the room she'd always loved. There was no rain, no damp cabin, only the crackle from within the confines of the sculpted fireplace mantle and a faint crash of surf that no window or wall on the island would ever block out.

Gran Vanna's beautiful accent wasn't weaving a tapestry of insightful conversation any longer. From across the table, Caroline realized she'd stopped listening and was unaware of how much time had passed.

Her grandmother studied her. "I'm still willin' to pay a penny for your thoughts, sweetheart. In fact, I'd give everything I have to help."

Caroline gulped against a rising choking sound, wringing the pretty embroidered stitches around the napkin in her lap. "No one is safe. Anything can happen at any instant, and there's nothing I can do to stop it. I can't just live right or be right, and no precautions are enough. As the Bible says, the same rain falls on the evil man as it does the good one. All those broken pieces of the mosaic, they cut, they hurt, they leave me bleeding with scars all over my heart, and I can't make sense of the pieces I've shattered into. I don't even know myself anymore! How can anything ever be the same again?"

With that, she stopped skirting the edge of her composure and threw herself over it, into a safe place to fall apart again. She needed Gran Vanna's help to make it to the afghan-adorned sofa, where she cried with abandon.

The familiar casual chatter around the tables in the Castaway's Pavilion Room soothed Chad. The haunting, soft melody of David Arkenstone's song, "Homecoming," set an unobtrusive background mood, at once both contemporary and ancient.

Reproductions of the most well-known paintings by generations of Painter Place artists hung throughout the upscale restaurant, changing quarterly. This room had the theme of the famous annual Island Summer Dance events. Bright paper lanterns hung along the walls to simulate the gaily lit Painter Pavilion, ensuring patrons would catch something of the magical excitement. The walls and floors mimicked the weathered planks and railing of the real Pavilion, while the ceiling transformed into a starry night over the ocean.

He and a few friends owned the restaurant. The Castaway was named in tribute to the first Painter to inhabit the island across the waterway, and they defied the odds when Patrick placed the Castaway on the map as one of the best establishments on the coast of South Carolina. Others warned them they'd never make it in this business without selling alcohol, but people drove for miles to the small town of Whitehaven to spend a couple hours of their evenings here. Anyone who wanted to get wasted knew it was simply a matter of going somewhere else after dinner. As he and Patrick often told people, if they couldn't do without a drink for a few hours, they had a problem they needed to deal with.

Joined tables accommodated the dozen family and friends he'd invited to gather for a dinner to welcome Caroline home. His younger brother Cole and wife Shannon were back from London, and his older sister Sandy and her husband Ben had come up from Charleston.

Chad hoped his dinner party would help his wife feel at home again, instead of looking around as if she were seeing some things for the first time or drifting somewhere else. So far, it seemed to be working. Cole had a clever comeback to one of Joey's taunts about some British music he'd picked up while working in London, making the corners of Caroline's soft, sculpted lips lift in amusement. His eyes lingered on the tempting satiny pink shade of lip color that coordinated with her dress and sultry eye shadow. It was nothing like the siren call of "take-me" red lipstick worn by Isabelle, who was now in a secure cell somewhere awaiting a trial.

He winced that this jarring comparison sprang to his mind when admiring Caroline. He still prayed every day that all thoughts of Isabelle would be sealed away in a dark closet that the Lord wouldn't open often to humble him. He was forever grateful that God threw his confessed sin as far as the east is from the west, as the Bible taught. But the harshest part about toying around with a book of matches in your life, or even just accidentally encountering something filthy, was never being able to wipe your memory clean. It was easy to feel guilty or dirtied by it over and over.

When he told Caroline a few days ago that he was giving an impromptu dinner party in her honor, she asked him to select the dress he'd like her to wear. He chose one that always sent his pulse rate up a few notches. It was an amethyst purple, like her birthstone, and the clinging sleeves covered any remaining hints of bruises from the jungle.

She was wearing the single diamond earring spray he once bought for her in Charleston when they were dating, a gift to celebrate their two-week anniversary. Her hair was pinned to tumble over the ear at her opposite shoulder in loose waves, and her wrist sparkled daintily with the diamond eternity bracelet that was the first gift he gave her after coming home from college. He presented her with a meaningful gift on every week anniversary for one month, to mark the four years he could not see her or give her gifts. Why she had worn them tonight, out of all the jewelry he'd given her over the last ten years, was a mystery he planned to ask about later.

But for now, he smiled to see some old sparkle return to her eyes. She enjoyed Sandy's romance reports about how her Grandad's housekeeper and Jack were becoming better acquainted.

The housekeeper had come up with some fantastic new menus that showed off her cooking skills to Jack, while still pleasing Dr. Rush about Granddad's dietary restrictions. There was little of the soul food Charleston was famous for on Phil Gregory's plate.

The subject of romance stirred up an impatience in Chad. His intentions for this party were a success so far, since his wife seemed to be warming up to feeling at home again. But the longer he watched her in that dress, the warmer he became himself. He tried not to meet her eyes too long and convey where his mind had wandered. After what she'd been through, getting back to normal in their relationship should be her idea.

Behind her, two local businessmen on their way out of the Castaway after dinner glimpsed the group. They invited themselves inside to welcome Caroline home. Chad chafed at the boisterous intrusion, wishing the waitress had remembered to close the large doors. However well-meaning the intentions of their acquaintances were, reminding Caroline of the public attention to her ordeal could ruin the evening.

The men gestured for the family to keep their seats, patting Caroline's shoulder with their best wishes. Chad breathed a sigh of relief that they hadn't asked her questions. Then they turned their attention to address the men at the table, as if the women weren't present.

"We were talkin' over dinner, and we can't decide if we feel safer with all the investigators gone, or if we were better off with 'em here," one of them quipped jovially, shaking hands with Chad and Patrick. "Lots o' the guys, we wish they'd o' left that hot flamingo dancer behind! Whew, boy! We don't get many like that one passin' through, 'cept maybe on the big screen at Movies on Main. Just talkin' 'bout 'er made the steam rise off many a man here in lil' ol' Whitehaven!"

His friend took a toothpick out of his mouth. "I reckon a sensation like that's gonna live on in imaginations around here for a while." He made gestures to go along with an exaggerated storytelling voice, using the toothpick like a maestro's wand. "She had that look 'a danger about her, ya know, like the bad girl in a spy movie. Stirs a man's blood. Hey now, we'll run and let y'all finish dinner while it's hot!" He pointed at Patrick and told him how great the steaks were tonight, and that the recipe for the special seasoning better not be a secret.

The duo exited the Pavilion Room, one slapping the other's back and howling in laughter at another joke about the things Isabelle had stirred up in their imaginations. An embarrassed silence stalled over Chad's dinner party. Beside Caroline, her sister Marina reached to clasp her hand while sternly chiding her brother Patrick for not reminding the visitors about crude conversations around the ladies.

"Maybe they talk like that at home and their wives don't care, but in the Bible, Ephesians says Christians are to avoid crude jokes and topics like that. It certainly doesn't fit the parameters of Philippians four, verse eight. When you say nothing to remind them of that, it's the same as approving of it, so they'll do it again. They may talk and people will think you took part!"

While a red flush crept up his neck, Patrick glanced at his wife Natalie, who narrowed her eyes and nodded. He sputtered, "Why do I have to be the one to say somethin'? Besides, they don't go to our church. I hear they just get feel-good stories about parables on Sundays and don't bother carrying in their Bibles to look at the scripture themselves."

Marina's husband Danny wiped his dark blue cloth napkin over his mouth. "That's no excuse for any of us, Patrick. Marina's right, and I'm just as guilty. Pastor Payne would've found a friendly way to let them know their conversation wasn't appropriate or respectful to the women at the table. I'm sorry, ladies. I'll be better prepared if it happens again."

Caroline sat still, a thunderstorm brewing in sea-blue eyes she locked onto her husband's. He was embarrassed at the crude discussion about Isabelle, and at his failure to interrupt the acquaintances to cut the topic short. His well-crafted plan for the evening was in ruins, and he was unprepared for what would happen next. There'd be no escaping the maelstrom if the emotion behind Caroline's eyes broke free of the Southern Belle boundaries.

"Does everyone at the table know what happened between you and Isabelle?" she asked evenly.

At his slight nod, she rose. Chad stood, as manners dictated, expecting his wife to excuse herself to the ladies' room to recover, in which case several other women would follow to console her. But she addressed him, and he marveled at how she transformed a soft voice and mesmerizing eyes into such lethal weapons.

"The Jaguar explained to me how it is with guys, dealing with visual stimulation women wouldn't even notice. But if your imagination secretly drags 'dangerous' other women into the intimate side of our marriage, you'd better make sure it's a *phenomenal* experience for me!"

She slapped the table with the exclamation point after her last word, sending the bubbles in her sparkling water dancing along the glass. With eyes narrowed, she snarled, "If this is an inevitable fact of life with a man, there'd better be a benefit on my part for sharing you, or you'll live your life wondering who's inhabiting my imagination. I have many nominal talents, Chad Gregory, but the one thing I excel at is my ability for a creative interlude from reality!"

Stung, he stared open-mouthed at the spitfire across the table. Did she say she'd dare to imagine a stand-in for him? Reeling, he watched her snatch her ivory fur wrap and platinum metallic clutch purse from the nearby bench and march her high heels out the open door.

With his heart in his throat, Chad stared as his wife walked away in the amazing dress he'd picked out for the party. He heard Danny gasp, Cole stifled a choking sound behind his napkin, and Joey was overcome with a cough. Beside him, Patrick shot up with a disapproving scowl and called out sharply, "Caroline!"

Chad threw his napkin on the table and untangled chairs to run after her, turning sideways to get past customers near the door as they put on their coats. He flashed them a white smile when they greeted him, but he rushed away.

He spotted her in the parking lot in the brisk chill of a coastal winter evening, looking around for where Azariah had parked her Ferrari. Jogging up behind, he gently took her arm and pulled her into a shadow around the corner of the building. Easing her back against the wall, he kissed her.

She stiffened, then responded roughly, as if she wanted him to hurry and get it over with. He read her message loud and clear. He should give up, save his pride.

Frustrated, he pulled back and opened his eyes. Struck by blue lightning in hers, he blinked and pulled farther back in instinctive defense, but he needn't have. She turned her face away so he couldn't kiss her again. The welcome mat he searched for was nowhere in sight. His heart sank, but then his resolve surged. This wasn't over, not by a long shot.

Chapter Twenty-Six

If I get married, I want to be very married.
– Audrey Hepburn

Cole Gregory cleared his throat, sighed gustily, and draped his arm nonchalantly around his wife, Shannon. He was the first one to speak at the table of shell-shocked friends and family left in the Pavilion Room. "Well, I'm just speakin' for myself of course, but I'm so glad to be back at Painter Place! Whitehaven's a small town, but there's never a dull moment. I'd have hated to miss this confrontation tonight. It's one of those times when you really just had to be there, to see Caroline's eyes and hear her voice. I'm sure it would only have suffered in the re-telling. Uh, I'm pretty much done here at the Castaway, though. I want to go home now with my wife and ponder all possible meanings of the term 'phenomenal experience.'"

Shannon blushed prettily and feigned indignation, poking him in the side of his dinner jacket with her elbow. "Now you are actin' like the two men who were in here! Aren't Caroline and Chad comin' back in?"

Cole snorted and set off his dimple with a grin. "Are you kiddin'? Our guest of honor tonight just baited a trap my big brother can't resist. Did you see his face when he ran out? She's never been more irresistible to him, pullin' his leash. There's nothin' in the world Chad Gregory would rather do more than to be *phenomenal.*"

He reached a lazy arm for a sip of the remaining tea from his glass, then continued his analysis of his brother's predicament. "It's time they got this over with, anyway. He knew all along he wasn't gettin' away with what happened, and after he's paid for that, he's got to come up with a way to rise above a legend like the Jaguar. That major adventure with the wild cats changed Caroline. My brother has her caged in the Lambo by now, and he's headin' to their beach house to see who tames who."

Joey's wife Casey blurted, "You don't know the half of it. She's holdin' a trump card he'll never see comin' in a million years."

They all turned startled looks to her smug expression. Patrick scowled and exclaimed, "What, there's not enough intrigue tonight? Joey, spill it! Did somethin' happen between her and the Jaguar, to get even with Chad?"

Joey sputtered this was the first he'd heard about Caroline holding a trump card. No amount of begging would move Casey to reveal the mystery she hinted at, but she announced that while she had their attention, she hoped every man at the table took this lesson to heart and sought God's help with his thought life from now on.

Azariah rose and asked Nadia to ride home with someone else while he kept tabs on Chad. If they went to the beach house, there was nothing to protect them but a security gate and an alarm system. She shook her head vehemently and pushed back her chair. "Oh, no, you don't! I'm not missing this for the world."

"It'll be a late night."

"I'm a big girl, and no one's waiting on me." Nadia tucked her hand around his arm while they said quick goodbyes.

Cole pulled Shannon closer, kissing her soft dark hair. "What'll we tell Mama and Dad back at home? Bein' phenomenal sounds like somethin' that'll keep my big brother out late, like prom night."

Shannon laughed and pulled away, standing to raise her glass in a toast and encouraging the other ladies to do the same. "To our courageous Caroline, for the inspiration! May her life always be phenomenal."

Outside in the shadows, Chad turned Caroline's face back to him with fingertips on her chin, but her expression was scathing, and he considered backing down. Their breath became mists between them, and she shivered, so he gathered the slipping fur around her. With his arm circling her shoulders, he turned to lead her to his Lamborghini. He felt a surge of triumph when she dragged her eyes away from the gleaming bright yellow of her Ferrari where Azariah parked it, relinquishing her plan to leave alone.

But a new look on her face made him wary, one that reminded him of old westerns where people circled the wagons. It was a relief to see Whitehaven locals saying goodbyes to friends and strolling to their vehicles, since Caroline was too well-bred to cause a scene that might start rumors about their marriage. Chad waved nonchalantly at friends from church while he opened the passenger door for his wife.

He was walking around the back spoiler when it occurred to him that after almost ten years of marriage, they'd never had a knockdown, drag-out fight. There was no doubt in his mind that he was facing the first one tonight. He pulled his door handle roughly with a surging thrill. Fine! That was just fine with him. He had some things to get out of his system, too, and a fight on that scale would be just the place to unload.

Sliding into the driver's seat, he adjusted his tailored dinner jacket to get buckled in. He started the Lamborghini Countach, and it purred while he waited for other Castaway patrons to pass, flashing the expected smile and waving back at them. A commercial for a local auto dealership came on the radio, with the boisterous voice of one of the crude men in the Pavilion Room minutes before encouraging folks to come get the best deal around from his inventory. Chad cut him short with the push of a button, but then, lyrics about jungle love boomed out of the speakers. With a derisive snort, Chad pushed the button to turn the radio off.

At the entrance to turn onto Pavilion Way to cross the bridge to the island, he went the opposite direction. Caroline looked surprised, then narrowed her eyes in suspicion. He reached over to take her hand and rested it on her thigh before turning to concentrate on the road.

She allowed him to hold her limp hand. But she'd pushed herself into the Jaguar against the goat cart, and he wondered what the Jaguar had whispered into her ear. Somehow, no one had noted that in any of the reports. And that move of sliding the Glock she'd just shot a man with suggestively over her body...

With a white-knuckled grip on the steering wheel, he didn't bother cloaking the sarcasm in his tone. "Was it like old times, wrappin' your arms around Chris Shepherd again? Guess you two had a lot to catch up on—you know, him bein' dead and all."

Her head snapped around to glare at him, lips parted as if a million scalding things were ready to pour from them. In an adrenaline surge, he pressed their joined hands deeper into that silky amethyst fabric. It would be an epic evening.

"Your mistake. Chris Shepherd wasn't there. The Jaguar was."

Laughing derisively, he nodded. "Oh, yeah. Excuse me. You're right, Chris Shepherd's superhero persona showed up. Bet that was a pleasant surprise! And you can't beat him havin' a selective memory of his past, of bein' madly in love with a *gringa* who's no longer on the market. She never was in the first place. He was always in way over his head, but you can't blame 'im for tryin'. So, answer the question! Did you enjoy it? You know, his kiss on your neck, your kiss on his neck, the 'I'm-first-in-line-when-your-husband-goes-down' attitude? Oh, and who can forget all the cozy chick-flick moments of singin' harmony with a guitar by a campfire? And then there's the real story, the whole 'spurned-girlfriend-gets-her-ultimate-revenge' thing. Most girls don't get to live that dream, but then, you're not most girls, are you, Caroline?"

He knew he was ranting now and almost regretted going this far when he looked from the road to her expression. Almost. He was heady with the adrenaline rush, unpacking things he'd bottled up because there was no "proper" outlet for them.

Oncoming headlights made him tear his eyes from the seething drama in hers while he kept the Lamborghini on his side of the line. He could hardly wait to see how she handled what he'd just dished out.

Caroline kept it simple and deadly, denying nothing. "At least I was the center of his world!" she hissed.

Chad winced. When had she become so good at this? And she was only getting started. "Your own selective memory replaced me on a sleazy sidetrack when you realized I might not make it back. Maybe you should have married a racy supermodel and gone to live in Las Vegas, where risk is always on the menu. As for revenge on Chris Shepherd, it isn't necessary against a true heart like his, just a cheatin' one. If you think the 'spurned girlfriend gets revenge' stories are rich, wait until you experience the newly updated 'spurned wife' version!"

It took an effort not to give her the satisfaction of seeing him gaping. Had she just slammed him and praised the Jaguar all in one comeback? He shouted, "Answer the question, Caroline! Did you enjoy bein' with him again, havin' him handle you like that, like he never could when you were dating?"

"How did you imagine the dangerous *senorita* in your daydreams, Chad? Did you enjoy that?"

With a frustrated growl, he jerked his hand from hers and slapped the console. He was furious. By evading his question, she answered it. But his fury was tempered with fear. Even if he could force his mouth to describe to her what happened with Isabelle, the pastor said some things might do more harm than good for a marriage. He wasn't answering her question, either.

She held up her empty palms, mimicking confusion. "What, we need show and tell for this, maybe in some exotic place? Or did it happen in one of our places, Chad? We're adults here. Find the right verbs and adjectives!"

"It's not what you think!" he exploded. "I don't imagine everything, and never in our places. You'll just have to live with that much."

"Yeah, well, sure, I can do that, Chad, and you'll have to live with that much about the Jaguar!" she came back, every bit as venomous as the snakes in the jungle. He detested the smug look that told him there was plenty he'd like to know. Then she said, "And your use of the word 'don't' smacks of present-tense consistency. In that case, your college days were downright distracting. My dad was wise to test you! I was so naïve."

"Your dad knows how guys think because he's done it too! It doesn't mean he'd run around on your mom, and you know it. She's everything to him!"

Guiding the Lamborghini Countach onto the driveway pavers and up to the security gate, he punched in the code and looked over at the back of her head. The Jaguar had done his job well. She certainly wasn't afraid of the dark outside her window anymore.

This tactic would get him nowhere. He lowered his voice. "I was supposed to consider alternatives to you in college, remember? So yeah, I allowed some room for possibilities, but with limits. It wasn't the same as what I imagined it would be like if you were all mine, admittedly with no limits. It's what got me through, hoping at the end of four years I could come back and you'd still feel the same way about me."

The gate closed behind them as he navigated the rest of the driveway. Parking in the garage of the beach house he'd built for her, he came around to open her door. It was show time, here where he bought the land after Hugo, creating their own escape from the responsibilities of Painter Place. It was alternately a love nest when they craved privacy, a weekend get-a-way with the kids, or a place to stay to make room for his Uncle Justin's family when they visited from England. It was all theirs, brimming over with happy memories.

But she didn't get out of the car. He couldn't persuade her to come inside if he was towering over the low profile of the Lamborghini, so he knelt to one knee beside her. "Come on, Care. We need to air this all out, in private."

"Nothing's private with you, Chad! Our whole family and then some know about what happened between you and Isabelle. Do you have any idea how demeaning that is for me? Can you imagine how I feel when I hear men gush over her, knowing you had the same thoughts? I'm not enough for you, and now everyone who matters to me knows it. I won't be tryin' anymore."

Her voice choked with tension, and he felt a fresh stab of concern. Was their intimacy forever damaged? Alarmed, he reached for her hand. But she jerked away and said she wanted to go home.

He scrambled for something that might entice her to follow him inside. She hadn't been herself since coming back from the jungle. He tried a soothing tone. "You're trembling, Care. Come on, let's get warm first and calm down. I can't take you home yet. I don't want my parents to see you like this."

She shot him a sidelong glance. "I'm sure you don't."

He stood in a flash of anger. As in the parking lot at the Castaway, she had no real options. He didn't bother to cloak the steel in his voice when he announced, "I've got the car keys, and it's goin' nowhere soon."

Shivering, she set her jaw before getting out, knocking aside his offered hand. Stung at another rejection, he dragged his eyes from those long legs and the curves in the drape of the amethyst dress. Sorting his key ring, he couldn't resist a jab. "If I go in front of you to unlock the door, can I expect a knife in my back?"

"Are you hopin' I have one strapped to my thigh again, like I did in the jungle? Maybe you've got a thing now for dangerous women with hidden knives. Isabelle could've killed you with the one she pulled out when she landed on top of you."

He whirled to face her. The soft glow of the porch light above them illuminated one half of her body, and the other was shadowy, as if she had a light and a dark side. He narrowed his eyes, recognizing which one he was dealing with. "You just spent over a week sleepin' with your old boyfriend, so it's not far-fetched to wonder if you've still got his knife strapped somewhere. A momento, maybe. You seemed to enjoy the way he slid his still-smokin' Glock to make out with you."

She hissed. Her eyes narrowed now as she leaned forward. "At least when I was on top of the Jaguar, somethin' good happened."

This took his breath away. He gulped to recover and mounted his own comeback. "Boy, if that's not the understatement of the year!" he shouted into the night, spreading his arms wide as if announcing it to the audience of palm trees. "It was good for him, good for you, but not so good for me! I'm the only one in this little trio who wishes this jungle adventure never happened!"

There, it was out. He hated her reunion with the Jaguar and an unforgettable bonding of their friendship, while he agonized over her safety, the future of Painter Place, and Gregory Global. He took a purposeful step toward her, pointing his finger and using his deadliest tone. "I'll be gettin' to the bottom of some things that happened there, like when the Jaguar's cameras were off, especially that night at the stream. All it takes is time and patience, and I'm a master at both."

He turned his back and bit his trembling lip, mounting the veranda stairs at a brisk pace and shaking with the desire to force that information out of her. What was she trying to hide when she'd sketched the Jaguar, then asked him to switch off his body camera? He imagined her eyes roaming over him, admiring and memorizing intimate details.

Turning the key and pushing the ornate ironwork door open with a rough kick, he stood aside haughtily to let her pass first. Then he slammed it, turned the lock, and keyed the reset on the alarm system. Savagely pulling off his tie, he made his way to the thermostat to adjust the heat setting. Marching to the master bedroom, he flipped the switch for the gas logs in the fireplace and inhaled deep breaths to calm down.

Back in the foyer, he watched Caroline push the button on a small sculpted shell lamp. Bracing one hand against a table, she gave her purse a sullen toss and reached down to remove her high heels. She kicked them ruthlessly under the table with her bare foot.

Chad came toward her in the shadows, watching as she ran her fingertips over the inlaid mosaic tiles on the foyer tabletop. She seemed lost in thought, though he couldn't imagine why the tiles were so interesting tonight.

One word came to his mind to define her. *Magnificent.*

Observing her while she was unaware, he was seized with how beautiful and dignified she was, how exciting and mysterious, how cool and yet sizzling, how fragile and yet incredibly strong. His heart was in his throat as he stepped up behind her, surrounding her in his arms, pulling her to him while he rubbed his face into her hair. *The way a jaguar marks his territory with his scent glands*, he realized, remembering what he'd learned with the twins about the big cat.

"No," she murmured. "All the talk about her has you in this mood. You said we'd get warm and calm down."

"That's what we're doin'. First we get warm, and later, we'll calm down. And trust me on this, you take all the credit for my mood."

He didn't relinquish his embrace, but loosened it, recalling advice not to push her after what she'd been through that night in the jungle. But he sensed there was only one way their first real fight would end. Making up was the reward for enduring the battle.

Inconveniently, the image of the erased words in her sketchbook flashed in his mind. Running a gentle hand up and down her back, he ventured, "Care, did you ever ask the Jaguar to turn off the video feed?"

She stiffened and tried to pull away, but he held on. Exasperated, she exclaimed, "Why am I the one being questioned? The problem tonight is you!"

"So, my concerns that we may have another problem, an old boyfriend problem, don't matter?"

Her tone became defensive. "I turned his camera off when he broke down at the scene of the murder of Chavarria's wife, to preserve his dignity in a time of grief. He needed comfort from someone who knew more about who he was than the guys on his team. He held me and cried a while. Then I asked him to turn it off later, while he was on watch, to persuade him to befriend you. After all he'd done for me, I didn't want him to evaporate from my life again. But not because I'm in love with him, and he knows it. You made the first move to allow us to stay in touch, and because I admire and appreciate that, I'll tell you whatever you want to know about both times. But not right now."

"You know nothing about him gettin' rid of his camera at the stream?"

Annoyed, she tried to push him away again. "Which time at the stream?"

He scowled. "There was more than one?"

Now she seemed wary, collecting her thoughts, and he grimaced. Another mystery to explore.

"You heard the Jaguar's account," she retorted. "I don't remember, and I won't try. All I know for certain anymore is that I didn't come back here as the same person who left for Charleston. Frankly, I'm afraid of the new version of myself. I don't even know if I like her!"

Chad sighed at the raw pain in her voice. In his impatience, he'd pushed her too hard, for his own benefit. It was time to change tactics in this siege.

"Well, I love her!" he drawled playfully. "Wonder what those men in the Castaway would say about dangerous-looking women if they'd seen you shoot at drug cartels last week? The heiress of Painter Place would become the number one hot item for the daydreams of men in town. I'd become the local legend who gets to live out those dreams. They don't know who you are, Caroline Amanda Painter Gregory. But I do. Your secret life is safe with me."

He felt her relax, so he nuzzled her ear around the dangling diamond spray and pulled the fur up closer around her. He whispered, "Why'd you wear the jewelry I gave you before we were engaged?"

She whispered a reply against his dinner jacket. "Because back then, you told the little boy in Charleston I was the only one for you. I was the only one you wanted, the one you'd waited for."

He inhaled a ragged breath at this insight into her grief. How had he missed this? Why had he been so rough tonight, venting his own jealous frustrations? She truly thought she was sharing him with other women.

"That hasn't changed, Care. I'm so sorry I crushed you like this. I detest what happened, and I'm embarrassed that it's part of the record on this whole fiasco, something our boys might hear about someday. Azariah is my witness at how I tried to avoid that vamp. The crude talk in the restaurant, that's not how I think, and you know it in your heart. Please, Care, I beg you to forgive me, once and for all, never using my mistake against me again. I promised you we were goin' to adjust to life after the jungle, and I'm committed to that."

He gently kissed her temple. "Remember that day after Hugo when your uncle Wyeth was in meltdown mode? My dad said his perceived betrayal between them had shipwrecked Wyeth's trust in him. If that's what I've done, Care, we've gotta work it out, like they did. We're in this duet for a lifetime."

She seemed to mull this over, then replied, "Does that mean I get to beat you up, like Wyeth almost did to your dad?"

He laughed out loud. "Why bother? You could just sic your spooky golden-eyed cat on me."

Encouraged, Chad began a fresh barrage of kisses, whispering declarations of how crazy he was about her, how much he'd missed her, and how empty his life was while she was gone. All the while, he'd maneuvered her toward their room as if they were slow dancing to the rhythmic surf that pounded the sand outside.

"It's just me and you, Care, in my heart and in my mind. It's always just been me and you. It's all I've ever known."

He searched her face in the shadows cast by the firelight. Before she'd been taken, they'd been able to talk as well through a look as they did with words. Maybe better. Now, he saw only unreadable mystery.

But mysteries didn't intimidate him. They were something to be explored and conquered.

"Tell me where we are, Caroline, whether the new you can love me again."

He waited for a few moments, then the luxurious fur slid into a hushed heap on the floor. The siege was over.

Breathless with anticipation, he renewed his resolve to make good on his promises. Taking her face in both his hands, he whispered, "Remember me? I'm Chad Gregory. If you'll save your heart for me, I'll always make our love story phenomenal."

Clad in a shimmering nightgown and matching robe, Caroline tugged at Chad's hand on the way into the kitchen at the beach house. Light from a lamp and soft music on the stereo filled the living room where Azariah and Nadia sat on throw pillows around the coffee table, playing cards. A small carton of gourmet cookies was open beside some empty cups of coffee from a drive-through donut shop.

Azariah raised an eyebrow at Chad, whose unbuttoned dress shirt flapped open over an old pair of jeans. He said calmly, "Caroline's mom called me to make sure she's all right, and your dad called. Both wanted me to remind you she's supposed to be resting, per doctor's orders."

He plopped down his card. Nadia smiled slyly at Caroline and played her next card. Azariah sighed and grunted.

Alone in the kitchen, Chad's playful embrace around Caroline's middle made it difficult for her to stretch to the top pantry shelf for the potato chips that were kept out of sight of the kids. His teasing nibble at her shoulder almost made her drop a bottle of ginger ale, and she giggled that he had to stop, or they'd be cleaning up the snack instead of eating it. He took it out of her hand and set it down, pressing her against the cabinets for an ardent kiss. Eventually, he let her pull away to scavenge more food, while he reached for two elegant fluted glasses to place under the ice crush function on the fridge door.

Caroline found a half bag of chocolate chips wrapped in a twist tie among the few items left in the house. Then she reached around her husband while he investigated the fridge, pulling the flaps of his open shirt away to run her hands over his stomach muscles. He groaned and pressed one hand over hers, reaching for a mason jar of Maggie Jane's honey-almond butter spread and warning her that if she was hungry, she'd better stop.

She went to find spoons, a fork, a butter knife, and some leftover party napkins, which she tossed into a tray. Chad gripped the tray handles and passed the coffee table, assuring Azariah they'd leave soon to get him home before the Ferrari turned back into a squash.

In the master bedroom, he settled the tray on the rug in front of the fire, pouring sparkling ginger ale into the two glasses and handing one to Caroline for a toast. They looked solemnly at one another as he cleared his throat from his last potato chip. "May our love survive and thrive with every challenge we face, allowing no one and nothing to come between us. May Painter Place and Gregory Global thrive with integrity intact, no matter what comes against them. And may our kids thrive and be prepared when we pass along their inheritance."

He closed his eyes to swallow the ginger ale, and she hesitantly copied him. He leaned over to seal the toast with a kiss, and she grasped him behind the neck before he pulled away, pressing her cheek to his. "What is it?" he asked, concern coloring his tone.

She struggled to answer, and he slid the tray away to wrap his arms around her. "Are you okay?"

When she could speak, it was little more than a whisper. "We're having another baby."

Stunned, he searched her face to see if she was joking. "What?"

Caroline set her glass down. "Remember Christmas Eve, after we put presents under the tree and you wanted me to open your gift of that nightgown, the one I wore before I left for Charleston?"

He pulled her close again and said close to her ear, "Of course I do. How could I forget?"

"Me either. And I didn't want to break the mood by tellin' you somethin' was different besides bein' surrounded by Christmas lights."

Chad sighed. She'd known the exact nights she conceived the twins and Savanna Caroline, telling him something was different each time. He'd joked about it the first time but marked his calendar at work the next day on a whim. The next time, he marked it with excitement. This was the third time, and he knew she was right.

Caroline continued, "Everything was so hectic with the family on Christmas Day and afterwards, so whenever it crossed my mind to mention it, it was never a good time. I planned to tell you on our date night, before everything fell apart with Global and you were so upset. But it was too soon for a test to know for sure, anyway, and I didn't know how I felt about it. We didn't plan for this, and I can't handle the three we have and still get anything done at the studio."

He gently pushed her hair back from her face. "Are you sure now?"

"Yes. I confided in Casey and asked her to drop by with a test to make it official. At the compound, I told the doctor it was possible, so he was careful with prescriptions. But I didn't want it to be a factor while I was in danger. If the mission had failed, you'd blame the Jaguar and Global, and he'd blame himself. My family would be devastated, and you'd always wonder what your child would have been like. My mom suspects. She used the code to trigger a memory for the Jaguar about the stars fallin' because if I didn't make it out, our baby would perish with me. There were two of us."

The things Chad saw on the helicopter tour with the Weaver flashed before his mind, and he imagined his baby nestled deep inside of Caroline, somehow surviving every risk she endured. He needed time alone to absorb the impact of this new twist. If she'd miscarried out in the jungle, she and the whole team would have been endangered.

He studied her face and found his Caroline there again, but shadows lurked everywhere. He couldn't fathom how she'd coped with this during her ordeal, or what she must have endured knowing the worst might happen. But prayer and time would heal her, he had to trust in that.

A baby! Chad's heart welled up with excitement. He rasped, "I'll take care of you. I'll get a nanny and housekeeper if we need them, so you can keep up your share in the gallery. Don't worry about anything. Just be as happy as I am."

Chapter Twenty-Seven

Imperfections we all have,
but we also have compensations.
-Hans Christian Andersen,
The Teapot

The Painter Gallery was buzzing with activity for the exhibition to celebrate Caroline's birthday. Shelly, the manager, had filled the reception lobby with balloons and plenty of bling. Local Whitehaven vendors had catered and decorated in the color theme of gold, silver, and crystal. A special display was set up to sample chocolate from the Chavarria plantation. Soft instrumental music flowed throughout the facility, and Caroline's work from the past year was showcased in the main lobby gallery.

Nadia was dressed in an understated yet stunning evening gown, as if she were a guest at the party. She no longer limped, and she remained unobtrusively near Chrissy and Wyeth. Azariah kept his usual watch over Caroline, Chad, and the children. Caroline's aunt Juliette and her husband Cameron Fisher brought along their daughter Mia and her bodyguard, and Caroline wondered if Weaver had his own cameras set up. She sighed ruefully.

As the host, Wyeth addressed guests and approved reporters selected by their publicity liaison, Jordan Wallace. Jordan, her husband Derrick, and their toddler son, Dustin, stood near the press section of the room.

Caroline's uncle began with accolades to his niece, announcing that one of her most unusual paintings from back in 1985 had just sold again to an anonymous collector. The highly publicized original painting, *Sea Cliffs*, had sold within days of its creation that year to the highest bidder. He was notified that afternoon that the collector had sold it for a large profit. As Wyeth recounted for the crowd that the painting was an impromptu plein air work filmed for a video in Mevagissey, Caroline flushed to think she'd talked about the painting in the jungle. *Surely the Jaguar didn't...*

She glanced at Chad as Wyeth told everyone where they could find limited prints of the newly collected painting in the gallery and copies of the video. Chad's distracted expression told Caroline he was estimating how a sale like this brought up the value of all the rest of her work. Then, his expression changed, and he turned to lock eyes with her. She knew he recalled mentioning the painting via their "date" over the video feed that day in the jungle rain.

Wyeth got Chad's attention so he could announce that tonight's event was in Caroline's honor, his family was also celebrating the news that she was carrying their fourth baby. After a flurry of surprised applause and congratulations, enthusiastic reporters asked for the promised brief interview.

They were led to one of Caroline's larger featured paintings, a view of the island's marsh, graced with sprawling oaks and dripping moss that swayed in a gentle breeze. The children scampered over, and Chad gathered Caroline next to him in case questions ignited one of her flashbacks. Rhett and Rayce were used to the rules when their parents were being interviewed. The twins stood relaxed and still, wearing suits and ties, their expressions composed. But Savanna Caroline reached up for her daddy, who scooped her into his free arm. Excited about being in a new dress at a party, she beamed, announcing to the reporter that it would be her birthday, too, in three days. She looked for confirmation from Caroline about how many fingers she held up.

The reporter grinned and wished her a happy birthday. He told her she was enchanting, then he gave a quick signal that they were live. Other journalists came to stand by, jotting down notes.

He faced the cameras first to announce that he was live at the Painter Gallery in Whitehaven, South Carolina, and had the privilege of attending a reception to celebrate Caroline Painter Gregory's birthday. The cameras panned to her and her family. "It must be such a relief to celebrate your thirtieth birthday back at home. There were times when you wondered if you'd see this day. We understand that you can't speak to the details about your ordeal, but do you keep up with the news coming out of South America, concerning the continuing fallout there?"

Caroline felt Chad's arm grow tense around her. She responded, "I learn the unfolding events through briefings with agencies who have a direct knowledge of what's happening, not the guesswork on television news. I'm focusing on my family and getting back into the studio with Uncle Wyeth."

"Will the theme of your next body of work be the Amazon jungle, inspired by your experience, or is that subject too painful to interact with as you would depict it on the canvas?"

Caroline stood silent, lips parted, as millions of shades of green unfolded and sunbeam spears pierced the shadows. The calls of birds and chattering monkeys filled her mind. She recalled the drawings she left out in the forest for the tribe. Unconsciously, she spread her slender fingers as she remembered resting them on the pictures torn from her sketchbook, praying God would be glorified in her efforts.

A discreet squeeze of Chad's hand around her waist brought her back to reality, and she hoped a quick smile covered her hesitation. She turned from the jungle to her role as the heiress of Painter Place, the next artist in the generations that spanned hundreds of years.

"The Amazon is a remarkable place on the planet, full of incomparable beauty and wildlife. But I planned my next series of paintings before Christmas, and nothing has changed my heart about following through. Next year's work will celebrate my Tenth Wedding Anniversary in September."

She turned a beaming smile up to Chad beside her. He basked in her attention and winked.

"Your anniversary and the birth of your next child extends into hurricane season. Mr. Gregory, it's well known that ever since Hugo, hurricane season makes you nervous. With another baby on the way, are you also nervous about the risk your enemies pose to your family?"

Chad's eyes darted to Jordan Wallace, who had approved the reporters present at the event. She rolled hers and made her way over to deliver a warning to the press. Then Savanna trilled, "Mommy's goin' ta have a baby, and I'll be a big sister!" She smiled and reached over to touch Caroline, saying sweetly, "Right, Mommy?"

Rhett and Rayce turned startled looks up to their dad to see how he would handle Savanna's rude interruption, but another journalist behind the reporter got the best of the impromptu opportunity. She called out, "Sweetie, would you like a baby brother or a baby sister?"

Savanna took to the spotlight like a natural, with an authoritative little Gregory attitude. Putting a finger to her chin and looking up at the balloons, she created an adorable pose, pondering a decision that might well change the world. "Oh, I'll take another brother. His name is Jag. You know, like the good guy on TV who saves Princesses 'n' stuff."

Caroline hoped Chad's sharp intake of breath went unnoticed as Savanna stole the show. She glanced at his handsome profile and offered him a weak smile. How would they ever backtrack this? The media would run with it like a touchdown in the Super Bowl.

With his jaw clenched, her husband dropped his arm from around her waist, so he'd have both to carefully set their daughter down. Her time in front of the cameras was over. Savanna primly adjusted her sparkling dress and leaned back against his knees, then took Rhett's hand with a dazzling smile.

The reporter turned a blank look around at the journalists to see if anyone knew about a hero named Jag who had been saving royalty on TV, but they shrugged and shook their heads. In the meantime, little Savanna encouraged her brother Rayce to grasp her other hand, though neither twin seemed sure it was a good idea to stand linked to her as they stood facing the world in front of their parents.

"My mommy's home now. We're a fam'ly!" Savanna announced in a singsong voice to the reporters and cameraman.

The Panther, Puma, and Jaguar had risen to their feet all at once. The Princess was having a baby! Cameras flashed as her charming daughter provided the perfect end to the reporter's interview, as if this was rehearsed. But the Prince's smoldering eyes told them it was not.

The reporter lost his moment with the Prince, his question long forgotten in the buzz of excitement. Now he focused on baiting the King, Phillip Gregory. But Gregory was expertly putting him off with respectful but brief answers that told him nothing he didn't already know about Global's unexpected role in taking down the two most powerful drug cartels in South America.

"Did that guy ever play James Bond in the movies?" the Puma muttered to the Panther. "He'd be the perfect Bond, minus alcohol and women."

The reporter switched tactics, asking if the rumors were true that Phillip Gregory might leave Global in the hands of his brother and two sons to run for political office. He hit pay dirt with Gregory's unguarded reaction of shock.

"I have no aspirations for political office."

"But sir, isn't it true that well-placed people are begging you to run?"

The Panther pushed a button on the remote to make the screen go black, saying that they were on call for a mission and couldn't afford to have the Jaguar mewing and medicated over seeing people from his past.

The Puma eyed the Jaguar, letting out a long whistle before he exclaimed, "This baby better be a girl, or the Prince has to come up with a reason his son can't be named for you."

Scowling, the Panther added, "With the press breathing down our necks here to know why your plantation was ground zero for the cartels, and all the interviews with locals over the jaguar story, they're bound to link the legends with her! They'll figure out where she's been, and who she's been with. The guy there tonight was unprepared."

"But the timing's off," observed the Puma, shaking his head. "They'll still know it's Gregory's son, even if she had an affair down here. It's too soon for her to know she's pregnant if it was the Jaguar's. Anyway, it's an amazing name! Jag Gregory. That little Savanna Caroline, her daddy better be armed to the teeth when she gets to be a teenager. She's gonna rock many a poor guy's world!"

The Jaguar turned to point his stunned expression out the window at the cocoa trees. "She hid this from us so she wouldn't be any extra trouble." He covered his mouth with his hand and closed his eyes. Then he ran his hand through his hair in agitation. "I made her miserable, demeaning her when she couldn't keep up, then I pushed her to get out here to the plantation during the storm. She was exhausted, injured, and in pain. Little wonder she fainted. It's nothing short of a miracle she didn't lose the baby, and it would be my fault!"

The Puma came closer. "You're the Plumber. You rescued them both, like in the game."

"No!" the Jaguar exclaimed. "No, I didn't. She and I, we both knew who would get her out alive. The Plumber's a helpful friend who will do what he can, but he'll fail sometimes. The only Hero she can ultimately depend on is God."

They jumped at the call on the radio, grabbing up their packs and getting details on a mission from their new boss-in-training, the Weaver's assistant. Outside, the three wild cats that now called the cocoa plantation home paced restlessly around a new specially equipped Land Rover, then streaked off toward the jungle as the team piled into it. The Princess' birthday had become the date of their first mission since rescuing her, so it was unclear what role the cats would play.

Team members checked and readied weapons and equipment while the Puma started the engine. The Jaguar pushed a button on the CD player before strapping on his knife. Christian rock music the Princess had given him boomed from the speakers, and he sang along. "Stepping out my door isn't safe no more, but I know it's where I want to go."

It had been a wonderful birthday, but Caroline disliked crowds and was glad the party was over. One last look at her reflection in the master bathroom reminded her the nightgown Chad had given her on Christmas Eve suited her.

Fur-trimmed wedge slippers masked her entry into the bedroom where her husband was turning back the covers on her side of their bed and singing intermittently. It was a little thing, so normal, yet so extraordinary. Watching him, she mused that things many would presume to be unremarkable about her life were priceless.

Wearing Carolina blue sweatpants and a gray muscle tee shirt, he lit a scented candle and sang out, "All she wants to do is, all she wants to do is dance, and make romance." A spin around with his air guitar sent his straight blonde hair flying into a roguish look that made her grin.

It was then that he noticed her, and she beckoned him with open arms. Never missing a beat, he abandoned the make-believe guitar for a pretend microphone, dancing toward her, on stage in a duet with the radio. His expression said she was the luckiest fan in the world, and he spun around with his free hand pointing at her.

"As we taxied down the runway, I could hear the people shout," he sang, scowling now. "They said 'Don't come back here Yankee,' but if I ever do, I'll bring more money, 'cause all she wants to do is dance. And make romance."

"Chad."

"What?" he managed, breathless from his performance.

She raised her arms again, and this time he grinned and sauntered into her embrace. "That's right, she's the birthday girl, and all she wants to do is dance."

The stereo wrapped them in the voices of the Vogues now, and they swayed to the music. "You're the one that I'm dreamin' of, Baby you're the one that I love..."

"Happy Birthday," he murmured huskily.

"Too bad I didn't get what I really wanted." She brushed his neck with her lips as she spoke.

He quivered at the tickle of her lips and chuckled. "Oh yeah? What did I forget?"

She sighed softly. "A dangerous kiss."

In that twilight place of half dreaming, just before Caroline fell asleep on her birthday, the big spotted jaguar came up to look right into her eyes. She stared into his golden gaze, waiting with bated breath, until he turned to run into the thick, green, infinite wild tangle that was the jungle. *Watch over him*, she whispered in her mind, and somehow, she knew he heard her.

Tonight, he ran with the Jaguar on a dangerous mission. Someone like her would get to go home.

But no one, anywhere, knew what tomorrow would bring.

Epilogue

The Jaguar and his team lazily pushed the new porch swings at the re-built hacienda, compliments of the Prince and Princess. It was a warm, sticky day, and they'd been overseeing operations on the cocoa crop. They appreciated the iced sweet tea and lemonade, all gifts from a South that was north of the plantation.

Carlos sipped his concoction of lemonade poured into his tea to give it a tang. "I can see how the Prince's suggestion will have a long-term improvement of the crop," he commented. "Is that one of the trade secrets he came away with from Panama?"

The Jaguar looked down into his own glass, veiling his response. "Gregory doesn't give away trade secrets. He asks questions that lead me to think of something, or else he makes suggestions. That's all."

Carlos cleared his throat. "Right. Okay, then, another subject. What about this thing the Weaver has planned? Retirement must be more boring than he lets on. What's his deal, sending some girls down here to decorate the hacienda now that construction is over?"

The Panther snorted. "They aren't 'girls' and they're trained to break your leg before you have time to wink at them. They're the ones who are bored, between missions, and they contacted him about his effort to help us rebuild. Interior design is their back-up career. We have a cocoa plantation to fall back on and they have a real job waiting, too."

"I'm not buying that, and neither is the Jaguar, are you?" The Puma slapped the Jaguar's shoulder. "He's just wants us to be more socially well-rounded and make friends."

The Jaguar stood up and stretched, then strolled toward the open front door. At his familiar footfall, the jaguar under the porch made some rumbling sounds. "I'll let the Weaver have fun playing his little joke to restore the hacienda, but they'd better leave my painting alone or I'll be the one breaking legs. And they can't decorate with frilly pink and purple things."

Carlos got up to follow him in. "But if they decorate in the colors of the Princess' painting, we'll all be blind! This is a rough-and-ready man's world down here!"

Now the Panther set his sweet tea down, raising his voice in their direction as Carlos disappeared. "You guys don't get it. You're proving the Weaver's point! It's good for all of us to make female friends. Who knows, if we ever get wounded and quit this business, we might marry one of these girls. They'd understand us."

Carlos came back out, chewing a mouthful of a beef jerky stick he held in his hand. The Jaguar came to stand in the doorway, leaning back against it and crossing his arms. He looked off into the cocoa trees and the distant edge of an ever-encroaching jungle. "Maybe that's the future for you guys, but that's not what I'm called to."

"The Weaver has one picked out with you in mind, so play nice," teased the Panther, grinning as he leaned back into a swing.

The trill of the phone sent Carlos ducking inside to pick it up. In no time, he was back at the door and grabbed the Jaguar's hand to shake it heartily. "Congratulations, man! Jag Gregory was just born. The Weaver wants you on the phone. He's at the hospital, in a South that's north of here."

Did you like this book? The kindest thing you can do for fellow readers is to take a minute to write a short review or rating online at your favorite bookseller. Authors really appreciate this, too!

Want more from the Painter Place Saga? Check out Southern Sky Publishing[1] or your favorite online bookseller to continue the story!

Be sure to see the **character list** *and the* **book club discussion** *questions that follow. Also, feel free to visit the artist's website for updates, blogs, free coloring pages, music and newsletters!*

Connect with Pamela Poole:

YouTube Channel: Pamela Poole, Artist and Author[2]

Artist Website: Pamela Poole Fine Art[3]

Publisher Website: Southern Sky Publishing[4]

Beneath the Surface

Discussion Topics
For Book Clubs

Within the chapters of Jaguar, characters reveal how their prayers for future generations affect situations and outcomes in the setting of Painter Place. Have you prayed for future generations in your family? Will they be able to draw strength from your spiritual legacy?

The Jaguar had to live with a "no" to his prayers because he wanted something that led him away from the path God called him to. Caroline reminds him that getting what he'd asked for would never have been enough, because he was meant for so much more. Can you relate to the Jaguar's disappointment? Have you ever been like Jonah in the Bible, running from what God called you to? Did your faith grow when you saw that He could be trusted?

In Jaguar, readers are given a chance to get to know Phillip Gregory more. Though he thrives on success, he knows he's not the source. To become a great man, he filled his life with timeless examples of greatness and kept his eyes on them as ideals. Phillip knows that what he models in character for his sons will be vital in not only their personal lives, but in the future of the company his family has run for generations. What character traits and reputation will you leave behind as your legacy to your children?

To better understand how to depict the thoughts and actions of men, I did some research when writing my novels in the Painter Place Saga. If readers are intrigued with some of the situations and thoughts described in *Jaguar* about a man's perspective on things a woman wouldn't notice, a quick resource to read is *For Women Only* by Shaunti Feldhahn.

The most eye-opening fact for me was that men gauge their respect for another man by his choice in a wife. Men with wives who don't speak to them with respect, and whose wives do not take care of their appearance, are often pitied by many other men. It costs them promotions and jobs, for if a man doesn't make a good choice in a life partner, how can he make good choices in the workplace? If you are a wife, are you showing honor and respect for your husband in your words and actions when communicating with him, especially in public? Why, or why not? No matter your weight or features, do you try to look your best for your husband to reflect his wisdom and taste?

While this story is fictional, there are real people in real places who have remarkable experiences as battles in the spiritual realm occur around them. Missionaries tell true accounts of amazing events in their endeavors to bring light to dark places. Do you have stories of encounters such as these? Resources for further discussion could include research about the mission work of Jim Elliot and Nate Saint, including Elisabeth Elliot's bestselling book *Through Gates of Splendor* and an account of the same event in the movie version of the book *The End of the Spear* by Steve Saint.

Author's Note

Only those involved with creating a novel can appreciate the work it takes. My faithful friend, Michelle Castro, has been an encourager and beta reader for Painter Place from the beginning. For the third novel, *Jaguar*, my friends Linda Shoemaker and Christin McCall joined her. Many heartfelt thanks to these ladies for your patience during the polishing process of this diamond in the rough! Consider this finished product part of your own accomplishment.

My son, Andy Poole, is ever an encourager, and seemed to enjoy supplying research about Mario video games for *Jaguar*. My husband, Mark, makes loving sacrifices so I can pursue my calling as an artist and author.

I have so many friends! Your prayers, support, and encouragement keep me going. May the Lord multiply back to you the blessings you've given me!

About the Author

Pamela Poole is known for faith-filled suspense stories where history, mystery, and spiritual truth intersect. Her novels in the *Strange Sands Suspense* series and the *Painter Place Saga* offer clean, compelling mysteries grounded in a Christian worldview. She writes stories that both engage the mind and encourage the heart.

Books in the Painter Place Saga
Novels
Painter Place, Painter Place Saga 1
Hugo, Painter Place Saga 2
Jaguar, Painter Place Saga 3
Landmark, Painter Place Saga 4

Legends (Short Stories)

The Wind Song of the Marsh, Legend 1
King's Ransom, Legend 2
The Castaway and the Mermaid, Legend 3

Devotional
Inspired Artistry – Embracing the Creative Calling

The Strange Sands Suspense Novella Series
Strange Sands Suspense — where faith confronts the unseen.
The *Strange Sands Suspense* series follows architectural historian
Mercedes Annalee Ellison as she investigates historic properties
along the South Carolina coast—only to discover that the past
often carries spiritual consequences into the present. Routine
preservation projects quickly become encounters with hidden
passages, ancient vendettas, and unsettling artifacts tied to the
unseen realm.

Rooted in a clear Christian worldview, each faith-filled novella blends mystery, suspense, and spiritual warfare with themes of obedience, calling, and trust in God. Clean, gripping, and thought-provoking, *Strange Sands Suspense* is perfect for readers who enjoy inspirational suspense where light confronts darkness and faith makes the difference.

The Old Cedar Chest, Strange Sands Suspense 1, Hilton Head, SC

The Hidden Hallway, Strange Sands Suspense 2, Savannah, GA

The Freedom Staircase, Strange Sands Suspense 3, Charleston, SC

The Dark Passage, Strange Sands Suspense 4, Bluffton, SC

The Devil's Drawer, Strange Sands Suspense 5, Beaufort, SC

Book 6 is coming in 2026! St. Augustine, FL

Accolades for the *Painter Place Saga*

Painter Place, Painter Place Saga 1
"If you are looking for a well written, CLEAN, sweet romance with a good story-line included this is for you! Would I recommend this book? ABSOLUTELY!"
-Liz, Top 100 Reviewer

Hugo, Painter Place Saga 2
"Another tremendous read by this author Pamela Poole. Book 2 in the Painter Place Saga doesn't disappoint as we remember the category 4 hurricane that came in with a vengeance in South Carolina. Continuing with family drama we are captured with the lives of Painter and Gregory families. I highly recommend reading this saga. You'll never want it to end."
-Gingy, Reader Review

Jaguar, Painter Place Saga 3
"This is the first book I've read from Pamela and the first I've read in the Painter Place Saga. Whew, there were things in this book that just left me speechless they were SO good!!!"
-ASC Book Reviews

Landmark, Painter Place Saga 4
"For young and old alike, this beautifully written story dares to hope that relationships can stand the test of time - without sacrificing personal modesty, integrity, and values."
-The Pen, Reader Review